THE
MADMAN

Book I
Welcome to Scientific Democracy

STEVEN T. STEVENSON

THE MADMAN
BOOK I WELCOME TO SCIENTIFIC DEMOCRACY

iUniverse books may be ordered through booksellers or by contacting:

iUniverse
1663 Liberty Drive
Bloomington, IN 47403
www.iuniverse.com
844-349-9409

ISBN: 978-1-6632-3188-8 (sc)
ISBN: 978-1-6632-3190-1 (hc)
ISBN: 978-1-6632-3189-5 (e)

Library of Congress Control Number: 2021923499

Print information available on the last page.

iUniverse rev. date: 07/30/2024

To my muse,
for always floating through my head like a little
butterfly and being eternally beautiful.
You know who you are. I have always loved you, and I hope
that we run into each other as children again someday.

CONTENTS

PART 3: PEOPLE WHO NEED US DON'T KNOW WHAT IS BEST FOR THEM

PART 4: YOUR OBEDIENCE HAS BEEN PREDETERMINED

PREFACE

This strange work is set forth as part one of two, but it is actually part two of three. If you read the companion novel, *The Book of Steven*, you will be aware that Steven's last adventure was through a heavenly world where he was told that any course of action was preferable over simply ending himself. However, that is easier expressed in the weightless ether of heaven than it is to surmount down here, when the combined forces of this material existence come crashing down on you all at once and you discover that you were nothing more than a pawn in someone else's scheme.

These works are not for everyone. They are not set in a safely impossible dystopian future that you can dismiss as never being capable of coming to fruition. In fact, *The Madman* represents the fictional extremes that can and will result if humans continue to let themselves be walled off by social persuasion and generally accepted notions.

However, these combined works are also a fun adventure and love story, and for those who have the patience to wade through the material, Steven's ultimate three-part journey may provide inspiration and intellectual stimulation in an era when humans need to desperately revisit the impersonal world they are creating, so that they may hopefully begin to rekindle the human soul.

The generations before us knew that the world is in fact a fairly uncomplicated place and that finding one's purpose in this human existence is entirely possible. It takes hard work, that's for sure, but as you will see by the end of Book II to *The Madman*, even modern-day challenges can be surmounted with enough effort and belief, and the battle you face is really no different than that of anyone who has ever come before you.

Whether you have the courage and desire to go on your own human journey in this regard is for you to decide, but I am hopeful that Steven's inspiration, challenges, and messages will be of some aid to you along the way.

INTRODUCTION

Greetings, and welcome to new life. Before the excitement overtakes you, however, I should warn you that the world you have come to inhabit has nothing to do with you. It never did and it never will.

Since the first roads were paved to establish this society, the designers knew that even if by some random chance you came to inhabit their country, there would be nothing you could do to halt their efforts, no matter how hard you tried.

In order to make your stay easier, they have furnished all the distractions a person could ever want. They have even been so kind as to leave you with the illusion that your life is heading somewhere, which it most certainly is not.

The schooling, the career path, the spouse, and the kids—you mark these things as evidence of a life filled with purpose. In the end, however, they might as well be imitation tin trinkets flung down to you from a parade float on high, keeping you occupied at street level while the great menagerie moves on. After all, the parade masters always save the true spoils for themselves and know well that it doesn't take much to keep you suspended in patriotic subservience.

So gather your trinkets while you can, and try not to disappoint. Above all, do not ever forget that your purpose is to serve this land and not the other way around. You will not survive the life you were born into, regardless of any designs to the contrary.

The spirit of the nation rolls on despite you, consuming every ounce of your marginal value in the process. Once it has finished, of course, your insignificant corpse and the ones of those you love will ultimately wind up as little more than handy by-products, to be recycled as fuel for the next generation of lobotomized subjects. In the meantime, your continued obedience has been predetermined.

Please enjoy your stay, and don't smoke.

PART I

This Land Is Our Land—The Stranger's Journey Begins

ONE

On the day I was born, I was drop-shipped directly to an orphanage, and by a mechanical drone of all things. CentRex—short for Center Express—Mail, postage prepaid. It's not even necessary to have a family member abandon you on the front steps anymore; the government now takes care of that with one-click efficiency. The crate they shipped me in is still at the orphanage, by the way. It doubled as a bassinet, and I can almost picture it in my mind to this day. Now, thirty years later, I've been drop-shipped into this city from that same orphanage. Actually, they sent me on a bus, but it feels pretty much like the same thing.

It certainly could have been worse. At least I wasn't lobotomized in utero like some of those other poor bastards. I often wonder if that hurts. It must not; that's probably how they get away with it. I would think that if it hurt, someone would seek vengeance—if anyone still knew what that word meant.

I personally have never wanted to have children, but I can't tell you for sure where that idea came from. They never gave us much instruction in the way of human sexuality when I was a kid; they mostly just left it to us to figure out—and boy did we.

Stepping out of the shower on the first morning in my new apartment, I recall a warm summer night at the boys' home when one of my brothers screwed me. It happened more than once, and after that, I did the same to some of the younger guys at the home. I had no idea what that meant at the time.

I guess he wasn't technically my brother. We all just called each other that, but to my knowledge, none of us were actually related by blood. I can't imagine that most people are these days either, with the way that technology seems to go.

This apartment they gave me is nice, but something feels very strange about it. Nearly overnight, I was plucked from the environment I grew up in and where I always had to share living space with multiple inhabitants, and now I have a spacious studio loft all to myself on the thirtieth floor in this foreign city. When you grow up poor like I did, everything you get that you didn't work for yourself feels strangely tainted, and no matter what I try, I simply cannot shake the unexplainable sense of dread that this new change has filled me with. There is also a bad smell to this place that is not otherwise explained by the self-composting toilets they installed in all the units. The toilet actually smells remarkably fresh, however they make that work.

Never mind, Steven. You know that it's not good to waste time wondering about useless things. Stability is good for the economy, and the economy is good for me. Everything else must be endured for the country. Right. Off to my first day at work.

* * *

All my experience to this point has been spent in the open country. The city I've been planted in is, by contrast, a maze of monstrosities—one skyscraper after another, with no clear view of anything resembling a horizon. Once you've entered that maze, it is hard to believe that you can ever escape it.

The taxi I was riding in seemed to zig and zag endlessly through the tall buildings, though it was otherwise in no apparent hurry, and the driver read his paper while the car did all the work. Out my window, I noticed signs everywhere directing people to a nearby hospital, and the self-guided car seemed to be following them as if through some gravitational telepathy. Then, as we came within a few blocks of the vortex the signs were pulling us into, we suddenly turned left and reached our destination.

The center itself is where I arrived. It is not a hospital of any sort, as far as I know, but it is supposedly the apex of all government operations. It doesn't look like much from the outside—just six stories; a dwarf compared to all the skyscrapers surrounding it—but where those bodies occupy one city block or maybe two in girth, the center is ten blocks wide by ten long. It is painted a nondescript white from the outside and looks more like a giant warehouse than anything else.

But once you are up close, there is no mistaking what it is. The words "CENTER FOR SCIENTIFIC DEMOCRACY" are stamped prominently on a granite monolith standing sentry in a lush green out front. The entire building is framed by a rectangular strip of grass that must be fifty yards wide on each side, and meticulously manicured. Other strips of concrete crossing the lawns allow access to various exterior doors.

Across the green expanses to the right and left, the center is flanked by two sentries: a coffee bar and a medication dispensary. Those appeared to be the staples of this town, as people were lined up for blocks in front of either station for their morning fix.

Never having had the need for either, however, and not yet permitted access through any entrance except the main one, I passed through a giant automatic door, scanned my thumbprint at the front desk, and was directed up to the sixth floor. Walking through the lobby, I noticed that all the walls had thick white padding on them. Ghastly pictures of civic leaders also stuck out prominently, hung at heights seven feet off the ground, and my first impression was that the self-driving taxi had taken a wrong turn and that I had in fact been dropped off at a mental institution.

Shaking off the notion, I boarded the elevator, thankful that no one else was on it, and tried to slow my breathing. However, as the doors closed, the paneling on them suddenly morphed into a giant electronic screen from top to bottom, so instead of being able to concentrate, I was forced to stare at a blabbering face that pitched advertisements for exotic vacations that were being offered in a raffle of some sort.

By contrast, the elevator motor was completely silent, and the ride seemed deliberately languished—probably to increase attention to the screen. It seemed as though at least five seconds passed as each successive floor ticked by, and I was sweating palpably despite the cool air pumping in through the vents. I saw my destiny slowly approach as the floor numbers increased, and fear filled my gut like a lead weight. I had no idea how I got here; nor did I know what they expected of me, and I was quite certain that I hadn't done anything to deserve this.

As the door opened on my intended floor, a pleasant-looking, clean-shaven man of about sixty was there to greet me. He was tall with wispy gray-black hair and carried himself well. Glancing at his midsection, however, it was obvious that his primary activities kept him at a desk, and he was wearing a pressed gray suit which was complemented by a pair of impeccably shined leather shoes. At probably thirty years his junior, I was by contrast in the prime of my life, well-toned from rigorous exercise, but also wearing the only suit I had ever purchased while at the orphanage—and a used one at that.

He smiled and held out a hand to me. "Hello, Steven, I'm Dr. Jacob Cronosson. I am the director of the center." I took it, and he gave me a firm shake, but before I could even respond in kind, he quickly added, "Oh, and by the way, happy thirtieth birthday! I must say that you come very highly recommended by your professors, and we're glad that you will be joining us!"

His warm greeting did not ease my fears, and all I said was, "Thank you, sir. I'm glad to be here." He nodded in acknowledgment and motioned us toward his office. We walked through a door marked "Director," and he gestured toward a chair on the other side of his desk; then he took his own seat and picked up a document to study—apparently my résumé.

While he was reading, I stole a glance at dozens of pictures hanging on the wall to my left. These weren't the calloused, stern men and women of determination like those I had seen in the lobby. Rather, these were all young-looking gentlemen, fresh and eager in their appearances, and they all seemed to be photos taken at college graduations somewhere.

Leaning back in his chair, the director spoke up and startled me back to attention. "It says here that you majored in significant social media activity from 2006-2020, and your degree was in applied sciences in social communications." He looked up expectantly, apparently not noticing that I had been staring at the photos.

I sat up sharply and my voice cracked. "Yes, yes it was. My senior thesis was about the patterns in social communications reflecting a greater connection to first-order emotions during that period."

He nodded with some small level of interest. "Isn't that something? I guess there are patterns in everything." Then he went back to the document. "And you also minored in international political economy. You wrote a paper on US intervention in Latin America and questioned the overall utility of using surplus US crops to weaken demand for corresponding Latin American crops during the twentieth and early twenty-first centuries." His eyes rose approvingly. "Very clever! I must say, no one else but you seemed to think that crop subsidies were much of a controversy back then."

A trickle of sweat ran down my neck, and I involuntarily tugged at my shirt collar and then meekly tried to offer a defense to the project, which I was in fact very proud of. "Well, I was a bit apprehensive about writing that, but at the time it just seemed wrong to be holding other people down so we could maintain a global dominance in agriculture." The director just continued smiling and listening, and then I cleared my throat and added, "So ... you're not upset about it?"

He dropped my résumé on the desk and chuckled. "Of course not! Why would we be?"

Feeling a small bit of tension leave my body, I responded tentatively, "Well, that was the first and only time that I did something truly questioning what I was learning, and it made me very nervous to do it. I remember that my professor frowned upon my efforts severely."

He waved a dismissive hand and said, "Oh, Steven, that's what they're supposed to do. Young minds always want to grow beyond their surroundings, and it's the professors' jobs to keep them in check. But questioning when you are young is always a good thing. You can't do any harm until you get out and start working in the *real* world anyway, and by then all your silly notions have been sufficiently tempered. But we want the best here, Steven, and that certainly appears to be you."

Still feigning confidence, I responded, "Yes sir, I hope so."

He leaned forward and raised a challenging finger, adding with a small hint of expectation, "Of course, it's easy to excel in academia, but the real test will be how you perform productively in society."

I choked again. "Yes … yes sir. However, if you don't mind me asking, what is 'here'? I must say that despite everything I learned in school, I am thoroughly ignorant as to what goes on at the center."

He nodded confidently and replied, "By design, my good chap, purely by design! Ordinary people cannot be trusted to know what we do, and most of them wouldn't want to know anyway." Giving me the small nod of a confidant, he added, "But remember: you're not one of the *ordinary* ones, are you?"

"No sir. I guess not."

He leaned back again and folded his hands behind his head, saying assuredly, "Young man, you should take more pride in your situation than that. You have been hand-selected from a crop of your peers to participate at the epicenter of human development. Now I'd say that's not a bad start, considering where you came from?"

Trying to follow the path of confidence he was offering, I repeated, "No sir, I guess not."

I stole a glance back up at the wall, and this time he caught me. He followed my gaze up to the pictures and scanned them admiringly. "Oh, you're probably wondering who those boys are?"

"Yes sir. The pictures caught my attention, but I didn't want to interrupt."

Looking back down at me, he opened his arms wide in a peaceful gesture and said, "Steven, relax! You're in safe company here, and your question proves the point. There's no need to be apprehensive at all!"

I gulped. "And why is that, sir?"

"Because those boys on the wall are just like you!"

I looked up at them again in wonder. "They are?"

"Yep. At one time, they sat in the very chair you occupy now and were starting on their own stupendous journeys. They were once part of the same Orphan-to-Citizen program you've been selected for, and those boys are the highest-grossing orphans we've ever had."

I looked up at them again. "Wow! And they came from the same place I did?"

"Well, technically not the exact same location, but from orphanages around the country. And like you, they were all specially selected to be given a leg up in life so they could reach their true potential in our marvelous society."

As I lowered my gaze, the dread from the morning returned nonetheless, and the director saw it and tried to continue leavening the atmosphere. Smiling broadly, he said, "I told you, relax! Steven, my boy, you are destined for great things, and this is the perfect place for you to be. Everything else that we do here will soon be made quite clear to you." He grabbed my résumé off the desk, efficiently shoved it into a file folder, and then said, "And speaking of new beginnings, I thought that we would start you in the incubator lab. How does that suit you?"

Overcompensating again, I darted up in my chair and responded, "That sounds interesting!" I tried to calmly add, "I mean, as I mentioned, I pretty much have no idea what you do here, so starting out in one place is probably just as good as the next. But the incubator lab sounds a bit technical … I'm not sure that I'm qualified with my background."

He laughed. "Oh Steven, don't worry about it! We have people at the lab who majored in playing video games, feng shui for left-handed people who like the color blue, and underwater basket weaving." Leaning forward confidently, he insisted, "Now I think you'd agree that you are certainly more qualified than them?"

"Yes sir, it would seem so."

Waving another hand, he said, "Oh, of course you are. Steven, my good lad, don't worry about a thing. One of the hallmarks of any stable society is encouraging young people to find their little niches in life, and the rest, of course, sorts itself out. Anyway, we'll teach you everything you need to know on the job. We have a nice entry-level position over in the lab that we have hand-picked for you, and I have no doubt that you'll fit in just fine."

My face slackened a bit at hearing that. However, the reality of what he was saying also took me by surprise, and I asked, "So I wasn't supposed to have studied anything in particular to get a job here? I mean, this is the most prestigious organization in the whole country, and I would have thought that it required specialized training to get in."

He just smiled and shook his head lightly. "Steven, my good boy, we don't care what you know! All we care about is that you can follow instructions and learn what we put in front of you. That's what really counts." He rocked gently sideways in his chair and added with a chuckle, "Oh, and a modicum of clever curiosity never hurts, since it keeps things from getting boring for us!"

I finally sat back and took in a bit of the relief he was urging. Shaking my head lightly, I said, "Huh. Well, having to go through twenty-five years of education for an entry-level job seems like a lot of 'instruction,' especially if everything you're going to require me to do will be learned on the job?"

The director smiled broadly and replied, "All part of the process, my son, all part of the process, but it works quite well and has so for generations! After all, you don't have to be anywhere until you're thirty, and studies prove that your intellectual curiosities are at their peak until your mid-to-late twenties, so—"

Suddenly, an intercom on his desk buzzed. "Director, we have an incredible breakthrough in the lab! You must get down here immediately!"

"Right-o. Thanks, Jones." The director clicked off the intercom button with a decisive thumb and said, "Steven, let's dispense with these paltry formalities. There is much to do and learn while you're here, and you'd best get started. Come now and I'll walk you down to the lab and introduce you to Dr. O'Dwyer, who has run the operation for the last thirty years. You'll get along with him famously!"

Before he got up, however, he paused momentarily, reaching into a drawer and pulling out a device that he then held out to me. "Oh, and by the way, here's your new cell phone."

I tried to refrain from cringing and said, "Phone?"

"Sure. You'll need it so you can talk to people, pick up messages—that sort of thing. You've seen one of these before, right?"

Taking it in my hand and turning it over to study it, I said, "Well, I had a cell phone at the orphanage, but it was a much older model. They gave it to me when I turned twenty-one."

"Oh good, then you'll be able to work this one just fine. All you have to do is push that little button with your thumb and the phone will activate."

I hesitantly complied, and the phone lit up with a series of beeps; then we both stood up and headed out of the office. I shoved the phone in my pocket and followed him to the elevator, intending to further examine the device later.

We rode slowly back down to the ground level as I pretended to be studying something on my shoes for most of the ride. However, I felt the director turn toward me, and I obediently snapped to attention as he said, "If you will recall, there was a time when other countries actually tried to rebel against our subsidies programs." His comment came out nonchalantly as he was still looking up at the screen on the wall, but there was an obvious hint of patriotism in his voice.

I quickly responded, "Oh yes, I remember reading that."

Without breaking his gaze from the advertisement playing in front of us, he added with studied confidence, "It couldn't have worked, of course. When it comes to economic dominance, we are inevitable. Besides, if there is one thing that our foreign policies have accomplished over the years, it is to let our neighbors do well, but never *too* well."

The doors opened, and we emerged back into the lobby. His last comment was completely lost on me as I looked up and met the steely eyes of some former leader. As we walked past the rows of portraits, I said, "Hey, did any of the boys in your office make it up on this wall?"

The director seemed caught off-guard by the question and paused for a moment; then he said absently, "Oh, perhaps. I'll have to check the records when I get back upstairs. Don't worry about that for now. Just come with me and you'll be well on your way."

We proceeded around the far side of the reception desk, and behind it to the left was a large automatic door that was guarded by electronic key entry. The director scanned his card, and we passed through to the other side, where we entered into the quiet hum of machinery. The room seemed to continue on infinitely, although the line of sight in the foreground was blocked by row upon row of tall metal objects.

Our first human encounter was with a meek-looking shortish creature standing several yards inside the lab who was holding a clipboard and rocking back and forth with nervous excitement. He pushed up his glasses when he saw us, and then he smiled awkwardly, and the director motioned me toward him. "Steven, meet Jones."

Jones timidly extended a scrawny hand to me, hugging his clipboard with the other. I stepped forward with nervous excitement, grabbing his outstretched hand and giving him a reassuring pat on the shoulder, and said, "Hey there, buddy—" However, my initial physical contact caused him to collapse onto himself like a Slinky right before my eyes. My brain may have deceived me, but I think that he actually hit the ground faster than the clipboard, which bounced off noisily to the side.

The director grabbed my arm and pulled me back sharply. "Jesus, Steven, be careful! Jones has screen in his esophagus!"

Still trying to take in the whole experience, all I could muster in dazed surprise was, "Huh?"

He pushed me out of the way and responded curtly, "Oh, it's the newest craze. Never mind." Kneeling down impatiently next to the formerly upright Jones, the director said, "Now what was it that you needed to tell me?"

The latter was in apparent distress but still tried to finish his duty as he looked up with urgency and clutched at the director's pant leg. "*Rayon ankle socks ...*" Gasp. "*... linked to ...*" Gasp. "*... Alzheimer's!*"

The director frowned at the hand wrinkling his freshly pressed suit; then he stood up and motioned for a few of the onlookers to come over, responding flatly without even looking down at our injured colleague. "Very good, Jones, I'll take care of it. We'd better get you to the hospital."

The director appeared to be exercising visible restraint not to simply shake Jones's lingering grasp away, and Jones looked up at him fondly and finally unclenched his hand, letting it fall limply to the floor. *"Thank you, sir. And if I don't see you again ..."* Gasp. *"... it was nice knowing you."*

Trying to mask his annoyance, the director carefully smoothed out his trousers and turned in the other direction, motioning me to follow him. "You too, Jones." And then we walked on.

Several yards away and still reeling from the event, I said, "What was that all about?"

The director was intently shaking his leg as we walked, trying to make sure that the wrinkle Jones had left would fall out on its own. He shot me a momentarily confused look and said, "Oh, Alzheimer's almost bankrupted us once, so now we keep a close eye on it."

Still in shock, I retorted, "No, what happened to that guy? I barely touched him!"

He shook his head momentarily and answered, "Jones is just the victim of another health fad. People are always trying to self-improve these days, and now they have a screen installed in the esophagus to cut down on calories. It's a one-way valve that lets nutrients down, but not all the waste. Bulimia is now as regular as breathing—which I find a little unappealing—but the devices do eliminate GERD, which we were never able to do before." Right before we rounded the corner, he finally shot a glance back at the remnants of Jones that they were scraping off the floor and added, "The most unfortunate side effect, however, is that most people these days are as brittle as glass."

As Jones passed out of sight, I said, "Don't they exercise?"

"Oh, sure, but it's mostly just virtual yoga. People stopped doing traditional exercises when a series of articles came out revealing the gross and dangerous things that physical activity can cause." He stopped for a moment and turned to address me. "But Steven, you do have to be very careful about coming in contact with most of the employees around here. Years of selective breeding have left us with a stock of people who, while being adequately suited to their jobs, are nonetheless lacking in a certain robustness. You'll notice that all the doors here are automatic, and I doubt if old Jonesy could have even opened a manual door if he tried." Appearing satisfied that the pressed crease in his trouser leg would recover, he smiled again and said, "Anyway, on to more important things!"

We rounded another corner and came upon Dr. O'Dwyer, who was a broad, stout man in a white coat and seemed to be about the director's same age, although Dr. O'Dwyer sported a white beard. He was busily recalibrating one of the machines as we approached, and the director and I stopped a few feet away from him, where the director announced, "Here we are, Steven. Let me introduce you to Dr. O'Dwyer. Dr. O'Dwyer, Steven here comes very highly recommended to us, and he's an orphan."

I cringed visibly. Turning his attention away from the machinery to address us, Dr. O'Dwyer hardly seemed to take notice and simply stood up and stepped toward me. "Oh, good, fine, fine. Hello, Steven. Gordon. Gordon O'Dwyer." He reached out a broad palm to me, and I grabbed it gingerly as his own grip nearly crushed my hand.

Trying to meet his strength without wincing, I said, "Oh my, that's one hell of a handshake you've got!"

He grinned at me in a show of dominance and doubled down; then I thought I heard a bone crunch. "Yes, Steven, I played a bit of rugby when I was away at school!"

I finally had to let out an involuntary grunt and pulled my hand away in surrender. "Argh. Oh, well, good to meet you."

Satisfied, he wiped his hands on his pants and said boastfully, "Yep, you'll find out that actually digging in at the center and getting to the work we do requires a certain level of robustness, and some of the others are not physically cut out for everything that goes on around here." He rolled his eyes and added, "And heaven only knows how they ever got their jobs in the first place." Then, perhaps out of official duty, he sighed and remarked, "But they're necessary to the overall effort, I suppose." The director nodded affirmingly at him.

Still trying to discreetly shake off the pain, and not having the slightest idea what was in store, I said, "Yes sir, I guess so."

Obviously aware that it was his turn to take over the orientation for the director, Dr. O'Dwyer stepped toward me and threw a guiding arm over my shoulder; then he turned me around to start surveying his domain. "Leave all of that aside for now. Steven, it is a very exciting time to be here. Never before in the history of our species have we had the power to exploit the true potential of human energy like we do now."

Moving with him felt a little like being nudged by a tank, and he started leading me down one of the rows, not paying any mind to our former company. From behind, the director cleared his throat, obviously snubbed by Dr. O'Dwyer's lack of etiquette, and said loudly, "Ahem. If you two will excuse me, I have to get back to my office."

Dr. O'Dwyer responded without looking back at him. "No problem, Jack. We'll take good care of Steven."

The director said over my shoulder, "Terrific. Say, Steven, why don't you stop by on your way out this evening and we'll grab a nightcap."

I looked back at him as Dr. O'Dwyer ushered me down the hall. "Oh, okay. Thank you, Director. Thanks for everything!"

He smiled and waved reassuringly at me. "Don't mention it."

Dr. O'Dwyer continued where he had left off. "Anyway, Steven—"

I stopped momentarily, thankfully able to somehow force him to halt his progress. "Wait, can I ask a question?"

He pulled his tree-branch arm away and looked at me with obvious annoyance. "Yes?"

I pointed back toward the elevator and said, "Did you see that guy who was just carried out on the stretcher?"

He was still trying to decipher a sufficiently weighty reason for my interruption of his grand tour. Not finding one, he confusedly replied, "Who, Jones?"

"Yes."

"Sure. What about him?"

"Am I going to get in trouble for whatever I apparently did to him?"

Dr. O'Dwyer let out a chuckle. "Oh, heavens no! Insurance pays for that. You'll find out while you're here that we have a highly advanced society where petty little things like personal injuries are handled as easy as pie."

Slightly relieved, I said, "Really?"

"You bet. Jones has an insurance policy he inherited at birth that takes care of all of that, so you don't need to worry about a thing."

Hearing that brought equal parts relief and everlasting angst to me. I was aware that all citizens were automatically assigned insurance policies of some sort at birth, although the actual details of the program were unclear to me, as orphans were not allowed to be part of the program for some reason. I viewed it as some kind of generational wealth benefit that I lost out on, and it had always made me both angry and determined to make my own way in life.

Perhaps sensing that this was a sore subject for me, Dr. O'Dwyer threw his arm around me again and, as we started walking, said dismissively, "Anyway, despite you being an orphan, we're taking good care of you now and you are in the best place you could possibly be under your circumstances. Don't worry, because your government benefits will more than make up for any shortcomings you may have experienced before you got here."

Completely unsure of what that all meant, all I could think to say was, "Oh, okay. Thanks."

It didn't seem that he even heard me, and as we rounded a corner into a vast room where people were busy tending to various workstations, he simply continued. "Anyway, we'll start you out with the lobotomies. Lobotomies are, of course, just an unfortunate result of the modern world. Americans have always had a love affair with cheap, readily available labor, and we've discovered over the years that the lobotomization process is the best way to keep the American miracle going."

His comment immediately shocked me, and I froze in place. Dr. O'Dwyer turned toward me and laughed, saying lightly, "Don't worry, Steven; we don't lobotomize orphans!" I let out a sigh of relief and he added, "After all, your parents committed suicide before you were born, right?"

That comment brought me back to reality, and I responded shamefully again, "Yes sir. That's right."

Dr. O'Dwyer just tilted his head with clinical confidence and responded, "Well then, you've got bigger things to worry about." Then he waved me to follow along and said eagerly, "Now come over here and I'll show you the brain splitter!"

*

TWO

We arrived at one of the vast conveyors that moved the incubation bubbles along, and the machinery and components were housed behind a large, clear glass enclosure that apparently prevented contamination. Sitting in front of us was an empty amniotic bubble, and there was a little eight-inch square hatch on the top of the bubble that provided interior access. There was also a fill tube near the top of the bubble on one side and two drain tubes flanking the bottom.

Dr. O'Dwyer motioned to the technician sitting at the station to get up and take a break, which he readily agreed to. As the worker stood up, he patted himself on the shoulder and appeared to aimlessly start wandering off in no particular direction, while the machinery in front of me instantly went on hold.

I watched him walk away momentarily and noticed that he seemed to be in some kind of delirium, as he nearly bumped into several walls while he was strolling away. When I turned to ask Dr. O'Dwyer about it, however, he was already busy at the controls. He activated some kind of override while still standing, and he said, "Here, let me show you how the process works. Step one, push that button—genetic material is deposited into the placental incubator." Now forgetting our departed colleague, I watched as a little sperm-and-egg capsule was dropped into the incubator and the fill tube quickly introduced a pinkish fluid that filled the bubble except for a few inches at the top. "Step two, push that button—incubator starts. Now come down the hall with me."

We walked about fifty yards past others who were also doing the same thing I had just witnessed, and as we approached the first person performing the next stage of the process, Dr. O'Dwyer motioned for that technician to get up, and we took his place at the controls. He depressed a series of buttons rapidly and said, "Three months later, hold this down and the lobotomy takes place."

Now inside the bubble was a little human gestating peacefully in amniotic bliss. When Dr. O'Dwyer clicked the controls, the top of the bubble automatically opened and a robotic arm descended into the fluid, and I watched as it made two quick cuts on the side of the scalp. A second arm joined the first and mechanically insufflated a little wire into the incision, and then a third made two quick sutures and the wounds were closed up. This all happened in about three seconds.

Dr. O'Dwyer hit the stop button, and the machine paused while a little LED countdown indicated the total time that could elapse before the next lobotomy had to be performed. Apparently the next fetus could sit for sixteen more minutes before its fate was sewn shut. Dr. O'Dwyer turned to me and said, "Now come down here into the loading dock."

We exited on the far side of the lab into a vast warehouse filed with crates and trucks, where there was also another set of stations. The conveyor system had followed us the whole way, and we walked up behind one of the technicians and Dr. O'Dwyer said, "Step three, six months later, push that button—new birth."

He didn't bother making the technician get up from that station, but we watched as he pushed the magical birthing button and a panel on the far end of the incubation conveyor opened up, rolling the amniotic bubble onto a soft cloth. Surprisingly, they left the bubble closed, which Dr. O'Dwyer explained: "We don't actually release them from the womb in here. That happens upon delivery so that the new family gets to unwrap their little bundle of joy at home—well, with the help of a fetal delivery specialist."

Surprised at the result, I shook my head and observed, "So you're shipping people little egged humans?"

"Pretty much." Another technician walked over and scooped up the capsule, carrying it away, and with that it appeared that we had reached the end of the birthing lesson.

I said, "Huh, the job doesn't seem that complex?"

Dr. O'Dwyer responded, "Oh, it may look like that right now, but that's only because we're a bit slow today. Normally these fetuses are barreling along the conveyors and the process at each station has to be repeated continuously, at the rate of about twenty per minute."

My eyes shot open at the notion of so many humans having their brains diced open during the workday, but Dr. O'Dwyer simply motioned me to follow him, and we walked back to the second station, where the technician was still on his break. The next lobotomization victim was sitting in front of us completely unaware, and Dr. O'Dwyer continued. "Now when you're down here on the lobotomy station, you have to be careful and listen for the machine to click three times. You can't just tap the button once. You have to hold it down until you hear 'click-click-click.' If you don't hear three clicks, you may not have gotten it all the way, but if you do it right, this happens."

He demonstrated again so that I could fully grasp the procedure. *Click, click, click.* "See? The display changes from a sad cherub face to a happy one." The fetus we were watching did not, in fact, seem to even register the procedure, and as I glanced at the fresh stitches that had been put in place, two faint drops of blood from the incision sites descended slowly and diluted into the pinkish fluid.

I winced involuntarily and asked, "Are you're sure they don't feel anything?"

Dr. O'Dwyer responded sarcastically, "Are you kidding? We'd hear nothing but complaints if they did! Steven, one of the government's greatest functions is ensuring that our citizens do not feel any pain. Heaven knows they can't handle it these days."

"But how do you know that fetus didn't sense the process?"

He resumed his lecture voice and answered, "Precisely for the reason you just inquired about. We have been tracking these things for more than five hundred years and understand every single aspect of human development in the womb." He paused and shot me a look of sheer arrogance, adding, "Well, we understand every aspect of human development everywhere else, but that's not what you asked me. The earliest months of gestation involve the formation of very basic structures; however, the fetus won't start establishing its identity until around twenty weeks. At twenty-four weeks, the brain takes off growing on its own, and by then it's usually too late. By sixteen weeks, of course, pain-sensing hormones have already formed, which we try to avoid disturbing at all costs.

"So we perform the lobotomization process at the three-month mark to avoid all those pitfalls, and that is also a time when the cranium is relatively soft and easy to penetrate. Timing it the way we do, we can perform our little procedure without causing any harm and can also get in and out and make the bridge connection in plenty of time and still allow hair to grow where the scar was. Hair growth, of course, begins in the fourth month of development."

I subconsciously felt around the side of my head and asked uneasily, "So you can't see the scar at all?"

He just laughed at my continued squeamishness and said, "Not unless you look with a magnifying device! Surgical techniques have become excellent in that regard."

I realized that I probably looked ridiculous digging into my scalp, so I let my hand drop and tried to deflect by asking, "Where do they go between each station?"

Dr. O'Dwyer pointed to behind the glass and said, "The conveyor tubes run horizontally back and forth behind this enclosure, and we also have multiple rows stacked on top of each other. After each station, the bubbles descend back into the bowels of the lab and just move along at a measured pace while we track and monitor the fetuses' overall development."

As I stared at the newly lobotomized victim sitting in front of me, who still had a leg up on me in life even after undergoing this process, I asked curiously, "Hey, so that little fetus in there has an insurance policy?"

He nodded and replied, "Yep. Well, technically it won't issue until the parents open the box at home, as we do still have some minor glitches in the process and lose a unit or two from time to time. But yes, he will eventually have his own insurance policy."

"And what's that worth?"

"Oh, I think that they're up to around four hundred fifty million these days."

I nearly choked at hearing him say that. Stepping back, I involuntarily exclaimed, "You've got to be kidding me? How can everyone just be handed that much money when I didn't grow up with squat?"

Dr. O'Dwyer responded offhandedly, "Well, Steven, it's a little complicated, but don't worry; it all winds up getting spent in the end."

I still felt as though I were being gypped somehow but didn't understand enough to protest further, and I didn't want to jeopardize this new job. Dr. O'Dwyer simply turned to walk away, so I followed.

We moved on and rounded the corner to a station with several people busily clicking away at some aspect of lab procedure, and Dr. O'Dwyer saw them diligently in action and smiled. Turning back to me, he said, "And, Steven, the hardest thing about this job has always been keeping the fetuses from being what they want to be."

Despite everything I had already learned during the day, my eyes nearly popped out of their sockets. "*What?*"

With clinical ease, he responded, "Oh, as you'll find out, what we do here is largely to fight against the unfortunate side effects of human evolution. One of the most disheartening of all is the body's natural instinct to try to adapt to changing circumstances." I just stood there in awe, and he continued without taking any notice. "Anyway, if the process is done at the right time, the rest of the brain will develop to compensate, but the necessary bridge will still be intact. If you do it too soon, however, the cells will completely work around what you've done, and then you won't have gained anything."

As I was frozen in horrified contemplation, some eager-looking goon ran up and handed Dr. O'Dwyer a clipboard, which he looked over briefly and signed with a deft stroke. Then he turned back to me and continued the discourse without pause. "I tell you, many years ago we had a fetus who was developing at an incredible rate. By two months, it was already forming neural connections that most don't have until they're ten years old. We went ahead and did the procedure at the three-month mark, but it didn't take. The boy's brain just busted right through the junction wire, and we wound up having to redo it multiple times and used a splicer that was fifty times stronger than what we use on most of the regulars. Fortunately, the process finally took in the end."

"And what happened to him?"

Absently, he said, "Nothing. What do you mean? He lived a normal life and died."

"But you said that he was developmentally gifted?"

He nodded proudly in recollection. "Sure was—probably would have turned out to be a real phenom!"

Exasperated, I said, "So why did you destroy that potential?"

Dr. O'Dwyer shot me a sideways look of condescension and answered, "Steven, we can't upset the system just because *one fetus* doesn't want to follow the rules. If we did, every parent out there would be claiming an exception because their child supposedly could be the next this or that." With a curt nod, he added, "Which, by the way, we know for a fact does not happen these days. Nope, the process is put in place for a very good reason, and keeping that stable is of utmost importance."

Still completely bewildered and out of my element, all I could do at that point was shrug. "Yeah, I guess so."

As we moved on, he added, "Anyway, that kid probably would have wound up with genius depression."

"Huh?"

"Oh, most of them do. They do just fine as kids when they're chugging along absorbing everything that you put in front of them, but then they wake up one day and realize that they are overeducated and overtrained for the world they find themselves in. That usually leads to psychosis, drug addiction, and other problems."

"And what causes that?"

Still using his narrating voice, he responded, "Well, with few exceptions, our society has been developing into stable, regimented order for a long time. You might say that as of right now, we are at the apex of that process. The only downfall is that certain anomalies may wind up feeling like outsiders from time to time, but fortunately we know how to take care of that well enough."

"Yes, but you are also lobotomizing an entire population."

He shook his head firmly and corrected, "Oh, no, not true at all. In fact, by law only 17.5 percent of all fetuses are selected for this process. The damn hippies won't let us raise the number any higher. Of course, parents can always request the procedure, and—"

I jerked on his sleeve without thinking and said incredulously, "What? Who on earth would willingly want their kid to go through that?"

Dr. O'Dwyer gave me a disapproving look, and I pulled my hand away, embarrassed; then he answered plainly, "It's actually very popular these days."

"You're kidding me?"

"Not at all. We call it the 'Daisy Buchanan.'"

"What?"

"The order form; it's called a Daisy Buchanan request."

"Why?"

He shook his head lightly and said, "Oh, who can remember things like that? It was probably named after one of the first to request a lobotomized child."

"Well, what if it's a boy?"

He elbowed me sharply in the ribs, nearly knocking me over. "Ha! Steven, there's not much difference between them anymore!"

As I was rubbing my tender flank, Dr. O'Dwyer looked over his shoulder momentarily and, making sure that no one else was close by, leaned over and lowered his voice. "One more thing—if you're heavily wedded to one kind of sexual orientation or another, you'll want to be careful. Everyone is into onesies these days—guys, girls, guys who used to be girls, and … whatever they call the rest. So you might want to check under the hood before you take someone home with you, if you know what I mean."

I stammered, "Oh, I'm not … er … okay. I still just can't believe it."

Straightening up, he said, "Well, they make the garments to fit males and females."

"No, no, not that! A parent willingly asking for a lobotomized child?"

"Steven, you understand the lobotomization procedure, right?"

"Yes. One incision in the posterior temporal sulcus, one incision in the left intraparietal cortex, one snip, and then a small wire snaked in and sutured to each structure."

He raised a skeptical eyebrow and challenged, "But do you understand what we're doing?"

"Um, no. Not entirely. Lobotomizing them in some fashion?"

Dr. O'Dwyer swept a broad hand in front of him and corrected. "No, no. It's not even technically correct to call them lobotomies. That's just a popular term that developed along with the process. However, we don't actually cut any of the structures out of the brain. We merely make a bridge."

"Yeah, but why?"

We started walking again as he continued. "A long time ago, we discovered that deep within the brain lies the part that makes people want to find purpose in their lives. It is a horribly troublesome nest of synapses that actually used to make people need to feel connected to some greater truth in the universe.

"So we severed the connection. Well, that's not completely accurate. At first we just severed it—snip, snip to both sides of the temporal sulcus—but then we discovered that if we did that, the synapses would automatically regrow. We tried a number of additional approaches and eventually discovered that the best combination was to sever the connection on one side and then reroute it so the electrical signals went straight to the region of the brain associated with instant gratification.

"That way humans' sense of purpose is linked directly to the most basic needs of childhood: warmth, food, sleep, and, most importantly, encouragement. As long as those are fulfilled, there aren't any problems; and as you'll find out, not only is there no pain, but it's an entirely seamless process as far as the person is concerned.

They will never have any sequelae from the procedure, unlike some things that happen *outside* of the womb."

I couldn't even respond, and before I knew it, we entered a door marked "Splicing Department," where hundreds of people were bent over little machines, peering into eyepieces and rapidly pressing buttons. As we toured, he continued: "Steven, everything else we do here starts with the genes, and in here is where we do our magic. Of course, it's still an evolving science, but we've worked out most of the bugs." While he was still explaining, we walked by one of the workers, and Dr. O'Dwyer proudly patted her on the back for emphasis in midsentence, which caused the eyepiece on her microscope to suddenly fill the space where her eyeball used to be.

She screamed and sat up startled, covering the wounded socket with her hand, and Dr. O'Dwyer looked down at her and said, "Oops, sorry about that! You'd better take the day off and go over to the hospital."

We moved on without pause, and he continued the tour. "Initially we removed the gene that caused colon cancer, but it turned out that it was also the gene for inherited behavior, or whatever the family dynamic was that led to cancer in the first place. The result was that the next generation behaved completely different from the prior one, and the offspring were almost unrecognizable to their parents. That's when we got the idea to just randomly assign kids to parents from birth—well, random in the sense of the genetic material that makes them up. Now fetuses are just a hodgepodge from different people, but the parents can't tell the difference anymore, and the kids imprint on whomever is put in front of them."

I blurted out sourly, "Sort of like being adopted?"

"Pretty much."

"I wonder why that didn't happen to me."

He mused for a second. "Hard to say. Statistically, males are very hard to adopt out. That could be why."

"Do you have female orphans?"

"Of course."

"Huh. I never saw any at the orphanage."

Dr. O'Dwyer responded dismissively. "Well, they're usually snatched up very quickly, or wind up being prostitutes." He looked over at me as I stared at him in disbelief, and he quickly added, "Anyway, you grew up in a boys' home. Let's move on."

I just shook my head and kept following him, but I was now wondering about the extent of changes they could make to fetuses in the lab, and I asked, "So do you assign genders at birth?"

He laughed. "Oh, Steven, there's no reason to do that! After all, so many people change genders by age five that we wouldn't know where to start guessing anyway!"

My mouth dropped open, and I exclaimed, *"You let five-year-olds have gender reassignment surgery?"*

Dr. O'Dwyer turned to me absently and said, "Of course. Steven, it's a horrible prison sentence to be born in the wrong body."

"So let me get this straight. You can't vote until you're eighteen, and you can't drink until you're twenty-one, but you can have gender reassignment surgery at age five?"

My guide was completely unfazed and responded plainly, "Yep. Sometimes the kid and their parents will undergo the process at the same time, and we run family discounts on transition surgeries to help with that."

"Is it expensive?"

"Oh yes, but it's covered by insurance, and if they can't afford it, the parents can always refinance their kid's insurance policy. That does leave the kid in double-debt when they grow up, but it's sure better than having to accept the gender you were born with."

Still flabbergasted, I asked, "Does anyone actually do that?"

"Mostly only people in lower classes."

"It seems it would be cheaper to just borrow Mom's or Sister's clothes."

He laughed and slapped me hard on the back. "Ha! Steven, nobody cross-dresses anymore!"

As I struggled to recover from the fierce blow, I asked, "Why not?"

He just shrugged and responded, "Why would they when they can get gender reassignment surgery before they reach puberty?"

Seeing no response from me, he added thoughtfully, "Besides, with everyone wearing pretty much the same clothes, we make a lot more profit on the surgeries than we ever could on fashion."

I frowned at that last comment, and he continued deflecting enthusiastically. "Steven, you'll really have to wait until you understand everything before you judge too much. I tell you, it's pretty neat what we can do these days. With the option so readily available, we don't even issue birth certificates with genders on them anymore, and with male-to-female sex changes, the nanobot can be programmed to simulate a woman's menstrual cycle. Of course, if they change back, it's hard to turn off the nanobot, but they don't seem to mind."

His nanobot comment was lost on me, but I shook my head incredulously and said, "Wait a minute. People get reassignment surgery and then have it reversed?"

"Sure—happens all the time. Unfortunately, there is no gene for regret, but that's part of gambling on what sex will suit you best for your life."

Frowning, I said, "Now that's just ridiculous!"

Giving me a directly accusing look, he replied, "Steven, you'd hate to wake up one day to realize that you had changed yourself into the wrong body, wouldn't you?"

Deflecting quickly, I said, "Look, that has nothing to do with me. Let's leave that aside."

Pausing momentarily to study me from head to toe, he responded skeptically, "Sure, sure." Then we moved on.

As we continued to tour, I finally asked, "And just to make sure I'm clear on what you do in the splicing department, you create people basically the same, right?"

He put a hand on my shoulder to halt me and said, "Wait a minute there, Professor Einstein. We eliminated the most common hereditary diseases for everyone. That included spina bifida, Down's, and a few others, and the basic childhood diseases package is free. It covers the top five—that is, in addition to the vaccinations we provide for the top five childhood illnesses—but everything else after that costs."

Disapprovingly, I asked, "So, you make people pay so they won't have a kid with a congenital heart problem?"

"Of course. It's too far down on the list." Flashing me an indignant look, he said, "Steven, we already provide them with cell phones and nanobots. The government can't pay for everything. Geesh!"

That was the second reference to nanobots, but I figured that we would cover it eventually on the tour, so I didn't bother interrupting. Instead, Dr. O'Dwyer simply added, "And it was a good thing that we got into the business when we did. Can you imagine that people used to go to other countries to purchase a kid that was made up of DNA from different mothers?"

It didn't appear to surprise him at all that I could not, but as we passed row upon row of workers all doing some sort of splicing task or other, I considered the possible benefits. My thoughts eventually turned to a buddy of mine at the boys' home who was, after a certain age, always ashamed and always on bottom, so I finally asked, "Do you do genetic male enhancements?"

Dr. O'Dwyer smiled and said, "Naturally! That's one of our most popular add-ons. After all, without those we wouldn't have any male frontal nudity in Hollywood!"

"Is it expensive?"

"Sure, but not as much as you might think."

"What other things do you do?"

"Oh, we can do really interesting things these days! We splice in bits and pieces of celebrity genes that produce very good-looking one-offs. Of course, we can't make them look *too* good. The binding agreements with celebrity donors all state that distillates must be one feature or more removed from actual appearance for the birth to be valid."

Just then, the bell rang; the splicing workers stood up, and most of them started slapping themselves on the back. I finally asked Dr. O'Dwyer about this phenomenon, and he explained that most people wore virtual reality contacts that activated by patting oneself on the back. I had no understanding what those were, but shortly thereafter, people were bouncing off the walls.

As we rounded a corner and exited the department, we entered some kind of central printing room where even more workers were busy doing nothing at the moment. Dr. O'Dwyer stopped and shook his head momentarily, saying to me, "Christ, it is a miracle that we can get these people to work at all. I tell you, there was a period when the mere threat of a weighty existence could nearly crush humans. Almost concomitant with the awareness of self came bouts of suicide, and a piece of paper could nearly decimate someone back then. We largely fixed that, but we do have to watch out for Newtonian ennui these days."

"What's that?"

"An awful condition where the human comes to realize that gravity is at work all around them."

"Is that a big problem?"

Dr. O'Dwyer responded emphatically, "*Huge.* Fortunately, if we can spot it early enough, we can attempt to intervene."

"How early do you look for it?"

"About the seventh month of gestation. You can often notice the baby slumping lower in the artificial uterus than the other unaffected ones do, although that happens more with the males than the females. There are, of course, also biological markers for it, and in some non-lobotomies, it can start the second they come out of the artificial womb. The condition causes extreme symptoms of sleepiness, crying, constant need for attention, and the urge for irregular feedings at night. Here, read this."

The cover of the pamphlet he handed to me read, *Understanding Your Newborn's Mental Health Disorders, 32nd Ed.* I said, "You give this to parents with their newborns?"

"Of course. It's mandatory reading." While I was perusing the document, he added unexpectedly, "And I swear, the music that Newtonian ennui has caused just blows me away."

I looked up at him and said, "What's it sound like?"

He responded disgustedly, "People crying. For some reason, lobotomies are tremendously soothed by it, but music is pretty disposable these days anyway as a result of the condition." Nodding in my direction, he added another random comment: "Never mind what zygote depression has done to the arts."

"Zygote depression?"

"Yep. That is a whole different malady marked by unusually sluggish activity in cell division. It creates long-term problems typically associated with depression, insomnia, Alzheimer's, and a host of other conditions."

I shook my head and asked, perplexed, "Wait a minute; I thought that Alzheimer's was caused by rayon socks?"

Dr. O'Dwyer deflected that one with ease. "Oh, it could very well be, but buying rayon socks is also likely linked to zygote depression. Just like the other forms of early-onset fetal misdevelopment, intervention at a young age is absolutely key."

My bewilderment growing by the second, I put down the pamphlet and said, "What do you do?"

"We get them into Baby Einstein goggles as early as possible, and sometimes the stimulus of the goggles helps stave off the long-term symptoms. Otherwise they risk going completely insane in later life."

I stepped back and said, astonished, "Wait a minute. You get kids *hooked* on those devices starting at age two?"

Dr. O'Dwyer frowned at me and scolded, "Oh, that's an awful way to put it."

"But is that true?"

"Well, frankly, yes. But consider this, Steven: why would any parent want their kid to grow up less familiar with technology than their peers? You have no idea what kinds of self-esteem problems that could cause." He stole a glance at my face and could see that I wasn't overly convinced; then he added confidently, "Trust me; if it was your kid, you'd want the best for them."

I muttered sourly, "I don't have kids."

Satisfactorily wrapping up that particular debate, he said, "Well, there you go."

"But can't the child just develop on its own?"

Dr. O'Dwyer shook his head fervently in response and said, "Oh, we can't risk that! That would be entirely too dangerous given our sophisticated economic model."

"Well then, why don't you just throw out the ones with zygote depression?"

He shot me a sideways glance and chided, "Now that would be a little barbaric, don't you think?"

"Is there a cure?"

"Not a total one, but we have discovered that you can delay the eventual effects, and we've also done what we can to take the burden off these poor souls through modern technologies. Living in a virtual world for as much time as possible during the day helps alleviate symptoms, and constant reaffirmation and bribing help as well. The first two years of life are the hardest because the baby can't be fitted with goggles until then. We ship them with the crate anyway, but if the parents try to use them before age two, they just fall off."

Still completely confounded by everything I was learning, I said, "Are you sure there isn't an easier way?"

Now perplexed for his own part, Dr. O'Dwyer responded sarcastically, "What are you talking about? This *is* easy! The goggles help the baby learn to just accept whatever is put in front of it."

"But that's what I mean. Are you sure that you can't just let them develop on their own … Somehow?"

He responded emphatically, "Heavens no! Steven, a person's whole life is a series of very precarious steps, and missing any one of them can lead to psychosis and disaster."

As we moved on, I considered the things in my own life that he probably viewed as precarious missteps, but I was determined to make it in this society and confident that I could handle anything that came my way. Then we entered the implant department, where Dr. O'Dwyer said, "Steven, this is where we implant the nanobot regulator. We do the basic implant here, and they get refills on a monthly basis."

"Implant? For what?"

"The nanobot that helps deliver essential medications to people."

"What medications?"

"Estrogen and Pitocin."

"Why do you give people those?"

"To help ward off aggression."

"Huh. Do you give people any other drugs with the nanobot?"

"No, it's just those two to start with. We add other medications PRN throughout life. Sometimes people need higher doses of certain things, and we usually deliver those right to their doors, but the health module isn't just for drugs. It also sends notification if your blood pressure ever gets too high, and it monitors … other things. The newer models can also automatically download software updates to people."

"Software?"

Dr. O'Dwyer responded abruptly, "Don't worry about that for now. Oh, and by the way, you don't have any of this stuff in you; and neither do I, for that matter."

"Why not?"

"Well, for one thing, Steven, we work at the center. We don't need that level of medical precaution because we can always get what we need from the government benefits we enjoy. Yes, my boy, you are very lucky to work here. Best employee program in the country!"

"I guess so."

"Anyway, the module automatically attaches to the gallbladder once we implant it, and from there it does all of its wondrous work."

He seemed to be satisfied that we had finished the conversation on that particular topic. However, I hazarded an additional question which set us off on another series of exchanges. "Yeah, but what happens if you have to take the gallbladder out?"

Dr. O'Dwyer's face blanched a shade, and he responded emphatically, "Oh, that can *never* be done! In case you didn't know, the gallbladder is an essential organ and people can die without it."

Frowning at him, I said, "Are you sure? I remember learning about gallbladder surgeries in a book I read at the orphanage."

Dr. O'Dwyer responded firmly, "You should really stop reading outdated textbooks. Look here." He pulled up a medical text on his phone. "See? 'Gallbladder—Removal of this organ will result in sudden, immediate, and even instantaneous death.'"

I peered at the instructions and clicked "next" to see if it said anything else. On the following page, it said, "Appendix. Should be removed before age forty-five to prevent Parkinson's disease." Looking up at Dr. O'Dwyer, I asked, "What's that all about?"

He responded lightly, "Oh, science proves that having your appendix removed can lead to a 20 percent reduction in developing Parkinson's, in approximately 20 percent of all cases."

I said sarcastically, "That sounds like a pretty unnecessary procedure. Do they do a lot of those?"

"Oh, yes. About 60 percent of our citizens will undergo that operation. However, we do it through the anus these days, so there's no scarring. As you can imagine, our photogenic population of lobotomies hate to have visible scars."

I took an astonished step back and asked, "But they like instruments shoved up their asses for an unnecessary procedure?"

Dr. O'Dwyer just smiled in response. "Oh, they don't mind that at all!"

Shaking my head, I said, "It still sounds pretty ridiculous to me."

He looked down at me and replied firmly, "Steven, if it were your family member, you'd want the best for them, wouldn't you?"

Responding in slightly redundant fashion, I said, "I don't have any family members, sir."

"Well then, there you go." And with that, he turned to walk on.

Trotting to catch up, I said, "But how do you know that doctors aren't doing it?"

"Doing what?"

"Taking out radioactive gallbladders?"

Dr. O'Dwyer just waved a confident hand and said, "Because by the time they're fully trained, doctors are too invested in our system to try anything radical and understand well enough that 'do no harm' applies to the state as much as anyone else. Besides, gallbladder anatomy is not taught in basic medical courses anymore. It's reserved for specialists, the same as we do with pharmacology."

He quickened his pace, and I hurried to stay with him; then he added in lockstep, "Anyway, it's hard enough for the doctors to keep up with what we do teach them. Medical information doubles every year, and we find a new organ in the body every five to ten years. Heck, we've found more organs in the last fifty years than in the first five thousand." Pausing to reflect momentarily, he said, "Yep, the human body is an ever-changing and fascinating organism!"

We turned to move on, but still focused on the nanobot implant I had just learned about, I asked, "Wait, are you forcibly drugging people?"

"Not at all. We can't do that unless you are a danger to the populace. The estrogen and Pitocin can't even be turned on until you exhibit some signs of antisocial behavior."

"How early does that happen?"

"Usually by about age five or so."

I just shook my head and said, "It sounds a bit artificial to me."

We had just entered a new room that looked like a warehouse, and Dr. O'Dwyer halted suddenly and turned toward me, retorting confidently, "Steven, using medications to relieve the pain of life is in our genes. Even the Neanderthals self-medicated."

I said, "Oh. Well, do you also give antidepressants with the nanobot?"

He laughed that one away lightheartedly. "Of course not! We don't need to automatically give antianxiety meds or antidepressants to anyone. After all, some people never wind up needing them."

Skeptical, I said, "How many?"

He shrugged. "Well, I don't."

I frowned and insisted, "How many of the *ordinary* ones?"

Finally, he relented. "Okay, all of them do, but it's easier to distribute those kinds of medications individually than in the nanobot. Look, here are the crates we ship them in."

"The nanobots?"

"No, the newborns. And we give them a year's supply of probiotics and—"

"Seriously?"

Dr. O'Dwyer shook his head knowingly and said, "Steven, infants' digestive systems are horribly irregular, but it's usually nothing to worry about as long as they get the right medications from the get-go. Also, we include an inhaler, the goggles you already know about, and several pamphlets. Here's *Understanding Your Newborn's Mental Health Disorders*, which you've already seen. And here is *Medication Dosages to Promote Early Regularity in Infants*, and here's one of our most popular titles: *The Girl Who Wouldn't Take Her Medicine.*"

I opened the last one and scanned through it. "Butterflies in stomach, fear growing, spelling test, wanted to hide in bed ..."

He continued explaining, "They're all mandatory for the parents to read to the child before age three. We also have *The CentRex Stork Brought Me a New Sibling*. That one helps to explain to children how they came to be."

Looking up at him again, I asked, "But how do you know that they read all of these?"

He pointed to the crate. "Right here. Look. There's a push-button contract on the outside that they have to depress to open it, and part of the contract says that the parents agree to read to their kid."

"Or what?"

He gave me an incredulous look. "What do you mean 'or what'? We've never had a problem with that. Steven, people understand that what science says these days is best for them, and that benefits everyone. You've probably heard that motto about stability, right? If we still had paper money, we could print that motto on every scrap of currency, but there's no need. Most people would rather be comfortable than free, and it's not necessary to remind them of that. Without us providing them with a system that allows them to take their lives completely for granted, they would be totally lost, so as a result, when we say that something needs to be done, people obey."

Suddenly, he clapped his hands together and said satisfactorily, "Well, that about does it for the day!" As he walked by, he gave me a pat on the shoulder that I thought might have dislocated something, but I pretended not to be affected and simply nodded and smiled at him. After that, all I could do was make my way back to the director's office, nursing my shoulder and feeling eerily disquieted about everything I had seen thus far.

*

THREE

The lab was nearly empty by then, and as I made my way through the mechanical rows, I felt a sense of incredible unease at the whole process. The level of human control they were exerting in that place was astounding, and I couldn't imagine how they were able to get away with it. None of this was taught to us in school—and probably for good reason, as I'm sure that most people would rebel if they really knew what was going on. The notion of people simply being handed such large sums of money at birth also bit into me fiercely and just reminded me of the tremendous disadvantage my parents left me with. Still, this was the only opportunity I had to try to raise myself from my prior surroundings, and I was going to stick with it as best as I possibly could.

When I arrived at the director's office, he was just finishing up something and looked up expectantly. "Hi, Steven! How did everything go?"

Trying not to reveal any of my disquietude, I simply sat down, still rubbing my shoulder, and observed innocently, "Wow, what a whirlwind of a day."

Closing the folder he was writing in, he gave me a concerned look and said, "Did you hurt yourself?"

"No, but Dr. O'Dwyer is ... a pretty brusque guy."

He chuckled, apparently having gotten over the social brusqueness he experienced earlier that day. "Oh yes, but people in authoritative positions often must be, since science proves that workers in bad moods perform better than those in happy moods. I myself sometimes have to remember that Ol' Gordon's persona is just another motivational tool that we have here, but you're tough enough, and you'll learn a lot from working with him." Leaning forward eagerly, he said, "Hey, I'll bet you could use a stiff drink!"

I shook my head anxiously and replied, "Oh, I don't normally."

"Come on! Let's go out and celebrate your new job! After all, one of the hallmarks of a stable society is the ability to cut loose from time to time."

I hesitantly agreed, but before we got up to leave, the director added a new level of discomfort to my day by reaching into his desk and pulling out yet another electronic contraption—a digital watch with nearly the same functions as the cell phone I was already carrying. Before even reaching out to accept it, I asked uneasily, "Wait, why do I need one of those?"

"Oh, to call people."

I pulled the phone out of my pocket for the first time since it had been given to me and gently waved it in front of him as a reminder that I could already make calls if I needed to, although I had no intention of doing so.

The director adopted a peculiar expression at my dislike of technological devices and asked, "What's the matter, Steven? Didn't you have any of these things at the orphanage?"

"Not really. We had a rotary dial phone at the orphanage, and the first time I ever saw a computer was in college."

He just leaned forward insistently and said, "Well, these are required government-issued devices, so you'll have to get used to them."

I took the watch from him, and he instructed me to press the little thumbprint activator on the device, which I did with extreme reluctance. Then I quickly shoved the phone back in my pocket, strapped on the watch, and issued a half-hearted thank-you.

Satisfied at that, he smiled assuredly and said, "Good! Shall we go?"

"Sure, but I have plenty of questions, and I hope that you can answer them for me."

"No problem. Let's go to Fontana's! It's one of my favorite places to cut loose!"

The bar was several long blocks away, and when we got there at four thirty, it was already packed. We selected a quiet booth, and I ordered a soda water, which initially disappointed the director, but he understood that I still had questions.

He continued his explanation while he nursed a beer. "Oh, no, of course not. See, we started by trying to eradicate childhood diseases. We were working on repairing gene mutations that led to spina bifida, Down's syndrome, and the like. It was all a very good place to start; then people came to us and asked us to do more."

"Like what?"

"Well, kids were being born mostly healthy, but we still couldn't get rid of all of the awful killings. Honestly, Steven, there was a very dark time when there was a mass shooting of some sort every single day, and it was tearing us apart. So we tried to get rid of guns to stop the problem, and the killers went to knives. We got rid of knives—well, everything but the plastic ones they use in school cafeterias—and they started using pressure cookers. We got rid of pressure cookers, and the next thing we knew, the Boston Strangler came back. So we finally did away with the reason why people do all of those things in the first place."

"Which is?"

"Awareness of self. And it worked like a charm!" With that, he took a long, satisfying pull on his beer.

"How did lobotomizing 17.5 percent of the population solve all of that, and how do you decide who gets lobotomized anyway?"

Setting his glass down again, he answered, "To start with your last question first, we originally used genealogy searches to determine who to lobotomize."

"What?"

He smiled briefly and said, "Oh yes, and the funny thing is that people had already paid for them themselves! A preselected lobotomized birth was prescribed to everyone whose family could not demonstrate ten generations of fine, upstanding living. Those were, as studies showed, the real at-risk population, and that first measuring stick weeded out a lot of dangerous people who came from families with criminal backgrounds and others who had just been drifters in society."

"Isn't that a little elitist?"

He shook his head. "Not at all. Don't forget, Steven, that you are part of the affirmative action program that proves that we create a level playing field for everyone." As I was mulling over his "level playing field" comment, he added, "Anyway, we had to eliminate mass murder. The one thing about having people accept whatever you feed them is that it makes them easy targets."

I took a thoughtful pull on my drink and scanned around the bar, wondering how many of these people had been mechanically deprived of their awareness. Most of them looked blissfully content, but that could have just been from the alcohol. I finally said, "So how did you come up with 17.5 percent?"

The director responded, "Originally we could only lobotomize 3 percent, but it turned out to be a hugely popular program."

"You're kidding?"

"I know what you're thinking—what parent would willingly do that to their child, right?"

I involuntarily stiffened in my chair. *Holy crap! Was he recording my earlier conversation with Dr. O'Dwyer?*

The director took no notice, as he was studying his half-empty glass, and answered distractedly, "Steven, you'll soon realize the tremendous benefit that comes with being lobotomized. For some people, it absolutely makes sense, and science proves that."

"So you convinced 17.5 percent of the population that they needed to have lobotomized kids?"

After downing the rest of his glass and belching nonchalantly to the side, he revealed, "Actually, it's closer to 35 percent."

I shot up in the booth. "*What?*"

"Seventeen point five percent is the number of people who can be statutorily *ordered* to have lobotomized kids. The rest are all made up of the voluntary lobotomies."

"Yeah, the Daisy Buchanans, right?"

He smiled. "Very good! You're learning fast!"

"But that's more than a third of the population that is lobotomized? Why don't you just substitute out someone who wants a voluntary lobotomy for someone who is forced to have one?"

The absurdity of my question forced a hiccup out of him, and he shook his head incredulously and said, "How? Steven, no one ever knows what they actually get. Even though they may request a lobotomized child or have one assigned to them, the actual process is totally randomized because of antidiscrimination laws, so all they'd be trading is a chance for a chance."

I sat up again and asked in astonishment, "You mean that the parents will never know at all if they got a lobotomized kid?"

"Nope. Well, after they reach a certain age you can tell when you're talking to a lobotomized person—if you have the right training, that is."

"But do the people who request a lobotomized kid have to pay for it?"

"Of course. It's not as much as the ones who request a non-lobotomized child, but—"

I gasped. "You make people *pay* to have a kid who isn't lobotomized?"

The director responded nonchalantly, "Naturally. Steven, procreating is not an inherent right, and people have to pay to play."

I took another sip of my soda water and tried to let the shock dissipate. Then I said, "So 17.5 percent of the population is made up of criminals and drifters?"

He had already ordered another beer, and he laughed briefly at my continued misapprehension. "Oh, heavens no! I told you that was just the original measuring stick, but the original percentage was also much lower. As the percentage increased because of economic and other demands, we had to broaden the criteria. Over time, we also had far fewer people who were either committing crimes or refusing to participate in our economy."

"So what happened?"

"Well, next we went to the welfare rolls." As he took the beer brought to him, he nodded to me and added, "But that's a no-brainer. After that, we moved on and started lobotomizing fetuses whose parents had never reached a leadership position in their lives; then we lobotomized those whose parents had never won an award of any kind."

"Award? Like what?"

"Oh, fairly significant ones. I'm not talking about the awards that they automatically give kids for athletic participation before the game even starts. I'm talking about something recognized on a larger scale and which shows a lifetime of dedication and achievement."

"But isn't that setting the bar a little high?"

The director shook his head assuredly and responded, "Quite the opposite, since we've been very generous in the selection criteria. We expanded it to every form of award: Nobel, military, VMA, CMA, ACM, Viewer's Choice, Grammy, MTV Video Music Awards—you name it. And with the sheer number of awards shows we have these days, that covers a lot of people.

"However, with the population constantly growing while the number of lobotomies that we're allowed stays the same, we are continually having to revise and expand the criteria. These days, if you know someone who won a major award, or once had a photo taken with one of them, you can also be selected for a non-lobotomized child. We also do drawings, raffles, and other contests, and ten people from every award show and ten people watching at home from the audience are randomly picked to be in a drawing to have a non-lobotomized kid. They receive follow-up phone calls and have to answer a mystery question, and then they can qualify." Taking a quick swig of his beer, he added confidently, "Overall, it's a pretty egalitarian system."

"How much do they have to pay to have a non-lobotomized kid if they're not one of the lucky ones selected?"

"About a hundred million dollars."

"Holy hell, that's a lot of money! How do you ever get them to pay that much?"

"Well, most don't, since people in lower classes rely on their insurance money for life's essentials and can rarely save enough from working to keep it replenished. However, I already told you that lobotomies are really no worse off than everyone else, and most people, in fact, take it to be a blessing, which is why so many will actually pay to have a lobotomized kid."

Still skeptical, I said, "Oh yeah, how much does that cost?"

"Ninety-two dollars and fifty cents. But we also give them a rebate coupon for one hundred fifty thousand off the purchase of a new car."

I sat up and demanded, "What? So why do you charge them for it in the first place?"

He responded plainly, "Mostly just to cover a small administrative fee." Then he signaled for another drink.

As I was still trying to understand everything, and still nursing my soda water, I said, "So." I paused, still trying to do the arithmetic in my head. "All you've really done is price the cost of having a non-lobotomized kid out of the reach of everyone except those who wouldn't ever be stuck having one in the first place?"

He set down his glass and half-frowned, half-belched at me. "Oh, Steven, that's a dreadfully dreary way to look at it."

"But is that right?"

He shrugged. "Pretty much."

I shifted uncomfortably in the booth and said, "Sounds like a trap to me."

The director responded assuredly, "No, no. Steven, we actually have the freest system in the world, and our citizens are happier than they are anywhere else. Trust me; you'll see."

I responded truculently, "Yeah, maybe."

Slightly defensive, he said, "Look, you can't see the whole picture yet. These laws are for their own protection. Think of it this way—you wouldn't argue against traffic signals, now would you?"

I shook my head. "How the hell are traffic signals related?"

The director responded indignantly, "Well, people complained about those when they were first invented, but traffic signals help slow people down and keep us safe."

Still riddled with confusion, which wasn't helped by the non sequitur nature of his comment, I said, "Wait. I don't understand how the lab births fit into all of this, or how you got this all started in the first place."

The director leaned back and answered, "Well, that's a little more complicated. See, a long time ago, there was a great uproar to make this country great again. However, the problem was that the entire world had changed, and it was going to be impossible for people to take life for granted the way they used to when we were able to exploit over half of the world's population. So we had to change the game.

"The year 2062 brought with it several watershed events. America had managed to establish a colony on the moon, and that colony opened the first non-GMO responsibly sourced sushi restaurant. It was an absolute pinnacle moment for humanity's reach into space. Everyone realized that if we all started to cooperate, we could move our reach farther and farther out and hopefully make first contact with alien life. That new hope caused countries to put down their economic swords and reorganize the international economy into something that would further space exploration for all."

Astonished at his narrative, I leaned back and asked, "All of that because of a sushi restaurant?"

The director nodded firmly. "Oh, yes. Nothing could possibly evidence our modern sensibilities to advanced cultures greater than selling responsibly sourced sushi in space. We also eventually emerged as the world leader in the export of lobotomization techniques, which allowed us to achieve permanent economic dominance and beat everyone in the race to colonize the planets. That was also the year that we ended the great debate—about circumcisions, that is." I thought about diving into that topic, but just let it go. He continued. "Anyway, with the first Charter Toward Galactic Equality, world leaders decided to do away with the old economic system. It had become so muddled with esoteric difficulties, pitfalls, and loopholes anyway that it was much better to move on to an entirely new system, and we now operate according to IVF."

"What's that?"

"The International Valuation of Fetuses. Steven, the insurance policies we operate under are also now standard in every country. The value of the policies for a country's citizens is based on a formula that measures quality of life multiplied by economic prosperity. As you may know, a US fetal insurance policy is worth four hundred fifty million dollars. A corresponding policy for someone born in Nigeria, for example, is worth twenty-five million. The value of other countries' policies vary similarly all over the world."

I sat forward abruptly. "Wait a minute. Are you telling me that a baby born in the US is worth more than someone born somewhere else?"

The director acted as if I just learned that today ended in a *y*. He laughed and said, "Of course, Steven! It's always been that way! Heck, people even come here from other countries just to order babies, all in strict accordance with economic might. And since we own the majority shares of all the space colonies, it is also in accordance with intergalactic economic law."

The lunacy of it all was almost too much to bear. I felt as though I had left my home country and arrived in an alien environment, and everything they did felt completely artificial and fake to me. All of that talk about money that was just automatically doled out to those little egged humans that rolled off the assembly line also made me very irate, and I finally asked, "Well, why don't I have an insurance policy?"

He shook his head regretfully and responded, "Unfortunately, because your parents committed suicide, they voided the policy that would have been given to you. I'm sorry about that." Then he added with a reassuring smile, "But, hey, don't worry about it. I don't have an insurance policy either!"

Astonished, I said, "You don't?"

"Oh, no. Those of us entrusted with the duty to be public servants can't maintain insurance policies. That's just one of the breaks, but the honor of the position more than makes up for that." He leaned across the booth to nudge my arm and added, "And remember; you're one of us now. You'll get the same benefits that any government worker with your health history gets."

It appears that my frown had taken on a look of panicked desperation while I tried to sort everything out, because the director suddenly leaned forward and said, "Steven, relax! Now that you're working at the center, you're pretty much the same as we are. And you may not realize it, but we've taken good care of you all these years to make sure that you would be ready to eventually join us."

My eyes widened in astonishment. "You did?"

"Sure. Look at it this way—when you were a kid, you were sent to an orphanage. I went to boarding school."

"And that's the same?"

He nodded and finished his beer, excusing himself for belching again. "Pretty much, and that's why we usually bring you right in to serve with us when you're out of school."

"Do they use the allowance system at the boarding school?"

The director paused and then responded, a bit clumsily, "Well ... no. I mean, not exactly. The boarding school kids all exist off their parents' credit."

That floored me. "So I had to grow up excluded from even the basic element of the economic system shared by the rest of society?"

He sighed and gave me a look of gentle pity. "Yeah, and sorry about that, but without parents to qualify you for the insurance system, there wasn't anything we could do." Then he tried to brighten the mood again and said, "Look, Steven, I'm sorry that you have that burden to live with, but you'll be able to get over it with plenty of hard work."

That was the same thing people had been telling me since I could remember. I had been working my entire life up to this point and had now barely scratched my way into an entry-level job that I'm sure others were just handed, the same as they were handed insurance policies without having to earn any of it. I was still determined to make it somehow, but my resentment about their system kept growing with every new detail I learned.

The director could perhaps sense my worsening mood, and as

if on cue, he reached into his pocket and said nonchalantly, "Oh, I almost forgot to give this to you. Here's your new identification card for the lab."

Not expecting anything stupendous, I half-heartedly sat up to take it from him. "Thanks. Say, I don't remember ever filling out any employment paperwork. Do I still need to do that?"

"Nope. That was all handled when you scanned your thumb on initial entry."

"What about, er, a security clearance or whatever? Come to think of it, aside from the desk clerk, I haven't seen any security around here at all."

He chuckled lightly and said, "Oh, we don't use that anymore! We have hidden security drones flying around the building during working hours. They prescan everyone coming in and out, so there's no need for a physical security presence, but most people these days don't go where they're not supposed to anyway."

"What about armed guards?"

The director slapped his knee. "Ha! With lobotomies, who needs them?" Then he added, "We do still have a few around for public events, but not many."

"I see." I looked down at my new card, and it had a G-7 designation on it. I could guess well enough what the G stood for but had to ask about the 7 part.

"That's your citizenship score."

I looked up, surprised. "I have a citizenship score?"

"Oh yes. Now that you've joined us, we've given you a fresh score. For most people, it's a combination of their credit rating and their NarXex score."

"NarXex?"

"That's a measure of how often you utilize health services and what types of prescriptions you take. It goes from 1 to 10, with 10 being someone who doesn't use the health care system at all."

"So how did I get to 7?"

"Intensive psychotherapy when you were a baby." Then he added solemnly, "You know, because of the suicide of your parents."

I was sick of hearing about that by now, but I tried to play it cool. "Huh. I don't remember that at all."

"Well, trust me; it happened. Don't you remember people telling you about your parents when you were a kid?"

Disgustedly, I said, "Yeah, like a million times."

He shrugged. "Well, I'm afraid that's all part of processing the loss. Anyway, we do our best to give you a fresh start when you come to work for us. Since you were an orphan, however, we did have to keep track of your spending on health services until you grew up."

Trying to sound curiously unassuming, I said, "It seems a little odd to make me pay for something that I don't even remember."

"Oh, it may seem that way, but we couldn't treat you any differently than anyone else. Hey, at least we didn't let it interfere with you paying for college."

I was loathfully disgusted at hearing him mention that, since I had heard that many others never had to pay for school. Most of them did only go to online schools attended from their parents' apartments, but it sucked paying for my own education.

Still trying to piece everything together, I asked him how my own citizenship score fit into the whole mix. To my utter shock, he explained that the numerical designation represented a percentage of the same insurance money that everyone else received at birth. Suddenly realizing that I had been given what was apparently an incredible sum of money with this new position, I leaned back and exclaimed, "You mean that I have 70 percent of an entire insurance policy's worth of money available to me?"

The director simply affirmed, and nearly instantaneously, I was in awe at the notion of having so much wealth at my fingertips. However, something also seemed very peculiar about the whole scheme, and I asked him how the government could ever afford to just hand people such large amounts of money.

The director explained that long ago, during the dark times, the entire country had to be nearly shut down because of virus outbreaks, and at that point, the credit system in the US grew out of control and the notion of credit became worthless in this country, along with the currency that used to back it. I had read some of this as well in school, but my teachers also kept me from asking too many questions about an era that they considered better forgotten in new times.

The director also explained that robots had been employed on mass scale around the same time, which also had the effect of depressing wages earned by ordinary people. It was at that time that the US switched to guaranteed income for its citizens, which eventually morphed into the credit/insurance system they used today. He also explained that everyone not working for the government was classified from A through F, and that their numerical scores would rise and fall based on their spending and earning over a lifetime.

Still largely unschooled in the greater functioning of the system but also partially tantalized by now, I looked up from the shiny new card in my hand and asked, "Can people cash in on their insurance policies?"

He let out a belly laugh in response and said amusedly, "Sure, I guess technically they can! But no one ever does."

"Why not?"

He answered decisively, "Humans these days are focused on long-term goals, and the insurance program helps to facilitate that. If they made the rash decision to cash in their insurance policy, they would of course run into same problem that lottery winners have."

"Which is?"

"Steven, easy money weighs light in the hand and doesn't give you the feeling that you've earned it.[1] People who come into a large sum of money invariably wind up blowing it and dying broke. That happens to lottery winners and top athletes, and it happened to people who in the past tried to cash in their policies. Thankfully, we've been educating people about sound financial decisions for many years now, and they tend to listen pretty well."

I took that all to heart and reminded myself not to go overboard on any spending decisions until I knew a bit more how everything fit together. Then I asked him whether I would be able to get an accounting of my spending with this new citizenship score, and he leaned back and laughed. "Oh Steven, you're probably the first government worker who has ever worried about keeping track of spending!"

It took him several moments to recover from that hilarious notion. Then he diplomatically added, "Actually, most people never have to worry about it in their lifetimes, but we do send people notification if their scores ever get too low. We also monitor spending decisions by certain classes to make sure that they don't run out of money before their time."

He continued for a while to explain the intricacies of the credit/insurance system and the limitations the government employed to keep everyone protected in their purchasing decisions. I didn't fully grasp all of that at the time, as I was reveling in my newfound social status and actually started to feel very fortunate in those brief hours sitting with him at the bar. It almost seemed as if my life were taking a tremendous upturn for reasons which I could not fathom, and all I could think to say to him when he finished explaining was, "Listen, thanks for giving me this incredible opportunity and taking time out of your schedule for me!"

He gave me a knowing smile and replied, "Don't mention it! I'm always happy to help a newcomer fit into our glorious society!"

As I leaned back in sheer awe of the whole thing, the director took his own opportunity to signal for another round. An effeminate-looking creature of some sort came over—apparently, a replacement for our old server, who was just getting off her shift—and she brought the tab for the director to settle so the other could leave for the evening.

Realizing what was happening, and also now eager to show appreciation for what I had been given, I quickly offered to pay. However, the director gently declined and said, "Oh no, Steven, that's not necessary. Trust me; you'll need your credits for plenty of other things while you're around!"

With that, the waitress turned to him and held up a device which appeared to take his photograph; then she handed him the receipt. Looking down at it, the director nodded satisfactorily and proceeded to order two raspberry gin and cokes.

- THE MADMAN -

As she sauntered away, I asked him about the photo business, and he replied, "Oh, that. Well, we've recently adopted retinal technology into point-of-sale transactions so that the tip is automatically calculated based on your level of enjoyment for the encounter. It's a wonderful benefit, but you'll want to be careful and cultivate a firm '12 percent' look."

I leaned back and asked, astonished, "What the hell is that?"

"It's a look that conveys that you enjoyed the service as much as you should have based on your social standing but also recognize that service workers should never be overcompensated for their efforts."

I shook my head and asked, "Why can't I just pay with my thumb like I used to and then type in the tip amount?"

"Oh, you can in most places, but this new technology is cropping up everywhere, and you'll get the hang of it."

Not having been able to get the hang of anything that had been explained to me since arriving in that city, I shrugged gently and asked, "And what was that you ordered for us?"

He smiled eagerly and responded, "Gin mixed with raspberry-flavored cocaine!"

I shot up in my seat and said astonished, "*I can't drink that!*"

"Don't worry. The flavoring is distilled from gelatin, so it doesn't interfere with the narcotics."

"No, I've barely drank alcohol in my life! I can't handle hard drugs!"

He waved a hand at me and chided lightly, "Oh, Steven, don't be such a rube! We've been purifying narcotics for ages. The stuff we have nowadays is as harmless as table sugar, and it's absolutely guaranteed not to cause any dangerous side effects."

I whipped my head around at the other patrons and what they were doing. Turning back to the director, I asked confused, "But they sell drugs in public places?"

"Sure. These days, we have pot bars, heroin bars, and nearly every other type of bar. This happens to be a coke bar."

I observed uneasily, "That seems a little dangerous."

"Quite the contrary. Regulating drugs this way is a perfectly scientific method to keep them off the streets." Coaxing me along, he added innocently, "Look, it's okay; everyone does it!"

Our attendant came back with a tray and smiled at me expectantly. Realizing that resistance was impossible, and now also incredibly eager to remain in the director's favor, I smiled shallowly and accepted one of the glasses.

The director raised his own and toasted, "To the lobotomies!"

I simply nodded at him and said, "Oh, okay. Here goes nothing …"

*

FOUR

I couldn't tell whether the sun was out yet, but I didn't dare look, and my brain was pounding from a hellacious hangover. I shoved my head under the pillow to try to arrest the throbbing sensation behind my eyes, but I couldn't get back to sleep. Despite the drugs from last night, my dreams were plagued with images of giant mechanical arms sweeping down from the sky and slicing consciousness out of people's minds, and just like the lobotomies in the lab, none of the people in my dreams seemed to take any notice of what was happening to them.

I finally raised my head up and saw my new identification card sitting on the desk, and my thoughts suddenly turned to my newfound social status and what I could possibly do with it. However, my apartment was already taken care of by the government, and now I had two superfluous tech devices that I didn't need, so I couldn't imagine what I might do with the money they had given me. I remembered that the director had also revealed to me that he was at G-9 status and that I could get there as well if I worked hard enough and logged enough hours, and I started to envision that as a lofty goal to work toward, even as I contemplated what I might have to do to get there.

I finally surrendered to the notion of facing the day and threw the pillow on the floor, but my thoughts returned to the actual lobotomies in the lab. As I rose to shower, I admitted that I could have it all wrong. Maybe it wasn't so bad. I remember feeling fearless when I was a kid, and I considered that could just be how they feel all the time. When I was younger, people all around me were trying to tell me about the world, and I didn't care one whit. None of what they said mattered. What mattered was doing what I felt at the time, regardless of the risks, so maybe the lobotomies really were lucky.

As I stepped out of the shower and noticed my cell phone and watch sitting on the desk, I also flashed back to seeing the internet for the first time in college. Now *that* scared me to death. I couldn't imagine how anyone could ever hope to find truth in that electronic jungle, and I didn't have any interest in dialing back into that world with these government-required devices.

However, as I was drying off, one of the buttons on my watch started blinking a soft blue, and I began to worry that my watch or phone might be used to send me messages about my job duties. I couldn't afford to mess up anything at this point, so I hesitantly clicked on the button. To my surprise, the daily news update appeared.

Urgent Report: Government on Verge of
Collapse! End of the Country in Sight!

Terrified, I shouted, "Holy shit! I'm going to get fired before I even get started!" I dressed as quickly as I could and sprinted to the center. I shot straight up the elevator to the sixth floor, fidgeting nervously the whole time while the elevator was in no apparent distress for its own part. When I got off on six, I rushed into the director's office and found him toying with some electronic contraption.

Gasping for breath, I efforted, "Director … have you heard?"

He looked up with calm curiosity. "Heard what?"

I was doubled over and sputtered desperately, *"News headline … government … collapse!"*

He chuckled and went back to fiddling with the device. "Oh, don't worry about it! Some of those stories can be a little overdramatic at times, and I'm sure the problem will sort itself out." Glancing over at the clock on his desk, he looked up at me with mild concern and said, "Hey, you're going to be late. Better get back downstairs."

Still in shock, I turned and walked back to the elevator, my heart pounding in my chest. I headed back to the first floor, but the slow elevator ride only continued to fuel my anxiety. The world wasn't going to end, but I was close to being late for my second day on the job.

When the elevator hit one, I received another jolt that morning, in the form of an abrupt collision with a poor, unfortunate soul. As I was racing out of the elevator, I saw him about five feet in front of me and sensed the imminent collision. I tried to warn him, but I was moving through space faster than my words could come out, and all I could manage was "moooooo" before I bowled him over. He never saw me at all but rather seemed to be stuck in a suspended twirl of some sort and unable to react in time, and his body crumpled like a paper house from the force of the blow.

Coming to a halt over his disheveled body, I exclaimed, "Oh my goodness! I am so sorry about that!"

Unaware of what had just happened, Dr. O'Dwyer looked up from his clipboard and said, "Steven, there you are." Then he looked down and noticed the disassembled figure lying on the ground. "Oh, hello, Smith. Doing okay down there?"

Smith gasped in pain. *"Not ... not really, sir."*

Dr. O'Dwyer shook his head and chided, "Playing with your VR contacts again?"

Somehow managing to still be slightly embarrassed, Smith replied, *"Yes sir. I was on a ..."*—gasp—*"... break."*

"Well, we'll get someone in here right away to take you to the hospital. Don't worry about a thing."

"Yes sir. Thank you. And if I don't see you again ..."

Dr. O'Dwyer nodded gently and responded, "I know, I know."

The demolished Smith looked up and motioned me down with one finger, and I hunched down over his broken body as he gasped and tried to collect himself. Barely in a whisper, he said, *"Steven."*

"Yes?"

"Steven ..."— gasp—*"... can you do my work for me today?"*

Overwhelmed with shame for the incident, I stuttered, "Sure, I ... um ..."

Dr. O'Dwyer butted in loudly and grabbed my shoulder, yanking me to my feet. "Never mind that, Smith. Steven is still in training. We'll take care of it."

As a team with a stretcher rolled in, Dr. O'Dwyer turned me away from the carnage and we headed toward the rear of the facility. Looking back at the emergency crew's ministrations and still unnerved from the whole experience, I asked, "Why the hell do they let people walk around with those things on?"

Dr. O'Dwyer responded sarcastically, "Because lobotomies have no concept of time, but for some reason also can't stand a single lucid moment. So by law, we have to let them use the VR devices on all breaks."

Confused again, I said, "Wait, he's a lobotomy?"

Dr. O'Dwyer scratched his head momentarily. "Is he? Maybe. I'll have to check his records." Deflecting the conversation, he laughed and added lightly, "But he sure was a dork! That's all his dad's fault!"

"What?"

"His dad waited until he was sixty to order him."

"Is that bad?"

"Well, studies prove that the older your dad is, the more of a geek you turn out to be. Unfortunately it can't be helped these days, since men have been steadily ordering children at older and older ages."

Still trying to process everything from the morning, I said, "But you have lobotomies working here?"

"Oh, sure, in some capacities. Steven, we've even had lobotomies elected to the presidency."

There was jolt number three for the day, and I exclaimed, "*You have got to be kidding me!*"

"Not at all. Steven, don't forget de Tocqueville's famous internet post: 'The election of the president is only ever a cause of temporary agitation, but never ruin.'"[2] I was not at all familiar with that one, and he simply remarked, "Don't worry. You'll understand after a while."

We meandered back to the shipping department again, and Dr. O'Dwyer continued musing about the problem of the VR contacts and how best to let people get their daily information fix. "Sure, we could implant a neurotransmitter and have internet messages beamed right into the brain, but the economy is no good without free choice, and that would make people just respond like robots. And besides, if we put a chip in the brain, other people could just hack it, and then we'd be stuck with a bunch of sleeper cells floating around. Anyway, robots don't need therapy now, do they?"

"No, I guess not. But is poor mental health that much of a problem?"

He let out a sarcastic laugh. "Have you looked around lately? It's everywhere, and nowadays, people don't even know what's wrong with them until we tell them."

I was only half-listening at this point. We passed an assistant who smiled warmly at me, and without thinking, I gave him a reassuring pat on the shoulder, which dislocated immediately. Apologizing lightly, I said, "Oops, sorry about that. I keep forgetting." Trying to refocus, I turned back to Dr. O'Dwyer and attempted a thoughtful question: "Isn't this all still a little controlling?"

He shook his head proudly and observed: "Steven, what do you think we're here for?" I frowned at him, and he added lightly, "Hey, at least it's better than it used to be. Let me tell you, in the dark times we had babies born with opiate withdrawal, and AIDS. This all may seem like control, but in the end, getting rid of the bigger problems allows us to focus on the things that really make life worth living. Besides, parents were overdosing kids, so we had to take over."

"But doesn't the artificial nature of the lab affect the biological relationship?"

"Oh, no, we fixed all of that. Now we give the parents two weeks off from work after their orders arrive. It's just like getting used to a new pet, and then they're off to daycare."

I remembered the orphanage and said snidely, "So you just dump them off on someone else?"

"Not at all. We use highly trained child technicians."

"You mean nannies?"

"Yes. And lobotomies make the best ones. Oh, don't worry, it's not that bad. We have virtual chat at work so parents can talk to the kids, and they don't even notice the difference."

"Yeah, sure."

Defensively, Dr. O'Dwyer retorted, "Hey, you didn't notice that you were rocked to sleep at night by a mechanical crib, did you?"

I answered sarcastically, "Not unless that was a cause of the intensive psychotherapy I had as a child."

He responded automatically, "No, that wasn't it, but it's sure better than it used to be. I tell you, in the past we had parents who didn't even know how to put their kids to bed safely, and it's sure a good thing that we came along to fix it."

"I guess so."

Nodding in my direction, he continued. "Now we use specially trained people who *do* know how to put a kid down safely. The nannies, as you call them, also help prevent parental burnout, which was a huge problem in the past. Trying to be perfect parents was literally killing people, and for others, having a child and then dumping the child off so that the parents can work two jobs is the only way to get ahead."

We stopped by one of the crates being loaded with a newborn, and Dr. O'Dwyer looked down at the brand-new baby, adopted an uncharacteristically loving tone, and then added, "Besides, we've been following and cataloguing people's experiences for so long that we already know that you won't be much different, will you, little guy?" He waved to the technician to close the crate and wiped his hands together. Standing up, he said to me, "Anyway, with an entire society frozen in childhood, not much changes these days."

Still feeling myself slipping down the rabbit hole, I grasped. "Don't the psychiatrists and psychologists have something to say about this?"

He snorted loudly, "Are you kidding? It was their idea, and all made possible thanks to the grand patron, Sigmund Freud, who first showed us how to keep people busy with fixations on childhood for their entire lives! But without him, we'd be lost. Based on everything we know now, human beings could not possibly endure their environment without the distractions we give them."

My drug hangover was wearing off, and as I glanced around at the precision of human control being leveled in the center, a sharp chill ran through me. As innocently as possible, I finally asked, "Are you sure that all of this is necessary?"

"Oh, absolutely. Steven, humans could not possibly survive without all of the things we provide to them, and science has proven that to an irrefutable certainty."

But he could see that I wasn't convinced, so to prove his point, Dr. O'Dwyer directed me to the back of the lab, where we descended a long, winding flight of stairs through a door marked "In Utero Department." The sign was faded, obviously a remnant from earlier times, but the stairwell was encased in solid steel and must have been very thick judging by the lack of echoes. We finally emerged into a giant basement of some sort, and Dr. O'Dwyer pointed me down a vast corridor.

It was eerily quiet compared to the lab, and I half-expected some sort of monster to jump out at us. By contrast, Dr. O'Dwyer was completely at ease in the bowel of his workshop and narrated as we walked along. "Steven, there was a dark period when the lobotomies had to be performed inside the mother, and back here is where those used to take place. Then we pioneered births by incubation alone, and now we just do the lobotomies on the production line.

"The artificial placenta was, of course, the key to being able to gestate embryos in the lab. Plenty of others have suggested different techniques for ensuring stability—marinating fetuses in alcohol, coercion, force, slavery—you name it. But they never worked in the long run."

We turned a corner and headed toward a dimly lit door, and he continued authoritatively: "Just like the notion of sub-nine-month gestation. Let me tell you, that's pure fiction. Under optimal circumstances, the cake needs nine months to bake, and that's not going to change. And all that business about repeating mottos to make people better citizens—well, there's no need to do that. As we have discovered, once you give the lobotomies a good catch phrase, or even a new, interesting-sounding word, they'll repeat it like squirrels talking to each other in a tree."

Yeah, like "Stability is good for the economy, and ..." Wait, when was the last time someone actually said that to me? Why the hell do I keep saying it?

My hands darted back up to my scalp, and I felt around once more to make sure that I couldn't feel any scars. Dr. O'Dwyer saw me and laughed again, so I quickly dropped my arms to my side.

Arriving at our apparent destination, he pushed open a heavy unmarked metal door that opened into a sparsely filled room that held nothing but various scientific testing implements hanging in racks, and a giant, open-top metal enclosure centered in the room. As we approached, I saw that sitting in the enclosure was an organic substance like I had never seen, and it was pulsing and moving inside the box. It appeared to be a liquid of some sort, but it was concentrated all in the center, without spreading to the walls. It was also expanding and contracting in vertical fashion just like a seamless jellyfish and was metallic silver in appearance but seemed to change colors as it moved. It was, quite frankly, the most gorgeous thing I had ever seen.

Feeling as though we had just entered a haunted domain, I leaned over and whispered, "*What ... what is it?*"

Dr. O'Dwyer laughed and responded matter-of-factly, "A warm, shapeless pile of goo!"

Seeing no need to remain quiet, I straightened up and said, "Yes, I see that, but what is it?"

"The secret to humanity. It's called Narcissium. It has an atomic weight of zero, and as you see, it changes color with the slightest interaction."

"Yes, but what does it do?"

He laughed gently again and shrugged. "Almost nothing! Its properties won't allow it to, since it has no internal substance whatsoever. It's really incredible stuff. It could do almost anything if only it could learn to cooperate with other elements. However, it combusts with even the slightest amount of pressure or friction, and it also freezes at sixty-seven degrees and boils at sixty-eight. You can't put it into any container, because it just oozes over the side, constantly seeking the lowest center of gravity, and even more amazing, the Narcissium will climb walls if it believes that a lower center of gravity is nearby. If you try to put a lid on it and pressurize it, it vaporizes and reforms outside of the container, and it also won't mix with any other substances under any conditions or circumstances."

I was transfixed watching it undulate and morph across the color spectrum, and I exclaimed, "Holy cow!"

Dr. O'Dwyer nodded and said, "Yep, pretty amazing stuff. As you can see, Narcissium must always be kept in low light, and we have found that playing it soothing music also helps to keep it stable. You'll notice that the colors change, but it won't reflect anything back, since reflecting takes too much work."

"Where on earth did it come from?"

He responded proudly, "Oh, a truly magnificent and pioneering experiment that was the final discovery in the quest of human existence!"

Unable to take my eyes off of the substance, I asked mystically, "Which was?"

He recounted the details with brief initial annoyance. "Well, of course, it was a very 'controversial' experiment when we did it, but you may recall that we were still doing lobotomies in the actual womb back then, and it was a different time entirely. Anyway, we took one of the first lab-born babies and raised it perfectly. We applied the Buddha model to a T."

I shot him a confused look and said, "Who is Buddha?"

"Oh, he's the guy who taught us how to live in harmony with our environment by ridding ourselves of unnecessary suffering. Anyway, the child was kept entirely in the lab and was never exposed to any suffering, pain, ugly people, or the like, and you could say that he was the center of peace in the entire world. Then we gave him a rare form of leukemia."

Hearing that jolted me out of my trance, and I said, astonished, "What? Why?"

"Steven, we were on the quest to find the essence of all humanity.

That was believed at the time to be rooted in innocence, and of course, there is nothing more innocent than a ten-year-old with leukemia."

"Huh."

"Anyway, shortly after the disease took hold, we ran him through the Mega Huge Higgs Matter Collider."

My shock meter pegged. *You did what?*"

Dr. O'Dwyer said nonchalantly, "Oh, you don't know what that is?"

"No, I know exactly what it is! But it wasn't built for humans!"

"Of course not, but the discovery we made changed all of that."

"Was he hurt? Or did … did he wind up dying?"

Dr. O'Dwyer just shrugged. "Naturally." Then he looked down at my gaping mouth and added reassuringly, "Oh, I know what you're probably thinking, but when we explained to the child and his parents what we wanted to do, the child chose God instead of living in pain."

I shook my head furiously. "Wait, what pain?"

"Well, leukemia of course."

"Yeah, but *you* did that to him!"

He rolled his eyes gently, having obviously heard that one before. "Look, Steven, it's not like we could have kept the kid in here forever anyway, and he was bound to be disappointed in no time once we let him out into the real world—leukemia or not. Besides, we had already located the God particle through collider experiments, so this was an ideal way to also finalize the search for the missing link."

Momentarily forgetting my nontechnical background and recent inheritance of a citizenship score, I was thoroughly exasperated at this point, but Dr. O'Dwyer continued his discourse with complete calm. "So once we did the experiment, and of course after cleaning out all the pieces of skin, bone, and other shrapnel, we scooped up the remains and pulverized them with radiation. Then we ran the detritus through a 3-D element simulator/printer, and voilà, Narcissium was discovered!"

I stared back down at the substance and said, "Holy crap! That much came out of just one kid?"

He laughed and responded lightly, "Oh, heavens no! Under the wrong conditions, Narcissium replicates itself like a virus, but it doesn't consume any matter in the process. It is truly a very strange element—and also truly amazing." He shook his head and added incredulously, "To think; it was the missing link the whole time. We had completely forgotten to look for element number zero."

Still studying the substance, I scratched my head in disbelief and said, "It still seems like a huge price to pay for … that."

He waved a dismissive hand in response. "You sound like some of the naysayers back then, but the experiment was justified for the good of all. Remember, my boy, that if there is one thing that has made this country great, it is that we have always had citizens willing to sacrifice anything to keep us on top. People were even willing to starve on the streets just so we could build the collider in the first place."

Seeing that I was still in shock, he added with a reassuring nod, "Oh, and by the way, the family was greatly compensated for their sacrifice."

"And the kid?"

"We put up a statue to him."

"Where?"

He rubbed the back of his neck for a second, pondering how best to address that. Finally, he said, "Well, it used to be in front of the center, but we had to move it to make room for a new coffee bar." He quickly added, "Which was, of course, also in his honor!"

"You mean Cup O' Joe?"

"Yes."

"So the kid was named Joe?"

Pretending to momentarily notice something on the blank wall, he said, "Well, no. Actually, his name was Kenneth, but people liked to call him Joe."

I frowned at him and asked skeptically, "Yeah, like who?"

Dr. O'Dwyer responded uneasily, "Well, the guy who did the experiment, for one. Anyway, people paid attention to the statue for a while and then just lost interest. You'll find that it is very hard to hold lobotomies' attention for extended periods of time." A little hesitantly, he smiled awkwardly and added, "Plus, we did need a new coffee bar!"

My shock didn't dissipate, and I demanded, "Well, couldn't you have put it somewhere else?"

"I'm afraid that would have upset the aesthetic plan for the lawn, and you see how nice that looks, right?"

As I stared at him in disbelief, he frowned momentarily and then regained his old forceful demeanor. "Steven, the important takeaway is that we have the longest running, most successful free country in the world because of citizens like Joe—er, Kenneth—and they don't necessarily get hung up over big rewards for doing their civic duty."

As I stood there deadpan, he laughed and added confidently, "Heck, there were times in this country's history when we had to draft people to go to war, and when they unexpectedly came back alive and we didn't have any jobs for them, those patriotic citizens were more than willing to starve to death for the freedoms they fought to protect!"

Still not convinced, I said, "Yes, I've read about that, but this is different. You pulverized a kid through a particle collider!"

"Of course, Steven. Come on, we can't run every test on mice, you know. After all, most mice experiments don't work the same on humans anyway."

My stomach was turning, but Dr. O'Dwyer just continued on his scientific roll. "Oh, and we also repeated the experiment on every other manner of life: cows, chickens, ostriches—you name it. They all went straight down the collider, but nothing else living on earth produced Narcissium. However, we did discover something remarkable that all life forms have hidden deep inside them."

"Which is?"

"Dark matter. A nefarious buildup of particles nestled unsuspectingly throughout all organic tissue."

Hearing that temporarily halted my nausea at thinking about the poor kid and replaced it with skepticism. "Oh yeah?"

"Absolutely. We also discovered that dark matter is the number-one cause of obesity."

I wasn't buying this one and challenged, "And how did you find out that living creatures are made up of dark matter?"

Dr. O'Dwyer responded offhandedly, "Through the collider experiments, of course. We configured the machinery to harness the strong magnetic force from the universe, and then we calibrated it so it would not respond to any forms of matter found in organic life."

Dubious, I probed, "No metal in pockets?"

"Nope."

"No fillings in teeth?"

"Nope."

"How about some buckshot accidentally left in an animal?"

Now back in his comfort zone again, he waved a scientifically calculated hand and said firmly, "No, Steven. All of our experiments are perfectly controlled, so that's how we know that life forms are made up of dark matter."

I took one more stab. "Could it be that the collider is attracted to something else?"

"Of course not. Look, the most basic truth of all science is that when you have ruled out all other known explanations, the one you're left with is the right one. Besides, we've proven the experiment time and again. Bigger, fatter animals have more dark matter than smaller ones and hence smash against the collider wall with greater force."

He looked at me to see whether I would try again, but I simply shrugged and added another inquiry. "Wait. You said that dark matter causes obesity?"

He nodded definitively. "Oh, it most certainly does."

"I thought that was from lack of exercise?"

He had obviously heard that challenge before, and holding up a finger, he retorted, "Good thinking. That is, of course, another problem we face. However, even with regular exercise, people still gain weight, and even if they maintain less input than output, they still suffer the same problem. Plus, nothing could explain insulin resistance until we stumbled upon the real culprit. Steven, you have to understand that this nation leads the world in the accumulation of dark matter inside its citizens." Shaking his head, he said mournfully, "It was truly killing us until this little experiment came along."

"Huh." Suddenly visions of thousands of people being slammed through the collider popped into my head, and I asked uneasily, "Um, was Kenneth the only human you pulverized?"

I was thankful when he smiled again and responded, "Oh, yes! Having obtained all the data we needed, we never repeated the experiment on another human. But we did find out that the collider has other wonderfully redeeming uses, since it's a great way to puree beef, chicken, pork, and nearly everything else."

"Why the hell would you ever do that?"

"So that people can eat it with esophageal screens, of course. The collider process also reduces the carbon footprint from foods that used to create a lot of emissions." He nodded proudly to the notion of that wondrous machine doing its work, wherever that was taking place, and said, "Yep, the collider is truly worth the seventy-two trillion we paid for it!"

Not sure whether my confusion was outweighed by my annoyance at that point, I asked, "Where the hell did the screens come from again?"

"Oh, years of diabetes drugs not working. The screens are a new way to regulate blood sugar since exercise doesn't work anymore."

Confounded again at hearing that, I said, "Wait, why doesn't exercise work?"

Dr. O'Dwyer responded dismissively, "Oh, it became too much of a mess for people to deal with. First it was good for you, then people got addicted, then they just turned to diet supplements and, finally, diabetes drugs to try to lose weight. What we never knew until the collider experiments, however, is that people have trouble losing weight because of buildup of dark matter, and the problem usually manifests itself around age thirty." Glancing over at me reassuringly, he said, "Fortunately for you, you're in good shape."

"Yes, I've always liked working out."

"Well, you're lucky. For most people, if they don't learn to exercise early, they'll never start."

"Do you even encourage exercise?"

He nodded confidently. "Oh, yes." Then his assurance faltered a bit. "Well, we try. We have a program to encourage ten minutes of physical activity per week. Most people don't make it, I'm afraid, so we do what we can to adapt nutrition to keep people healthy."

Recalling my physical encounters thus far with papier-mâché lab workers, I asked skeptically, "You call these people healthy?"

Dr. O'Dwyer responded lightly, "Well, no, but it's their own choice. You'll find out that it is impossible to run a stable democracy without letting people do what they want. Plenty of leaders have tried to rule with an iron fist and failed, and of course, now we know why."

My confusion came around full-circle, and I asked, "Why? Wait— does it have something to do with this?"

"Yes. Steven, Narcissium is what makes up humans. See?"

I looked back at the pulsing substance. "*That?*"

He relented slightly and said, "Well, okay, no. Not exactly that. However, Narcissium is the essence of what we have distilled from peering deep into the nature of humanity and the universe, and as far as science is concerned, that is what the missing secret to life looks like."

I raised an eyebrow and said, "Really?"

"Oh, yes, and as we found out through years of experimentation, force was never able to make that substance do anything. The only way to get it to work was to give it what it wanted. You see all of the mirrors around the enclosure?"

"Yes?"

"Those are essential to a stable society, and this goo showed us why. Everything else we've learned has also allowed us to make a quantum leap in scientific democracy."

I wasn't sure whether or not I was buying anything he was saying at that point. However, a row of glass objects next to the enclosure caught my attention, and I momentarily changed the subject. "Hey, what are these beakers for?"

"Oh, those. We were going to give out the Narcissium as gifts to people when we first discovered it."

I reached for one of them and said, "Can I have some to experiment with?"

He quickly slapped my hand away. "Are you kidding? The substance won't even let you get near it."

He reached his hand over the wall to demonstrate, and the blob instantly retreated, just as I had done when he struck me. Dr. O'Dwyer added knowingly, "It does that every time, since Narcissium has a natural aversion to authority. That stuff has never been out of the lab, and we haven't been able to touch it since we put it in here. We still have the beakers, but they're useless since there's no way to get that substance into them. Still, we can run interesting tests by using devices to manipulate the goo. As you can see, it refuses to be cornered for fear of being trapped and instead just sits in the center and retreats if you try to touch it."

"Does it ever attack?"

He shook his head and said plainly, "Nope. It just devolves to a lower molecular structure to avoid confrontation. But thanks to this pioneering development, what you'll find here at the center is that we excel at being able to maximize human potential, despite the paltry base we have to work with."

I stopped rubbing my sore hand and scratched my head with the other, and then I asked skeptically, "Let me see if I understand this. You're talking about their souls?"

Dr. O'Dwyer nearly doubled over laughing at my nonscientific ignorance. Still holding his stomach, he looked at me and said, "Come on, what's a *soul*? I'm talking about what humans are really made of! Look, Steven, it's impossible to ignore the scientific proof. Sure, that substance has plenty of energy, but without ability to channel it, it's directionless, as you can see."

Trying to mask my momentary irritation, I said, "I guess so."

Dr. O'Dwyer responded definitively, "Steven, humans are incredibly complex beings with the ability to do nearly anything. They are, in fact, changing so rapidly that scientific evidence doubles every year, and we know just what they're capable of too."

"Really?"

"Yes. We've been measuring output for decades through constant monitoring of heart rate, caloric expenditure, respiration, and the like."

"How?"

"Years ago, when there was a big fitness craze—you know, before we found out that the real cause of obesity was an excess buildup of dark matter—people used to wear this trackable technology around that constantly measured their energy output. We studied it for years and mapped just how much energy can be squeezed out of a human in one lifetime, but we now know that without proper guidance, at bottom humans are little more than this goop and won't produce anything."

Hearing his comment about tracking, I looked down at my watch in horror, but Dr. O'Dwyer dismissed my fears by explaining that they had long since discontinued that particular tracking program. I was slightly relieved, but my head was spinning by now, while Dr. O'Dwyer's apparently was not. He clapped his hands together triumphantly and said, "Well, that's probably enough for now, so let's get you back up to the director's office and you can finish out the day!"

As we headed out the other end of the corridor, I noticed a sign above another huge door. Warmth seemed to be emanating from behind it, and I stopped for a moment and asked, "What's behind here?"

"That's the heating system for the center."

"The door says 'Crematorium.'"

Dr. O'Dwyer responded proudly, "Oh, yes! Thanks to our modern advancements, people no longer hold the silly superstition that the soul"—he paused to let out a brief chuckle—"comes back to visit your final resting place, so now cremations are used to heat the center instead of natural resources."

Despite the warmth, I shivered when he said that and remarked, "That seems a little barbaric to me."

He gave me a knowing nod and replied, "Well, it's better than dependence on fossil fuels; that's for sure."

While I was lost somewhere between perpetual confusion and

nausea, Dr. O'Dwyer was apparently in elitist heaven. I realized this as he suddenly slapped me on the back and added boastfully, "Steven, I tell you, you're actually quite lucky to have been born right in the middle of all of the action! If you had been born in another state, you couldn't really see all these miraculous advances in modern society as they were being created, but you are truly fortunate to be here. In this very building, we process everything for distribution across the country, and everything is uniformed for stability. The weather may change in some parts, but people are all the same. Heck, it used to be that life expectancy would go up or down depending on where you lived in this country, but no more, all thanks to our center!"

As I was struggling to repopulate my lungs with air following Dr. O'Dwyer's forceful proclamation, he turned and directed me back up to the surface, leaving our sacrificial companion to his exiled state, alone in the empty basement.

*

FIVE

When I arrived, the director was at his desk as usual, and I flopped down in the chair and said, "Wow, what a day! Is work here always this exhausting?"

The director nodded assuredly and replied, "Yep. Remember what he said—you'll need grit to stay on top of things. But don't worry about it right now. You're probably ready to cut loose and relax, eh?"

"Well, um ..."

"Hey, you're gay, right?"

I shot up in my chair. "Am I gay? Wow, no one has ever asked me that!"

The director flashed me an astonished look and said, "You're kidding? It's now a standard question on all elementary school applications."

"Well, um, no. I mean, not really."

He smiled assuredly and said, "Why not? Come on, Steven, don't be ashamed! Gay it up!"

Hesitantly, I responded, "It's just ... not really my thing."

Finally relenting, he said, "Oh, fine, I have another place we can go."

"Okay, but no more drinks."

"No problem!" He eagerly grabbed his coat, and we headed out.

We hopped into an autonomous-driving taxi and the director made small talk with the driver about a recent soccer match that was supposedly very riveting. I couldn't follow along, since I hadn't yet bothered to turn on the television they had furnished my apartment with; nor did I have any particular interest in learning anything about soccer. Instead my mind was focused on that poor kid who was shot through a particle collider just so they could prove something—an entire life wasted in the name of scientific discovery.

However, my musings were interrupted by the director's jubilant announcement as we reached our destination. "Ah, here we are!"

Looking out the window at a row of dazzling lights on the building, and equally dazzling images of scantily clad women being advertised on the screen out front, I said, astonished, "What is this, a *whorehouse?*"

Firmly correcting me, he said, "No, Steven, these are comfort companions. We don't call them whores or prostitutes anymore."

The director paid the cab bill with his thumb, as taxicabs still hadn't adopted retinal technology, and we both got out and walked toward the building. A woman in a dental floss bikini greeted us at the entrance, and she had a tray filled with various pills and a substance that looked a lot like cocaine cut into little lines. The director looked over at me expectantly and nodded toward the offerings.

Guessing at what they were, I said nervously, "Oh, I'd better not. I had enough trouble with the drinks from the other night."

The director prodded me along. "Come on! I told you that this stuff is totally pure!" He picked up two clear tabs and handed one of them to me, and I rolled it in my fingers as he took his and popped it into his mouth and smiled. The woman looked at me expectantly as well, so I just shrugged and followed suit.

Our hostess directed us down the hallway past various doors which were opened up to plush bedrooms. Things were quickly becoming euphorically hazy, and as we passed one of them, I grabbed the director's arm and said, "Wow, that girl is gorgeous!"

Appearing to be pleasantly lucid at the moment, he remarked casually, "Yes, lobotomies often are." He nudged me toward her room. "Here, go on in. You can see that she's interested in you!"

I halted in the doorway and said, surprised, "What? She's a lobotomy? Oh, no way! I can't do that!"

He smiled and kept pressing me gently. "Steven, what's the problem? She's no different than any other girl you'll meet out there."

My mind may have been fuzzy, but something from the scene still registered as wrong. I looked at him and said incredulously, "How on earth could you make a lobotomy into a ... companion?"

He held up his hands innocently and responded, "I didn't do anything. It's just what she was born into, but with her good looks, this was a natural fit for her. Go ahead and ask her. I'll bet she's perfectly happy!"

I shook my head firmly and took a step back. "Look, I don't care. Just give me one of the normal ones."

He shrugged and said jeeringly, "*Okay*, but the next one may not be as attractive!"

I believe that he was technically right. The next one didn't seem to be as good-looking, but by the time the pill I took started working, it didn't much matter. The room I wound up in also had a silver tray filled with plenty of lines of coke, and I accepted the companion's offer to several snorts. I vaguely remember doing a few more lines off her body, and the rest was a carnal blur. Waking up the next day back in my apartment, I realized that it was still the middle of the week and I frantically rushed to make it to work on time.

After struggling through the day, I was back in the director's office. He seemed very relaxed for the afternoon, obviously satisfied with the outing from the night before. I had been drinking water all day but still had terrible cottonmouth, and nothing I tried got rid of the taste of hooker spit. Attempting to appear put together, I said, "So do they automatically get lobotomized kids, or what?"

The director responded lightly, "Oh, the ladies who perform companion services can't have kids—or get married, for that matter."

"Why not?"

"Well, over the years we have come to an understanding with them which reflects their value to our society. See, some people can't get married or don't want to, and other people get married but then the excitement fizzles. Comfort companions fill that all-important societal role of immediate carnal gratification with no strings, so in exchange for the privileges and protections we give to them, they agree not to have kids or to get married."

"What protections?"

The director responded assuredly, "What they do used to be illegal. Thankfully, now it's anything but, and it's protected and regulated by the government."

"But the companions are given the same upbringing as other women, right?"

He rocked in his chair and said lightly, "Mostly. However, if they're going to just wind up as companions, we don't bother with as much formal education. It's not really necessary in that line of work, so instead we just give them scripts of things to talk about."

I don't remember much talking going on last night. "Um, how do you know that they're going to wind up that way?"

He smiled knowingly. "Steven, we've been monitoring this for a long time. It's really pretty easy to tell."

Flashing back to last night, I said, "I still can't get over how gorgeous that one was! The other one was okay, but the first one was ... Wow!"

The director nodded and replied, "You'll find that common among the lobotomies—in there, out here—and they are some of the most attractive people in our society."

"How the hell does that happen?"

He scratched his head and answered, "Something strange in the whole process we haven't quite figured out. There is a direct correlation between how well the lobotomy procedure sets in and how attractive the person turns out to be. It must be something about the eternally youthful nature they inherit with being oblivious. They are also, by the way, the biggest users of the health care system."

Now sensing a flaw in the grand scheme, I said dejectedly, "Why? Let me guess; lobotomies die early?"

The director quicky rebuffed me. "Not at all. They live just as long as anyone else. However, lobotomies have this strange fixation on youth, and they consume more plastic surgery services than anyone."

I was starting to itch. Trying not to show it, I said, "Even when they're already born beautiful?"

"Yep. You could say it's a bit of an addiction. For some unknown reason, they can't stand to look any different than they did when they first became aware of themselves. I tell you, there was an interesting study long ago. We showed movies to lobotomies with their favorite stars, then we showed them movies with the same stars when the stars were twenty years older. Turns out that they couldn't even recognize them, and it appears that lobotomies have some kind of inability to understand the aging process. We're still tweaking the system to figure out where it all comes from."

I was vaguely listening to him by that point. All I could think about was the brothel and going back as soon as I could. The director mumbled on for another half hour and then stood up, having somewhere to be just then. We shook hands, and I casually made my way out of the center.

After that, I was at the brothel in less than twenty minutes. I spent the whole evening with a naked girl who could have been a lobotomy for all I knew, but I didn't care. She never asked me anything about my background, citizenship score, or my job. We just did drugs and screwed, and that was fine with me.

As we lay there in the evening glow, I hazily inquired about her past and how she came to be in that line of work. She couldn't recall any specific details before that day, and in my euphoric state, I didn't see anything wrong with that at all.

I did bother to ask her whether she ever wanted to do anything different with her life, to which she gave a vacant smile and simply climbed on top of me. As we started to move once again, all she said was, "Steven, what could possibly be better than this?" I had no response and just let the rest of my thoughts ride away with her.

* * *

I rushed into the lab just after the first break ended, and people were slowly deactivating their VR contacts and heading back to their desks. The director was there as well, standing over one male who was being treated for an apparent concussion dealt by an unmarked post in the corner. I realized that I still reeked of hooker perfume, and it felt as if the drugs were leeching through my skin.

The director saw me and said, "Steven, there you are. I thought that you were going to call in sick today."

Tucking in the last bit of my shirt as I rushed up to him, I said nervously, "Oh, no, of course not! Just running behind because of … an elevator malfunction in my building. What time is it, anyway?"

I looked down and saw a new message blinking on my watch: "Hey Steven, I found out that you're not gay! Wanna get married?"

I said, "What the hell is that?"

The director glanced down at my watch. Shaking his head momentarily, he responded, "Oh, you must have joined some newfangled social networking group. They're everywhere."

I looked up, confused, and said, "But I haven't even used this watch yet?"

"Well, don't worry about it. Friday is a holiday, and you'll have plenty of time to play with it over the weekend."

Still trying to pull myself together for the morning, I said, "Why is Friday a holiday?"

"As part of our labor regulations, we have to give the workers a day off at the start of every month. As you may know, trying to get lobotomies to work is like trying to get your cat to pull a dog sled, and boy do they love their holidays."

My thoughts immediately turned back to the girl I was with last night and what we would be doing over the long weekend, and I moaned unconsciously under my breath. Meanwhile, the resuscitation crew kept ministering to the employee on floor in front of us, and as they raised the stretcher and snapped the legs into place, I jolted back to reality. Quickly trying to show concern, I said, "Oh, is he okay?"

The director responded absently, "Who? Oh, him. Yes, he'll be just fine. I tell you, one of these days we'll have to give these people helmets just to be able to survive. Fortunately we have the best-functioning health system in the world."

By then my late arrival appeared to have been forgotten, and I eagerly kept the conversation rolling. "Oh, good. Say, I meant to ask you how your citizenship score got down to G-9?"

The question threw him off guard a bit, and he stammered, "Er, I had some surgeries."

"What kind?"

"Hangnails."

"Huh. I've never experienced that myself. Must have been expensive?"

"Yes, a bit." He sighed heavily and finally confided, "But I'm also on my third wife. You want to talk about costly? Two divorces have regrettably also played a part in my overall score."

Again trying to appear concerned, I said, "I'm sorry to hear that."

He tried to lightly play it off, smiling easily and responding, "Oh, it's not such a big deal. My last wife just wasn't a good fit for me. She left me for an F-10 and is now playing cat games somewhere."

"Cat games?"

"You know—sitting around all day, getting up to do a few yoga stretches, eating, going to bathroom, napping—cat games."

"Oh."

He flashed me a brief, uncomfortable smile and quickly changed the subject. "Anyway, people used to have to choose between having health care and cell phones, but no more. These days they can afford to have both, and the prices for health care are uniform all across the country thanks to our programs."

"That used to be different?"

"Oh yes. In the past, you could go to one doctor in New York and one doctor in California for the same treatment, and they would cost wildly different amounts. We fixed that problem and made health care uniform and accessible to all, and now you can even get a therapy session with your fast-food order."

"Seriously?"

"Sure. Having a master's degree in psychology is a requirement to work in fast food."

"How did that get started?"

He looked down at his watch, apparently realizing that he was late for something, and responded distractedly, "Well, most people these days can't decide what to eat without having their inner child massaged a little. Anyway, gotta run. Have a good day, and stop by my office when you're done."

By midmorning, my skin was itching, but I tried my best to follow along as Dr. O'Dwyer continued the tour. He said, "Later, I'll show you how the jobs are done in the ordering department. All lobotomies nationwide are processed right here at the center, and we provide next-day delivery anywhere in the fifty states. You can even order with one-click shipping."

I said, "Do people ever regret their buying decision?"

"Oh, sure. We get a lot of people who will OWI—that's 'order while intoxicated'—but it's usually not a problem. We provide a full money-back guarantee up to the time of birth. We do, of course, have fetal specialists who will contact the buyers and see whether they really want to change their minds, and most people can be convinced to go ahead with the purchase. Excuse me for a second. I'll be right back."

Fortunately, my headache was going away a bit. Just then, however, a girl suddenly popped up right in front of me and said eagerly, "Hi, Steven!"

I nearly toppled over backwards. "Jesus Christ! Where'd you come from?"

Confused, she pointed momentarily over her shoulder and said, "What? I work right over there. Anyway, here's an easy one! What did they name the ten thousand and fourth earthlike planet that they found sixty-four million light years away?"

I couldn't tell if this was a real conversation or a bad trip. "What the hell are you talking about?"

She smiled and poked at me. "This is the weekly quiz!"

"For what?"

"To win a vacation, of course! What did they name the ten thousand and fourth earthlike planet that they found sixty-four million light years away?"

I tried not to faint with the concentration and simply replied, "You've got me."

"E-10004, silly!" She shook her head and skipped off in the other direction, and all I could do was close my eyes and rub my face. *She must be a lobotomy.*

Dr. O'Dwyer appeared seconds later. "Sorry about that. Where were we?"

I snapped-to again. "Um, regrets, sir."

"Ah, yes. Regrets. As I was saying—"

I interrupted him and said, "Dr. O'Dwyer, can I ask you a question?"

"Sure."

"I've been noticing that most of the women around here seem to be in pretty good shape." I recalled the companion from the night before, who had tried to choke me while we were having sex—and who had done a pretty good job of it too.

He nodded. "Yes, that's quite true."

"But most all the males are ... Well, as you said before, it's hard to tell the difference anymore."

Dr. O'Dwyer raised an eyebrow. "Ah, so you've noticed the fairer sex?"

"Who?"

He chuckled and said, "Males, of course! Well, that is simply the result of a concerted demasculination program that we've been running for over a hundred years. Most everyone these days—and I mean boys, girls, boys who used to be girls—and whatever they call the rest—are given doses of estrogen and Pitocin at peak moments of agitation. For the males, the meds help to bring a more levelling perspective and encourage a feeling of well-being, but for the girls, it just makes them wilier." He pulled me aside and added knowingly, "By the way, you might want to buy some sex toys. You may have already found out that women are practically insatiable these days."

I puffed up confidently and said, "Oh, don't worry about me. My equipment works just fine!"

"No, it's not that. You'll see. You wouldn't be able to keep up with them even if you were Casanova. Most of them are into hardcore stuff as well, thanks to the wonderful plethora of romance novels that now feature rough sex. You may have seen them on the shelves in the grocery store available for instant download to VR contacts?"

"I ... um, no, not yet. Anyway, are you sure that demasculinizing males is necessary?"

Dr. O'Dwyer straightened up again and said confidently, "Of course. Steven, an absolutely brilliant study done many, many years ago discovered that men suffer from young male syndrome."

"What's that?"

"A ridiculous and outdated need to compete in their environment and establish themselves by shows of force and aggression. The study also discovered, of course, that women have no such need, so we just got rid of what it meant to be a young 'man.' Most males are generally gay now, and transgenderism is at an all-time high. In fact, pseudomale viewership of cooking shows has skyrocketed over the past century or so."

"What about the girls?"

Dr. O'Dwyer just laughed. "Oh, they already liked cooking shows!"

"No, I mean—"

He knew where I was heading and cut me off. "Steven, they were never a problem in the first place. The real problem was that the boys weren't more like them."

"Seriously?"

"Yes. Besides, we discovered long ago that estrogen suppresses expression of the dopamine receptors, and that, of course, helps prevent Parkinson's disease. So, as a result of our medication program, the boys benefit greatly through increased memory and resistance to developing Parkinson's, and being neutered for all practical purposes is really a small price to pay in comparison."

With that, we exited out the back of the center and proceeded to a large annex building where females were lined up outside. I had no idea where we were going, but when we entered the building, I gasped in horror. This was where they performed tubal ligations on all females as a mandatory part of the lab birthing efforts. Females underwent mandatory tubal ligations around age thirteen, and then their eggs were harvested after that to supply the center.

The notion had never crossed my mind when I was having unprotected sex at the brothel, but seeing row upon row of females with their feet in stirrups and being attended to by the staff physicians made me feel a bit ill. We toured a bit, and I pretended to listen to Dr. O'Dwyer's explanations but was grateful when we were finally outside again.

As we crossed back to the center, I thought to ask, "Can they get them untied?"

He paused for a second to contemplate the notion. "Well, I guess so. Technically, the process is reversible." Then he waved the idea away and said, "But it never happens. That wouldn't apply to prostitutes, of course, and the others wouldn't dare. Women are terrified of live births."

"Seriously?"

"Oh, yes. Steven, mothers used to almost die in childbirth, and preeclampsia was rampant in the dark times. Plus, natural childbirth was becoming impossibly painful."

"But how did you start the tube-tying process? I mean, people used to have natural births, right?"

Mockingly, he said, "If you can believe it, yes, and it's sure a good thing that we finally took over! Ironically, the tube tying got started because some nutjob tried to outlaw contraception. Real lunatic, I tell you. He almost led us to the brink of destruction at one point, but he also helped to break a logjam in social conditioning. His policies, and the fight to reverse them, got us over the sexual politics of the past hundred years or so that were based almost entirely on contraception, and eventually everyone had to agree that having babies born in the lab was really the only way to ensure equality of the sexes."

After a pause, Dr. O'Dwyer added unexpectedly, "That was, by the way, the same brilliant president who posted on the internet that the placenta doesn't belong 100 percent to women."

"What?"

He didn't even register my question and instead started on another roll. "After decades of back-and-forth, someone realized that he was right. The natural placenta is formed from the combination of egg and sperm, but half of that belongs to the man, and the placenta is what makes the entire birthing process work. Now, it obviously doesn't do anyone any good to own half of a placenta, but that's what led us to realize that we could end the whole gender equality debate by adversely possessing the other half of the placenta. After all, without us, people would have never gotten together in the first place to have kids." Resting a hand on my shoulder, he shook his head and lamented, "Steven, if you can believe it, back then the mothers would eat the entire placenta themselves and never even share any of it with father."

I stood there baffled, with the image of someone consuming even part of a placenta instantly calling up my nausea from before, but as we reentered the center, Dr. O'Dwyer simply continued. "Now, of course, we have Dolly, the artificial uterus. Just deposit anything you want inside of her, and nine months later, a baby pops out!" He jabbed me in the ribs and said playfully, "That's a little joke! Actually, the whole process is monitored constantly for foreign particles. In fact, it was the discovery of air pollutants in a mother's natural placenta that helped push the movement for the artificial placenta over the top."

By now my head was really spinning. It could have been from the drugs last night or the scene we had just witnessed, and I said, "How the hell did you ever get away with this?"

Dr. O'Dwyer just shrugged. "In the end, it wasn't too hard. Sure, people were upset at the time, but people were upset about seat belts in cars too." I still couldn't grasp the relationship to automobiles. He added, "Then came the great social media post on equality: 'All humans are brethren.' It used to be 'All men are brothers.' We could never figure out how to deal with that until the famous post came along, and that started the movement toward all births taking place in the lab."

I shook my rapidly fogging head and responded, "It still seems like a radical idea."

Dr. O'Dwyer leaned into me momentarily and declared, "Steven, leadership is convincing people to follow what you already know is right. Now, you want to be a leader, don't you boy?"

I snapped to attention again and said enthusiastically, "Oh, yes. Yes, sir!"

He stepped back, satisfied with my answer. "Good. Anyway, the same guy who caused all of the stir about contraceptives also caused the people to distrust us—" He shot me a knowing look. "For a short while, that is. Now when the girls' first periods come along, we welcome them into womanhood by tying their tubes. The girls are, of course, greatly relieved, and after that, medical technicians harvest the eggs from ages fourteen to eighteen."

"Then what?"

"Then what, what? Then they go off to online school, get married, order a baby, and the process starts all over again."

"Oh."

Dr. O'Dwyer added proudly, "Tubal ligations, of course, solve one of man's oldest problems—how to have fun in the sack without paying for it. It started with gays in ancient times, but now everyone can get away with it." As an afterthought, he added, "We did try to disable sperm once, but that didn't work."

"Does the process harm the girls?"

"Heavens, no!" Then, hesitating slightly, he added, "Well, not really."

I cocked my head skeptically and said, "What do you mean, 'not really'?"

"Well, the tubal ligations do make some women crazy." He laughed and added, "That is, crazier than they were before!"

He made a gesture as though he was going to punch me in the arm, and I flinched away and asked cautiously, "Why?"

Dr. O'Dwyer scratched his head and said, "Something about the sutures, I think. We're experimenting with different fibers since there may be some kind of evolutionary reaction to the ones we use now, and it could also be because we use Prolene sutures instead of Vicryl. Anyway, we're looking into it."

"But is the process worth that harm?"

He replied indignantly, "Of course! Don't worry, Steven; it's perfectly manageable, and anyway, it makes for a more stable society."

"Really?"

"Sure. Let me tell you, in the dark times, we had unwanted kids running around everywhere and mothers locking their kids in bathrooms for months on end. It was truly awful."

"But is it legal to keep women from being able to have children? Of their own, I mean. Well, naturally, I guess?"

He nodded assuredly and said, "Absolutely. The Framers were wise enough to nestle that government right conveniently in the dormant commerce clause."

"The what?"

"It's in the Constitution. See, the dormant commerce clause traditionally allowed the federal government to overrule anything the states did that interfered with interstate commerce, but over time, we realized that the Framers also meant it to overrule anything the *people* might do that could have a similar effect." He added confidently, "It's basically the same way we managed to turn protections in the Bill of Rights into things that applied to private citizens."

I had no idea what he was talking about, having never learned any constitutional principles in school. Then he said, "And because humans are now shipped across state lines after birth in the lab, that makes procreation literally our baby!" Dr. O'Dwyer let out a little chuckle at that clever pun. Seeing that I was not amused, he quickly added, "Ahem. We would have used the interstate commerce clause, of course, except that the Framers didn't have one-click shipping for newborns in their time. But they'd sure be proud of us now!"

With that last comment, he looked over at me with slight suspicion, and I quickly nodded in patriotic affirmation. Satisfied, he continued. "Anyway, there was plenty of precedent for adverse possession of the placenta before we got started. They already had state laws allowing men to sue to stop abortions, and judges were giving away reduced sentences in exchange for people getting vasectomies. Besides, all the woman has of her own is the uterus, and that's not the key at all. It's just a sack, and in prison, they used to call it 'the purse.' But once the artificial placenta came along, we had our own little fetal docking station to be able to replicate everything the mother would have done on her own—except better."

All of the frank talk about manipulating parts of the female anatomy made me turn green, but I managed to ask, "And everyone just went along?"

By comparison, Dr. O'Dwyer was completely unfazed. "Oh yes; it was actually quite easy. See, we had already been storing frozen eggs for women so they could wait until the right time to have a child. When the technology was ready, all we did was find one volunteer willing to have the first lab-born baby from her very own eggs, and after that, everyone else just followed suit. And with the infrastructure we had already developed for direct shipping of consumer goods, lab-to-door births were pioneered."

I started to get the chills and said, "The whole notion still seems a bit radical to me."

"Oh, not at all. Don't worry, Steven; the whole process is exactly what our citizens want and is very beneficial to straight males as well."

I responded in an artificial and overly eager fashion that raised one of Dr. O'Dwyer's eyebrows. "How so?"

He just grinned and replied, "As you'll find out, in response to tubal ligations, female body parts grow in a desperate attempt to attract a mate. Interestingly, if you have two girls as roommates, their body parts will grow at the same time!"

"Do lobotomies still have to go through the process?"

"Yep. Of course, we have to lobotomize fewer girls than boys, since girls are already going to wind up tied in knots. Ha ha!"

I didn't laugh with him. Instead I asked, "What do you do with all of the eggs?"

"We have storage tanks at the lab, and we currently have enough eggs stored to keep replacing our population for centuries."

"What about sperm?"

He waved off the notion and said lightly, "Oh, we don't store as much of that. Male sperm count has been dropping steadily for ages, and by the time males are forty, it's pretty much useless. Getting fresh specimens is essential, but there are always willing donors."

"Who pays for all of this stuff?"

"The people, of course."

"But the government owns it all?"

"Yes, in trust for the people. It's the same as for property owners."

"Huh?"

"Steven, all property owners who possess shares of the land hold it in trust for everyone else. That's why people below the C-5 class can't own property. They simply haven't demonstrated the self-control necessary to ensure that they can protect the people's property with the level of dignity and respect to which it is accorded."

At the same time that the notions of what he had been explaining were too much for me to comprehend, he simply stopped for a moment and surveyed his lab proudly. Then he boasted, "Anyway, we predicted this glorious development nearly 170 years ago—and got there in even less time!"

I tried to see what he was looking at and asked, confused, "Predicted what?"

Turning back toward me, he responded emphatically, "Elimination of the gender gap, of course."

I shook my head in disbelief and said, "That's what this is all about?"

"Of course. Women were always hampered in what they could do professionally because of having to have kids, so naturally, we eliminated that problem."

Still confused, I said, "But they still do have kids."

"Sure, but now anyone can: single moms, single dads, two dads, two moms. However, everyone is free to reach their glorious, full potential in life, regardless of their natural gender."

As I was still trying to reconcile that comment with everything I had seen thus far, he added thoughtfully, "Of course, being single affects the heredity process. If your kid dies before you do, everything will go to the state. Most people who don't want to actually get hitched enter into common law marriage with their service animal just to be safe."

I jumped back and said, *"Their what?"*

"Their pets. You know, you see them everywhere—the little dogs, or cats, or iguanas people have on leashes. They help keep people calm when they're out in public. Anyway, the pet inherits the remainder after the owner dies, and has a good life; and when the pet dies, the rest goes to us."

Trying to avoid being led down that distracting rabbit hole, I insisted, "But you're just producing kids like they were products, and they're automatically rolled out on an assembly line whenever you see fit?"

Dr. O'Dwyer shook his head definitively and responded, "Oh, no, quite wrong. We only produce a new life when it is ordered. Sure, part of that is determined by the economy, but the choice to order is ultimately up to the individual consumer." Patting me on the shoulder reassuringly, he added, "It's basically the same as how nature began, and nature always knows the right time for couples to request a new bundle of joy in their lives!"

Taking a precautionary step backwards, I said, "I'm sorry to say this, but it sure doesn't look that way to me."

Dr. O'Dwyer paused and frowned over at me, responding authoritatively, "Well, Steven, despite whatever you may think, we can't *force* people to have children, and we certainly can't just produce more if they're going to wind up as unwanted orphans. The whole system is completely voluntary and works quite well. Trust me."

I shook my head. "It still seems like a hell of a lot of kids. And just to be clear, the decision on actually making the babies is left up to you, right?"

"Well, to the center, yes."

"Do you produce twins? Or, I mean, more than one kid with each order?"

"Oh, we can if we want, but most people don't order twins because they want their own unique bundle of joy."

That notion was almost too ridiculous to consider, given

everything that I had seen thus far. Letting it go, instead I asked, "Do you screen people before they order?"

"Of course. Prospective purchasers have to meet certain economic thresholds. They have to demonstrate six months of stable employment and have enough in their policies for the purchase."

Finally starting to connect the dots, I asked skeptically, "So you're just making money selling the people back to themselves?"

He frowned. "Oh, that's an awful way to look at it."

"But is that right?"

Dr. O'Dwyer just shrugged. "Pretty much, but without us, they'd be lost. In reality, Steven, the government is like the head of a household. We love all people, and the gratitude we get for ensuring their well-being is the pride we feel as protectors. The money is really just an aftereffect. In the end, everything we do is for their own good, and we take better care of them than their parents ever did—all without the messy ties of random biological selection.

"And the economy is, in fact, the best tool that nature has ever had for informing us about the correct way to bring new life into the world. Science proves that natural instincts must be planned, since people's goals are more long-term now and kids interfere with that unless the timing is right."

I hazarded another risky question. "What about copulation?"

He laughed and said, "What about it? Stop reading outdated textbooks! Here, look at this." He pulled up an online dictionary on his watch.

I read: "COPULATION - intransitive verb: to order a fetus from the Government." I looked up in surprise and said, "Huh."

Dr. O'Dwyer added assuredly, "Steven, copulation was always a troublesome act, so once we figured out that most of it involved things that were duplicative and unnecessary, we streamlined the process."

"Unnecessary?"

His attention was momentarily caught by something in the distance. Still, he kept talking and added, "Yes, like the female orgasm. It has nothing to do with reproduction, but females got them because they could have become males at a certain point along the developmental process. Since it's an inessential function, however, we got rid of it, and of course, a famous study proved that there were never any long-term benefits to breastfeeding, and—"

He finally looked back at me and noticed my jaw sitting on the floor. Reassuringly, he said, "Oh, don't worry; we gave them their orgasms back after we started the tube-tying process."

I just shook my head, still trying to recover from the lunacy I had been hearing all day. Through the effort, however, my cottonmouth suddenly returned, and I found myself involuntarily licking my lips. Dr. O'Dwyer saw this and also noticed me starting to scratch my neck; then he just smiled and pulled something out of his coat pocket and said, "Developed a little dependence, huh? Here, have an opioid patch."

I took the patch out and slapped it on my back. Almost instantly, a gentle, euphoric wave swept over me, and I let out a sigh of relief. "Thanks. Hey, why do they let people take drugs in the first place?"

Dr. O'Dwyer waved a lighthearted hand and said, "Oh, it's not a big deal. After all, we don't make addictive drugs anymore."

"But the bars are filled with people taking drugs at night."

"Yes, but they're not addicted. Like you, they may be a little dependent, but you're dependent on food and water, so there's not much of a problem there." He put his hand gently on my shoulder and finally said, "Listen, why don't you just go home and take a nap?"

Seizing at the desperately needed break, I sighed heavily and said, "Thanks. I could sure use one."

After that, I headed straight for home, completely forgetting that I was supposed to stop by the director's office.

*

SIX

Despite being nearly exhausted, I tossed and turned all night, coming in and out of vivid dreams that were filled with images of young girls in the countryside being used like Pez dispensers to produce lobotomized children. By the time I woke up, my interest in returning to the brothel was nonexistent.

Shaking off the dreams while I was in the shower, the first thought that came into my head was about standing up the director from the day before, and I dressed in haste and ran to the center. After making a beeline up to his office, however, I was politely informed that he was gone for the day, so I went back downstairs and set to work.

The next day, I stopped in again. Hanging on the wall in his office was a gigantic new poster depicting something wonderful that had just been discovered in space.

Initially he didn't notice me standing in the doorway. I knocked on the door and nervously walked in, greeting him sheepishly. "Hello, Director. Sorry about the other day. I, um, got caught up with work and didn't have time to stop by your office."

He raised an amused eyebrow in response. "Yes, Dr. O'Dwyer told me. Had a little hangover from the brothel again, huh?"

Blushing, I admitted, "Oh, yes. Sorry about that!"

He just smiled and responded, "Don't worry at all. It's very healthy for young men to be out exploring. I was mostly just wanting to see if you were up for another outing, and when you didn't show up, I had my answer."

I sat down and said, "Well, sorry again." Nervously wanting to change the subject, I asked, "Hey, what's that poster for?"

He answered proudly, "We're in the middle of a three-year promotional event for SWAGSA! They need to raise money for a new mission, since we're trying to find a missing planet in our solar system."

SWAGSA stood for the Science, Weather, and Aeronautics Governmental Space Agency. They were responsible for nearly every aspect of scientific development above and below the Earth, although as an orphan, I really couldn't see any benefit to their efforts. I shook my head and said, "You have to advertise for that? I figured that the government would just take it out of policies and not waste time with advertising?"

The director responded plainly, "Steven, people aren't dead. They still notice when we take money from them. Of course, space exploration is only a fractional percentage of any person's overall insurance policy, but we still have to justify our efforts with public support. After all, the planetary colonies need all the help they can get."

"Do the posters work?"

He laughed. "Oh, that's not the main marketing campaign! What we usually do is subliminal advertising through movies, television, and the like. Lobotomies love movies about interstellar travel, and whether they know it or not, every time they watch something about our journey through the stars, they feel more and more at ease with what we're doing. Of course, we've only colonized as far as Pluto right now, and the next stop after that is quite a long jump, but if we can find that damn missing planet, it might make interstellar travel easier. Then we'll be well on our way to colonizing another habitable planet after this one."

"Why is SWAGSA short of money?"

Rocking gently in his chair, he responded thoughtfully, "It's not so much that they're short; it's just that the unanswered questions of the universe are so *vast*. SWAGSA already adopted out the Earth and all the other planets to generate revenue. Citizens own little pieces of galactic property and pay taxes on those, but we need to make another tax increase to cover new ventures. If we don't sell the campaign correctly, of course, people could get upset because they believe that it interferes with other purchases. As you probably know, lobotomies are obsessed with technology upgrades."

Just then, he looked down at my arm and said, "Hey, your gender identity monitor is going off."

I glanced at my watch, and it was glowing. Suddenly confused, I said, "My what?"

He pointed. "Your watch. It has a gender identity monitor."

"What the hell is that?"

"The monitor measures how you're feeling on a spectrum between male and female."

I looked up at him, exasperated, and said, "On a *what?*"

He responded plainly, "Steven, you may not know this, but we're all 50 percent woman—or more, in some cases."

"What?"

"Yep, you're at least half woman, and your vital signs, where you've been during the day, people you've talked to, what's on your evening schedule, and some other factors all determine where you are between being a man and a woman. Your watch crunches all of that data and tells you where you are between being gay and straight, and yours is glowing reddish-purple, which is on the verge of partial gayness."

I shifted nervously and tried to dodge the technological insinuation. "I, um ..."

He waved at me, easily letting me off the hook. "Don't worry about it. It's only a tool, but it's a very useful tool."

I shoved my hand down in the arm of the chair to hide the timepiece and inquired with innocently redirecting curiosity, "How could that be of any use?"

He just smiled and politely pretended not to notice. "Oh, lots of ways. For example, parents used to have to monitor texting, who kids were hanging out with, and the like, but between the nanobot and gender identity monitor, that problem has gone away. As long as the kids are maintaining a mood on the side of mostly gay, they're pretty docile and rarely get into trouble. Then, of course, there's the newest craze—those VR lenses. You know about those from your little encounter with Smith."

Thankful that the conversation changed, I assumed an air of concern and asked, "Oh yeah, what happened to him? Is he back yet?"

Appearing to ponder that momentarily, the director said, "I don't know. I haven't seen him, but I'll check around. Anyway, have you tried the lenses?"

"Of course not. My eyesight works just fine."

"That has nothing to do with it. The eyepieces are about seeing more than you can, and they actually help people live in the enhanced Multiverse reality we created for them."

"What the hell is a Multiverse?"

"It's a virtual reality platform where people can go to experience life that they can't handle in physical form." As I rolled my eyes, he added thoughtfully, "Plus, by transmitting messages directly to the lenses, we've gotten rid of the distraction people used to encounter looking down at their devices."

I shook my head and muttered sarcastically, "They get rid of more than that."

"What?"

"Nothing. But what's wrong with *real* reality?"

The director shrugged innocently. "Oh, nothing—for people like you and me, that is. But some people need to escape from time to time, and the eyepieces help with that."

Acridly, I said, "Yeah, like every thirty minutes of every hour."

"Well, that's part of it. The contacts also take pictures and let people surf the web and watch television. People can even do reverse-convex selfies."

I shifted sideways in my chair, not having the slightest idea what that was, and said, "That sounds a bit ridiculous."

"Not at all, Steven. Selfies save lives, and the lenses are also the quickest way to send instant messages. They're so fast, in fact, that they occur in the blink of an eye!"

"Huh?"

He laughed and said, "The lenses send messages just by blinking! They take into account where you are, what you're doing, and who you're sending the message to; then the AI software picks from a list of the most likely messages you'd want to send and blasts one off without you having think about it. With the contact lenses, people can IM you and ask you anything."

Just then, my opioid patch started to wear off, and my stomach immediately responded. I inconspicuously tightened my gut in the seat and abruptly changed the subject. "Hey, I've been looking for the men's room around here and haven't found one anywhere. All of the bathrooms just have a picture of a eunuch-looking character on the front of them, and girls go in there as well."

He gently rocked back in his chair and laughed. "Oh, there are no separate bathrooms in our society! With normal copulation eliminated, it's not what you do in the bathroom but how well you manage the opportunities presented to you in life that really matters between the sexes."

I squirmed in the seat and said, "That, um, seems weird to me. You mean there are no separate bathrooms anywhere?"

The director responded lightly, "You can still find them over at the church, but they're just old-fashioned that way."

"Why do they still have them over there?"

He shrugged. "Dunno. I guess no one ever asked the clergy for integrated bathrooms."

"Well, I went in the one here once, but all I heard was the sound of people barfing."

"Yep, that's just from the esophageal screens."

"Gross!"

He responded plainly, "Well, it's better than having to exercise, but I told you that it was also a little unappealing. Of course, the Romans used to vomit between big meals as well, so it's a well-established practice."

Hearing that made my gut hurt again, and I stood up hastily and said, "Excuse me, gotta go."

After leaving the church, I felt better—and not just because I was finally able to use a public bathroom with some privacy. I was also slowly realizing that the director's initial comments about welcoming curiosity and questioning were true, and neither he nor Dr. O'Dwyer took umbrage with my skepticism about what they were doing in that society. I was still going to play their game as best as I could, but at least I could challenge them in a respectful manner without potentially jeopardizing my status or employment. Feeling myself start to fit in to this new existence somewhat was at least a small relief.

I wandered for a while without paying attention to where I was going, and I eventually passed by a place called Ophelia's Pond. On one end of the pond was a video billboard showing images of new births from the lab, so I sat down on a bench and watched a few of them. All the children looked very happy and were absolutely beautiful—obviously a fresh batch of lobotomies.

Standing up to head home, I wondered how babies could go from being that cute to becoming these detestable creatures as adults. My thoughts were disturbed, however, by a commotion on the other side of the pond, as a girl standing there suddenly screamed at the top of her lungs and plunged into the water. I watched curiously for a minute, and it appeared that she was starting to drown; then I sprinted around the side of the pond and dived in after her. However, halfway to reaching her, two men in scuba suits suddenly emerged from the depths and grabbed my arms, hauling me toward the shore.

Surveying their odd catch, one of them popped out his breather and exclaimed, "Hey, what the hell is a male doing in here?"

The other shook his head and said, "Oh, he's probably just off the deep end of his gender identity spectrum." They escorted me to the edge of the pond and instructed me to get out. Two other divers had pulled the girl out and were administering CPR to her.

As I slogged home with my underwear creeping into places unknown, I returned to feeling as uncomfortable and unwanted as I did most days at the orphanage.

The next day, Dr. O'Dwyer explained the incident to me: "They post pictures and videos of every new baby on that billboard at 7:30

p.m. each day, and couples and some singles make it part of their evening pastimes to go to the park and watch the new arrivals."

I said, "Can't they watch the newborns on the internet?"

"Nope. They're only available on the screen at the pond, but you're lucky. You get to see all the births firsthand in the lab—well, when you have time on your breaks, that is."

"What about the girl trying to drown herself?"

"Oh, that happens all the time. It all started years ago when we tried the Buddha experiment with one of them." Seeing my immediate concern, he added, "Not to feed her into the particle collider, mind you, but just to see if the experiment would work on a female. However, right after we tied her tubes, she went nuts and ended up drowning in the pond."

"Let me guess—Ophelia?"

He scratched his head and responded unsurely, "I think so. We originally believed that it was caused by an unexplained food allergy, but over time we came to discover that it was part of an evolutionary relapse."

"Huh?"

"Well, as you may know, humans used to be amphibian, and the current thinking is that the suture fibers cause the female psyche to revert to prehistoric times, thereby causing the fixation with the pond. We're pretty sure that's it."

"What about the girl from last night? Same thing?"

Dr. O'Dwyer responded reassuringly, "Oh, no. When they pulled her out, they discovered that she was low on vitamin K."

A bell suddenly rang, and Dr. O'Dwyer clapped his hands together and said satisfactorily, "Well, time to go home, Steven!"

I looked around confusedly and replied, "But it's only noon?"

"We're giving them a half day today. It helps with motivation, and anyway, we can't have these people working all the time, since we have to give them time to run errands and contemplate necessary purchases."

As he was walking away, I found myself suddenly jonesing for the brothel again—not for the girls, but for the drugs. I figured that

I would give it one last go but promised not to get involved with any of the companions this time.

I was almost to the door when I ran into the director. He came up and patted me warmly on the shoulder and said, "Hi, Steven! Heading out for the day?"

Sensing that I had somehow been detected again, I responded nervously, "Oh, yes. I was just on my way to … the grocery store."

The director just smiled and said, "Fine, fine. Say, why don't you stop by my place tonight and have dinner with the missus and me?"

Bloody hell. I forced a smile and responded, "Oh, sure, that would be nice!"

"Great, see you around seven!"

*   *   *

I dejectedly shuffled back to my apartment, put the brothel out of my mind, and slapped on a fresh patch. Walking through the front door of my building, I noted for the first time the addresses of my neighbors. We all lived in the same building, but each unit had its own unique identifying address—not just 1-A, 1-B, and so forth. The buzzer for my apartment said "1075 Melrose Drive," which was very strangely only one number off from the address of the orphanage where I grew up. But my next-door neighbor's address was 1525 Conestoga Lane. Weird. And they were all like that. In my building, we had four hundred different physical addresses for all the units.

I left my building and went to the next neighborhood over— which was technically twenty-five feet away—and all of the buildings there were set up in the same fashion.

I went upstairs and showered, and then I caught a cab out to the director's place. He lived in a high-rise building, the same as everyone else in town. However, his building had only sixty-five inhabitants, each with their own floor.

When the door opened, he smiled at me warmly, still dressed in the same clothes from that day, and his wife popped into view just behind him. By contrast, she was decked out in a translucent evening gown with low shoulders, and the gown didn't leave much to the imagination, either above or below. I finally made it to her face and saw that she had apparently gotten a transplant, as her youthful-looking eyes were wrapped in a crocodile purse.

The director greeted me first. "Hello, Steven."

"Hello, sir."

"Let me introduce you to my wife, Rhea."

She made for me immediately. "Oh, look at this dashing boy!" Studying me from head to toe, she said curiously to the director, "He's an orphan, huh?"

I responded quickly, "Yes, ma'am, I am. Or, I was. I work at the center now."

Beaming at me, she replied, "Oh yes, Jacob told me all about the great things you're doing over there! I'll bet that you're glad to be earning an honest living now, what with you growing up under a different economic system?"

"Actually, I didn't even know that until very recently, but it wasn't too bad."

She put a hand on my shoulder and said, "Well, we share your pain. Don't think that just because you grew up isolated, you had it any worse than anyone else. My parents were *very* harsh on me!"

"Oh really?"

"Absolutely! My mother wouldn't let me buy designer clothes until I was at least fourteen!"

I tried to be sympathetic. "Must have been rough."

She pantomimed fainting with her free hand and said, "Oh, it was awful! It took me years of therapy to get over!" Then she dropped the pity routine and said eagerly, "Come, come; let's sit down and get more acquainted!"

We walked into a giant living room decked out with velvet furniture. It may have been my imagination, but I thought that the temperature rose a few degrees right as we stepped into the room, and I suddenly got the sensation that I was walking into the den of Hades. Still completely at ease, the director took a seat in a broad armchair. I sat down on a loveseat as the director's wife immediately nuzzled up next to me. Her perfume was overpowering, and I started to perspire, but the director didn't seem to notice anything strange and just sat there smiling.

His wife advanced eagerly. "So, tell me, are you dating?"

I fidgeted nonchalantly and tried to inch into the tiny space next to the arm of the couch, but I was trapped. "Um, not exactly. They keep me pretty busy at work."

She smiled wantonly and said, "Hard to believe for a strapping young man like you! I'm sure you'd be able to find a girl, or a guy, to suit you."

I shuffled in the chair and said, "Yeah, I'm not really gay."

Her eyes widened, and she inched closer. "Well, my, my! A real virile specimen, huh? Do you have much experience with women?"

The director came to my rescue and responded reassuringly, "Oh, I took Steven to a comfort companion the other day."

My face turned crimson, and I pulled at the collar of my shirt. She petted my arm approvingly and said, "Oh, good! So you've been broken in a bit?"

My crotch started to respond involuntarily, and I crossed my legs and said, "Huh?"

The director cleared his throat and chided briefly, "Dear, please. Give the boy some time to settle in."

She backed off a few inches and giggled innocently. "Oh, sorry! But now that you're thirty, you are sure to be a hot commodity! As you know, thirty is when people start to get married, order a new baby, and settle down."

By law, marriage and ordering a lab baby were limited to those thirty years or older. I had no idea where either limitation came from and thought to ask why people had to wait so long in society to get started on things.

The director's wife laughed and replied, "Oh, that's nothing! Fifty is really the new forty for starting a family!"

The director chimed in. "And forty is the new thirty for finding yourself!"

As if finishing off a duet, she said, "And thirty is the new twenty for starting out on your own!"

He quickly added, "And twenty is the new ten for coming out of adolescence!"

They laughed in unison. "Ha ha ha!"

I tried to laugh too, but it came out flat. Clearing my throat, I leaned forward even farther and said quizzically, "Okay, but how did you decide that thirty was the right number for marriage and ordering a lab baby?"

The director's wife took the opportunity to inconspicuously steal a glance at my butt. When I caught her, she smiled and sat up as well, assuming a proper posture, and responded proudly, "For a long time, there was no age limit for either getting married or having children, but then we set it to eighteen to protect the tender youth. After years of scientific study, we finally came to a consensus that getting married before thirty was simply too early, since lot of women surveyed said that they looked back and wished that they had waited to get married."

Interrupting her, the director sat forward a bit as well and said, "Excuse me, dear. Steven, that is of course correct, but from my department, it had a lot more to do with young people having an incorrect understanding of what 'making it' means."

She nodded. "Oh, yes, quite true, dear. Thank you. Steven, it was truly awful back then. People would have a child, and then the parents would lose jobs, or the mom or dad would have a drug or gambling problem or the like, and the poor kids would grow up with virtually no parents at all. People thought that graduating from college was 'making it,' or getting their own place, or their first job. They never understood that it takes a lot more than that to guarantee a stable upbringing for a new little one."

I responded with light sarcasm, "You don't say?"

Pleased to be on a soapbox for the evening, however, she simply ignored my comment and continued. "Of course, we tried years of contraception education and nearly everything else, but the kids just couldn't listen, and so many didn't know about proper methods to use anyway or couldn't remember to use them correctly." Then slumping back on the couch, she adopted a pouty face and added sullenly, "And then that whack job came along and ruined everything!"

The director nodded. "Yes, he did. And Steven, the real problem with birth control restrictions is that it drove people to buy from other countries. That was, as you can imagine, very bad for the economy."

His wife perked up again and rested a hand on my shoulder blade, continuing proudly. "Fortunately, after that, a million people put on little pink knit hats, and the artificial placenta eventually came along, and then we went to tube tying, and that was the end of messy live births!" Nodding emphatically at me, she added, "It was a great relief to us women, let me tell you, and setting the limit at thirty both for getting married and having kids gives people a wonderful advantage in life!"

I asked, "Do people ever get married under thirty?"

She laughed and tousled my hair. "Oh, heavens no, you silly boy! That's a serious felony and carries a long jail sentence. Haven't you heard, 'Under thirty, serving twenty'? Ha ha ha ha!"

The director jumped back in and continued lecturing. "Of course, Steven, that rarely happens these days. Fifty is really the new thirty for those sorts of things, and most people wait until their midforties or so before getting life together. Some people do get married right at thirty, and if so, they usually like to marry another thirty-year-old. It gives them that 'high school sweetheart' kind of feel."

His wife added thoughtfully, "However, most people don't reach their real earning potential until their fifties or sixties, and of course, that is very important to stability."

I asked, "Earning potential?"

She replied, "Sure. That's the point where the parents die, and you get to inherit what they have left over."

"Don't people get there by working?"

She responded lightly, "Some do, but many of them have to rely on their parents to finally get a stable footing. Of course, when you get married, you do get to inherit half of your spouse's policy as well."

I said, bewildered, "Before they even have a family?"

She replied, "Oh sure, and it works out quite well. Their parents don't have them until they are in their forties or fifties, and by the time the kids are ready, the parents are usually almost done." She inched closer to me and prodded somewhat suggestively, "Say, have you thought about starting a family?"

I squirmed back into my corner and said, "Um, not yet. I'm not sure I'm ready."

She pressed against me and pinched my cheek. "Oh, you're probably still just restless from growing up wild in the boys' home!" With that, she let out a playful little "grrrr" and her hand slid down onto my upper thigh. Then she added, "But watch out. There will be plenty of women turning thirty this year as well, and they'll be itching to order a child." She rubbed her bare leg against mine, and her hand continued to travel toward my crotch. Seductively, she invited, "And of course, there are the older ones who are available!"

The director lectured without taking note, "Yes, Steven, and you'll want to be careful. There was a monumental study years ago that established that being good looking can lead to trouble."

His wife said thoughtfully, "Oh, that's true, dear." Turning back to me, she added, "And my, you are definitely that!"

I cleared my throat again and shifted back toward the arm of the chair to get some free space and hide my growing erection. Trying to keep the conversation moving to avoid further advances, I asked, "So, what, people just date until they're old enough to marry?"

She beamed. "Sure, but they also get to play cute games of house until then!"

I said confusedly, "House? Most people appear to live in apartments?"

The director responded assuredly, "Well, we give people virtual houses to live in, and each unit has its own unique address—not numbers or letters, but a separate physical identifier. That system works very well to keep people content."

Sitting in their plush, whole-floor condo, I looked at him skeptically and said, "Are you sure about that?"

He responded, "Of course. In the past, most lobotomies regretted home buying anyway, so it's much better this way. Oh, and they're also great for home deliveries, since most lobotomies are agoraphobic. Having homes closer together saves on delivery costs, and lobotomies don't much care what a place looks like as long as it provides shelter and Wi-Fi. The vast majority of them will avoid all physical contact unless it benefits them directly anyway, and of course, you've experienced some of that."

I shifted again and cleared my throat; then the director's wife said eagerly, "Oh, and don't leave out the sex games! I remember those years well!" In her best bedroom voice, she leaned over and said to me, *"And, Steven, we still play plenty of them around here!"*

I tried to shift her weight off me again so I could sit up, and then I hastily changed the subject again. "Ahem. Do you two have children?"

His wife leaned back dramatically and clutched her bosom, responding fondly, "Oh, I did! Two beautiful boys from my second marriage. But they're gone now, off on their own adventures."

"Where do they live?"

She sat forward again and responded lightly, "In a building about three blocks away, but we hardly ever see them because everyone is so busy." Then she put her arm around me and gave me a long squeeze. "Ah, I remember when we first ordered them! Such a delight! Of course, we had plenty of practice beforehand."

I asked her what she meant about practice, and she explained that in school, students are given a polyurethane doll they have to pick up for three minutes every twelve hours or else it cries. Otherwise, they just leave it plugged into a light socket and it's fine.

Then she looked at me and said, "My, my, you remind me so much of them! Such a handsome boy!" She absentmindedly unbuttoned the top of her blouse and threw her leg over mine, and the director just sat there smiling cluelessly. Leaning in seductively, she said, "Steven, if you want, we could go upstairs for a good romp before dinner! I have some nice taboo porn we could watch! Why don't you let Momma give you some instruction!"

The director sat up approvingly and responded, "Yes, fine idea, and that will also give me an opportunity to test out my new camera equipment! Steven?"

My eyes bulged at the mere suggestion. Trying not to show my extreme shock at the indecent request, I quickly stammered, "I, um, maybe I shouldn't. I'm not, er, exactly feeling myself today."

She pulled away dejectedly and said, "Oh darn! Such a dashing young man!" Turning to the director, she propositioned wantonly, "Dear, would you like to come upstairs with Mommy and have a go at it before dinner?"

He shook his head lightly and responded, "Sorry, sweetie, I should probably pass too. I'm waiting for a new shipment of ED medications, and I'm afraid you wouldn't be very satisfied."

Her momentary frustration was apparent, and then she lit up again and said, "Oh well, at least I still have my trusty Hitachi! Hold still, Steven. Click. Thanks, I'll see you boys in a bit!"

As she walked out, I started to feel nauseated and coughed, choking on some vomit. The director looked at me, seemingly concerned, and said, "Steven, are you okay?"

Trying to quickly regain composure, I said hoarsely, "Oh yes, just fine. Probably some bad shellfish I ate earlier." I deflected the conversation so I could recover. "So you and Mrs. Cronosson are in an open marriage?"

He said, "Actually, it's Pollitt."

"What?"

"Her last name. It's Pollitt."

"She didn't take your name?"

He tried to laugh lightheartedly and replied, "Oh, no, there's no need for that these days! The insurance benefits transfer just as well even if you don't take someone else's name." Then he added lightly, "But as you'll find out, by the time you're on your third, the holy 'bonds' tend to be a lot looser. Women like to be able to shop for upgrades these days, and as a result, monogamy is basically dead. And a good thing at that, since it was too hard to begin with."

Still clearing my throat, I efforted, "Kind of like raising your own kids?"

"Precisely. Well, of course, I don't have children of my own. I've always just stuck to helping youngsters like yourself, but I've also helped her raise her kids and know all about the hardships. Steven, what we have found out through years of rigorous scientific study is that the entire process of being born is simply too hard for humans to endure, so we do what we can to soften the whole experience."

My windpipe was finally clear, and I said, "And what if people don't like what you're doing?"

He slapped his knee and responded, "Ha! There's no such thing, my boy! Besides, people who would want to fight it all would be doing so based on some outdated notion that they are more than themselves, which science has simply proven is not true."

Grateful to finally have some room to breathe on the couch, I said, "Well, it still seems a bit strange to have open relationship with someone you're married to."

He waved a hand at me and replied casually, "Oh, laddie, you'll find that 'cheating' in the new era is not like what you may have learned as a kid, since we've opened the barriers pretty wide. That was all based on a landmark study years ago about mismatched libidos among spouses. See, science has proven that cheating is essential to maintain a healthy marriage. It's so healthy, in fact, that not letting your spouse cheat on you is grounds for divorce—unless, that is, you can go three to four times per day to meet their insatiable needs."

Upstairs, I heard a soft bang. He apparently didn't notice, or pretended not to, and I said, "Seriously?"

"Oh yes, but that's also because we changed the rules about what cheating means. These days it's not cheating to have cybersex, phone sex, or VR goggle sex; flirt; or perform oral sex, anal sex, or a whole host of other activities. We've simplified things so that we can pretty much comport ourselves just like the animals do."

I shook my head and said, "What the hell does that mean?"

"Steven, it is well documented that we maintain certain animal instincts within us from our prior evolutionary form, and of course, if it can be found in nature, it means that we can do it too." Patting the arms of the chair he was sitting in, the director added, "Yep, this wonderful universe has provided us with predesigned guidance about such principles, so we don't have to worry ourselves with debating the answers!"

"Well, but animals don't have to wait to have offspring."

He shrugged indignantly and said, "Humph. They do if we have any say about it! Steven, you can't imagine the huge population of homeless people—and animals—that came around before we started regulating things." Shaking his head with practiced sympathy, he said, "There is nothing worse than a creature born without any family to take care of it."

I shot back defensively, "Hey, what about me?"

He just offered a light apology. "Well, there really was nothing that we could do to prevent your parents from committing suicide and you becoming an orphan. Sorry, but that little detail was just beyond our control. Anyway, you'll want to be very careful about getting started as well. Girls are no longer competing in a world based on physical aggression or in a world based technically on genes, and their tactics are entirely different these days."

With continued growing unease, I said, "Thank you, I will, but something still bothers me about all of this. How do you know that you're not taking things too far?"

He replied confidently, "Because, Steven, our entire society has advanced one careful step at a time, all through the rigors of the scientific method. That way we're sure that every decision we make is firmly rooted in sound principles." I stopped to ponder that based on what I had seen of *his* society thus far, and he added, "Anyway, the important thing is that the sanctity of the home is not disturbed, since that terribly upsets the inheritance system."

A faint sound coming from upstairs slowly grew into audible moaning, but I politely pretended not to notice and asked, "And does she, um, work?"

The director nodded proudly and said, "Oh, yes! She teaches an adultery class at one of the online universities on Wednesdays and Fridays!"

I choked again. "They actually *teach* people how to cheat on their spouses?"

He waved an innocent hand and corrected. "Oh, no, nothing like that. More like, she teaches people how to recognize and understand the urges that someone or their spouse may have, and to do so without letting it cause financial turmoil."

My discomfort now increasing by the second, I said, "It all seems a little strange to me."

He responded assuredly, "Not at all. Remember: even Jesus was a big supporter of adultery. Oh, who can forget that famous internet post: 'Throwing stones at your neighbor's window hurts more than just the glass'?"

Just then something toppled upstairs and shattered on the floor, and I corrected, "Um, I'm pretty sure that he didn't say that on the internet."

He heard it too but pretended otherwise. "Oh, he he! Right you are! Must have been someone else. Anyway, the practice has been condoned for years, and it really makes for happier households."

The moaning continued, and it sounded as though something as large as a dresser crashed down. I nodded assuredly at him and said, "It's a good thing that you gave female orgasms back to them."

The director looked up at the ceiling and, still smiling obliviously, said, "It sure was, and a small price to pay for all of the great benefits they bring to a household!" Looking back at me, he added proudly, "Yep, without her, our relationship would have been a mess. Luckily, when we got together she already knew the best way to smooth out the transition and make it less financially devastating."

"You said it was expensive?"

He nodded firmly and responded, "Oh yes. The wedding cost nearly a third of an insurance policy, as most of them do, but the rest for us was not as expensive as it was for others."

By now, it actually sounded like the bed was jumping off the ground, and we heard her scream, "Come to Mommy; come to Mommy!"

The director adjusted his tie distractedly and finally said with mild embarrassment, "Oh, and don't mind her. Everyone has a fetish or two these days. That's perfectly normal and something we like to encourage!"

Cocking my head in disbelief, I said, "You call that normal?"

He laughed and replied, "Well, technically there is no 'normal' anymore! It's really all just a range of permissive behaviors."

Holding back the urge to throw up again, I tried to be reassuring. "Well"—cough—"you're certainly a lucky man."

He smiled proudly. "I'll say! She's held together relatively well over the past few years. Sure, she had kids early on, but she didn't gain any weight."

"What?"

"Oh yes. Most of them blow up like balloons when they order a child, but she maintained her same girlish figure."

Having now completely lost my appetite, I stood up hastily and said, "Um, I just remembered that there's somewhere else I need to be right now."

Perhaps not terribly surprised, the director stood up as well and motioned me to the door. "Oh, no problem. Young men and their adventures never rest!" He patted me on the back as I left and bade me well for the evening.

As the door to their apartment closed, I headed for the elevator as quickly as possible and, once outside, tasted the fresh air and reveled in the quiet solitude. After walking for a short distance, my stomach slowly recovered, and finally climbing into a taxi, I looked back at his building standing in the distance. All I could think was that I wouldn't wish his existence on anyone, and what an ugly one at that ...

*

SEVEN

As if to top off all of the absurdity heaped upon me thus far, the day after my indecent encounter at the director's condo, I was graduated to my station performing lobotomies in the lab. I admit that the first one I performed was very eerie and terrifying, and I was thankful that no one else was around when I finally did it. I simply took a deep breath, closed my eyes, and held down the button until it clicked three times. When I opened my eyes again, all I could see as evidence of the butchering I had just performed was a tiny fresh scar and traces of red slowly diluting into the gestational abyss.

I looked around momentarily before starting the next one, and my coworkers all appeared completely oblivious to the nature of their efforts and clicked along without any signs of recognition. As a result, I simply turned back to the machine and kept at it, watching the random selection process take place as each successive fetus was either lobotomized or not, depending on the fate that had been predetermined based on their social standing, ability to pay, and potential luck in the nationwide raffles that took place nearly every day.

During one of the morning breaks, Dr. O'Dwyer stopped by, and I happened to comment to him about the more bothersome aspects of society I had seen and learned about, to which he simply responded, "Yes, it's true that we have had some ugly periods in this country—slavery, Vietnam, riots, detentions, torture, covert support of military dictatorships, and, of course, aggressive subsidy policies. But they were all for the good of the country." Smiling confidently at me, he added, "You do also have to keep in mind all of the money we raked in on movies depicting those dark events once the dust settled, and when that's added in, heck, those dark times were actually a boon for everyone!"

I just rolled my eyes, but he kept trying to boost my confidence in the system. "Now, of course, things are virtually perfect. Everyone is completely free to live the way they want."

Giving a gentle nod to the machinery behind me, I retorted, "Except lobotomies."

He just shook his head and said dismissively, "That's just a minor sacrifice for the greater good. Steven, having to lobotomize our citizens is peanuts compared to all the freedoms we enjoy. You must understand something fundamental about scientific consumerism. As purchasers, we want to be able to relate to the people who perform services for us, and that never worked with robots—or with foreign workers, for that matter. The only way to do that with our own people and be able to get them to accept their lots in life is through lobotomization."

I cocked an eyebrow at him and insisted, "You're still sure that they're necessary?"

He frowned momentarily at my continued questioning, but then he smiled and corrected himself mildly. "Sorry, Steven, I have to remember where you came from. Trust me; we studied this for years with call centers. We would farm out customer service work to foreign countries to cut down on labor costs, but the consumers weren't happy. Even if we gave the workers fake American-sounding names, the callers still knew that they weren't dealing with one of their own. Nope, going to lobotomies was the only way to solve that problem." He put a consoling hand on my shoulder and added, "Now I know that it seems like a harsh thing to do to a human, but—and you'll realize this later—the lobotomies really are better off."

Relenting and trying to steel myself for the next thirty-minute shift, I finally said, "Yeah, maybe."

Suddenly, however, a bell went off overhead and Dr. O'Dwyer

clapped his hands together and said, "Well, that does it for today! Have a nice evening!"

My eyes lit up. "But it's only ten thirty."

"Oh, today's a quarter day. We're trying to reduce worker burnout, so go and enjoy yourself!"

Walking out, I thought about going back to the brothel, but recent events had completely weaned my interest in women. Instead I stopped into a liquor store on the way home and bought a bottle of whiskey. After that, I just lazily walked around town letting a warm mist fill my head—anything was better than thinking about the mess they had turned humanity into.

I didn't realize it, but I had pretty much come full-circle and wound up right back in front of the center. As I stumbled past the coffee bar, a gentleman looked up and said, "Hey, Steven, want a nice cup o' joe?" I shuddered quietly and moved on.

After another day of selectively mutilating my fellow countrymen, where everyone miraculously managed to work until 2:30 p.m. before a three-quarter day was called, I decided to stop by the director's office. The conversation started with me fending off his first offer for an outing to celebrate the day's good work. "Look, I'm done with brothels. I am simply exhausted with all that goes into male–female relationships."

He smiled warmly and nodded. "That's perfectly understandable, so we'll do something else!"

Seeing that it was still early, and willing to accept the social company to keep from drinking alone, I hesitantly nodded in anticipation of a brief outing at a bar. However, the next thing I knew, we were at a bathhouse called the Back Door. Looking up at the neon sign, I retreated several steps and said, "What the hell are we doing here?"

He responded innocently, "I thought we'd try something different this time. I'm sure you'll like it!"

I froze in place and muttered nervously, "I … I don't think so."

"Come on! Look at your gender identity monitor. It's glowing bright purple! Trust me, it'll be fun!" He was right—about my monitor, that is.

A bare-chested male slicked in oil greeted us at the door. "Hello, and welcome to our club!" He grabbed my arm and ushered me along, adding enthusiastically, "No reason to stay up front! In here, you'll find the best things near the back door! Come right with me and we'll get you prepped."

Immediately confused, I said, "Prepped?"

The attendant replied, "Yes, that's a little shot we give you to keep you safe while you play in here."

I halted halfway through the lobby. "I don't know. I don't really like needles."

The director smiled and prodded me. "Oh, it's harmless! Just a little prick!"

"What's in it?"

The attendant responded, "PrEP mixed with meth and amyl nitrates. The solution keeps you safe and also helps to dilate ... your senses."

I said, "Safe from what?"

"The PrEP helps to inoculate you against HIV."

"Is it 100 percent effective?"

The attendant said, "No, but you'll be fine."

Whipping around toward the director, I exclaimed, "What the fuck?"

He just smiled and pushed me forward. "Oh, don't worry! Everyone else in here is on the same thing, so it's really like double protection for you, and your odds of catching anything are statistically very low. PrEP is also now part of most people's monthly cocktail of drugs."

"How do you know if someone has taken his?"

The director responded matter-of-factly, "You just do. Anyway, partners have to disclose their STD status or else it's a crime."

I finally sighed heavily and relented, proceeding into one room to receive the prophylactic shot. After a few minutes, I noticed that the director was gone, but I was, in fact, loosening up and didn't much seem to care. The attendant came back to find me and led me into another room. After lovingly unbuckling my belt and helping relieve me of my trousers and underwear, he said, "Now come in here and we'll finish the rest of the preparation."

Dreamily, I said, "What 'rest'?"

"Steven, you may not remember this from your experiences as a kid, but the large intestine is three feet of crap. We have to clean you out to be able to have anal sex."

That woke me up again, and I tried to protest briefly. "Oh, I'm not sure …"

He just kept smiling and pressing me forward. "Don't worry; girls go through the same thing—well, when they do anal, that is!"

Looking back at him through the rapidly approaching fog, I said, "Huh. They make it look so darn easy in the movies."

He responded knowingly, "Yes, they certainly do!" With that he gently patted my backside and led me in.

After that, things got a bit fuzzy. From my recollections, being cleaned out in the bathhouse is a mix between a trip to the dentist and going through a car wash. First, they propped me up on a horselike contraption, and then two attendants set to work at either end of me, brushing and rinsing, scraping and scouring. Somewhere in the middle of it, I also caught the faint smell of bleach—"so that my taint would have the right tint," as one of the attendants explained. Just about the time they were spritzing my insides with something called "Eau de Venus" and hanging a miniature pine tree air freshener from my prostate, my memory gave out.

I woke up later that night considerably spent and covered in lube. After another unceremonious rinse job, they threw me in a cab, and I made it safely home.

The next day, I stumbled in through the front door of the center, my head still fuzzy from the night's activities and my posterior quite sore. One of the guards saw me come in and greeted me. "Hey Steven! It looks like you had fun last night! I hope you got your shot?"

I barely registered the comment. "My what? Shot? Gosh, I hardly … Wait, I do remember getting a shot at the start. Did I ask the others if they had gotten theirs?"

"Well, you must have enjoyed yourself! See?"

He had pictures of me loaded on his phone, and there I was, spread out in all my naked glory. Nearly petrified, I glanced around quickly and saw a few other people walk in, and they grinned knowingly as they passed by. Apparently the pictures were circulating all over the lab, available to anyone with a smartphone or VR contacts.

My jaw dropped. "*Oh my God!* Where did you get those?"

"From the bathhouse's website. Look. New pictures are uploaded every day!"

"Jesus Christ! They didn't tell me that!"

"Steven, don't worry about it. Everyone's doing it! Anal sex is the most natural thing in the universe. Here, look at this. We even put out a manual on it which is modeled after India's famous one."

Still shocked and now growing angry, I said, "What the hell does that mean?"

He responded innocently, "Well, India is, of course, the birthplace of human spirituality, so it can't be wrong."

I lowered my head and just made my way to the elevator. As I rode up, there was a quick flash on the screen of my exploits, apparently as some kind of public advertisement for the bathhouse. Christ, I hadn't done anything like that since I was a kid, and now it was apparently public knowledge. After that, I vowed never to go back to the bathhouse and decided to start taking the stairs at work. The rest of the day, I stayed quietly at my station and tried to avoid everyone.

* * *

The next morning, I had to go see the director, but when I pushed open the door to the stairwell, the alarm went off and thirty people wound up in the hospital in shock. The director explained to me that there was an alarm on the stairs because no one used them except in case of fire, and I eventually talked him into disabling it so that I could "get some exercise."

But everywhere I went, I kept running into people who had seen my sexual defilement. The video made its way around the social media circles, and as a result, my message inbox multiplied times ten thousand. Every time my phone beeped, it was a message inviting me to have sex somewhere, and then girls I used to casually say hello to started trying to introduce me to their gay friends. Finally, I confided in the director and asked for help.

Standing firmly on the other side of his desk, I said, "Look, I'm into women."

He responded reassuringly, "Steven, it's okay! Your gender is just what you were born with, but don't forget, gender is a spectrum. By the way, have you checked yours yet today?"

Coldly, I said, "No."

He smiled expectantly and offered, "Want to go back again tonight?"

"Oh, no. No way." Fumbling to try to hide my shame, all I could think to say was, "That was … that was just a waste of energy."

Rocking back gently, he observed, "Well, sure, having anal sex is wasted energy, but there's no reason to copulate anymore, so what's the difference?" Seeing that I was unconvinced, he smiled and added confidently, "Steven, once you get rid of procreation, the rest is just about pleasure!"

Shaking my head, I countered, "Now, I'm not sure that's true."

"Think of it this way. If a person you like happens to have a duck bill on their head, and the bill is what gives them pleasure, then you have duck bill sex. No problem!"

Still unnerved by the whole experience from the other night, I said sarcastically, "Sure, and I'll bet that these days people do that too?"

The director smiled. "Oh, not too many, but there are some!"

Seeing that I was getting nowhere with him, I went back to work and just kept my head down and stayed at my terminal. My watch kept going off with new messages, and I eventually just turned it off.

* * *

The director found me late the next day, appearing considerably distraught as he hurried up to my station. When he got there, he said with mild panic, "Steven, where on earth have you been?"

Immediately defensive, I answered, "Here working. Why?"

"I tried to get in contact with you. Why didn't you respond?"

"Oh, I guess my watch was turned off. What happened?"

The director adopted a regretful expression and said, "I'm afraid we have a bit of bad news. We accidentally injected you with HIV."

I jumped up and exclaimed, *"What the fuck?"*

The director shook his head apologetically. "Yes, I'm sorry. It was just a bad mix-up. Apparently one of the pleasure technicians grabbed the wrong vial."

I clenched my fists and leaned in toward him aggressively. "What do you mean, *'wrong vial'*? Why would you even keep something like that around?"

He took a step back and shrugged innocently. "Well, some people just want to get it over with. Don't worry, though, since we know how to control the disease."

"The hell you do! Are you sure I have it?"

"Not 100 percent, but you'll have to wait a few weeks to find out for sure. Here's a test to take and send into the lab—not this lab, the STD lab at the clinic, around the corner from the hospital."

Still furious, I shouted in blind anger, "Goddamn it! I didn't even need that fucking shot! You told me that everyone was already inoculated when we went into that place!"

He appeared to be strangely amused by my sudden flash of anger, but rather than punishing me for lashing out, he instead switched to documentary voice and responded casually, "Oh, you actually never can tell. If someone forgets to take their dosage, PrEP turns out to be totally ineffective and instead creates HIV drug resistance." He chuckled and added lightly, "I'm afraid that we're subject to the same problem we used to have with females remembering to take contraception—if you don't take it, it doesn't work!"

Fuming, I demanded, "Well, why can't you fix it the same way you did with women?"

He said amusedly, "How, by sewing up their genitals?"

Fiercely, I shouted, *"How about by not dragging me to a fucking bathhouse in the first place?"*

He responded innocently, "Well, it sure looked like you had fun!"

Shamefully left with my drug-induced amnesia, my only response was, "I ... don't remember. But why don't you just give PrEP with the nanobot?"

He shook his head and responded assuredly, "Steven, there's no room in the nanomeds for PrEP. Besides, not everyone needs it."

Exasperated at the mere suggestion, I said, "Come on, pretty much everyone is gay!"

The director responded with slight indignation, "Well, I'm not."

I shouted at him, *"Then why the hell did we go to a bathhouse?"*

He backed up innocently again and said, "I'd thought you'd like it. Oh, Steven, don't worry. HIV is just another chronic disease, so it's nothing at all to fret about. If you catch it, the postexposure medication just comes out of your citizenship score." Apparently satisfied with that explanation, he walked away, and I sat down again, burying my head in my hands.

The next day, I sent in my test and tried to stay focused. The girl at the station beside me stood up at one point and walked by me, and I overheard the conversation she started. "Dr. O'Dwyer, I hate to bother you."

"Yes, dear? Remind me of your name again?"

She bounced up momentarily on her toes and smiled. "I'm Susie!"

"Oh, good. Please go on."

Then her face dropped and her somber tone immediately kicked in. "Well, I know that I'm supposed to work today, and I've only been on the job for three days, but for some reason I just don't want to work."

He assumed a concerned expression and pulled up her file on his watch. "Let me see. Right now we don't have anything in your chart that would let you take the day off, but why don't you go to the doctor and get checked out?" Looking back up at her, he added thoughtfully, "It sounds like you might have a latent case of Newtonian ennui."

She gasped and turned white. "OMG! Am I going to die?"

He gave her a reassuring pat on the arm and said, "Probably not, but run along and they'll take care of you."

Her face lit up again. "Great!" Then she turned back to me, batted her eyes, and asked politely, "Hey Steven, can you handle the rest of my work today?"

The line of fetuses could be conveniently recalibrated so that units allocated to one worker's station were redirected to another's in the event that one of the workers was absent, which I had already experienced before. That meant double work for me and no further breaks for the day, but I simply grunted and nodded, and the girl smiled at me and skipped away whistling.

Dr. O'Dwyer came up to me, rested his hand on my shoulder, and said, "Thanks for doing that, Steven. I don't know how long she'll last here, and one of the problems we face is constant turnover. What did she say her name was again?"

Wearily, I answered, "Susie."

"Thanks. I tell you; people get injured all the time, wind up going to the hospital, and then new ones come in. I can never keep any of them straight."

After struggling for a few more hours, I finally got up and exited through the back door, leaving someone else to lobotomize the next fool to come down the line.

*

EIGHT

I passed the next several days in suspended uncertainty, and the monotony of my new job was not helping, either. One ... two ... three—no lobotomy. *Click-click-click*—lobotomy. One ... two ... three—no lobotomy. *Click-click-click*—lobotomy. *Click-click-click*—lobotomy. *I swear if that fucker got me infected with AIDS, I'm going to take this whole place apart—citizenship score be damned!*

An overeager female suddenly appeared in my peripheral view. "Hi Steven, whatcha doin'?"

Dully, I said, "Working."

She came up and stood right behind me, impervious to my efforts to ignore her, and said intrusively, "Can you guess which seven world leaders went on a rafting trip down the Ganges River last week?"

Refusing to look up, I answered curtly, "What?"

"Can you guess which seven world leaders went on a rafting trip?"

I snapped around. "How the fuck should I know? Aren't you supposed to be working?"

She turned white, and a small tear started to well up, and then she tried to regroup while still sniffling. "Steven, this is part of my job! I'm supposed to go around and see whether everyone is paying attention to the elevator raffle!" *Sniffle.*

"Well, I'm not. Can you leave me alone?" *Sniffle, sniffle.*

She walked off, but five minutes later another functionary tapped me on the shoulder. I looked up aggressively, and he just handed me a note and scampered off. The note read: "Steven, _____ had to go home. Please finish work for her. Signed—G. O'D."

One ... two ... three. *Click-click-click.*

"Hi, Steven. What are you doing?"

Holding back the urge to murder someone. "Working."

"Can you guess the manufacturer of the hydroponic reverberator on the Pluto space station?"

I whipped around maniacally and demanded, "Are you fucking kidding me? Is this part of another raffle?"

Another pink face turned to white, but the tears were slow to react—possibly the result of clogged tear ducts. The unfortunate male creature standing in front of me stammered on, "Uh, uh, yes. The VMAs are tonight, and this is one of the questions that they may call viewers at home with. And I was ... I was ..."

"Would you please leave? Now!"

"*Waaaaaahhhhhh!*"

It looked as if I had cured that problem—the crying one. Unfortunately, I would still have to work on making people also disappear at will, as he just stood there looking pitiful and dripping snot around my workstation.

Finally I sighed and said, "Look. I'm sorry. I didn't mean that."

Hearing this, he recovered slightly and remarked, "Well, I've never heard someone be so ... mean!"

I repeated insincerely, "I said I'm sorry."

He sucked up a long string of snot and smiled pitifully at me and then said, "I guess I understand, what with you being an orphan and all."

I leaned into him menacingly and demanded, "What's that supposed to mean?"

"Oh, nothing, nothing. Listen, I'm feeling a bit lightheaded, and I need to go to the doctor. Do you think that you can finish my work for me today?"

"Fine."

He pepped up immediately. "Thanks, Steven! You're the best!"

An hour later, another unwelcome visitor appeared. "Hi, Steven, what are you doing?"

I'm not going to answer that. Don't look up; don't look up. I felt a tap on my shoulder, and I finally turned around. "Oh, um, hi. Didn't see you there."

"Look, I have to leave early today. Can you do my work for me?"

I shook my head with regret. "Sorry, I can't. I'm an orphan."

Sharply, she said, "So? That doesn't keep you from working. Why don't you try to shoulder my burdens and have some *real* problems in your life?"

I sighed. "Okay, okay, fine. What's killing you?"

She beamed in response. "My personal battle with bipolar disorder!" Holding up her phone, she said proudly, "Look, it's on my social media account!"

I cocked my head and retorted, "You know, if you share it with a hundred million other people, it's not really a 'personal' battle anymore."

Her eyes blazed at me. "*What did you just say?*"

Mine just rolled back. "Never mind. Yes, I'll do your work."

Suddenly another girl popped into the scene, and she had a rack like a moose. Chipperly, she said to the other, "Did I hear you say that you have bipolar disorder?"

"Yes."

"Oh, me too! Are you taking a mental health day?"

"Yes!" She frowned sideways in my direction and added, "Well, now that Mr. Grumpy has been nice enough to agree to do my work for me."

"Hey, let's go do something together!"

"Okay!"

"Um, Steven ..."

I already had my back to them and responded automatically, "Yes, fine. I'll do her work too. Just please leave."

Dr. O'Dwyer walked around the corner seconds later. Grinning broadly and letting out a whistle, he said, "Did you see the rack on that girl? Thank goodness for tubal ligations, eh?"

I was still fuming and trying to concentrate. "Huh?"

"Breasts have always been a strong attractor, but breast implants were also linked to cancer, which helped get us into the tube-tying business. We convinced people that having their tubes tied at the onset of puberty would cause the body to increase estrogen production, and they were ecstatic."

Bitterly, I responded, "I thought that was all just made up."

"Well, you tell me, pal. Haven't you seen all of the huge breasts and rumps on women these days?"

"I guess so, but I just thought she was a fat ass. I never suspected that it was because of the tube tying."

Sharply, he chided, "Steven, you can't say that anymore! It's no longer correct to call people fat or obese. Instead you have to say that they have an excess buildup of dark matter."

I turned back to my work without responding, and then Dr. O'Dwyer nudged me playfully and added, "Anyway, if you weren't mostly gay, you'd think she was pretty hot too!"

I looked up at him fiercely. "I am not mostly gay!"

"Totally gay?"

"No!"

He grinned coyly and pressed, "What about the bathhouse?"

Gritting my teeth, I responded sharply, "*I was drugged.*"

"Well, I saw the video, and it sure looked like you were having fun."

I was now in the red and I slammed the auto shutoff button and said angrily, "Look, I didn't want to go in the first place, and I certainly did not authorize anyone to publish the tape that someone else made while I was there!"

Dr. O'Dwyer just waved a hand at me and said, "Oh, don't worry. When you entered the front door of that place, you signed a copyright application with your thumb. All naked photos of you are legally protected and can't be reproduced for financial gain—except by the bathhouse, that is."

I turned back to my machine and mumbled sourly, "I'm not sure that really helps anything."

"Hey, look at it this way, it could be a big boost to your career!" I turned and scowled at him, to which he just grinned and continued ribbing. "Oh, come on. I'm sure that it was no real shock to you. Didn't you fool around with the other kids at the boys' home?"

I finally stood up and exclaimed, *"What do you want from me? I didn't know what it meant at the time! It was just something we did as kids!"*

He shrugged and said lightly, "So why stop now?"

Unable to respond adequately at that point, I sat back down and looked at my shoes. Finally, I said searchingly, "I don't know. I just feel like at this point in my life I should be attracting myself to females."

He put a hand on my shoulder again and urged confidently, "Oh, Steven, that is an outdated, preprogrammed response to your surroundings, which you probably got from a horrible book written during the dark times. You should just give in to your urges. Come on, gay it up!"

I shucked his hand off me and responded aggressively, "For the last time, I am not gay!"

He took a step back and grinned sarcastically. "Okay, okay. Geesh, touchy, touchy. Sounds like someone needs to get some psychological counseling."

Finally I took a deep breath and said, "Sorry. I'm just a little on edge from having to do everyone else's work."

Dr. O'Dwyer shook his head regretfully and responded, "I'm afraid that can't be helped. The law says that if you can prove you can't work, you don't have to."

Disgusted with the notion, I asked, "Do they still get credit for not working?"

"Of course not, but most of them don't care. As you may know, lobotomies are not motivated by financial gain. They believe that they will inherit enough from their parents to survive, or marry someone with a higher citizenship score, and most lobotomies will work only as hard as the rules make them." He chuckled and added, "They are actually very clever in that regard! For the ones who have two or more jobs, they have to figure out how to avoid working at multiple locations at the same time, which can be work in and of itself."

Dumbfounded at the notion, I said, "Don't they worry about running out of money?"

Dr. O'Dwyer cocked his head at me and asked rhetorically,

"Do those really seem like the actions of someone who has any real concept of it? But we can't change the labor laws. Just try taking something away from a lobotomy and they will whine and cry like you have never heard anyone whine and cry before. That is, of course, largely caused by zygote depression, which so many suffer from." He patted me on the back lightly and added, "Thankfully, you're our little workhorse around here and you'll be moving up the ladder in no time!"

Completely exhausted by then, I said, "It still seems wrong for them to get out of work."

He responded assuredly, "Well, don't worry. We also keep track of the types of excuses they use. A whole different rating system applies to that—for promotions and the like—and once people start making excuses for working, you can usually tell that they're not ready to take on more responsibility."

I sighed heavily at the thought. Giving me a final, light pat on the back, Dr. O'Dwyer said chipperly, "Anyway, you'll probably be the last one here today, so be sure to turn out the lights when you're done. Thanks!"

* * *

The next day, my fantasies while performing my monotonous task vacillated between homicide and self-lobotomy. *Click, click, click. One ... two ... three. Click, click, click. One ... two ... three ...*

Click, click.

Click.

Click.

What the fuck? Whether I push this button or not, the machine keeps doing the same thing. The only thing that actually halts it is getting up out of this chair or pushing the stop button.

My watch suddenly went off. "Report to Dr. O'Dwyer's office immediately!" Terror set in, and I was in his office in less than thirty seconds.

Shaking his head disapprovingly, Dr. O'Dwyer said, "Steven, I'm afraid that I have to give you a bad performance review."

"Why?"

"For not running your machine correctly."

I tried to plead with him. "But the machine does the exact same thing whether I press the button or not."

He just shook his head again and said, "Yes, but we have to find something for people to do. Did I tell you about the trouble we had when the robots were around?" He looked down and made a deft mark in my folder; then, looking up again, he said, "Anyway, since that's just your first screwup, I'll only dock you half a point."

I whined dejectedly, "Half a point? So, I'm now down from G-7 to G-what? 6.5?"

"Yep. Sorry about that, but we have to keep employees motivated. The next time it will cost you a whole point." He stood up, grabbed the card hanging from my belt, and snipped it off the lanyard. He handed me a freshly printed card that said "G-6.5," and then he added, "By the way, the director wants to see you."

I bowed my head and sluggishly went upstairs. When I walked in, the director stood up from behind his desk with a deep look of concern on his face and said, "Steven, what's bothering you? I heard that you got a bad performance review today?"

Bitterly apologetic, I stood near the doorway and replied, "Look, I don't want to complain and get docked. You probably lose points for that too."

He beckoned me in compassionately. "No, no. You can always speak freely to me. Don't worry about that. Come on in!"

I stepped into his office cautiously and took a seat. Measuring my words, I finally said, "Well ... is everyone around here completely deranged, or what?"

Sitting down, he considered that for a moment and then replied thoughtfully, "Oh, I'd imagine that everyone at work has a mental health disorder of one kind or another. A lot of them suffer from fear of push buttons, PTSD since birth due to humming machines, and other things. Why?"

My eyeballs nearly popped out of their sockets, and I sat up and exclaimed, *"How do you hire people to work here who have PTSD due to humming machines?"*

The director shrugged and responded, "We have to. The law says so, and we have to hire lobotomies as well."

I just shook my head and said, "I still can't believe that part."

"Come on, Steven. Can you imagine doing that job for the rest of your life if you weren't lobotomized?"

I sighed and responded, "Good point."

"Is there anything else wrong? You seem pretty stressed out today."

All I could say was "No, not really."

"Well, we're closing at noon, so you can take a little break."

Having just been docked and needing to work it off, I protested, "What? Why? We closed early the last three days?"

The director responded lightly, "Steven, people with mental health problems can't be expected to work a full day, and it's not good anyway. If they spend too much time at work, it cuts down on consumer spending, which as you know is a vital part of our economy."

My temper flared again. *"Spend? Spend with what? None of them work, so how the hell do they have anything to spend?"*

He calmly replied, "Insurance, remember? Well, that and inheritance. Besides, science proves that high blood pressure in young people can lead to early dementia, so we can't push them too hard."

As I sat there still fuming, and already longing for early-onset dementia to get me out of this mess, the director suddenly beamed at me and switched gears. "Anyway, don't worry about it. We have a special treat for you!"

I leaned back in surprise, completely off-balanced by that comment. "You do? But I just lost a half point?"

He responded lightly, "Oh, don't worry about that. You'll make it up in no time, and this has nothing to do with that."

Cautiously, I asked, "So what is it?"

"As part of your work benefits, you're entitled to a government car!"

I immediately shook my head and declined. "Look, I appreciate that, but there's no way that I'm going to dive into an expensive consumer purchase. I'm trying to work my points up, not down, and I'm sure that a car is ridiculously costly, especially if part of a lobotomy order includes a one-hundred-fifty-thousand-dollar discount on the purchase."

He laughed. "Steven, didn't you hear me? The car is part of your work benefits, and it's completely free to you with your government employment!"

"Really?"

"Sure! Every government worker gets a free car in our country!"

"Huh. I guess it's okay then, but I don't know how to drive."

He just laughed. "You don't need any special training for that! We call driving 'using the force' these days!"

"What?"

"Don't you watch the *Star Wars* movies? Using the force—it doesn't require any training at all!"

"I, um ..."

He said reassuringly, "Look, don't worry about that. Just go down there and pick out something nice, and I'm sure you'll feel better once you're behind the wheel of a fancy new automobile!"

* * *

I took a cab out to the lot, and a salesman in a short-sleeved shirt and tie sprang up when he saw me and started approaching. It didn't look as if there were any other customers there that day, and the rest of the salespeople were just milling around.

He greeted me warmly at the door. "Welcome to Government Motors, Steven! The director phoned and told me to expect you. Congratulations, you've taken your first step toward a new life of freedom!"

I shook his hand cautiously and said, "Thanks."

We walked into his office and he started into his pitch. "Please have a seat and let me tell you all about the exciting venture you're about to embark on!" I sat down, and he stood right in front of me; then he held up his hands and said excitedly, "First, close your eyes!"

I just sat there staring at him, so he urged, "Come on, trust me! This is an important part of the process!"

I finally gave in and closed my eyes, and he said, "Okay, now picture the perfect automobile. Do you see it?"

Having only ever ridden in busses or taxis, I pretended to contemplate the idea and said, "Sort of."

"Good. Just stay focused on that and keep your eyes closed. Now open your mouth and stick out your tongue."

My eyes shot open as a cotton-covered stick was jammed into the back of my throat. "Ick! Hey, why'd you do that?"

Efficiently depositing the swab into a plastic bottle and closing it up, he said plainly, "To collect a DNA specimen."

"For what? I thought this didn't require any special training."

He smiled and said, "Oh, it doesn't!"

"Then why do I need a DNA test to drive a car?"

As he dropped the bottle through a little window in the wall, he responded gaily, "It's not a DNA test; it's a personality test! And we have to take yours because, despite diligent efforts to locate the same, we don't seem to have any data on you. That's very odd, since most people already provided voluntary DNA results as part of their genealogy searches."

I spit out the cotton remnants and said, "But why do I need the personality test?"

"Oh, that. To determine the options you might want, of course."

"Why are vehicle options based on my personality test results?"

"All options are based on your essential nature, and that's in your DNA."

"My what?"

"Your essential nature. By giving people the option to make their cars behave like they do, we are encouraging people to embrace the truth about themselves. It's all a very healthy part of modern society!"

I scrubbed my tongue one last time, already disliking this whole outing, and said, "Whatever."

The salesman paused momentarily, appearing unsure of how to respond to that and maintain professional chipperness. Probably gauging that I wasn't putting up any real resistance, however, he finally said, "Oh, good! The results take about an hour, and in the meantime, we can take a test drive and I'll give you a rundown of the options available to you."

We headed out in a monstrous luxury SUV model of some sort that was roomy and comfortable, and the engine purred quietly and melodically the whole time. My chauffer led the way, scrolling through the brochure of functions on the dash computer while the car did the rest. He said, "Of course, you don't have to choose this particular model. You qualify for anything in the D-7 to E-6 range, and that includes all mid-sized sedans and SUVs."

Looking over at him confusedly, I said, "Why can't I get something in the F range?"

That was apparently the funniest thing he had heard all day, and he burst out laughing. Finally he stopped when he noticed that I was not also laughing and said, "Excuse me, Steven, let me just check something. Oh, you're an orphan. They may not have explained this to you, but you can't get into the F class."

"Why not?"

"'F' stands for 'filthy rich.' You can't get into that class unless you're born into it. Heck, we don't even sell F-class cars here!"

I sighed annoyedly and said, "Let's just get on with it."

We drove along, and he continued to explain the features. Finally I stopped him and said, confused, "Wait, doesn't the car just go from point A to point B?"

He slapped his knee and replied, "Ha ha ha! Heavens, no! When we first created autonomous vehicles, that was all they did, but since all cars are governed to go the same top speed, we had to include apps to make them more commercially attractive. And with computer precision these days, we can make your car a perfect extension of who you are."

"Why is the car autonomous?"

He paused and then responded thoughtfully, "Well, lots of reasons really, but mostly because lobotomies can't adjust to changes in the road. Here, now let me demonstrate a few things. For urban traffic, we call this the Bump and Run Program. It comes on automatically at traffic lights if you're behind someone. See? The car in front accelerates at a steady pace, but since our car has Bump and Run, we can accelerate and decelerate rapidly several times over to give the impression that we're trying to push the car in front to go faster! Isn't that fun?"

Flatly, I replied, "A riot."

"Now we can pull up next to the car and watch this. As we come up to the stop light and get ready to proceed—Zoom!—we can take off and leave them in the dust behind us! That's called the Jungle Dominance Mode! Pretty neat, huh?"

Dully again, I said, "Pretty neat."

"Here's the My Car's Space Is More Important Than Your Car's Space Program. If our car is driving along and an obstruction is blocking part of our lane, any normal car's programming will slow and stop until the obstruction is removed or there is enough room next to us to make a lane change. However, with this app, our car will occupy part of the lane next to it to make room, even if there is another car already there. As long as the other car doesn't have competing software, it will automatically have to move, and so on, and so on."

"Huh."

"We also have the I'm Constantly in a Hurry Mode."

"What's that?"

"That app only activates on weekends. You can see the drivers on Saturdays or Sundays darting furiously up to each intersection only to have the brakes slammed on—never mind that the lights are all on automatic timers and much slower than they are during the week. Now, for shopping trips, we also have the Parking Lot Sand Shark Program. With that activated, the car will wander around for twenty minutes looking for a spot that is ten feet closer to the building. It's very popular!"

I frowned at him. "Are you serious?"

"Oh, yes! Steven, do you know how many people suffered PTSD in the past because they couldn't park close enough to where they wanted to be?" I just stared straight ahead and didn't dare respond to that one. "As for options that are available for either in-town or highway traffic, we have the Ride in the Blind Spot Program, which does exactly what it sounds like. And this is the Tailgate Program. As you may have seen, some people don't feel good unless they're tailgating someone. Now let me shift out of that, and here is the Box-In Program!"

We had cornered an unsuspecting lower-class car on the road, but the other driver was fast asleep in his car and oblivious to us. Appearing embarrassed that the ploy didn't stir any fear in the other motorist, the salesman attempted to deflect: "Ahem. It usually helps if you have a significant other on the road with you, but sometimes you can find a fellow traveler in a comparable model with the same software to help you fully execute that program's features."

We left the other vehicle in the dust and found another road victim who *was* aware and who immediately dived under the dash at seeing our rapidly approaching vehicle. I gripped the dash myself as the car suddenly accelerated and then slowed right behind the other vehicle, and the salesman boomed excitedly, "That's the Big Truck Maximum Overdrive Mode! It's only available on larger models, of course, and lets you bear down on people at a ridiculous rate of speed and then come to a sudden deceleration just behind their bumper. Wasn't that fun? Did you see how that old lady cowered in fear? Ha!"

I was at a loss for words. Rapidly switching the controls again, he demonstrated the Sunday Driver Mode, where we wandered recklessly across any lane we wanted to, the Uber-Self-Interested Hypochondriac Mode, which caused the car to randomly brake, adopt whatever speed it wanted to, and periodically pull over to the shoulder for self-checks even though we were still in traffic, and the Fear of Being Left Alone Mode, which kept our vehicle within six feet of the car in front of us, despite the fact that we had passed into a relatively empty stretch of highway.

We suddenly darted through an interchange, and he continued

the nauseating tour by explaining the step-up algorithms in the programming that permitted upper-class cars to ignore pleasant yield requests from all lower-class cars when merging. The salesman also explained that C-class cars were always stuck in the slow lane by default, and D-class cars could use the middle second lane, while E-class cars could use the first middle lane—that is, the one closest to the outside lane—and F-class cars naturally got the outermost lane.

I learned that some lower-class citizens couldn't even own cars, which he didn't delve into in any great detail. Then he added eagerly, "Since you're probably getting an E-class car, you can ignore requests from everyone except F-class, and your car will even be fitted with emergency lights!"

I shot him a startled expression and said, *"Like the police?"*

"Not exactly, but they look like police lights to most lobotomies, so you still get the same benefits!" Then, apparently considering the company he was with, he looked over at me cautiously and added, "Technically, you *don't* have the right to pull anyone over. However, we can program your car to pull out in front of all cars except F-class and force them to yield down to as slow of a pace as you want. Isn't that great?"

I tried to shake myself out of the trance the car and speech had put me in and said uneasily, "That actually seems a little aggressive."

He replied reassuringly, "Not at all. It's a tremendous blow to the ego to have to follow someone in a cheaper car."

"But how do these apps force other cars to behave in certain ways?"

"Steven, the modern technology in these cars allows them to talk to each other. You could call it a bit of trash-talking. A more luxurious vehicle can 'talk' the other car into moving out of the way or doing a variety of other functions, and it's really just an electronic version of societal pleasantries that have existed for centuries. Heck, cars don't even have horns anymore. Now they just electronically tap each other on the shoulder."

I looked in the mirror and saw that my face had started turning green. He had noticed it by now and rapidly dialed down the controls.

Still eager to pitch more features to me, he said confidently, "Oh, I can see that you may be a little timid for all of that. You strike me as more of the Slow-Down-And-Let-People-Have-The-Right-Of-Way-Because-I'm-A-Good-Samaritan type. Here's what that does."

The sickness kept coming on, despite our more leisurely pace, and I efforted disgustedly, "What do people do, drive using their inner child?"

His eyes lit up. "Oh, that would make the cutest bumper sticker! 'My Inner Child Is My Co-Pilot!' Do you mind if I use that?"

I just closed my eyes and said wearily, "No, please do, but can we just get back to the car lot?"

The salesman remained nervously compliant, still pressing toward his expected sale and said, "Oh, sure, I guess you've seen everything you needed to, huh? I'll just click home and we'll be back in a jiffy!"

After a bit, we started to come to a halt. I opened my eyes and noticed a train of stopped cars ahead of us and asked, "Hey, why are we slowing down?"

"There's an accident. This particular model comes with the Rubbernecking Program, and the car automatically slows down if there's an accident, even if it is not blocking the roadway."

I shook my head and said, "That's ridiculous."

He responded confidently, "Oh, the Rubbernecking Program is very popular these days, especially with the contest they're running where the first person to get to an accident and report it is automatically entered into a drawing for a vacation!"

While we were stopped, he took the opportunity to open up another line of inquiry. Pulling his electronic pad out again, he said, "By the way, what do you normally do when you drive?"

Staring blankly at the motionless vehicles all over the road, I said, "Huh?"

"Do you take drugs? Watch movies? Surf the internet? I need to know so we can determine your proper level of distraction to install in the car. We can also put a valium dispenser right here in the middle console."

Shaking my head in exhaustion, I said, "I don't know. I've never driven a car before. Say, can we just get back to the dealership?"

"Oh, sure, no problem. Let me switch off the Rubberneck and I'll have you back in no time!"

Two hours later, we pulled into the lot, and I was glad to have my feet safely on the ground again. The salesman told me to wait with the car while he ran in to the office, and he returned moments later with some paperwork. Delighted at the sale he was about to close, he said, "Okay, we'll just go over some of your options based on these test results! Oh, and with your car acquisition, you also get a year's subscription to one of our most popular magazines!"

The magazine he handed to me was entitled *Not You!* On the cover was a picture of two wealthy people leaning out the door of a jet that was flying over a dilapidated neighborhood, and they were laughing as they dumped the plane's chemical toilet on everyone below them. I thumbed quickly through the pages and said, astonished, "People actually read this?"

"Of course! The magazine showcases things that people in certain classes can do that others can't. Lobotomies eat it up!"

I chucked it on the ground at my feet. Having sensed something not quite right about this whole experience, I said suspiciously, "Let me ask you something. I just get this car for free?"

"Sure."

"Do I have to take a driving test?"

"Nope. Well, not really. All you do is push right here with your thumb. See there, just under the handle on the driver's side of the door? That's the actual driving test."

Eyeing the push-button module on the car, I recalled that in addition to hearing Dr. O'Dwyer's explanation about the obligations triggered by depressing the mechanism to open a newborn crate, I had also received two contracts in my email from activating my phone and watch, both of which stated that I had agreed to support various international manufacturing coalitions that I had never even heard of. Dr. O'Dwyer assured me that they were all harmless, but I wasn't interested in unknowingly giving away more of my rights for technology acquisitions.

I took a step back and said, "Wait a minute. Can I read the contract?"

He was temporarily stunned at my request. "The which? Oh, the push-button contract that comes with the car?"

"Yes."

He fumbled uncertainly for a moment, then said, "I, um … I guess so. I'll have to go and look for one though. No one has ever asked us for that. Hang on; I'll be right back."

He returned after forty-five minutes and said, winded, "Sorry about that! I had to go down into storage to find one!"

He handed me the 164-page contract that was triggered by the push-button on the handle, and I flipped through the pages and then threw it on the ground next to the magazine. Starting to experience jaundice at the notion of car ownership, I frowned at him and asked accusingly, "So what *else* do I have to do?"

As a bead of perspiration appeared on his forehead, he smiled uneasily and said, "Oh, not too much! We make very robust cars these days, so you only have to deal with inspections and tune-up every ninety days. Oh, and then there's the annual inspection, and the semibiannual cosmetic checkup, and … other things."

"Seriously?"

"Oh yes. Since the manufacturers all insure these vehicles, they require frequent checkups to make sure that there are no maintenance-related accidents, and the terms of your lease agreement also require the cosmetic checkups. But don't worry; you don't have to remember to do any of it."

"I don't?"

He smiled broadly. "Nope! We keep track of the schedule for you and just have someone pick up your car when required and leave you with a loaner until we're done!"

"How the hell does that work?"

"Well, because of all of the technology in the cars these days, we know where you are constantly, and one of our technicians just comes to wherever you are and performs the swap-out."

I didn't like the sound of any of that and asked uneasily, "How long does all of that take?"

"Oh, about a week."

Skeptically, I demanded "Wait a minute. How much do the maintenance fees and rental fees cost?"

The salesperson began to perspire and shuffled nervously, obviously feeling his government-paid commission slipping from his grasp. Hurriedly, he said, "Oh, it's nothing to worry about at all. That only amounts to a small fraction of your insurance policy. Here, just give me your hand and we'll finish this deal!"

Before I could remind him that I wasn't eligible for insurance, he grabbed my hand as if getting ready to fingerprint me, and we struggled for a moment as he grunted. "Now, just reach out that little digit and—"

I wrenched my hand away in disgust and wiped it on my pants. Bitterly, I said, "Sorry, Chuck, I'm not interested."

His name was not Chuck, but he tried to continue playing the good salesman nonetheless. Smiling clumsily, he said, "Well, can we talk about it further while I drive you home?"

Turning to leave, I responded curtly, "No thanks, I'll walk."

*

NINE

The following morning, I ran into the director coming through the lobby, and he smiled over his coffee and said chipperly, "Howdy, Steven! Pick up a new set of wheels?"

I was way beyond grumpy by then and responded flatly, "No."

"Why not?"

I shook my head and answered abruptly, "The whole process made me sick. All those damn programs for following and cutting in and cutting out are just promoting passive-aggressive behavior!"

Adopting an expression that showed he was ready to deliver another lesson, he put a hand on my shoulder and led me toward the elevator. Responding casually, he said, "Steven, passive-aggressive behavior is the hallmark of civilized society, and it's a fair tradeoff from the alternative. You wouldn't want aggressive-aggressive behavior, especially on the road. We had that when the self-driving cars first came out. People couldn't stand to not be able to let out their pent-up rage on other drivers and would halt in the middle of the road to assault someone."

Hearing that just confirmed my suspicions about the process, but in a chipper tone, the director added, "Besides, people who can afford to own cars, especially luxury ones, have worked hard to get where they are. They deserve to feel a bit of freedom with that, and in that regard, the car signifies social status above all else."

We stepped out on six. "I thought you said that most people inherited their wealth."

He retorted automatically, "Well, keeping it together generation after generation is its own kind of hard work."

"How do you know they didn't just buy it from someone else?"

As he sat down at his desk, he said firmly, "Oh, that is strictly forbidden, since resale to private persons is a no-no. There's nothing worse on the road than someone driving a car that is out of their league, since it creates incredible safety hazards. The car is naturally not matched to the driver's personality, so they don't know how to operate it properly and it completely screws up the whole system."

I took my own seat. "Really?"

"Absolutely. Gray market goods are something we must continuously watch out for, since people out there are always trying to buy used products from those in higher classes. That causes great difficulty in being able to identify people by their natural social order, and it's as bad as if someone stole your citizenship score. Let me tell you, there is nothing worse than having someone in a lower class than you drive the same car as you do." He took a sip of his designer coffee and added reassuringly, "But if anyone ever does buy a gray market car, you can usually tell by the bumper stickers."

"How's that?"

"Bumper stickers help to tell about class. Someone who worked hard and could afford to buy a true luxury automobile would never deface it with a bumper sticker. That's part of what holding property in trust is all about."

Disgusted, I shifted in the chair and said, "Well, have you read that scummy magazine that's out there? *Not You!*?"

He nodded and smiled. "Oh yes, that's a very popular one!"

"How the hell is that possible?"

"Steven, you still have a lot to learn. See, in the past when we used to have hard economic times, people would discriminate based on wealth. The wealthy would see someone who was poor and immediately retract in fear. As it turns out, that was all based on fear about different interests."

"Huh?"

"The trust system works so well because people abide by it. They recognize that property is valuable and treat it as such. The poor used to be discriminated against because they didn't have the same interest in preserving property, and magazines like *Not You!* help the lower classes want to be like us. So as a result, we don't have to discriminate against them anymore. See?"

"Yeah, I guess I do."

He smiled coaxingly and said, "Are you sure you don't want to go back to the dealership and look around at some more models?"

I stood up and responded plainly, "No, thank you. I think I need to go home and rest."

*   *   *

Later that night, I was lying in bed trying to sleep, but I was becoming increasingly convinced that the whole society was fucked up, and I couldn't tell if I would make it much longer in that place. The money I had been given with my citizenship score just felt like a dirty trap, and I wasn't going to sell my soul to electronic devices, lecherous advances, and lobotomizing my own brethren just to survive.

I sat up and said defiantly, "Well, whatever happens, I'm going to get some of that Narcissium to play with. They'll never notice."

I scanned myself into the back door and made my way down to the basement. The whole lab was empty, and once downstairs, I entered the Narcissium room and closed the door. The substance seemed to automatically sense my presence and formed into a tight ball in the middle of its pen. I grabbed one of the beakers from the shelf and opened it; then, somehow sensing this as well, the Narcissium curled like a cat's tail and seemed to purr a bit. I held the beaker over the wall of the enclosure and waited. Suddenly a small portion of the Narcissium broke off and shot right into the beaker and sat there quietly humming away inside the glass vessel.

I put a cork in it and ran excitedly out of the basement. I crossed around the side of building, and just as I was running past the coffee stand, the Narcissium suddenly started to stir and seemed to leap right out of the beaker. It actually oozed through the pores in the cork stopper, and then the substance disappeared into the lawn several yards from Cup O' Joe.

"Holy shit!" I looked down and noticed a small amount of residue on my hand. After wiping it quickly on my jeans, I sprinted home.

* * *

The next day, I got to the lab without expecting anything different, but when I arrived, I saw a tiny flower growing outside on the lawn right where I had been last night. It was the most beautiful plant I had ever seen, and it had metallic gray leaves, but they continuously changed colors in the sunlight. I gulped and looked around to see whether anyone noticed me, but it seemed the coast was clear. However, by the time I got inside, the news was already buzzing.

Dr. O'Dwyer set to action immediately. "That's terrific news, Johansen! Natural discoveries like this are always good for us! Now go out there immediately and build an enclosure around it."

Confused, I said, "Why?"

Dr. O'Dwyer responded confidently, "If there is one thing that science teaches us, it is that you must take anything new that pops up on the lawn and box it in as soon as possible. We have to be careful about letting life run rampant on its own, since we have too much at stake these days to take any chances."

Someone ran in and said eagerly, "Sir, sir, the plant is growing at an incredible rate, and its trunk is now two inches in diameter!"

Dr. O'Dwyer nodded knowingly in my direction and said, "See what I mean? Wilson, good work. Go out with Johansen and take this metal rod and drive it right down through the center of the plant."

Again I asked, "Why?"

Dr. O'Dwyer answered, "Oh, the tree will still grow, but we'll be able to run electricity through it and destroy it if it becomes a threat. It's just for safety's sake."

I said, "But how do you know all of that?"

As he watched the two workers rush out the door, Dr. O'Dwyer answered definitively, "Because, Steven, if there is one thing we excel at, it is stunting growth."

Fifteen minutes later, there was a wild commotion on the lawn as Johansen and Wilson both got sprayed with something from the tree. They wound up passing out and were immediately rushed to the hospital, and after that, anyone else who went near the thing had to wear a protective suit. It took most of the day, but they finally got a wooden enclosure built around our new addition to the lawn, and a long metal piercing stuck out of the top of it like a skewer. The person who inserted the skewer still wound up in the hospital even though he was wearing protection, and no one could quite figure out why. For my part, I just stayed at my station and kept my head down.

Late in the day, I had another unwelcome visitor. An overeager, underworked colleague of mine was desperate to tell me about the newest movie she had seen. Bouncing up and down eagerly, she said, "Steven, it's called *The 57!* And get this: the story starts with fifty-seven people who all set out on a Tuesday—which is, of course, the best day to buy condiments."

I clicked away dully at my station, barely able to elicit a response. "Why?"

She responded knowingly, "Because the subject has been heavily researched and documented. Weekend parties deplete stores of condiments, and new orders arrive on Mondays, so Tuesdays are when you find the best stock of products, and they're generally cheaper as well. Anyway, unbeknownst to each other, these fifty-seven brave souls all venture out on Tuesday morning to buy ... get this ... Heinz 57 sauce!" She was now hopping around as if she had to pee. "OMG, can you stand it? Can you guess what happens?"

Click-click-click. "No, not really."

"Well, all fifty-seven of these people get to the store and find out that they're all out of Heinz 57! Can you believe it?"

I paused for a second and asked, completely disinterested, "No, but why didn't they all just buy another brand?"

Suddenly she looked down at me, bit her lip for a second, and started to softly cry. I stopped the machine and turned to face her, now not only bored to death but also completely annoyed. "What?"

"Steven ..." she sobbed, "... I am trying to tell you a story ...and it is very, very emotional for me! You keep interrupting"—sniffle—"and you are obviously not taking the deeply personal feelings involved in this plot seriously enough! You are keeping me from getting to the best part, and that really hurts my feelings!"

I looked down at her ass. She apparently had an excess buildup of concentrated dark matter, and perhaps that was contributing to her emotional lability. Trying to stave off a meltdown, I sighed gently and said, "Sorry, please continue."

She regrouped and wiped her nose, once again undaunted in her quest to continue bothering me. "Thank you. The reason why all fifty-seven of these people couldn't just buy another brand is that all of them had individual precious memories from childhood of their parents using Heinz 57 at family dinners." Chiding firmly, she added, "There, Mr. Heart-of-Stone, does that help you understand just how serious this is?"

"Yes, sorry."

She sucked up a large collection of snot and regained her composure; then, bowling forward with renewed vigor, she said excitedly, "Anyway, it turns out that the delivery truck had been hijacked by some undesirables who wanted to sell the steak sauce on the black market. As you know, it can't be purchased by people who are not B-7 or higher."

I didn't dare respond. Instead I resumed the lobotomies I was performing, wishing that I could climb into the machine and give myself one right at that moment. She continued explaining that after being held hostage for fifty-seven hours, the driver finally told them that the sauce had just expired and had to be thrown away, so they let him go. She also explained that it wasn't really expired, but the "grubby outcasts" didn't know that, and so the driver was able to make it to town, and unknown thousands of people were saved from the same horrific fate that 'the fifty-seven' had to endure.

Click-click-click. Apparently a bout of Newtonian ennui had caught me, as I felt like falling out of my chair right then. Struggling to even form the words, I said, "That's it?"

By contrast, she was in full animation. "Oh, no, that was only the first half of the movie! The second half shows the stories of the original fifty-seven, who wind up, as you can imagine, in intensive psychotherapy!"

Now disgusted that I had asked that question, I said dully, "Yes."

"And do you know what their brilliant, clever psychiatrists do?"

"I can't wait for you to tell me."

Nearly jumping up and down again, she said, "I know, right! They put them all on a bus together and take them to the grocery store."

"Let me guess—on a Tuesday?"

"Of course! And all of them have to share the communal fear of being forced to face that harrowing danger again, and they all go into the store and there's plenty of Heinz 57 for everyone! But because their brilliant mental health professionals were able to help them get back up on that proverbial horse and conquer their fears, they were all saved!"

Click-click-click. I finally glanced over and noticed that she was openly weeping at this point. Smiling vulnerably in some notion of shared emotional struggle, she held out her arms to me and said, "Steven, can I have a hug?"

I replied with cold indifference, "No." Then I cocked my head and asked, "By the way, do you ever worry about how much you seem to cry about totally insignificant things?"

She turned white and said in panic, "OMG! You don't think ... that I have grand mal emotional lability, do you?" Her head whipped around frantically. "Where's Dr. O'Dwyer? I need to take the day off and go to the hospital!"

Overjoyed at the opportunity to be rid of her, I stood up eagerly and said, "I think he's over there!"

She sighed heavily and said, "Thanks, Steven, you're the best! Oh, by the way, can you finish my work for me today?"

* * *

Several days later, onlookers were still gathered around the tree's enclosure and completely mystified by the new wooden creature. It kept growing at a steady rate and was now six feet high and absolutely radiant. Owing to the tree's rapid growth, the spike had also disappeared somewhere in its bowels and was no longer of any tactical use. They thought about using a larger one, but Dr. O'Dwyer eventually abandoned that plan for fear of further scientific embarrassment at the hands of an unpredictable living organism.

I ran into him pacing near his office as a group of eager lab workers were listening to him complain out loud. "What an awful tree, and what a mess it's created! We can't classify it, and it won't abide by the limitations of decent horticulture. The damn thing behaves like a mammal, and if we take away sunlight from it, it doesn't suffer. It just switches to nonphotosynthesis to keep producing energy. Ordinarily, when you put a roof over a tree, it will wilt and die, but this one just waits patiently." Spinning around accusingly at the group, he added, "And we've detected that rather than growing upward, its root structure is getting deeper and wider! Ridiculous behavior! Yes, that's it. We're just going to have to figure out how to cut it down, but we can't seem to touch it without activating its defense mechanisms. Oh, what to do, what to do?"

A helpful plebe said, "Sir, couldn't we just put concrete under the roots?"

Dr. O'Dwyer's eyes lit up. "That's brilliant, Jefferson! If we do that, it will have nowhere left to go and will have to die! Get a crew out there immediately!"

Jefferson responded dutifully, "Aye aye!" I just went to my station and started working.

Later in the day, as I was coming back down from delivering something to the director's office, I decided to check the elevator and see whether my famous video had finally been taken down. It had, and they were running another one of those raffles, so I finally listened to the entire ad: "Order a new baby and get entered to win the vacation of a lifetime!"

Furious, I charged out and confronted Dr. O'Dwyer. Completely forgetting my place, I shouted, *"What the hell is that? You're bribing people to order babies?"*

At first he looked at me dumbfoundedly. However, when I filled him in about the advertisement, he calmly dismissed my concern. "Oh, it's not technically correct to call it 'bribing.' It's just part of the newest economic stimulus package. Steven, government stability, economic health, and various other factors are the things people have always considered when deciding to have a baby, and as you know, maintaining a healthy workforce is essential to any functioning nation."

Still exasperated, I said accusingly, "But you're advertising to get people to order them!"

Unapologetically, he retorted, "Well, governments have always used incentive programs to maintain their labor forces. China had the iron rice bowl, Japan used to pay their citizens to have kids, and other countries have used similar tactics. In reality, it's all about generating hope and confidence in tomorrow, and that's just good economics."

Indignantly, I challenged, "Well, I think it's wrong!"

He shook his head and responded assuredly, "Oh, Steven, it can't be. It's science. After all, studies show that lobotomies who have children report being happier than their contemporaries who don't."

I frowned deeply. "I seriously doubt that's true."

Attempting to permanently dodge my concern, he sighed knowingly and responded, "Then I'm afraid that it may just be a bit too technical and complicated for you to understand with your educational background."

I finally lost it. My test had just come back clean that morning, but the combination of the HIV scare, the idiots I had to suffer every day, and the mounting pile of bullshit answers I kept hearing finally got the best of me. I stomped my foot and said angrily, "You're goddamn right I don't understand! This whole system is a mess! Why don't you just let that tree live? Why don't you just let these people live? It seems like an awful lot of effort to try to keep things within your well-defined parameters, especially when most everyone around here can't seem to work more than two hours out of an entire fucking day!"

Dr. O'Dwyer turned directly toward me and studied me for a long minute, all the while wearing a decisive frown. Then he finally spoke in a low, accusatory tone. "You know, Steven, something just occurred to me. You may not be very well suited to work in the lab. Report to the director's office. He said he wants to see you." And with that, he turned sharply and walked away.

As I had come from destitution while living in the boys' home, the notion of actually losing my job now petrified me, and my legs started shaking involuntarily. I was also afraid that the other workers had witnessed my outburst, but it appeared that I blew up during one of the breaks. Lowering my head, I navigated around the morass of VR-distracted idiots who were busy running into each other and made my way upstairs.

Panic-stricken in the director's office, I whined, *"Am I fired?"*

The director gave me a reassuring look and said, "No, of course not, but Dr. O'Dwyer is right—the lab might be a bit technical for you." I felt my face sink, and he added, "Hey, don't worry about it! There's a recent opening at the newspaper, and maybe you'll feel better over there. As a matter of fact, I think you'll feel right at home, what with your major in social communications and all!"

I finally calmed down and took a seat. Still unsettled from the whole experience, I said, "Well, I appreciate the new opportunity, but I feel bad that I pissed him off so much. And it still feels like a firing."

He smiled gently and waved me off. "Not at all! Think of it as merely a change of scenery. After all, most people start out in jobs that don't align with their interests, ambitions, or long-term goals. Fortunately, science proves that it's good to change jobs every so often, since it helps to keep you fresh and motivated."

Despite what he said, my insecurity immediately returned at the prospect of a new environment, and I asked hesitantly, "You think that I'll fit in over there? It's been a long time since I wrote anything substantial."

He responded automatically, "Oh, you'll be a natural, what with your boyish good looks! After all, attractive people like you are our best asset when it comes to delivering the news!" He stood up to come around the desk, patted me on the shoulder, and said, "Look, don't worry about anything. Just go home and rest and report tomorrow ready to start your new job."

Realizing that I had dodged a colossal bullet from my behavior, I stood up and said, "Okay, thank you." We shook hands momentarily, and then I thought to ask, "Say, where is the newspaper?"

The director smiled and said, "Right here, on the second floor!"

*

Notes to Part I

---

[1]   Alexander Solzhenitsyn, *One Day In The Life of Ivan Denisovich* (New York: E.P. Dutton & Co., Inc. and Victor Gollancz, Ltd., Ed., Signet Classics, 2008), 35.

[2]   Alexis de Tocqueville, *Democracy in America*, trans. Harvey C. Mansfield and Delba Winthrop (Chicago: University of Chicago Press, 2002), 124.

PART II

Anything You Say Can and Will Make Us Money

TEN

The next morning, I was out of bed like a shot, eager to start over in a new environment, and I dressed quickly and jogged over to the center. My progress was halted, however, by the new barricade erected in front of the building. Tree branches were extending across the entire entryway, and by that time everyone was afraid to go near the tree. Instead a temporary sign politely redirected visitors to the back door.

I crossed under the warning tape and walked right up to the tree, gently patting the trunk. The tree hummed an audible hello.

Heading around the back, I recalled that, unfortunately, no one had ever thought to also install an automatic door in the rear of the center. When I got there, one of the workers was trying desperately to throw his whole weight down on the handle and wrench the door open at the same time. The door was not moved by his presence, so I gently helped him aside and pulled it open.

Gasping for air, he nodded a thank-you and walked in. Without thinking too much, I let the door close behind me, and I heard later on that there was a perpetual logjam out back for most of the morning.

After that, they instituted new policy and handed out pamphlets all around the building, explaining how to use the "buddy system" to open the outside door and apologizing for the temporary inconvenience that rampant nature had caused out front.

Arriving on the second floor, I came out of the stairwell to a scream of activity. A red-faced middle-aged man shouted over the PA system, "Okay people, we have 750 million anxious readers out there logging on today to see what's happening! Let's look sharp and remind them why they need us! Remember: be careful how you word articles. People don't like to be told what to do, but they love to fit in. Now, let's get out there and get it done!"

He finally noticed my presence and said, "Ah, Steven, there you are. I've been expecting you."

I shouted at him to make myself heard. "What's all that noise?"

"What noise?"

"Can't you hear that?"

"Oh, that. That's just people talking."

"It's not this loud in the lab!"

"Well, most science-minded people are introverts. Up here, you won't find many of those, but lobotomies tend to talk in the same way bats use sonar. Anyway, welcome to the newspaper. The director fully briefed me on your situation."

"My situation, sir?"

"Yes. That you're an orphan"—I cringed—"with a real talent for writing!"

"Um, yes, yes, sir. That's correct."

He looked me up and down and whistled. "Say, you're even better looking in person than in that sex tape you made!"

Floored, I stammered, "I, um, I did not make a sex tape—knowingly, that is."

The manager just waved a hand at me. "Don't worry about it. Probably be a big boost for your career. Ever do any reporting?"

"No, not really."

"Hang on." He paused to address a beep on his watch. "What is it? Okay, got it. Jackson, come over here."

"Yes, sir."

"Let's run an article that this new tree could be the scientific discovery of the century."

"Right, boss."

The manager returned to address me, and by then, the noise was starting to blend into the background. "I tell you, Steven, you're very lucky to be around right now. Most species are in trouble of being eradicated before we can even discover them, but not this guy. Luckily we're also working on programs to export life to other planets to help preserve it, but we're also already on our twelfth mass extinction this year."

Still nervous about being discovered as the source, I said nonchalantly, "Is the tree really that big of a discovery?"

He shrugged lightly. "Most likely, no. However, people are obsessed with believing that they were the first to witness this, that, or the other, so saying that will get them to read our stuff. In reality, the scientists will eventually link it to something, and it will just turn out to be an offshoot of a species we already know about. But in the meantime, they'll flock for miles just to take selfies next to it." He smacked his forehead with a sudden realization. "Shit, we should probably make up T-shirts! Crawford, come over here!"

"Yes, sir."

"Let's get some T-shirts made up to commemorate the plant discovery. And be sure to call it an 'alien' something or other."

"Right, boss!"

I said, "What's with the 'alien' bit?"

The manager replied, "Oh, lobotomies are obsessed with finding alien life. Years ago, we ran a bunch of articles where we referred to everything new we found as 'alien.' It was a big hit. Anyway ... Hang on a second." Someone ran up to him with a storyboard. "No, no. That's the wrong order. Let's run 'World Is Going to End Tomorrow,' then 'Boy Rescues Puppy from Well,' followed by 'Automaker Unveils Car That Massages Your Ego While You Drive.' Oh, and add 'Buddy System Announced for Hostage Situations.' Wait, make that the second. Yeah, that will be a good reminder of the program we're starting downstairs."

Thrown into momentary panic, I interrupted hastily and asked, "Excuse me, sir, but the world is ending?"

The manager replied casually, "Oh, probably not ..." He nodded at me and added for dramatic emphasis, "*Yet*. But the data shows that we are always just one second away from a global pandemic, which is very good for the news business, as you can imagine. So do you have any idea what kinds of stories you want to cover?"

"I'm not really sure."

"Well, do you like sports?"

"I played a little football when I was a kid."

He frowned and said dismissively, "Oh, that old barbaric game?"

"Barbaric?"

"Of course! We outlawed it in civilized society years ago. Too many concussions. The only sport we cover here is soccer."

"Is it any fun to watch?"

"Oh, sure. The game is a little slower than it used to be. By regulation, every two players are tied together so they look like figures on a foosball table, but as you know, safety is paramount these days."

"Do they play any contact sports around here?"

"Heavens no! There is a tremendous risk through contact sports of knocking the lobotomy hardware loose. Fortunately, most people these days just play esports."

"Oh."

"They do still have the Gay Bowl, but it's not quite the same. Have you seen it?"

"Oh, no. I'm, um ... straight."

"Sure, sure, fine, fine. Hang on a second. What is it?"

Another functionary ran up to the manager waving a report in his hand and exclaimed, "Sir, someone died from eating cheese!"

Confused, the manager said, "That's it? Was it rotten?"

"No."

"Was he allergic?"

"No."

The manager's face suddenly lit up. "Leapin' Louis Pasteur! This could be the definitive proof we've been looking for! Run it immediately, and get a task force started as well! We'll need a dozen reports to back this up by tomorrow!"

"Yes sir!" And then he scampered off.

I said, "Proof of what?"

The manager exclaimed, "That cows need to be sent through the particle collider before we milk them!"

Skeptically, I said, "You really think that's our business to decide?"

He nodded feverishly. "Oh yes! We have to tell people what to eat. Steven, these poor lobotomies can die from consuming cheese, fish, eggs, peanuts, high-protein diets, caffeine, and nearly every other staple food. Without us they'd never survive. I tell you; I've even seen some of them trip over white lines on the pavement." I stood there deadpan, and he added thoughtfully, "Of course, that could also be due to the VR contacts, but they need our help nonetheless."

He took in a breath and stretched his back. "Anyway, as you can see, I'm up to my asshole in alligators today. The best thing for you to do is read through the archives and get the lay of the land."

"Archives?"

"Yep. We've got everything on file—everything the government has ever written from the time that we kicked those limey bastards out of here through today. Once you get an idea for how stories go, we'll get you out there to start covering the news. Jamison, get over here!"

He appeared and said excitedly, "Sir, I was just looking for you! We found the most amazing discovery!"

"What is it now? Oh, that. No problem, I'll take care of it. Show Steven here to the archives."

Jamison studied me for a moment and said confusedly, "What for? He's too good looking to be a writer?"

The manager waved a dismissive hand at him. "Never mind that. He'll be out on the streets soon enough. Just show him to the archives. And Steven, here's a dictionary of useful terms for you while you're writing."

I accepted the booklet of terms from the manager, and Jamison ushered me along dutifully. While we were walking, he said, "Did they tell you what shift you'd be working?"

"Shift?"

"Yes. We cover the news twenty-four hours a day."

"Is that really necessary?"

Jamison replied, sounding astonished, "Of course! Steven, the government must be able to act at any moment. We elect second- and third-shift legislators just to be able to handle requests for new laws that come in at odd hours. As you'll see in the archives, a long time ago we cancelled summer vacation once to address some hot new issues, and it worked so well that we just made government into a 24/7 service, the same as the newspaper."

Ironically, on hearing that I started to perk up. *Maybe this will be the hard-working, energetic place I've been looking for!*

He added, "Anyway, the news is obsolete in about five seconds these days, but with the attention span of the lobotomies, that's all it really takes to deliver effective democratic updates to them."

We had finally reached the archives room, and in it sat a lone, dusty computer. Jamison said, "Here you go. We store everything in this little machine, and that will help to get you up to speed. It should be easy enough for you to figure out. Just turn it on and start searching."

I sat down at the terminal, noticing that there was a push button on the computer. The fear from my past instacontract experiences returned, and I studied the button from all angles. It didn't appear to have a thumbprint ID, so I hesitantly pressed it, and the machine came to life and started loading.

While it was starting up, my phone beeped. I hadn't looked at it for nearly a week. *Holy shit, seventy-six thousand new messages!*

"Hi Steven, heard you're gay!"

"Join our gay group!"

"Wanna take me shopping?"

"Wanna take me to the hairdresser?"

"Wanna have sex?"

"Wanna order a baby?"

"Hi, Steven, heard you're not gay!"

"Wanna take me shopping?"

"Wanna take me to the hairdresser?"

"Wanna have sex?"

"Wanna order a baby?"

"Guess the most popular sushi being sold on Mars today, win a cruise. Second prize: a nonlobotomized kid!"

What the fuck? I've got to remember to ask the director how to turn these messages off. Okay. Archives. Here we go.

Let's see. Citizens don't want to pay taxes, American Revolution, lots of people die. Birth of nation. Rest of Americans left alive very happy to be rid of Brits. Everything going well, logging and plantations in east. Civil war, lots of people get killed. Manifest destiny continues west and south, lots of people get killed. Everything going well following discovery of gold, lots of people getting killed. Industrial boom, everyone moves into cities. Lots of people dying. Suffrage movement begins, lots of people killed. A bunch of women burn to death in New York, worker's compensation system born. Safety increases, riots start, lots of people killed. World war, lots of people killed. Powers realign. Wall Street crash, New Deal. Government steps in. Another big war, lots of people killed. US comes out on top, industrial base booms. Desegregation and civil rights, lots of people killed. US in big debt. Take US off gold standard to fix debt. Unpopular war, lots of people killed. Oil crisis, lots of people broke. Cold War spending, economy picks up. Soviet Bloc falls, World Wide Web born. Trade in credit surpasses trade in actual goods. Stock markets flourish. Economy slumps, go to war. Economy slumps, change finance rules. Economy slumps, virtual markets created. Everyone goes gay. Economy slumps, leverage more natural resources. Legalize sports gambling, economy booms. Economy slumps, xenophobia explodes. Virus outbreaks, borders closed. Economy slumps, minimum wage increased. Economy slumps, credit market expanded. Robots mass-produced, economy slumps. Credit markets threaten to collapse, shift to guaranteed income. Robots removed. The cigarette is dead. What the hell is a cigarette? Oh, cancer. Got it. Economy slumps, credit/insurance system introduced. Run out of space for citizens, build more skyscrapers. Artificial placenta introduced as solution to gender equality. First baby born in artificial uterus. Lobotomies legislatively approved for 3 percent of population. Tax credits given for additional lobotomies. NarXex score introduced. Keep running out of space for citizens, first colony on moon. First sushi joint opened on moon. First colony on Mars. First sushi joint opened on Mars. Pluto Intergalactic Defense Colony established. First sushi joint on Pluto.

By the time I was done, the manager was gone for the day. Not knowing what else to do, I decided to just go home. As I walked out, several staff writers were there late, keeping the sleep-deprived public tuned in to whatever was happening at the time.

The next morning, I arrived an hour early, and the manager was already furiously at it. "People, somewhere out there is a dog who died protecting a little kid from danger or a girl who is playing checkers with her blind grandmother. Now go out and find them!"

He finally noticed me, and I said, "What was that all about?"

He wiped sweat from his forehead and responded emphatically, "Steven, we are paid—nay, our entire purpose in life is—to keep the public morale high. Seeing acts of real goodness like that always reinforces peoples' beliefs in today."

"Who pays our salaries?"

"The people."

"So the people pay us to reassure them that they're okay?"

He patted me on the shoulder enthusiastically. "You bet! It's the greatest system on earth!"

He finally sat down in his office to take a breather. He motioned me to do the same, and I accepted and said, "Say, from reading the archives, I would have thought that we'd have flying cars by now?"

He wiped his brow again and let out a regretful sigh. "We almost got there, but a series of economic setbacks during the dark times halted progress in that regard. Thank goodness movies, pharmaceuticals, and military spending kept us afloat. But once the lobotomies started, the need for flying cars just went away. Most of them don't travel very far outside of their own neighborhoods, and if they do, they wind up taking a flying bus."

"Flying bus?"

"They're called airplanes."

"Oh."

"Regular buses are pretty neat too. These days they have showers for the homeless."

- THE MADMAN -

I had no response to that, so I said, "Hey, I saw an old press release about a guy named Huxley predicting social control of fetuses. I can't believe people didn't see that coming."

The manager laughed. "You're telling me! But the whole development passed completely without incident. Here's a funny note—there used to be a book called *1984*, and one of the things the book predicted was monitors in homes."

"Monitors?"

"You know, little devices with speakers to listen in and record every conversation. When he introduced the idea, it was a little creepy, but when those very devices hit the market and started with chippy names like Alexa, Cortana, et cetera, no one even noticed the parallel. Then, when they finally quit trying to come up with cute alternatives and just renamed the devices 'Orwell,' I thought people would lose it. Turns out no one did."

"Didn't someone warn them?"

"Of course, but lobotomies have a hard time changing direction even when the wall is heading straight for them. That's probably the result of a million years of brutish living. It is, of course, also the reason why we have autonomous vehicles."

"Then why do we still scare them with news stories? You know, like 'The World Is Going to End'?"

"Because, Steven, it's good for them. The human body is still hardwired to feel better when it's scared. That is one evolutionary benefit among millions of deficits, and it helps us sell stories. Anyway, did you get the pattern for how we do things?"

I sat up confidently and responded, "Sure. The country's economy gets in trouble and you either kill a bunch of people to get it going again or you change the rules to generate more available credit."

He brusquely waved me off. "No, no, not that! I mean how we present these stories to the public. Oh, hell, there's no time. We need you out in the field to cover something that just happened."

I asked unsurely, "Am I ready?"

"No sweat. The formula is pretty easy. It goes like this: notable event, tragedy, expert commentary, hero, redemption, touching story about young person or dog or cat, new baby born, country heals and grows together. Look for that; got it?"

"Um, okay. What am I reporting on?"

"A rock climber just died on a very dangerous route on the south end of town. Get out there and interview everyone still alive, and get photos of the body if you can."

"How do I get there?"

"Take your car."

"I don't have one."

He rolled his eyes and said sarcastically, "Jesus Christ, where the hell do they find the people to send me? Wait." He checked my file on his watch. "Oh, you're still high enough in your G-status. Just take a cab. I'll have one outside for you in five minutes, and there's an app on your phone to call them to bring you back. Oh, and by the way, get the family to sign this."

He handed me an inch-thick document, and I said, "What is it?"

"Standard form release agreement. It gives us the movie rights to the story."

"You've got to be kidding me?"

"No. We get one with every story, even if it's not likely to turn into a movie. Just find someone with authority to sign it and bring it back to me."

*　*　*

I was back by early afternoon. "Okay, boss, I got all of the info, and here's the signed form."

The manager grabbed it without looking, and when he finally did, he pulled his hand away in disgust. "What's this mess on it?"

"Blood. It turns out the guy was only mostly dead, so he signed it himself."

Hearing that, he smiled and wiped his hand on his pant leg. "Oh, good! Is he dead now?"

"Yep. He died about thirty minutes ago, right before I left."

"Terrific! There's nothing more disheartening to a news writer than having to cover all the stuff leading up to death. It's much cleaner when the body is already cold." He pointed to the other side of the office and said, "Over there is a terminal for writing. See if you can get me a draft by the end of the day. We'll want this to be out in the midnight news blasts before his corpse hits the incinerator."

He handed the blood-soaked release back to me with visible distaste, and I headed to my station and turned on the computer. It was completely different from the computer for the archives, and the screen simply presented a flashing prompt.

Welcome to the News Wizard

Please select genre for story you are writing:
Health advice. Life advice. Purchase advice. Relationship advice. Scientific development. Human interest.
Human interest.
Does your story involve death or dismemberment?
Yes.
Good. How many dead?
What the hell?
One.
Terrorist attack involved?
No.
Natural disaster?
No.
Celebrity?
No.
Attempted rescue by dog?
No.
Warning! Story likely to have low reader appeal. Are you sure that you want to proceed?
Yes.
Do you have supervisor approval?
Yes.
Please enter supervisor's approval code:

Fuck ...

After finding the manager and entering the appropriate code, the computer allowed me to proceed with another prompt.

Topic of story:

Free climbing.

Milliseconds later, the screen auto-filled with fifteen references about dangers of the activity, the best types of safety harnesses to buy, and doctor warnings about lobotomies developing vertigo any time they are elevated higher than six inches off the ground. The only items left for me to input were the name of the deceased, the route he died on, and the number of unfortunate people or pets he left behind as a result of his foolish attempt at being more than who he really was.

WTF. I need more help. I hunted down the manager again. "Boss, can I get the computer to turn off the auto-suggestions?"

He initially looked at me as though I were an alien. "Take the computer off auto-fill?" He frowned and eyeballed me for a second, but finally sighed and gave in. "Okay, Steven, but you have to be careful about what you write."

"What for? Censorship?"

He took a step back and replied, astonished, "Of course not! Not in our free society! After all, we can't turn away the chance to make a profit." Looking down at my disheartened reaction to hearing that, he quickly added, "And for the purposes of maintaining good scientific journalism, of course!" Then he laughed nervously and patted me on the back.

Seeing that I was not smiling, he reached over me to fiddle with the controls. Clicking away, he said, "Most people don't have real keyboards anymore. They just get pads with big emoji buttons that simply enter prewritten messages. Only the news writers get real keyboards, but typing words still fills in prewritten stories." He entered a quick password, and the screen came up blank. "Voilà. There you go, Mr. Shakespeare. Have at it."

I nodded and said thanks. When he left, I cracked my knuckles and studied my notes from the interviews. *Shit. But I need a title. Where to start?*

I've got it! 'Man Sets Out to Conquer Self—Wins!'

My fingers set to work. "Today a twenty-seven-year-old man reached heights that most can only imagine. Neither gravity nor self-doubt could keep him from ascending to his dreams, and he held on to them until the day he died."

I stopped typing and sat back for a second. I could feel that this was going to be a great story, and it was only my first assignment. *Hey, I think the director was right. I think this may be my real talent!*

My fingers worked the rest of the afternoon almost with a mind of their own. I found the manager near the end of the day sweating over some recent catastrophe, and he wiped his brow with a handkerchief and held out his hand, saying unassumingly, "Let's see how you did."

Proudly, I handed him my creation. He started rapidly scanning the pages, and the frown he was wearing when I first saw him deepened. "Oh, no. No, no, no. Steven, say 'we' when you write."

Confused, I said, "Who the hell is 'we?'"

"You know, us. Saying 'we' makes you seem closer to the reader. It also imputes the collective will of the whole society, which is what we do here. Anyway, let's see what else you put in here."

After another minute of reading, he paused again and said, "This is a bit long. Remember: the average attention span of a lobotomy can only handle information in pamphlet size."

After scanning all the way to the end, he flipped the pages closed, slammed the article down on the desk, and looked at me disapprovingly. The sweat reappeared on his brow as he shook his head furiously. "No, no, no! We'll never be able to run this! Steven, this guy died free climbing. This is why the auto-format structure works. Free climbing has been advised against by all of the reputable experts."

Trying to mask my hurt, I said, "But I talked to him, and he and every single person I interviewed said that he was absolutely living according to his dream."

The manager just frowned at me and responded sharply, "Yes, but these early deaths are a tremendous disruption to the economy! Plus this guy was ignoring everything that science has proven about necessary safety precautions. Steven, we have to watch out for dangerous activities like these and warn people, not encourage this kind of behavior!"

I pleaded, "Why not?"

"Because. Steven, the poor lobotomies these days can die from swimming when they haven't even been in the water. They'd never survive without us."

Seeing my distress, he stopped and sighed, backpedaling momentarily. "Sorry, I have to remember where you came from. Look, we have a carefully regimented society, and the stories we write must reemphasize our values. People need to be reminded that science contains the only answers for them and that adhering to the mechanisms and support structures we put in place is the only way for them to avoid going totally insane."

Feeling the ground slip out from under my masterpiece, I urged, "But can't you tell one story about a guy who got to a height he was reaching for? That seems pretty upbeat to me!"

He snorted and replied indignantly, "Most certainly *not!* That could cause all kinds of psychosis. Steven, we had to lower the bar for hero stories to keep people from feeling bad. You may not know this, but the human form is incredibly weak. They once did this experiment where a kid was shot through a particle collider, and all that came out of him was goo. Can you believe it?"

Completely deflated, I just rolled my eyes and said, "No."

"And lobotomies these days have no sense of mortality. Without a sense of death, of course, you can't have a notion of coming of age, so we just don't tell those stories anymore."

Already frustrated by my first assignment, I said dismissively, "Well, if you don't tell stories like that, then what's the point of all of this?"

"Steven, our chief goal here is to figure out what our target audience wants and present that."

"Who's the target audience?"

"Fourteen-year-olds in the C-7 class or better who are mostly on the female side of the gender spectrum."

"Seriously?"

He nodded firmly. "Oh yes. Those are the ones with the most ability to affect spending decisions, which helps us generate huge ad revenues!"

Confused, I said, "I thought they had to rely on their parents' insurance at that age."

"They do, but have you ever heard a fourteen-year-old lobotomy scream at the top of its lungs when it doesn't get what it wants? In the old days, money used to jingle, but nowadays, that's what profit sounds like!"

I sat down defeated. My enthusiasm for this new job had been thoroughly doused, and I said hollowly, "Is that all we're doing here?"

He assumed an indignant stance and responded, "Of course not. The primary function of news is, and has always been, to reassure our citizens. As a matter of ethical principle, we are not directly profit-driven."

"Then how do people get raises?"

"Well, okay, the salary scale is technically based on the number of lobotomies who click on a story you write. And lucky for us, the more stories we write, the more lobotomies they produce!" He let out a big grin. Seeing that I was not amused, however, he added, "Look, going forward, just remember this rule of thumb: if the people are doing something that benefits the common goal, then all deaths are worth it. On the other hand, if you are doing something that people don't like, then one death is an unacceptable risk."

Meekly, I replied, "Yes sir."

He sighed again, gave me a reassuring look, and said, "Don't worry; there's no way you could have known that, being an orphan and all. I'll fix the story."

Just then my phone went off. It was another request for sex, and the manager saw me click it off angrily. When I looked up, he was staring at me curiously. I said, "I'm getting sick of people asking me to have sex all the time!"

He came around the desk and put his arm around me as I stood up. "Oh, Steven, you're too much of a hermit—and a prude. That may have been okay in the lab, but you're one of the faces of our newspaper now. You need to live up to the standards of working here. Get out and mix it up a bit. Say, when was the last time you were laid, anyway?"

"Oh, it's been a little while. I've been avoiding the requests from these women because they're all for sex *and* shopping."

"So?"

"Well, I'm worried about keeping my citizenship score up."

He ushered me out of his office and said firmly, "Look, don't fret about that anymore. You'll be making plenty of money at the newspaper. Now go out there and get some strange ass. That's an order!"

*

ELEVEN

The next morning, my rock-climbing story was up on the news board. It had been moved to page six under the Darwin Awards and was now all about the safety dangers involved in going out on a ledge when all the experts had warned against it. The article concluded like this: "And if he's looking down on us now, he'll tell all of you kids that the only courage you'll ever need is the courage to play it safe."

My disgust became venomous. Seconds later, a snout-faced girl came up to me and said, "Hi Steven! Name the six world leaders who went on a fishing trip together in Scandinavia last week!"

I snapped around. "What the fuck are you talking about?"

Undaunted, she pressed, "Come on! It's the weekly civics quiz!"

I suddenly remembered that I lost the last job for acting out and quickly adopted an innocent tone. "Um, I don't know."

"Steven, you have to play the civics quiz game! It makes us all better writers!"

I smiled politely. "Sorry, I'm busy."

She grabbed my arm and insisted, "Well, at least use the word of the day in a sentence!"

"Word of the day?"

Fortunately, the manager came to my rescue and separated her from me. "Sherry, move along now. Steven's an orphan, and he can't be bothered with things like that."

That day I left early to avoid ramming anyone's face through one of the padded walls. However, halfway through the lobby, I ran into the director, and he greeted me unsuspectingly with his customary salutation. "How's it going, Steven?"

I was initially terrified that he would be mad about me leaving early, but he showed no signs of noticing. Not knowing what else to do, I let down my guard and admitted what had happened. "Bad. I screwed up my first story."

He gave a concerned look and threw his arm over my shoulder. "Oh? How so?"

As we walked, I said, "It's hard to explain. The manager changed the whole idea. He said that what I wrote was too risky and traumatizing."

"Well, try not to worry about it too much, since that was only your first assignment. But remember while you're working there that people want to be educated, informed, and compassionate, but they don't want to be bothered with anything." My watch went off again, and he looked down momentarily at it and said, "What was that?"

I pulled away from him and replied, "That is also hard to describe. So far I've received fifty requests to have sex with people here at the newspaper—guys and girls—or at least I think they're from both."

He laughed lightly and responded, "Oh, that's just the glorious equality of the sexes at work! Don't worry about it. In the dark times, people were so stressed out that they were having less sex—which is, of course, a bad thing and is terrible for the economy."

"Yeah, I guess so."

"Also, it's good for people in the news to get in bed with others, and as frequently as possible."

I remembered the manager's comment about being a prude and finally said, "Yeah, maybe you're right."

Just then the director turned to me and asked, "Say, what are you doing later?"

Cautiously, I replied, "Nothing much ... yet."

He patted me on the back and said, "Let's catch a game! I have great seats for the soccer match tonight." Still trying to pay penance for the lab, and thankful that his invite didn't include drugs and sex, I reluctantly agreed.

As the director walked out, I clicked on one of the messages. The girl looked cute enough, so I responded and asked whether she wanted to meet for dinner tomorrow. She replied, "You bet!" Her reply also included a full-spread naked photo of herself. She suggested a reservation at eight thirty and meeting up two hours beforehand to have sex. I was at a loss to respond.

* * *

The seats were right up near the field. I would say near the action, but there wasn't any going on. The director was oblivious as usual, and staring out at the matchstick figures with a broad smile, he said, "Isn't this fun? Have you ever seen a soccer match before?"

Resting my chin on my hand, I responded bleakly, "No."

"It's very exciting!"

"Yeah, sure."

He turned toward me and inquired, "Steven, what's wrong? Are you still upset about that article?"

I looked up at him and responded with mild frustration, "A little. I mean, I wrote a very nice piece about a guy doing exactly what he wanted, and the manager cut it up and changed it into a safety pitch."

The director nodded consolingly and responded, "Well, death and injury from sports have always been very sensitive subjects. We like for people to be able to enjoy themselves without getting hurt, and when something is near and dear to our hearts, like keeping people safe when they're engaging in recreational activities, even one death is too many."

I happened to glance up at the jumbotron just as an ad flashed up on the screen: "Be sure to tune into the History Channel tonight for a special presentation: 'The Dangers of Ancient Free Climbing!'"

I looked away in disgust and muttered, "Bastards."

The director frowned at me and asked, sounding concerned, "Why do you say that?"

"How can they call something 'ancient' when someone was doing it four days ago?"

He dismissed my ire with ease. "Oh, Steven, that's just the way things go. Old fads and ways of living are easily retired these days.

After all, you wouldn't want to be out running around free on a range like a cowboy, now would you?"

I replied bitterly, "That's different. That was hundreds of years ago, not last week."

He shrugged lightly. "Well, there's not much we can do about the pace of change, but it's all for safety's sake. Think about this: Wimbledon grass used to cause injuries, football caused CTE, and running too much caused a sickle cell trait to develop that was deathly." He shook his head regrettably and added, "I'm afraid that these tender lobotomies just have too much these days that can hurt them. And don't even get me started on the number of people hospitalized because of Q-tips every year."

I sat up momentarily and challenged, "Okay, I'll grant you that lobotomies probably need specialized regulation, but does that have to apply to everyone?"

He leaned back in astonishment and looked at me. "Of course! We can't raise the bar higher than our most protected group! Plus, in these modern times lobotomies demand our immediate response to the problems they encounter. That's why we have nearly a billion laws on the books to cover our nearly billion US citizens."

I gasped at hearing that. "You really have that many laws?"

The director responded proudly, "Yep! But they're all necessary to ensure safety and stability in our country. Remember that these people have to be thought of like little children. They trust us to solve any and all issues that frighten them, and to do so as swiftly as the heroes they see in action movies—you know, the ones who obtain instant superpowers that used to have to be obtained through years of practice and hard work to defeat foes. That's why we have to pass a new law every time something frightening happens."

My depression now deepening again, I rested my chin back in my hand and muttered, "I guess so."

"Steven, think of it like this." He pointed down to the field and observed assuredly, "People are like the grass out there. Without us, they couldn't even grow."

"Isn't that being a little overdramatic?"

He laughed and slapped his knee. "Well, at least they wouldn't look as pretty!" I just shook my head, and he added, "Besides, as part of the deal with the insurance companies to get to our credit/insurance program, we had to agree to eliminate all inherently dangerous activities. People really don't mind too much, and look at how much fun we're having!"

Taking a deep breath, I tried to lighten up and returned his enthusiasm for the game. Then he rested a consoling hand on my shoulder and advised, "When you're at the newspaper, you just have to remember that readers are very fragile."

I shook my head and said, "What are you talking about?"

"They're fragile. The slightest missed phrase in a story could decimate them."

"You have to be kidding me!"

"No, not at all. Think about the people you met in the lab. You broke how many arms?"

Fidgeting with the recollection, I said, "Um, eight or nine, I think."

"Humans these days are just as fragile on the inside, and the slightest hint of anger, sadness, cuteness, or virtually any kind of emotion stirs them into a frenzy. You can use that to your advantage when writing an article and trying to attract an audience, but be careful not to overdo it."

"What do you mean, 'overdo it'?"

"Well, despite the fact that lobotomies can't remember anything, once you set them off on an idea, they'll run with it forever. That's why we are very careful about how we develop programming."

Still trying to find some levity, I asked, "How the hell did they get like that?"

"Oh, because more than half of our society is based on virtual reality these days. Some people, in fact, hardly ever interface with the physical world, and as a result, we try to make sure that things are pleasant for everyone on an equal level."

I said, "But doesn't that just mean that we're all tethered together by the same low standards, just like those guys on the field?"

Cheerfully, he responded, "Yep! But don't worry too much about it. There are still plenty of interesting ways to stay entertained, even for someone like you!"

Just then the referee threw a flag at a player who got caught heading a ball. I asked, "Why did they call him for that?"

The director said, "Headers are illegal."

"Seriously?"

"Oh yes. Studies show that 99 percent of all people who ever suffered a bump on the head died of CTE. Sixty-four percent of people who even watched a head collision died of it as well. Heck, lobotomies can get a TBI from the slightest disturbance. Why do you think we have padding all around the center?"

The reasoning for that finally made sense, and after a short pause, he glanced sideways at me and added, "You might have it as well. That's why you can't remember your therapy from when you were a baby. You should probably get checked out."

"Um, no thanks." My damn phone kept going off and buzzing against my leg. Finally I couldn't ignore it anymore and said, "Director, can I ask you a question?"

"Sure."

"I've been following your advice and communicating with several people on the internet."

He raised an eyebrow. "Guys?"

"Um, mostly girls."

"Oh, okay."

"Anyway, every time I respond to a message, they automatically send me a nude photo."

Adopting a paternal tone, he said instructively, "Oh, don't worry about that. That's just standard protocol these days. It's a form of preconsent to sex in case that winds up happening. As you know, we take consent issues very seriously." Then he nudged me and chucked lightly, adding, "It's also very useful so you can tell if you're actually talking to a guy or a girl!"

"Huh." And with that, I pulled my phone back out and started scrolling with renewed understanding of my prospects.

I looked up at the field from time to time, but the game meandered on in no specific direction. The goals were slow-coming, as the players kept getting tangled up in each other's legs. At one point, I looked down and saw that a new goalie had been put in for our team. He had a dog tethered to the side of the goalpost, and I said, astonished, "What the hell is that?"

"What? Oh, the animal? That's the goalie's service dog."

"You're kidding me!"

The director shook his head earnestly and replied, "No, it's no joke at all. The other team can lose an entire point if they get in the way of the service dog helping the goalie cope with his role."

I just shrugged and said, "Now I have seen everything." A few minutes later, I let out a calculated yawn and stretched. "Well, this is pretty boring."

The director's placid smile was unfaltering as he responded, "I know, but it doesn't matter! They love it, and we make a good deal of money on the betting."

"What, is the game fixed?"

"No, but we do have access to superior analytics and can pretty much predict who will win."

His comment was completely lost on me, as I didn't care one whit about getting involved in sports betting. Still, looking down at the players, I furrowed my brow and said, "It's just hard to believe that people can actually win or lose a game that isn't interesting in the first place."

The director laughed. "Oh, you'll find that to be true about a lot of other things in our society as well!" While I was pondering that, he quickly added, "Anyway, the game is really about promoting togetherness." He must have been right, as the players were presently all tethered together in a big heap. He patted me on the back and said chipperly, "Don't forget that famous internet quote—'Be different, but together'!"

Seeing no progress on the field, I scanned the stands and observed, "The stadium seems a little empty."

"Oh, sure, but people are still watching from home and from the space colonies. That jumbo screen feeds highlights to all the planets, but live sports also have to compete with television. We have six hundred thousand television stations with twenty-four-hour programming, and there's something for everyone. And the television schedules are transmitted to peoples' VR contacts with suggested programs to watch so they never miss a thing."

My phone went off, and it was about sex, dinner, and shopping, with no mention of television. This one sent a seminude photo only, so I clicked accept. When I looked up again, the field was empty except for the referees, and I said, "What happened to the game?"

"It's a therapy timeout. The other team is down by four goals, and the AI stats just reported that no team has ever come back from being four goals down with only thirty-eight minutes left in a game played at the opposing team's stadium on a Thursday in June. So the therapist works with them to see if the players will keep going, and if not, they can surrender at the twenty-minute mark."

"Huh. Say, I just remembered that I'm supposed to be somewhere. Mind if I go?"

The director turned and smiled proudly at me. "Not at all, young man. Happy hunting!"

* * *

Two days later, I was out on my first accepted encounter, which started out tamely enough. We went to the movies. I can't remember what the title was exactly, but I think that it was a spin-off from *The 57!* My date told me that Sophia had recommended it to her as a film that was sure to be an instant classic. I had no idea who Sophia was, but there didn't appear to be anything redeeming on the screen at all.

It involved a woman who returned to the supermarket decades later to confront her fear of not being able to find kosher pickles. At one point, she flashed back to something while studying one of the food labels in the store and fainted; then the movie ended with a dramatic score as she was taken away in an ambulance. I have no idea what else happened, as I was completely intoxicated by the perfume of the girl sitting next to me and half-hard the whole time.

I do remember that there was a lot of crying going on in the theater, but I have no idea what for.

Walking home afterward, the girl said, "Isn't it amazing that we're all susceptible to things like that?"

By then my interest and libido had waned, and I feared a dull evening of conversation ahead. "Yeah, sure."

We were walking back to my place by instinct, but when we had reached the front door, she stopped and said eagerly, "Oh, let's go to my place! My neighborhood has a real fission-fusion, Tex-Mex, wasabi cilantro feel to it!"

I looked at where she was pointing and asked confusedly, "You're talking about that place that is twenty feet from here?"

"Oh yes, but the vibe is completely distinct! You'll see! Let's go to my apartment and have food delivered!"

When we got there, she excused herself and disappeared into the bedroom while I searched for the takeout menu. Finding one, I proceeded to order whatever unique fare this neighborhood was supposedly famous for. From the other end of the phone, a polite gentleman said, "Hello?"

"Yes, I'd like to order the Tex-Mex wasabi cilantro special."

"Ah, yes! Good choice. Say, are you feeling okay today?"

"Um, sure."

"Any unusual dreams lately?"

WTF? "No. Not that I can recall."

"Are you having trouble getting up and facing the day?"

I pulled the phone away and looked at it for a second. Holding it back to my ear, I insisted, "Listen, can you just tell me how long it will take?"

The order-taker stammered, "Oh, um, about forty-five minutes."

I responded curtly, "Great, thanks. Goodbye."

I hung up the phone and shook my head. When I turned around, the girl was standing in front of me, already naked and lubed up.

I dropped the phone in my startled condition and said, "I, um, what's going on?"

She grinned seductively and replied, "Oh, nothing. I just like to have dessert before the food arrives!"

Two hours later, clothes and takeout boxes were strewn everywhere, and I was moderately satisfied with how the evening had turned out. That is, until she suddenly turned to me with wanton eyes and said, "Steven, I like you! Let's order a baby!"

I shot up. "*What?*"

She cooed, "Come on! I'm old enough, and you said that you're a G-7. That's pretty good!"

I shook my head and started to get up. "Yeah, but … Oh, you don't understand. Look, I gotta go."

* * *

The next day was back to business; the manager was working on another aneurysm. "Come on, people! Didn't I say remind them why they need us? Your stories are reminding them why they hate reading in the first place! Geesh!" Finally noticing me, he turned and said, "Oh, hi, Steven. I tell you, if only these idiots could remember anything. Most of them wouldn't have survived one second during the dark times."

"Dark times, sir?"

"Yes. At one point in our nation's history, newspaper circulations were in the tank and we were having to buy out writers' contracts, if you can believe it. Thank goodness for instant updates to VR contacts, which solved the whole problem. Sure, readers can block us by blinking six times, but blinking seven times resets the defaults. I tell you, without lobotomies and technology, these fools would starve. Anyway, how was your date last night?"

"Pretty good."

He ribbed me and let out a coy smile. "Pretty good? She said you rocked her!"

"Um, uh …"

"Don't be so modest! What goes on in the bedroom is public knowledge these days."

Seizing on that comment, I said, "Okay, then let me ask you a question."

"Yes?"

"We had sex before dinner. I mean, before I had actually taken … or before the takeout had arrived."

"So? You did it anally, right?"

Blushing, I replied, "Yes."

He patted me on the shoulder and said, "Steven, don't worry about it. Doing it that way makes perfect sense, and it's the easiest way to get around things. Hey, a guy like you should feel perfectly at home that way!"

I jumped back and demanded, "What the hell is that supposed to mean?"

Holding up his hands innocently, he said, "Oh, nothing. But look, everyone has seen your sex video, so they probably just assume that's what you're into."

"Oh. Well, what do I do now?"

"Ask her out again."

"No, not that. At work?"

The manager scratched his chin momentarily. "I don't know. Let's see, what are we missing for tomorrow? Here, do an article about the ten things people don't know about the new phone upgrade."

I looked at the assignment sheet he handed me. "Seriously?"

"Yes. It's very easy to do. We have endless files full of research about mundane things that people don't know about, and the lobotomies eat it up."

"Wasn't there just a new phone upgrade two weeks ago?"

"Sure, but the need for upgrades is constant, so we have to keep the stories coming constantly as well."

That particular project took about forty-five minutes to write, and I was back in his office before midday. The manager nodded approvingly as he read. "I must say, this is a very good piece. But Steven, when you write news articles, say that things are 'surprising.'"

"Why?"

He looked up and responded officially, "Because we set

the standard here and people expect us to know the most about everything. So if we say that it was surprising to us, they'll want to read it because it will surely be surprising to them. You can also say 'strange,' or 'awkward' or any number of other modifiers that will automatically pique the interest of your readers. Here, clean it up and have it ready to go this afternoon."

Finishing that project was easy; then I bolted home and got ready for date number two. She arrived in a sleek onesie with no makeup and was immediately impressed. "Wow, your apartment is a palace! Gosh, I sure hope that I get something like this one day!"

"Yeah, it's okay."

The next thing I knew, she took off all her clothes and was already lubed up and ready to go. Halfway through coitus, I said to myself, "This is just like being back in the boys' home! I don't know what I was so worried about!"

After that, we showered, and then she put on makeup and got ready for dinner. Grinning at her as I laced up my shoes, I said under my breath, "I think I'm starting to like this place!"

* * *

We took a cab to a nearby restaurant, and I struck up a light conversation on the way. "So what do you do?"

She looked up from her phone. "I work over at the pharmacy."

"Is it a good job?"

"Oh, yes! I'm the first one in my family to make it that far. If I can only get the apartment I want, I'll be okay!"

She talked on and seemed sweet enough but was obviously under a lot of pressure from her family, and her eyes appeared to be nearly on the verge of tears as she explained herself further. We continued at the restaurant, and I tried to sound positive. I said, "Do you like what you're doing? I mean, is it satisfying to you?"

Her eyes darted around nervously. "Oh, I don't know. I don't know who I am, but I'm not even fifty yet." Still trying to hold back tears, she added meekly, "Tee-hee!"

Suddenly our waitress appeared and greeted us chipperly, "Hi, how's it going, you two?"

My dinner companion looked up at the waitress, bit her lip, and suddenly broke down. The waitress leaned down and hugged her while she cried, saying lovingly, "Oh my, you poor child! Tell me what's troubling you!"

The blubbering mess across the table from me reported a lot of what she told me in the car through bits of sobbing and numerous hug breaks. The waitress carefully took notes on her pad when not consoling, nodding the whole time. "Uh huh. Yes, yes. Tell me a bit more about your father."

When my companion had let it all out, the waitress cocked her head in a clinically concerned fashion and said, "Well, it sounds like you're suffering from a bit of late-onset class dysfunction today. Let me recommend the filet mignon and a nice Chianti to drink. You should probably go see your doctor tomorrow as well and ask her to increase your Wellbutrin medication."

My date seemed to recover miraculously. "That sounds great! Thank you for being so kind!"

"Don't mention it. That's what we're here for. Now, you should be warned that the dish has a very high caloric content, so you'll want to watch what you eat for a few days, or at least throw up right after dinner."

Unabashedly, my date responded, "Oh, don't worry; we had anal sex before we got here!" I just buried my head in my hands.

The waitress jotted that down and said, "Oh, terrific! There's nothing quite like a good cleanse before anal sex to purge unwanted calories!" Then her eyes turned to me. "And you, sir?"

I looked up and fidgeted uncomfortably. "Um, I'll have the same."

She cocked her head to the other side and immediately readopted her patterned, concerned look. "Are you sure? Why don't you tell me about your childhood?"

"Oh, I'm okay. Can you just bring me the filet, please?"

The waitress frowned and scribbled something down on her pad.

She was still writing as she walked away, and I heard her mumble under her breath, "Having trouble coping with past ..."

I turned to my newly revived companion and asked, "What the hell was that all about?"

She was beaming and explained. "Oh, the restaurant is designed to help you find your bliss point for food! Lobotomies can never figure out what to order, and that's why food is just suggested to them based on their emotional profile for the day. But you'll love what they serve here!"

It took two hours for our appetizers to arrive, because of other therapy sessions that were going on around us. After that, our waitress came back another hour later holding a tray with four glasses on it. Two were wine; two were filled with pulverized steak. Setting the tray aside, the waitress wiped her hands together and said, "Can I get you two some straws?"

My companion replied, "Oh yes, thank you!"

Eyeballing my liquid fare, my own response was, "Do you have any filet that isn't ... pureed?"

The waitress just laughed. "Oh no, we don't serve Neanderthal food here!" Then she picked up her tray and walked away without further comment.

I quietly sucked down my steak as we dined in silence. Meanwhile, the girl across from me was glowing the whole time. When we had finished, the waitress reappeared with an expectantly open smile, and my date likewise smiled, but I couldn't figure out what I was supposed to do. Then the waitress pulled a little handheld device out of her apron and held it up to my face, saying gaily, "Cheese!"

I quickly smiled for what I thought was a postdinner photo. All too late, however, I remembered the director's words about paying for things. The faux-photo routine was apparently a well-known trick to garner generous tipping from patrons, and the total bill came to $3,487.50, including the 38 percent gratuity I had been lulled into.

While we were walking to my place after dinner, my ire from the restaurant was interrupted by a pedestrian death we came across that the ambulance service was still cleaning up.

I stopped to see if there was anything I could do, but the medic shook his head and said regrettably, "'Fraid not. This one couldn't be helped. Unfortunately, lobotomies will follow anyone across the street, even if the signal is red. They have some basic inability to not follow what someone else is doing, even if it's to their own peril."

Hastily moving us away, my companion pulled close to me and shuddered. "That sure was scary! I thought real death only happened in the news." Then, just as we got to the apartment building, she turned to me expectantly and said, "Steven, I had a wonderful time tonight! I know—let's go upstairs and order a baby!"

I stopped in my tracks, pretending that I had just remembered something. "I, er, um ... I can't."

"Why not? You have the perfect apartment, and you're good looking, and you have a great job!" Then she paused and stepped back. Tears started to form again, and she shot me a wounded look. "Wait a minute. Is it because ... you don't like me?" She was looking up at me with pure innocence as her makeup steadily streaked away.

I grabbed her shoulders comfortingly and said, "No, no, it's not that at all. It's just ... I remembered that they're doing a fire drill in our building tonight."

She sniffled in genuine surprise and looked up at the building. "Really?"

I slowly turned her away to leave. "Oh yes, and it's going to start any minute. You'd better go."

As I gently pushed her down the sidewalk, she blinked back at me with concern and asked, "Are you coming?"

"No, no. I'm, um, the fire warden. I have to stay behind and make sure that everyone gets out."

When we reached the end of the block, she finally turned and said, "Okay, but will you call me?"

I waived a steady hand goodbye, saying, "Sure thing." And then I turned and headed back to my apartment.

*

TWELVE

My next assignment was a little more challenging and involved a stranger who had wandered into town one day, walked into a restaurant, and started waving a gun. He initially fired several shots into the ceiling and then just ran around shouting at everyone, and the whole episode was completely unforeseeable in that compliant little society. In the middle of the event, one customer who just happened to walk in while the attack was in progress made immediately for the assailant and knocked him down. He was killed in the process of trying to pry the gun away and subdue the attacker but was able to stop the event, and the police eventually arrested the shooter. I was sent down to interview everyone at the scene.

No one had ever witnessed anything like that. While others were busy trying to remember whether the buddy system applied to active shooter situations as well, this one man decided to confront the danger. As a result, aside from the unfortunate intervenor who died, there were only some minor wounds to attend to from chunks of plaster that had fallen from the ceiling.

The title of my story was "Man Stands Up to Terror, Saves Hundreds." This was a work that I was truly proud of having written—not just because I thought it was a well-written piece, but because I had finally witnessed a genuine act of humanity in this screwy society.

Ten minutes after I hit print, however, the manager issued another round rejection. "No, no, all wrong! The instructions say that the first course of action is to run. Second, to hide. This guy definitely can't be celebrated."

Feeling my anger grow at the prospect of another gutted story, I insisted, "Why not?"

"Well, because he went right to the third step, of course. Steven, people are encouraged not to engage in any forms of self-help these days."

I just shook my head and demanded, "Again, why the hell not?"

The manager laughed and said, "Well, if they did, what would there be left for us to do?" He could see that I was not amused and quickly added in an official tone, "Look, science proves that it is best for everyone to wait out all emotionally charged events and save themselves for something bigger in life. Let's just change this around and focus instead on what a religious fanatic the shooter was."

I scratched my head, searching for the detail I had obviously missed from my interviews. "Was he?"

"Of course! He opened fire on innocent people!"

Seeing that my pleas wouldn't get me anywhere, I said, "Well, what exactly is a religious fanatic?"

"Someone who doesn't view religion the same way we do." He handed the draft back to me, adding firmly, "And be sure to refer to him as 'radicalized' as well."

"'Radicalized'?"

"Sure. All you have to do is say 'conspiracy,' or 'radicalized,' or something similar, and people stop taking it so seriously. It's very beneficial to overall mental health to reduce stress in articles. And be sure to put that in quotations."

"Huh?"

"Quotations. Lobotomies are fascinated by quotations. They may not remember a word you wrote, but they'll remember the quotations."

"I don't get it."

"Steven, quotations signify that something is *important*. Quotations can be used for everything from pithy and focusing comments to special terms in an article. They also show the reader that you have mastered a highly complex and technical vocabulary that they must memorize and repeat."

I held up two fingers on each hand to show that I understood and said, "Okay."

The manager frowned at me and sternly added, "Just don't forget when you write that there is good stress in stories and bad stress. Good stress is the kind we do; bad stress is the kind other people cause."

I shook my head and said snidely, "That seems kind of self-serving."

He glanced down at his watch, obviously short on time, and responded hastily, "Well, it's a little hard to explain. Look, just be careful about what you write. Oh, and while you're doing that, be sure to cross-reference ten or fifteen serial killers or mass murderers from the past when you talk about this madman."

I said, "I'm not sure that he killed anyone except the one guy who intervened."

"That doesn't matter. If you include references about similar lunatics, it will help readers associate the story properly. And by the way, let's also run some expert opinions reinforcing the avoidance program, and we'll post a picture of a kindergarten class full of lobotomies learning the proper method. That should do it."

I dutifully sat down to rewrite. Wanting to be as precise as possible, I opened the dictionary, looking for a word. I noticed that there were only about fifty words in the whole booklet, while the bulk of it was examples of how to make those fifty words match any situation. Some of the terms I ran across were as follows:

barbarian—(dislikable noun): someone who does not understand the benefits of our system of trading credits for goods, with the remainder paid in tax; see also *Neanderthal*—someone who doesn't follow social trends.

Luddite (noun): someone who opposes the most recent technology upgrades; synonym—*seditioner.*

naysayer (noun): someone who says no to government initiatives; see also *treason*—saying no to government initiatives.

science—(inviolable noun): the absolute truth about everything.

radicalized—(highly useful adjective): acting in a way that we do not like.

slavedriver—(defensive noun): someone who *genuinely* expects you to work more than four hours per day; see also *workaholic*—someone who works a full day.

I managed to incorporate seventeen of the fifty terms. The revised article, while completely alienated from what actually happened, seemed as though it would pass the manager's scrutiny.

He nodded at my revised draft and praised, "Very good! But we'll have to shorten it to make room for a promo we need to fit in about a new movie. It's a suicide story."

"Is it about the woman who shot herself on the air?"

His face lit up. "Ah, so you've seen it?"

"No, I saw the reference in the archives. You rerun that movie every six years."

"Yes, we do! It's a very popular remake! Anyway, I'll take care of shortening this." Suddenly he stopped, having noticed something else in my piece. Looking up at me and waving a stern finger, he added, "Oh, and by the way, Steven, 'science' is *never* written in quotations."

The next day, my article had been moved to the third page. The second page was about the Multiverse mob that had gone crazy over the recent "radicalized" behavior and was calling for the attacker's death. The level of public venom directed at the attacker, his family, people who once knew him, and nearly everyone else that the internet mob could think to decimate was shocking to witness. Anyone who could have ever been associated with the attacker was required to either denounce the lunatic's actions immediately and demonstrate allegiance to the mob's will by joining in the chaotic efforts or be subjected to brutal condemnation as a coconspirator or at least an unwelcome sympathizer. Almost instantaneously, public opinion far and wide went from benign and driftless to dagger-sharp and demanded the attacker's prompt execution for upsetting the sanctity of that peaceful society. The ripple effect of public rage also caused numerous other unsuspecting people to lose their jobs and livelihoods for failing to respond accordingly to the situation.

I flagged the manager down and asked about the situation with great concern. I didn't particularly have any sympathy for the gentleman who caused the incident, but the mobilized internet mob violence seemed far more of a deadly element than anything that guy had done.

Scanning the web posts briefly and then looking up again, he said dismissively, "Steven, these people don't have any real adventure left in their lives anymore, and getting to participate in internet mobs is the only excitement most of them will ever have. But don't worry; letting people vent on the internet is a staple of any healthy democracy."

"But I thought you said that people were supposed to avoid emotionally charged events."

"In public, yes. On the internet, however, it's an entirely different thing." Then he smiled reassuringly and added, "Besides, what good would all this technology be if we couldn't use it to instantly condemn people and make others feel better about themselves?"

I uneasily scratched the back of my neck. "I don't know; it all seems a little scary to me."

"It may at first, but a virtual mob is actually very useful. That tool has helped us root out separatists, racists, parents who don't read required stories to newborns, and a host of other troublemakers." Likely sensing my unease, he added, "Listen, don't worry about it. This little fervor will die out soon."

"Are you sure?"

"Of course. See, Steven, the way our society works is that a little crisis erupts and people get into a bit of a tizzy, and then they turn their attack on something else. In the meantime, it's our job to reassure them that everything is under control and learning how to garner the interest of the lobotomy mob is actually central to what we do." Turning to a colleague who was passing by, the manager said, "By the way, Zimmerman, let's run that 'Cosmic Radiation Could End World' story tomorrow."

I said, "But won't that cause panic?"

The manager replied, "Oh no. We're already preparing the action-adventure movie that shows how we solve the problem."

"Does that work?"

"Naturally, and in the meantime, the space program gets a nice little budgetary boost that no one argues with."

That was the second reference I had heard to the space program budget, and I said basely, "Yeah, what's so great about them that they get to hog all of the tax money?"

"Oh, it's not that. In fact, contributions to the space program are only a fractional percentage of the insurance program, but don't forget that they've given us some wonderful things that make this country safer and better."

Mockingly, I said, "Yeah, like sushi restaurants?"

"Well, there's that, but we also have an early-warning observatory on Uranus to detect asteroids coming toward Earth, and if you've seen some of the action-adventure movies on that subject, you'd know what a threat those are. We also have another observatory on Pluto watching for Martians."

I laughed incredulously and said, "Now *that's* dumb!"

Flabbergasted, the manager put his hands on his hips and demanded, "How can you say that? Did you see *Aliens 52*? What if creatures like that attacked Earth? Wouldn't you want to know about it?"

I jeered, "Maybe. But what if they come from the other direction?"

He scoffed back at me. "What *other* direction? If they're going to attack Earth, they're going to have to get past Pluto first."

"Not if they come from below."

He did a double take. "What 'below'? Steven, there is no below! We have our planets lined up in a nice little row, and scientific evidence proves that if aliens are going to attack us, they'll fly right by all of the planets in order." He shook his head and said dismissively, "If you had a scientific background, you'd understand all of this."

As he walked away, he stopped and added, "Oh, that reminds me, one of the astronauts is coming home from Mars next month, and we need to run a returning heroes promo on him."

I asked snidely, "What's heroic about serving sushi on Mars?"

"Well, he was actually making space blankets. However, his courage, and the courage of those other brave souls are paving the way for all of us to escape this planet should an extinction-level event happen."

I smirked and said, "You mean like an asteroid that comes from the other direction and isn't detected by the observatory on Uranus?"

The manager finally lost his patience with me. Punitively, he said, "Steven, I've changed my mind. I think that you should go back to your station and just keep writing. I have a nice *low-brow* assignment for you, and we'll leave the technical matters to those with more interest in—and respect for—our planetary efforts."

That night, I was out on a date again. I said, "Where do you live?"

"In uptown."

"Oh, that's ten feet away."

"Yes, but it's a totally different neighborhood from this one! It has a real raw, organic, fusion-fission Asian-Mediterranean feel to it. Let's go to my place and order in!"

Looking at her ass as she trotted across the street, I said, "Okay, but you call."

She smiled back at me and said, "Sure thing! But hang on, I need to stop in this store and pick up some more lube and anal bleach."

* * *

Not much changed for a while after that. The manager was up to his same routine, rounding up a story with the mobile correspondent on the other end of the line. "There's been a new attack. We're going to need six. Yes, biology, sociology, urban planning … No, I think that he's at Burger Bob's. Yes, check there. Yep. Get them ready. Oh, and his fourth-grade teacher. Find her as well. Apparently he scored very low on testing."

He finally noticed me and said, "Okay, now what did you find out about the victim?"

I was working on a bar fight story. "Well, boss, the victim himself says that he was just in the wrong place at the wrong time. He doesn't want to press charges and said that in hindsight he should have seen it coming."

The manager blew up. "Oh, that's the most ridiculous thing I've ever heard! Do not—I repeat, *do not*—write that!" He started pacing and muttered sarcastically, "'Wrong place at the wrong time.' How the hell would we ever sell stories if people took that kind of attitude?" Then he paused and turned back to me curiously. "Tell me this. Is he good-looking?"

I took a small step back and deflected. "I, um, that's not really my thing, you know."

He just frowned at me, insisting, "Never mind. Let me see his picture. Oh, oh, God, we can't run this! He's hideous!" Taking a step back to better survey the photo, the manager jeered, "Now that's a guy whose parents should have paid extra for a celebrity look-alike upgrade!"

I said, "What's the big deal?"

The manager handed the photo back to me and explained. "Steven, our strict policy regarding photos is as follows: if the person is a victim, you find the *best* photograph possible of them and use that. If the person is a villain, you find the *worst* photograph of them and use that. This guy should technically qualify as a victim, but it's obvious that he never took a presentable photo in his life."

I stood there waiting for the eventual disappointment to hit me, and seeing my slackening face, the manager said, "Look, just write the story like we had discussed before. With a mug like that, I'm sure that he won't be talking to anyone about what happened anyway. And leave out all that self-deprecating crap."

"Why?"

He exclaimed, "Because, damn it, it's victim shaming!"

I just stared blankly at him. He finally sighed and put a hand on my shoulder and said, "Steven, you have to understand the way stories work these days. The attention span of a lobotomy is about five seconds, so stories about heroes or people with excessively developed personality traits can't be adequately explained anymore. To gain the sort of robustness that makes up people like that takes training, and time—basically, things that lobotomies can't handle."

"So?"

"So obviously this guy had gone through some laboring ordeal in his life that made him sturdier than others. Telling people that he's out there will just make our readers doubt what we've been saying to them all along about never taking too much responsibility for their own lives. Nope, he's a clear-cut case of excessive stoicism, and that is very dangerous these days."

I started to crumple up the draft and said dismissively, "Well then, we might as well just trash the story."

He quickly grabbed it from my hand. "Oh, no! We have fewer grand tragedies these days, so we have to make the most of every single one. No, just write it like I said, and we'll run it tomorrow."

* * *

My computer was acting up again, and the message kept flashing at me:

> I'm really sorry to bother you today, but I think that you might have perhaps pressed the wrong button. If it doesn't upset you too much, could you please try that again? And sorry in advance for any undue emotional difficulty this interruption might have caused.

The message was followed by several warm, smiley emojis. I smacked the unit several times, but it was unfazed and the smiley faces wouldn't go away, so I finally asked the manager for help. He looked at the screen momentarily and then pointed me to one of the stations at the end of my row. "Oh, just use hers. She needs to go anyway."

Reluctantly, I got up and went down to where the other writer was sitting. The girl I was supposed to replace gave me a bubbly smile as I approached and said, "Hi, Steven, thanks for coming along to finish my article for me! You'll love working on it! It's an exposé about service dogs on Mars!"

WTF? I actually said, "That sounds interesting."

"Oh, it is! See you later!"

Sitting down to another ridiculous task, I tried to use her computer, but it was perpetually stuck on auto-fill. Even if I typed in a single letter, the computer just picked up and kept writing the story where she left off. One of the technicians came by, and I asked for further assistance.

He peered at the machine through his spectacles and said, "Why, there's nothing wrong with this computer at all. It simply auto-writes stories, which is very helpful for the lobotomies!"

"Can I turn it off?"

"Heavens no!"

"But my computer in college didn't have auto functions?"

He scratched his head and said thoughtfully, "Huh, must have been a real dinosaur. All writable technology is now auto-fill. Sorry, pal, you'll just have to make do."

He left, only to be replaced by another visitor in the form of an overly exuberant cherubic male figure who didn't seem to be affected one bit by the weight of his existence. "Hi, Steven! What'cha working on?"

Unenthusiastically, I mumbled, "Nothing. A ridiculous story about dogs in space."

He shook his head and said assuredly, "Oh, there's nothing ridiculous about that. Did you know that there is a terrible cat overpopulation problem on the moon?"

"You have to be kidding me?"

"No, not at all."

Sitting back to look at him for a second and ponder the notion, I said, "So you're telling me that the moon, which used to be devoid of any life at all, now has a cat overpopulation problem?"

He nodded with deep concern. "Oh yes, and it's terribly sad!"

"How the hell did that happen?"

"Well, the people we sent up there didn't want to be alone, so we sent the cats, and the cats didn't want to be alone, so they bred. I'm afraid that you can't fight nature, Steven." He shook his head compassionately and added, "Don't even get me started about the dog problems on Pluto or the goldfish problems on Saturn's moon!"

Trying to vainly arrest myself from falling into another time warp, I demanded, "What are you talking about, 'we can't fight nature'? There are humans and animals living in space? That sure sounds like fighting nature to me."

Assuredly, he replied, "Well, the universe was created for us, so that's not technically correct."

I paused for a second and then said definitively, "I guess we just need to make fewer humans so they won't muck up any more parts of the galaxy."

As those words started to register in his brain, the guy's face went completely blank. Behind his eyes was the kind of brewing realization of horror that takes weeks to fully register and will assuredly result in lasting trauma.

*   *   *

Friday was a boon for the writing staff when the manager made a midafternoon announcement: "People, people, listen up! For a limited time, we're going to bring back the use of 'game changer' as an accepted catchphrase for articles!" Murmurs of great approval went all around the newsroom.

He held up a cautionary hand and added, "Now, we can't use it for too long, because as we all know, the game never really changes anyway. But we'll keep it on the approved list for the next six months, and that should help you all improve readership for your articles."

"Hooray, hooray!"

Later that day, I performed a "game changer" search in archives and came back with 1,076,000 hits of the term in stories between 2000 and 2050. Shortly thereafter, the manager unexpectedly caught me at the archives terminal and immediately demanded, "Steven, what are you doing? I asked for that article an hour ago!"

I responded avertingly, "Well, I got sidetracked. My computer is still broken, and I'm not able to use the substitute one you gave me."

"Why not?"

Indignantly, I said, "Because it's stifling my writing!"

"What are you talking about?"

"Well, if you're going to force me to use a computer with auto-fill, then when I sit down to write, I type on the computer until I come up with an idea that can't be prefilled. That way I know it's unique."

He swiftly yanked me out of the archives room and stood there angrily. "Steven, it's time to get with the program! You have to remember that most people read these stories with their VR contacts, so the format for the story needs to be like this: horribly scary thing happens, click; very sad, click; authorities and experts respond immediately, click; interesting technical term or principle involved, click; problem solved, click; hero pinned with medal, click; buy product, click; next story. Got it?"

I frowned and said, "That's just pattern crap. It's not providing people with any real material."

"So? They wouldn't know what to do with it anyway. Look, people don't need to search for answers anymore. Just ask Sophia."

That was the second reference to the mystery person, and I said, "Who?"

"The little program imbedded in the gallbladder module that tells you everything you'd ever want to know—from how many calories are in the food you're eating to where you're supposed to be during the day."

Astonished, I said, "Are you joking?"

The manager cocked his head and responded, "Steven, do you honestly think that lobotomies can remember where they're supposed to be during the day? Hell, when we first starting lobotomizing people, we had to give them special apps just so they could remember to finish a task. Nowadays Sophia sends automatic updates to the eye screen on contacts, and people register them subconsciously. Didn't they teach you this at the lab?"

I stammered, "Well, my time there was cut short. But how does Sophia know how to tell people what they're supposed to be doing?"

"Oh, the sophisticated AI technology mimics human intelligence so that humans don't need to use it anymore."

Just then our conversation was interrupted by a weeping girl who walked up and lightly tugged his sleeve. She said woefully, "Mr. Manager"—snort—"... I have something very serious to discuss with you!"

The manager looked at her with mild concern. "Yes?"

"Well"—snort ... sob ...—"I sent Steven an instant message"— ... snort—"and he didn't respond to me for"—gasp ... snort ...—"three days!"

The manager put a consoling hand on top of her head and said, "There, there now. What was the message about?"

She finally broke down completely and blurted out, "*The word of the day challenge, and now it's all gone and ruined because we're on a new word of the day and my message was really clever and he didn't pay any attention to it! Waahhhhhh!*"

He gently patted the top of her head and responded, "That's okay, Stephanie. You'd better get over to the hospital and they'll take care of you."

As she trailed away in a stream of snot, I said, annoyed, "What's her problem?"

The manager responded, "Extreme PTSD caused by not getting a timely instant message response. It's terribly afflicting among young people."

Holding back the urge to spit, I said, "Humph. They should turn off those damn VR devices and get to work."

He shook his head disapprovingly and scolded, "Oh, Steven, don't be such a Luddite. The contacts are very important to workplace longevity. They take selfies, and as you know, there was a pioneering study years ago that proved selfies increase self-satisfaction. They're also a great way to keep track of people."

"What?"

"As they age, you know."

"Oh."

"The contacts are also the only way for introverts to network."

"Seriously?"

The manager smiled assuredly and said, "Of course! Most lobotomies are naturally agoraphobic and have trouble networking, but the eyepieces solve that problem. They send instant messages to anyone you want to talk to, and if they get an instant response, then they naturally feel more comfortable about networking."

As he walked away, I mumbled to myself, "Well, they should probably just stay at home where they belong ..."

*

THIRTEEN

On Monday, another catastrophe broke. Bursting into the room, one of my coworkers exclaimed, "Holy crap, someone just stole sixty-seven trillion dollars from the space program!"

I jumped up and said, "Do we know who did it?"

She nodded excitedly. "Absolutely, and they're under investigation right now, but no one can seem to locate the electronic funds and they may be lost entirely!"

I was not surprised that invisible wealth could suddenly vanish. However, rather than make a snide comment, instead I suggested helpfully, "Hey, we should talk to those guys and get the movie rights!"

The manager intervened. "No, no, Steven. For real scandals, we wait at least five years and then do the movie."

I shook my head in confusion. "Why?"

"Never mind. We'll get someone else with more experience to do the story." Then he started pacing in deep concern and added, "But this is going to be a huge problem for the people. We'll probably have to cut back on cell phone upgrades next month to make up for the cash shortage."

Jokingly, I said, "And while you're at it, why don't you just print some more people?"

He whirled around and exclaimed, "Great idea, Steven!"

"No, wait. I was kidding."

He gave me a delayed response while pondering something—probably the number of new lives it would take to erase that deficit—and then finally said, "Oh, I know. Excuse me. I need to make a phone call."

He came back several minutes later and shot me a sideways look, and I asked cynically, "Did you tell them to start printing more people?"

He frowned impatiently and responded, "Of course not. Did you need something else?"

"Not really. But how the hell can that happen in the first place?"

"What?"

"You know. Someone robbing sixty-seven trillion dollars?"

Seeming to have already forgotten the event, he said, "Oh, that. Well, the United States cooperates with dozens of developing nations to fund the initiatives that build parts for our space program. Sometimes irresponsible behavior along the chain can happen, especially when you put large sums of money in the hands of people who have never experienced that kind of spending power."

"You mean, like the credit/insurance program?"

"A bit, yes. Of course, we protect that much better at home than we can abroad through scientifically determined spending limitations. But don't worry; our economy has self-correcting measures."

"Like what?"

"Oh, we usually have a recession every eighteen months or so, and then things seem to work themselves out."

I frowned at him. "I'll bet."

He eyed me and replied curtly, "Let's leave the overtechnical economic issues aside for now. Why don't you just work on this story instead?"

I looked down at the assignment sheet. "'The Ten Things You're Doing Wrong When You Go to The Bathroom.' Are you kidding me?"

"Oh, no. It's a very important subject, and one that people don't know enough about."

Pleading with him, I said, "Do you have anything else?"

"How about this? 'The Ten Things That Cause You to Want to Buy a Car.'"

That actually could have been worse, but I didn't let on. Instead I simply asked, "Why is this important?"

"Steven, you have to understand how these stories work. Take a simple concept like buying a car or going to the bathroom and divide it up into all its constituent parts. Then slap some expert opinions in about each part, throw in some big terminology that people aren't familiar with, and voilà—you have a potential Pulitzer on your hands!"

Seeing that my talents were going to be put on hold for another day, I said, "Look, just give me the car assignment and I'll work on that."

"Okay. I'll just give the bathroom story to someone else whose writing is already in the dumps. Ha!"

I was just sitting down to write when another unwelcome interruption greeted me. He said, "Hi Steven! Tell me the name of the new Persian cat that the singer Vanity bought for her adopted half-daughter."

"No idea."

"Geesh. You're not much of a good citizen, are you?"

"Guess not. Now leave me alone."

When the news of the cell phone shortage hit the streets, people were completely despondent. However, medication sales went through the roof. I didn't much care for my cell phone—or my watch, for that matter—but my phone kept lighting up with sexy vixens who wanted to romp, so I tried another date to take my mind off of things. Unfortunately she insisted on eating out, as Sophia had suggested another restaurant where the fare was supposed to be unforgettable. I was merely hoping for edible.

The restaurant turned out to be quite a distance away, necessitating a taxi ride. Our driver was surprisingly comfortable with my date suggesting that she and I have anal sex in the back of the cab on the way to dinner, and the driver even turned around a few times to watch and snap pictures, since the car was driving itself. Despite the enjoyment getting there, however, my annoyance meter pegged when my date tried to insist that I borrow one of her matching spare onesies to go into the restaurant, and it only got worse once we were in the dining establishment.

The waitress greeted us warmly at our table. "Hi, how's it going, you two?"

I held up a firm hand and insisted, "Look, before you even start, I don't want to talk to you, and I don't want to discuss my emotions or my inner child. I want food!"

She was unfazed and simply responded lightly, "Oh, a bit of a Neanderthal, huh? How about a nice steak puree?"

I stomped my foot and demanded, "No! I want whatever you have that hasn't been shot through a particle accelerator! Go out and kill something live if you have to, but I want to eat something's flesh!"

My date grinned seductively at me when I said that, but I didn't pay her any mind. For her own part, the waitress raised a pensive finger to her lips and said, "Hmm, let me ask the manager, and I'll see if we can do anything."

Seventy-five minutes of banal conversation later, my dinner arrived. "Here you go, sir."

I studied the unrecognizable substance wedged between two buns and asked, "What is it?"

"A turtle burger."

"Where the hell did you get the turtle?"

"From the aquarium next door. You said you wanted something real, and turtles don't work very well in the collider, as you can imagine, since the shell messes up the whole process."

"Fine, thank you. I'll try this."

The meal was surprisingly satisfying. Unfortunately, it also completely made me forget about the tipping ploy that followed, and I overpaid once again for underwhelming service. My date also left the table momentarily to vomit, and when she returned, my libido was effectively ruined, which meant no dessert.

Afterward we took a leisurely ride home through and around the park, and I don't believe that the car ever got going faster than twenty-five miles per hour with all the city traffic. My companion, however, was in postgastronomic bliss, even after throwing up her meal. I was bored to tears again.

Turning away from the window, she said, "Thank goodness for

lobotomies! There used to be so much opposition to self-driving cars. Don't you just love this?"

"Yeah, great."

She suddenly slid over and grabbed my arm. "Hey, I have a great idea!"

Her breath reeked faintly of vomit, but I pretended not to notice. "What?"

"When we get back to my place, let's go online and order a new baby!"

That sealed the deal. My eyes darted around nervously, and I leaned forward and said urgently, "Oh, um, driver, could you pull over here?"

Suddenly confused, my companion said, "Why? What's wrong?"

I reached for the door handle before the autonomous vehicle had even halted and responded, "Oh, nothing. It's just that I forgot my doctor said that if I don't walk more, I'll die."

Her face blanched, and she said, "Seriously? That sounds pretty awful!"

I nodded earnestly and replied, "It is, and I think that it's catching. Don't try to follow me. Just save yourself."

As the door slammed shut, she rolled down the window and said expectantly, "Well, will you call me later?"

I was already on the other side of the street and replied over my shoulder, "Sure thing."

*   *   *

I was back in the director's office after another long day, and he had his feet up on the desk. Pleasantly, he said, "So how's dating life?"

I responded unenthusiastically, "Okay. It's hard to eat."

He chuckled. "Come on, nobody eats on dates! The vomiting from the esophageal screens tends to ruin the mood!"

I waved him off. "No, it's not that. Every time I try to order something, I wind up in an amateur therapy session, and it drives me nuts."

Appearing oddly curious, the director cocked an eyebrow. "Really?"

"Yes. I tried to order takeout the other day, and the first question was whether I had trouble getting up in the morning."

He put his feet down and said sincerely, "Oh, that's no joke. Difficulty waking up and facing the day can be traumatizing if not managed properly. We use 'best possible self' imaging techniques with people in yoga classes to combat that, and it helps them envision a brighter tomorrow."

I leaned forward and insisted, "Look, leave that aside. Isn't it possible to get food in this town without being diagnosed?"

The director said, "I'm afraid not, since the practice has become too popular now."

"How the hell did that happen?"

"Oh, it all started when people could go online and instantly receive a diagnosis and a prescription at the same time. The program became so successful that we had to triage to the service industry."

Acridly, I said, "Well, I'm sick of the damn questions."

Though I was expecting another excuse, the director instead surprised me with a useful suggestion. "Then why don't you just cook something at home yourself?"

My eyebrows shot up. "Great idea, thanks!"

It took a little while to find stores that actually sold real food, but in short order, I was stocked up to begin dining on various types of animal flesh in my apartment. I also learned how to hone my dating prospects, and the one I was hooking up with tonight at least said that she exercised regularly—hence, no esophageal screen. I felt moderately optimistic.

When she walked in, she said, "Wow, nice apartment! Let me put on my 3-D contacts and see what it really looks like. Oooh! This is a penthouse!"

Following her around the apartment from behind, I said, "Yeah, it's okay."

After sex, and dinner, and then sex again, we lay on the couch, watching television. The president was giving a speech with the vice president at her side. My temporary companion was transfixed on the images and gawked. "Aren't they gorgeous?"

I was bored to tears again. "Yep."

She snuggled closer and added, "Sure makes you feel proud to live in such a wonderful democracy, huh?"

I yawned. "Yep."

Mixing romance and patriotism, she said, "Sophia tells me that we have the first transgender wife-and-husband couple as president and vice president who also went to high school together and had lockers in the same row! It's glorious to be alive in a time with so much progress!"

"That's progress?"

"Sure. It hasn't ever happened before. Aren't you proud to be a part of it?"

"Thrilled."

Suddenly she sat up and looked at me. With bubbling exuberance, she said, "You know what would be the coolest thing?" I already knew where she was going and was planning my, or her, exit strategy. She continued without even waiting for me to respond. "We should order a baby!"

I started to open my mouth to protest, but her pleading continued. "Oh, come on! It'll be great! But I'd like to hurry up and get it done soon. I want to be back in my beach body by summer so I can wear a thong!"

I finally sat up, realizing that I was, in fact, talking to an alien species. Cocking my head, I said, "So let me get this straight. You want to order a baby?"

"Yes!"

"And I presume that we'll get married while it's processing?"

She nodded enthusiastically and said, "Oh, I'd like that!"

"Then, afterward, you're going to prance around in public with your ass hanging out?"

Her failure to register my concerns was evident. "Uh huh!"

I stood up immediately and announced, "Say, we have to leave."

The pattern confused look I had grown accustomed to seeing

at the end of my dates suddenly appeared on her face, and she said, "Why?"

Grabbing her hand to pull her up, I responded flatly, "Oh, they're coming to fumigate my apartment in twelve minutes. It's very poisonous. We'd better get you downstairs and into a cab."

She nervously fumbled for her clothes, while I had put on only my boxers and shoes. Looking at me with concern, she said, "What are you going to do?"

"Come back up here. But don't worry; I'll be okay."

"Will you call me later?"

"Sure thing."

* * *

I was pulled into an afternoon briefing session where one of the researchers addressed the manager. "Sir, sir, you have to see this! According to the most recent study, the surface of the earth appears to be caving in!"

The manager was not even remotely moved. "So?"

"Well, preliminary calculations indicate that all of the materials we've sent to the moon and the other planetary colonies for terraforming have weakened the integrity of the earth."

One of the others asked incredulously, "Even though we 3-D print all of the materials?"

The researcher responded decisively, "Yes, and there are sinkholes forming everywhere. Data also suggest that the earth's rotation is fractionally off."

Now the manager interrupted him and said, alarmed, "You mean worse than before?"

"Yes. I'm afraid it could actually start affecting climates everywhere in another thirty to forty years."

The girl next to me raised her hand and asked, "Can't we just Botox the sinkholes?"

The manager shook his head and said curtly, "No."

I smiled and chimed in helpfully. "Well, it sounds like we'll have to cut the space program!"

The manager waved me off and started pacing. "Oh, no, we're never doing that." After a minute, he stopped and snapped his fingers, announcing confidently, "People, this is an easy problem to solve! We just need to tell everyone that jumping up and down is no longer allowed. Let's get a study going to show that excessive jumping up and down causes damage to knee joints. That should take care of it."

In unison, four of them said, "That's a great idea!"

I butted in and insisted again, "But why don't we just stop terraforming?"

The manager responded indignantly, "What for? Steven, the moon's gravity has been increased by 0.0001 percent as a result of our efforts. That's a huge scientific accomplishment and makes it much easier to work. Nope, these people are just going to have to stop jumping up and down, and that should balance out the problem. Oh, and be sure to add that if they don't stop it now, it could cause irreversible harm to the earth."

Everyone nodded in approval, and he added, "Then let's do an article that says we've established that the gravitational pull of the earth is too strong and people need to be put in leg braces."

One of the researchers said, "Brilliant!"

The manager continued. "And as a show of solidarity, let's get most of the writing staff fitted with them—well, the unattractive ones who never go anywhere anyway, that is."

Everyone nodded in dutiful agreement. However, I mumbled, "That sounds pretty ridiculous to me."

The researcher next to me pushed up his spectacles and scowled at me, demanding, "Steven, are you saying that the law of gravity is a ridiculous thing? Let me tell you; it's not!"

I said earnestly, "Well, it just doesn't sound like something people will go for."

The manager settled the dispute. "Look, if climate change can be linked to diabetes, the uneven tilt of Earth's axis and rotational problems can be linked to kids jumping on the bed. Get it out immediately."

I said, "Climate change is linked to diabetes? I thought that diabetes was caused by dark matter?"

The researcher snidely responded, "Steven, you should stick to what you know best and leave the technical side to us. Yes, global warming causes diabetes. It also sends people to the hospital every day with PTSD. The environment is responsible for 99 percent of all deaths, in case you didn't know!"

I stepped toward him menacingly with my hands in a strangling gesture and threatened, "Well, oxygen shortage is responsible for 100 percent of those deaths!" Terrified, the researcher scampered around the corner and disappeared, and everyone else just stared at me with blank faces. Regaining my composure, I switched to a topic I *did* know about and offered another helpful solution: "What if we just produced fewer people on Earth?"

There probably isn't that much silence at a funeral. Finally the manager released the tension by saying apologetically, "Ahem. Sorry, everyone, but I'm afraid Steven doesn't have a science background. Please just ignore what he said. Oh, and while we're at it, let's rerun that series of articles about the right things to eat to keep global warming in check. Someone find out from upstairs whose products we're invested in these days, and we'll get the articles out ASAP." And with that, the crowd forgot all about me and my lack of economic patriotism and went about their business.

It would be fair to say that by then I was becoming fed up with the whole system and everyone in it. I could barely bring myself to accept another insta-date/screw, but the girl who sent the message was so hot! She also swore that she did not have any interest in kids, did not have any present shopping needs, and had not thrown up since she was a child. Still, I probably shouldn't have accepted. The sex was great, but afterward I guess I wasn't much company.

She snuggled up to me blissfully, pretending to be interested in my burdens, and said, "What's wrong now, Steven?"

I shot back, "Those bastards out there are ruining the earth, and they've made everything so complicated that ordinary people can't even go to the bathroom without consulting experts!"

Sleepily, she said, "Yeah, I read something about that. People need to be more careful. Thankfully, Sophia usually reminds me when it's time to use the facilities." And then she was out. I could tell that I wouldn't be able to ease any of my troubles with her.

* * *

Sitting comfortably behind his desk the next day, the director said, "Oh, the evolution of studies was very important, since it allowed us to gain the trust of our citizens again. Once we introduced scientific democracy, everyone realized that we were really here for their best interests."

Shaking my head, I said dubiously, "I still don't see how any of it matters."

He responded assuredly, "It's easy. We show them a study that says people do X, and then people do precisely that. As you may know by now, there's nothing wrong with a little self-fulfilling prophecy when you're the government, and it sure helps the economy move along. Then we follow up with an artist's rendition, and that seals the deal."

"It does?"

"Oh, sure. Once we do the artist's rendition or pass a law, they're basically enshrined in eternity."

"I just don't understand why you have to pass so many."

The director shook his head. "Steven, my boy, it's simple. If the government doesn't use the rights it has, they go back to the people."

"Huh?"

"It's right there in the Constitution. Fortunately for us, the Framers were wise enough to give us our own means of self-preservation, which is really just a natural right of any government."

"Says who?"

"Alexander Hamilton.[3] Anyway, the reason why our system works the way it does is that people aren't really using their rights anymore.

As a result, our government can run as efficiently as it was originally intended to, and without unnecessary interruptions. You'll eventually see that the whole system is very well thought out." I just sat across from him with my hopes steadily dropping. He finally noticed it and said lightly, "Hey, don't worry! If there was ever a real problem, I'm sure the people would fix it!"

I slumped down and sarcastically replied, "Yeah, right."

"They would! Trust me! This is all covered in *Federalist* no. 16."[4]

I raised an eyebrow and said, "Can I find a copy of that?"

Fumbling momentarily, he replied, "Oh, well, we don't keep many books around these days, but don't worry; it's there all right."

My deadpan look did not fade, and he finally rocked sideways in his chair and redirected. "Steven, is there something else bothering you? You seem pretty down, and I'll bet that there's more to it than this talk about studies."

Finally, I admitted, "Well, I'm getting a little fed up dealing with all of that crap at the newspaper."

Supportively, he said, "Don't lose heart. After all, you're doing a very important job!"

Shifting sideways in the chair, I challenged, "Oh yeah, what's so important about it?"

"Steven, you are helping to provide twenty-four-hour-per-day news to the people, and that's the most important resource we have."

"Well, excuse me for saying so, but it seems pretty useless to me."

He smiled. "Oh, it may seem like that, but with twenty-four hours to cover in a day, everything becomes news. And don't forget: it's not just for you. We also have the lobotomies to think about, and they need constant instructions. For some peculiar reason, we have found that they will follow nearly anything as long as we can prove that a thousand other people are doing it. Fortunately for us, the news constantly reminds them of that."

What he was saying finally registered a bit, and I sat up momentarily and said, "That can't be right, can it? About the studies, I mean."

"Pretty much. The way it works is that the thousand-person

survey then turns into a hundred papers on the subject, and whatever we've found is basically irrefutable after that. Anyway, science has proven that the government knows what's best for the people."

I leaned back in surprise and asked, "Really?"

He nodded firmly. "Oh yes. There's a very famous government study that proved it."

"Come on?"

He said assuredly, "Steven, don't forget that this is the country that was founded on *The Federalist Papers*."

"So?"

"*The Federalist Papers* were a collection of newspaper articles written by political actors under pseudonyms to convince the people to give up control to the government, and they were later taught in school as a model for how the government should work. Really brilliant marketing when you think about it!"

* * *

Everyone was in a fervor at the office the following day, and when I found the manager, he was busy approving the upcoming layout. "Yes, yes, we'll run global meltdown, then boy saves grandmother from drowning in soup bowl, et cetera."

Still, the noise from the commotion was deafening and otherwise unexplainable by what I heard him describing, so I said, "What the hell is going on?"

He turned the storyboard toward me. "Look at the headline. Nice, eh?"

It read, "*WAR!*"

My eyes shot out. "Holy shit! We're going to war?"

He handed the board to someone passing by and nodded to him in approval, and then we ducked into his office, where it was quieter, and he finally responded, "Oh, no, of course not. There are no real wars anymore. Fortunately, the spirit of our global economy has a tendency to soften people's manners and to extinguish the inflammable humors which used to lead to wars.[5] Heck, even dogs cease to bark after having breathed a while in our atmosphere, all thanks to the Founders!"[6]

"But don't countries still get into fights?"

"Oh sure, but all we have to do these days is apply gentle diplomatic pressure and the thing usually goes away." Sitting down, he added, "Most soldiers now also suffer from PPTSD anyway."

"What's that?"

"Pre-Post-Traumatic Stress Disorder. People get so worked up even at the thought of confrontation that they fall apart."

"How the hell did that get started?"

Leaning back, he said thoughtfully, "It was a very interesting part of scientific development. PTSD was, of course, a syndrome experienced by soldiers over two centuries ago. It was caused by seeing a traumatic and life-threatening event, such as witnessing a soldier get blown up right next to you, having a land mine explode under you, and the like. Over time, civilians adopted PTSD to cover everything from getting into a minor fender bender to the shock at losing a pet."

"Are you kidding?"

"Oh no, but you have to understand that the diagnostic criteria used for PTSD has stayed the same: life-threatening experience coupled with extreme emotional distress. However, what constitutes 'life-threatening' changes as our society evolves, and as you know, these gentle little lobotomies are frightened by nearly everything."

I looked out the window of his office and saw that several people had, in fact, fainted in all the excitement. He continued. "In any event, PPTSD emerged on the civilian front and was later adopted by military personnel. They figured that if civilians could steal their disorder, the soldiers could do the same. In truth, however, when armies began to experience serial suicides among their troops, actually fighting wars pretty much lost its fashion appeal."

Confused, I said, "Then what's with the headline? When I went through the archives, I saw tons of 'WAR' announcements."

The manager responded lightly, "Oh, lobotomies are obsessed

with wanting to be part of something big, so we announce a 'WAR' about every twelve months. They go nuts over it!"

"Well, what's actually happening?"

He shrugged and said, "Not much. A few countries want to get together and put up a competing sushi restaurant on Pluto, but it completely violates the International Agreement. The world leaders are talking it over on a skiing trip right now in Switzerland. Fortunately, we are the only country with a tactical missile site on the moon, so everyone pretty much follows our lead these days." Adopting a playful grin and changing the subject, he said, "By the way, how was your date last night?"

Thrown off guard by the question, I blurted out quickly, "Oh, fine."

He grinned at me. "Tammy said that you were kind of kinky!"

"What?"

"She said that you wanted to have missionary sex with her!"

"Is that weird?"

He nodded and said, "Oh, it's totally taboo. Makes girls think that you're trying to screw up their heads. Next time just stick to anal."

Annoyed, I responded, "Look, I'm tired of anal. Don't girls do anything else?"

"Not really. Why? What's the big deal? You've been with a prostitute, right?"

"Yeah, so?"

"Well, they do the same thing."

"Yeah, but those are prostitutes."

He just shrugged, and before he could respond further, his phone went off. "Sorry, gotta take this. Close the door on your way out."

*　*　*

The war scare passed, but the manager's stress did not. He was pacing again, and the cause this time was a persistently unexplainable force of nature, which thankfully still had not been tracked back to me. Furiously, he said, "That goddamn tree doesn't even have the decency to stand still so we can kill it!"

Innocently, I asked, "Do we know what it is yet?"

He mimicked spitting and responded, "Yes, a complete menace!"

"No, what species?"

"Oh, who cares! We don't need another discovery. We have had more scientific breakthroughs in the last ten years than we did in the previous hundred!"

"How?"

That derailed him momentarily and he responded, "Huh? Oh, well, we used to be hindered by actually having to verify things, but now we can just announce a new breakthrough when we get an inkling of an idea. It's very useful."

"But why would you change scientific thinking to permit that to happen?"

"Steven, that's easy—back to the old law of supply and demand. Once we were able to derive an inexhaustible funding source—i.e., members of the public who didn't question budgetary increases for new initiatives—we were able to change the parameters for public announcements. All we have to do now to keep the funding flowing is make sure we announce new discoveries on a regular basis. By the way, let's run an article that the hole in the ozone layer is caused by excess oxygen. That will cover up for the tree campaign that we're now cancelling."

By this time, I was more concerned about my wooded friend than I was about the rest of these humans, and my walk home was filled with increasingly hostile thoughts, which were unwelcomely interrupted with twenty-five new invites for sex blasting over my phone. I didn't want any company, however, and desperately needed sleep, but I was granted no immediate reprieve in that regard. Instead I ran into a shapely new neighbor while I was getting onto the elevator, and she blurted out, "Hey, Steven, nice sex video!"

I tried not to be distracted by her skin-tight, overburdened yoga attire. Staring up at the screen, I stammered, "Um, I didn't make that."

She started reaching into her purse to pull out her phone and offered eagerly, "Have you seen mine?"

I snapped my head away and responded, "Oh, God no!"

Just then the elevator opened at the next floor and a mother got on with her little son. I ignored the girl next to me, who was trying to bring up her sex video for public viewing, instead pretending to focus on the elevator screen. A video advertisement for genital piercing treatments popped up, and the little boy's jaw dropped and he just stared and stared in awe. A few floors later, the door opened again and the two of them got off.

As the door was closing, I hear the little boy say, "Mommy, when can I get my clit pierced?"

Lovingly, she patted his head and said, "We have to get you one first, sweetie. Probably for your eighth birthday."

He jumped up and down and exclaimed, "Oh, goodie!"

As the doors closed, I turned to my elevator companion in shock and said, "Jesus Christ! They show stuff like that on public advertisement?"

She shrugged without looking up from her phone and responded, "Of course. Why?"

"Well, do you think that's such a good influence for kids? Did you hear what he just said?"

"No. Did he say something?"

"Yes, he did!"

She finally stopped fiddling with her phone and turned to me. "Look, Steven, check the archives. Nudity doesn't bother us anymore. We're grown up enough to handle anything these days."

"Well, don't you think that's a little inappropriate in a place where a kid could see?"

She rolled her eyes and responded sarcastically, "God, Steven, you're such a prude. People get to be proud of their bodies these days, and there's nothing wrong with educating five-year-olds about the human form. Geesh. After all, kids used to get in trouble for having sex videos on their phones, and we changed all of that years ago."

"Seriously?"

Condescendingly, she replied, "In case you didn't know, a kid committed suicide over it. That means it's very serious. Someone like you should know that." I held my tongue until the elevator reached my floor, and then I quickly got off without looking back, glad to be out of there. However, as the door was closing, the girl stuck her arm out to stop it and said, "Hey Steven, by the way ..."

I reluctantly turned around to address her. "Yes?"

She looked me up and down and said invitingly, "I could really use some cock right now. You wanna come up to my place?"

The bile shot up my throat so fast I barely could react in time. Trying to recover a bit, I said, "Ahem. Sorry about that. You know, I just remembered that I have to go over to the hospital tonight to ... have my mesentery checked out. Yeah, it's been overacting terribly the last few days."

She just shrugged and said, "Well, here, I'll text you my sex video, and you can call me whenever you want. Bye!"

I stood frozen until the door closed, and then I rushed down the hall to my apartment and jumped into the shower to burn off whatever outer layer of skin may have been involved in that encounter. I also thought to carefully delete the video she had sent me. I did it while looking at my phone through the lens of a paper towel roll—something we were taught in school as a trick to avoid burning your eyes while looking at an eclipse.

* * *

I was back at my desk, struggling to capture the essence of what I had witnessed recently. *What's the word I'm looking for? Dictionary. Here it is. "Histrionic: Garden-variety behavior employed to maximize self-gratification marked by verbalizing and actionizing lobotomized need for immediate attention; sign of healthy social development." Crap. All these terms do is give people excuses to behave like total assholes!*

Suddenly the manager was at my side and demanded suspiciously, "Steven, what are you doing?"

"I'm writing an op-ed about my elevator encounter last night."

He leaned down to scroll over my draft. "Here, let me see. Oh, Steven, you can't write this. That's body piercing shaming!"

I responded defensively, "So? Half the articles you guys produce here result in someone feeling bad about something."

"Yes, but there's good shaming and bad shaming. Good shaming is when it furthers our societal objectives, and bad shaming is ... Well, never mind that for now."

He quietly reached over and pressed delete, and my op-ed vanished instantly. Straightening up again, he said, "Listen, I need you back out on the streets right away. There's a gang holed up on the far side of town who are calling themselves 'The J Street Troubadours.' Go interview them and find out what their beef is and get them to sign a literary release."

I shook my head. "What? I thought you said that we wanted movie releases?"

"For gangs we get the literary rights as well; then they're turned into movies. For most other things, they go straight to movies—especially for huge tragedies like cave-ins, collapses, earthquakes, and supermarket shortages. And the standard turnaround time for all real-life-tragedy-to-movie events is thirty days, so if you don't have them sign the waiver up front, it just delays things and ruins our averages."

I just sighed and took the assignment and dutifully started on my way.

*

FOURTEEN

The gang was holed up in the poor sector of town, even farther south than the A-3 apartment buildings. Most people wouldn't even go into that neighborhood, and the ones who did never went back. Even the autonomous-driving taxi was programmed not to get too close to that area, and the superfluous driver told me I would have to walk the remaining several blocks to my destination.

When I got there, I found eight guys all hanging out and sitting on dingy, broken-down furniture. They seemed to be having a good day and were all smoking hand-rolled cigarettes. I had never seen one, having only read about them in the archives, and the smell made me slightly lightheaded but wasn't entirely unpleasant. Surveying the group as I walked up, I also noticed that they were surprisingly well-groomed. For all I knew, however, they could have been marauders from *The 57!*

The one who appeared to be their leader eyed me suspiciously and spoke first. "Let me guess, you're the asshole from the paper who's here to find out what we want?"

Not sure what I had gotten myself into, I said, "Well, sort of. Hi, I'm Steven."

He took a drag of his cigarette and didn't bother offering me his name in response. Instead he said, "Well, tell me this, *Steven*. What kind of question is that? Is it a crime to not want to be a part of that ape circus you call a civilization?"

The rest of the group eyed me aggressively, but I tried to stand my ground. "Well, technically I don't think so, but I should tell you that all scientific evidence indicates that smoking kills and robs. You should probably cut that out."

The guy next to him laughed sarcastically and exhaled in my direction. "Hey, at least it's not heroin!"

I laughed nervously in response. "Heh heh!"

Suddenly my phone went off. It was my manager: "Steven, did you get the story yet? We need something to fill in on the evening edition below the article about a one-legged orangutan who plays checkers."

"Um, not yet boss. I'm still working on the details."

"Crap. Okay, we'll run something else." As the call trailed off, I heard the manager say, "Peters, get over here. We're going to have to run that flesh-eating neurotoxin story instead."

As I turned back, the gang leader laughed at me and said, "You carry a phone?"

I nonchalantly shoved the device in my pocket and retorted, "You don't?"

He shook his head and responded, "It's just another method of control, man." He gestured to the guys sitting around him and added assuredly, "Besides, everyone I want to talk to is right here."

I had a brief flashback to the orphanage, and then I quickly said, "Well, I need it for my job. Anyway, what are you guys doing out here?"

He just shrugged coolly. "Living, man, just living, except that we refuse to do so as part of that façade you call life."

I took a step back and said, "I'm not sure it's a façade. We actually have a very rich, well-put-together society based on sound scientific principles." *Christ, I sound just like the director.*

The leader shook his head in response, and another remarked, "They got you lobotomized too, Holmes. You don't live in no scientific democracy. You're a money slave."

I shook my head and protested again, "Now, I don't think that's right."

One of the others piped in. "Are you kidding? It's all about the money. What do you think they're selling out there? I'll tell you— human capital. All the gender equality, environmentalism, and pet overpopulation issues are just about getting people to willingly hand over their insurance blood money. And because they never had to earn it in the first place, those fools have no real concept of what they're giving away."

The gang leader jumped back in and said definitively, "Steven, their only real goal is to get people to sell themselves. Count the number of things in the news tomorrow that are designed to cost you more money. And as long as you can pay, you have value, but watch what happens when you're no longer any good to them. They'll discard you like an old oil drum, and the minute you try to live your own existence, they'll crucify you for it."

His comment sent a deep shiver down my spine; then he stood up boldly and added, "So you ask what we want? Nothing. We just want to be left alone. We want to stick together as a band of brothers and not be forced to accept what they're selling. Print that in tomorrow's paper if you'd like, errand boy."

I shuffled nervously and said, "Oh, well, I don't know if I'll write anything about this. They may put me on another assignment. I was just supposed to come out and talk to you."

One of the other guys responded coldly, "It doesn't matter what you do. There is nothing sacred anymore, and everything you do will be trivialized and sold. Shit, even the universe is for sale these days."

Another chimed in. "Steven, that whole society is strung out just trying to make ends meet before they die, and while your precious government may leave a few coins to the next generation, they still own the purse."

Growing uneasy, I took a step back and said, "Yeah, I guess so. Anyway, is there anything else you guys want to say?"

The leader sat down, and everyone remained defiantly silent, as they were apparently done acknowledging my presence for the day. Just then, however, some tweaker came around the corner and grabbed the front of my shirt. He was blabbering something that I couldn't understand through foul breath, and he was spraying spit all over me. I took one step back and dropped him with a blow to the nose. I heard the sound of bone crunching, and blood splattered all down the front of his shirt as he covered his face and collapsed on the ground.

One of the gang members jumped up and exclaimed, "Damn, man, what'd you do that for?"

My adrenaline was still pumping, and I whirled in his direction aggressively. "What the hell are you talking about? That asshole got in my face!"

Shaking his head, the other said angrily, "He don't know any better! He's just strung out because he can't hack it on the streets. Man, you're the asshole!"

My phone went off again to the sound of the manager's voice. "Steven, get back to the center immediately! Cancel the interview and get back here!"

I backed away slowly from the group with my fists still clenched, but no one tried to pursue me, and the cabdriver was thankfully where I had left him when I returned. I was still coming down off my rush as we pulled away, but because of traffic delays, by the time we got back to the center I was fast asleep.

When I arrived back on two, the manager was deep in conversation with someone. "No, no. Remember: all of these problems require an economic-friendly solution. Look at this example. 'Feeling jet-lagged? Science proves that spa vacations reduce the painful effects from long travel.' See how it works? Christ, how do you think we get paid around here? Oh, and be sure to add that eating Pluto sushi fights winter blues."

I stepped up as the other walked away. "Hi, Boss."

I could tell that he was not happy with me. Frowning sharply, he said, "Oh, there you are. What the hell did you do today?"

Innocently, I said, "What are you talking about?"

"You knocked out a drug addict on the street!"

"So?"

"Steven, you can't do that. He can't be blamed for his addiction."

I shot back defensively, "Well, he can sure as hell be blamed for getting in my face!"

The manager waved his hand at me and said firmly, "No, no, it doesn't work that way. You can't just haul off and punch someone. Don't forget, you're luckier than him, so next time, try to show a little more compassion and understanding."

I was fuming again and replied indignantly, "What the hell for? That's how we used to settle disputes in the orphanage!"

"Well, out here we have a much more sophisticated way of doing things. You have to abide by a basic code which says that with people below you, you can do anything you want as long as you show pity while doing so. But physical violence is strictly out of the question. Don't forget that as a member of this staff, you have a reputation to uphold."

"What reputation?"

"Steven, the whole purpose of the government is to substitute the idea of right for that of violence—indeed, to place intermediaries between the government and the use of force."[7]

I kept getting the idea that these guys were all reading from an invisible script. Not knowing where that came from, however, all I said was, "So what do I do?"

"It's easy. If you want to cut in line in front of someone in a lower class than you, just act like you're too important to pay attention and then quietly step ahead of them. When they try to confront you, give them a look like you can't be bothered with their lower class and then look away." Winking at me in confidence, he added, "Trust me; they'll get the message."

I said disgustedly, "Sounds like a pretty shitty system."

He responded assuredly, "Actually, all properly functioning societies depend on passive-aggressive behavior as the cornerstone of civilized interactions. Without that, having a bunch of money wouldn't get you anywhere, because someone could always just break your neck for being an asshole to them. Now that, my boy, is bad for investments."

Finally relenting, I said, "Okay, okay."

The manager nodded affirmingly and added, "And don't forget that all homeless people have mental health disorders. For most of them, we show compassion and send them to the hospital. However, those guys out there refuse to go for some unknown reason."

Still defensive, I said, "Well, I didn't know. Sorry."

"It's okay. I have to remember where you came from, but maybe you should try not touching anyone until you learn a bit more. Now tell me, what did you find out?"

"They don't want anything, and they won't sign the agreement."

He was genuinely surprised by this. "Seriously? Don't they know that signing on with us is the only way they'll ever be able to contribute to our economy?"

I felt as if we were talking about two different groups. "How can *those guys* contribute to our economy?"

"Lots of different ways. Steven, you have to realize that for every story we write, it gets posted, then reposted, talked about, blogged, discussed over coffee via instant VR chat, and the like. Posting and reposting and then talking about what people say on the internet makes up a huge portion of our economy, and the magic of the world revitalization we created when we gave the internet to everyone is that we also gave them the ability to prosper like we do. Of course, not all countries follow the model as well as they should, but it's not our fault if they don't take advantage of the opportunities we've provided to them."

I was still entirely dubious about his theories on the economy but decided not to get into that discussion. Instead I said, "Well, those guys just want to be left alone, and I'm pretty sure they don't have any interest in the internet. They even laughed at me for carrying a phone."

The manager just turned up his nose and said, "Humph. Neanderthals."

"Actually, I grew up without a phone or the internet, and I didn't feel like a Neanderthal."

"Yeah, but that's different. You were an orphan."

"So?"

"So we are constantly operating on an internet bandwidth

shortage. I'm afraid that after providing internet to all of those remote villages in Africa, we simply couldn't get to you orphans."

Ignoring the gently condescending pity in his voice, I simply said, "Anyway, what were you talking about earlier?"

"Huh?"

"Something about spa-friendly vacations?"

Finally recalling, he shook his head and corrected: "No. Economic-friendly solutions."

I stepped back and said, "So we really are just using stories to sell things."

The manager shook his head definitively and responded, "Oh, no, not at all. Steven, look, our salaries are paid by ad revenue—and, well, by a small tax bundled with the internet usage fee—but it's only a fractional tax. Anyway, if people don't click on stories, we don't get paid, and those stories are only important because they help people feel more comfortable about the state of the economy."

Finally grasping the truth, I said, "Ah, then you're using the news to control the economy!"

He was momentarily flabbergasted and responded defensively, "Not even! Geesh, as if someone could actually do *that!* Steven, in a free market, humans still control the most important variable of all—individual will. They ultimately decide whether or not to make purchases, and we certainly can't force them to do so. That would be downright un-American!"

"But they pay us to tell them where to spend money."

Just then his watch beeped, and he responded distractedly, "Exactly. And don't forget science proves that sauna bathing is good for your health. Excuse me for a moment." He spoke into his watch. "Yep, we'll get a wrecker over there ASAP."

When he finished, I said, "Was there a crash?"

"No, but traffic is in trouble. Thankfully the Safety Patrol will take care of it shortly." He studied me for a moment and then added, "Say, why don't you do a ride-along."

"Seriously?"

"Sure. It'll be a good learning experience for you. I'll have the driver pick you up on the way, and then tomorrow, go back to that gang and get them to sign the release. I want it on my desk by midafternoon."

* * *

As the driver steered us along blissfully, I said, "Holy cow, your tow truck is manually controlled?"

He responded in a flat, emotionless tone, "Oh, yes. If it weren't, I couldn't do my job. I have to be able to put this thing anywhere on the roadway where it's needed, and this is our destination."

We pulled over on the side of the highway. We weren't blocking anything, but oddly enough, as soon as he put on his lights, everyone halted. Surveying the instantaneous jam, I said, "Huh. Look at that. Traffic completely stopped just because we're parked on the shoulder. But why are people stopping on the other side of the road as well?"

The driver said dully, "The Rubbernecking Program they put in cars these days works no matter which side of the road the accident is on."

"But there's a five-foot wall in the middle of the highway, and most of them probably can't even see what's over here."

Absently, he said, "It doesn't matter. They'll watch it on the news in their cars while they slow down to pass. There's also a prize for people going in the other direction who spot the accident."

"Let me guess—a vacation or a nonlobotomized child?"

"No, no vacation for those folks. Just the nonlobotomized child."

Watching the cars rapidly pile up, I said nervously, "Are you sure we should be doing this?"

He responded vacantly, "Doing what?"

"Causing a traffic pileup for no good reason?"

"Oh, it's for a good reason all right. Volume in the express lanes was too low earlier today."

"What? So we're sitting here to make people pay to use the express lane?"

"Yep."

"Well, are you sure that we should be doing *that?*"

He responded unenthusiastically, "Oh, it's nothing new. We stage emergency events all the time to be able to test the auto-pull-over function in vehicles, and there's certainly nothing wrong with that."

"Yeah, but we're forcing people to pay money to use a lane that they otherwise wouldn't have to if we weren't sitting here."

He nodded absently and said, "Yep. People just don't understand that the express lanes are good for them—always trying to save a buck for something or another, which I've never really understood. Fortunately most people don't drive these days—and a good thing too. The population is so high that if everyone drove, the roads would be completely clogged."

That was the second time I had heard that notion, and it finally dawned on me that autonomous vehicles were created to keep most people from wanting to use the road. *Keep that one to yourself, Steven. You don't know who this guy is.*

I changed tactics and said unassumingly, "Nice day today."

"Yep."

"What are you doing tomorrow?"

The driver furrowed his brow as he stared out the window and said, "What's tomorrow?"

"The day after today."

He tried hard to think on it. Finally he gave up and said lightly, "Oh, I guess I'll just wait and see what they have on the schedule. I generally just try to accept whatever the day has in store for me."

Holy shit, I'm riding with a lobotomy! I've got to find out what this is all about!

I sat up and said, "Ahem. So did you catch the soccer match last night?"

"No. I don't watch it. I prefer old-fashioned football, but it's gone now."

"Yeah, what a shame."

He shook his head vacantly, apparently able to recall some details from the distant past; then he responded, "Football fell apart when they took away the kickoff; then they took away tackling as well. After that, the game changed to no contact, and it wasn't worth watching anymore."

I said, "Well, thank goodness they used football to legalize sports betting before they got rid of it, huh?" He just nodded in an absently compliant manner, and I decided to probe further. "Hey, let me ask you this: if most people don't drive, why is traffic so horrible?"

"Because of all of the delivery vans. As you know, most people are scared to go outside these days, so things have to be delivered directly to them."

"Interesting. Say, do you know how much money the government will make on our little venture today?"

He just kept focusing straight ahead, despite the fact that we weren't moving, and responded, "Oh, I don't know. I'm not very good with money. The toll rate goes up based on volume on the road, but I don't know numbers."

"Is this all you do—drive a tow truck?"

"Nope. Other days they have me out making potholes."

"What for?"

"Well, roads are made of technology that repairs itself these days, so we need to make potholes to sell tires."

"That doesn't sound very fair."

He just shrugged. "I don't know anything about that, but I do know that it's good for the economy, and that's sure a good thing for us."

"Let me guess? You're in the B-class?"

He said unemotionally, "Actually I'm an A-8. Of course, ordinarily it's not necessary to send someone out to impede traffic. Typically people are so fixated on their own self-interest to get somewhere that they'll encroach on someone else's path of travel and cause an accident. That usually happens when two upper-class cars try to get each other to yield, and accident scenes usually take about six hours to clean up, even for minor ones."

Looking out at the mass, which was in fact not moving at all, I said, "Why?"

"Oh, the police have to diagram everything, fill out reports, and interview all of the people stopped on the road to see if they suffered any PTSD, and then everyone has to have enough time to take accident selfies."

Now seeing people who had, in fact, gotten out of their cars to locate the best spots to take selfies, I asked, "I wonder why they don't disable the Rubbernecking Program on cars?"

He shrugged vacantly and responded, "What for? The same thing used to happen anyway before the Rubbernecking Program came along. Of course, the tolls are only a small fraction of the people's insurance policies, but they allow us to do very useful things."

"Like what?"

"Like provide free literature to parents with new baby purchases."

Leaving that comment alone, I asked, "So what'd you do yesterday?"

He scratched his head momentarily. "I can't really remember. I was either driving this truck or making potholes."

"You're a lobotomy, huh?"

He looked at me and nodded dully. "Oh, I think so. I certainly fit the profile, and I have a scar on my head. See?"

He turned his mostly bald head my way, and there was indeed a very faint scar running along the side. I asked, "Wow, did that hurt?"

"I don't think so. If it did, I probably would have noticed."

"Does it bother you?"

He just shrugged again. "Why should it?"

"Well, you obviously have trouble remembering yesterday or thinking about tomorrow."

Looking forward again with his hands on the wheel, he responded plainly, "So? What's the big deal? I can only be in one day at a time, and I might as well make the best of it." That notion seemed very strange to me at the time, but he just shook his lobotomized head and added, "I've never really seen what all of the fuss is about. I do what I do, and that's just fine with me."

"Sounds like you're pretty content."

Placidly, he responded, "I sure am."

We sat there for another minute, and I finally said, "Wait, won't people be upset that there's no actual accident?"

Starting up the tow truck, the driver said, "Not anymore. Two SUVs up ahead just tried to get into the express lane at the same time, and now that's blocked too. Our job is over for today."

* * *

I had him drop me off at home, where I had a short fling to round out the evening and then went to bed. The next day, the manager completely forgot that he had sent me out with the tow truck driver, and I ran into him first thing in the morning as he was pacing frantically around. He demanded, "Did you get the releases?"

"Oh, I was just on my way back there. Sorry, I got a bit distracted with another project."

He retorted snidely, "Yeah, like getting laid?"

I didn't have the heart to remind him and simply said, "Well, yes. Sorry."

"Just get it done!"

Half an hour later, I was back in the trenches, pleading with them. "Look, why don't you guys join the rest of us? You'd be a lot happier, and there are plenty of goods to go around in society!"

The leader, who I now know was named Jim, said, "Let me tell you, Steven, the way they're running the instant gratification program out there is the worst thing you can possibly do to a human. It's breeding nothing but generations of marshmallow fluff. Nope. The only way to be truly free is to rely on no one but yourself."

"But don't you want to be comfortable?"

"Ha! What's that? Owning a bunch of trinkets so you can be like everyone else? Steven, tell me this—do you even like the people you're around every day?"

I took a step back and stammered, "Oh, well ... I don't really socialize that much."

"Let me guess. You screw a lot of girls, or guys, or whatever, and that's pretty much the extent of your friendships?"

I scratched the back of my neck and admitted, "Yeah, I guess that's mostly right."

"Steven, all of the people you despise are driving cars programmed to behave just like they do, and their opinions change every time they blink. Just think about that for a second." I realized that he was right and realized why I was never interested in any of the girls I was with for more than two seconds after the conversation started.

Tommy, at his side, changed the subject. "Yeah and watch what happens if anyone ever emerges to challenge them. The first thing they'll do is yank away all those lovely freedoms they pretend belong to the people." That comment seemed to jar something loose in my mind, and as I was mulling over the notion, he added sourly, "All we want is the freedom to be left out of their game, and I'll bet that someone like you comes to take that away from us one day."

I looked up at him reassuringly and said quickly, "Oh, don't worry; I don't think they mean to throw any of you in jail."

Jim blurted out sarcastically, "Yeah, because the jails are already full of *orphans*."

Shocked, I said, "What?"

Just then, my phone rang, and the manager said urgently, "Steven, get back here right now!"

My cabdriver was his own interesting study. We were in a large luxury model equipped with the Bump and Run Program, and he had great fun using it to prod our fellow travelers incessantly as we returned to the center. When we got there, I took a moment to regroup at my desk; then I found the manager and broke the news. "No, they won't be bought off, and by the way, they call themselves the White Stallions."

The manager was genuinely surprised at hearing that. "Really?"

"Yes, and they even have gang jackets embroidered."

The manager frowned and started pacing. "Well, that's no good at all. We've already called them the Troubadours. We've even made up a catchy slogan."

One of the kiss-ups said, "Boss, the name they're using is also the name of the characters on that show you watch—*Blue Street Blues*."

The manager stomped his foot and said angrily, "Christ, you're right! Oh, now that just won't do! Go back and tell them to change to the Troubadours!"

I responded, "I seriously doubt that they will."

The manager paced for a moment, stopped, and said firmly, "Well, we're sticking with what we've got. Besides, there's no way that we're going to waste a catchy slogan! Here's what we'll do: write a story about how the Troubadour gang is secretly trying to hide their identity by calling themselves the Stallions. Yes, that should do it!"

The ass-kisser said, "Brilliant!"

I frowned at the manager. "Wait a minute. Are we just making things up now?"

Defiantly, the manager responded, "Steven, we don't have to make up the news to use it however we want to. Now go and find the worst pictures of those guys you can so we can run them with the story."

I said, "I already tried to photograph them, but they wouldn't let me."

The idiot chimed in again. "I know! Let's get surveillance on them, and we can cut out little frames of the footage! That way we can show photos of them out of sequence and out of context and make them look totally ridiculous!"

The manager waved him off. "There's no need for that. The worst pictures we find of people already come from selfies. They're automatically uploaded to the NSA database, and I'm sure we have something on those guys. We'll check it out later today. Steven, just go back and tell them to cooperate with us so we can add their special skills to our collective economy."

I said, "Really?"

His eyebrow shot up. "Of course! How do you think we're going to get the movie rights if we don't?" Momentarily reflecting, he said, "Or maybe we should give them a television miniseries. That might do the trick."

Quasimodo next to me said, "Why don't we just throw the gang in prison?"

The manager responded automatically, "Oh, that doesn't work

anymore. It builds up too much of a following and just draws attention. Plus our prisons are already too full of"—he paused for a second—"... other people."

Walking away, I started to wonder whether there was some truth to what the gang was saying, and I also started to feel the gap widen between me and everyone else in that society. As I headed back out, I found myself muttering, "I wonder if I could do prison."

*

FIFTEEN

I had just returned to the center and was waiting for the manager, but when he came out of his office, he was interrupted by one of my colleagues who had a very important message to deliver. "Sir, sir, we have the most amazing discovery! They just came out with a new watch that can tell you when the person *next to you* has to go to the bathroom! And thank goodness, too, because people were either going too often or not enough, but now they can use the buddy system!"

"Good work, Thompson! Get a story out on that right away. Now, Steven, what did you find out?"

I shrugged and said, "Not too much. One of the gang members has a cold, but that's about it."

The manager's face quickly sunk, and he asked, "Is he social distancing?"

Unfamiliar with that ridiculous term, I said, "Uh, not as far as I can tell."

He quickly covered his mouth and backed away from me. "Mother of God! They're using germ warfare to attack us!" Suddenly suspicious, he lowered his head and proclaimed, "It's probably a retribution scheme for what we did to the Indians."

Confused, I said, "How's that?"

"Unmitigated bacteria—that's how we cleared the country for westward expansion. However, our immune systems can't handle it anymore because we're all dependent on Tamiflu and Z-packs. That gang could single-handedly wipe out all of the lobotomies, what with their tender conditions and all!" He turned to the guy next to me and urgently demanded, "Snivels, get a story out on that immediately and tell everyone that the CDC recommends double flu shots this year—and the next!"

Snivels ran off obediently, and I said, confused, "Why would they need double flu shots?"

The manager responded lightly, "Well, flu shots are sometimes less than half effective, but by having people get two of them, it'll be like double protection. Flu shots also delay the onset of Alzheimer's, and we make a good deal of money selling the vaccines, so it's a win-win for the economy as well. It's not quite as good as having a new pandemic to announce, but it's still good enough."

I frowned, but he didn't notice, as he was apparently struck with continued thoughts about how best to turn uncomfortable events into profits. He said curiously, "Oh, that reminds me, is the gang selling anything?"

I responded plainly, "Nope."

He clasped his hands behind his back and started pacing. "Well, that's no good. That's no good at all. You can't have revolution without products."

"How's that?"

He stopped and said, "Steven, by definition, anything that can't be bought or sold these days has no value in our economic scheme."

Without even thinking of the potential consequences, I offered, "Well, they are writing some pretty good songs."

He looked up hopefully and said, "Really? What do they sound like?"

"I recorded a few of them. Listen."

"♫♫♫ *Fuck the government! They'll sell you a batch of fries while they lobotomize, and then stuff their mattresses with your ashes ...*"

He raised an eyebrow and said, "Hey, that's a pretty catchy tune!"

"And here's the other. It's more of a country and western theme."

"♫♫♫ *Mamas, don't let your babies grow up without Ritalin. They'll dump you down a chute and think it's a hoot; oh, mamas, don't let your babies grow up without Ritalin ...*"

The manager was tapping along with the beat and smiling. "Say, that's great stuff! Get the rights for those as well! They're sure as hell a lot better than that crap the lobotomies listen to."

I said, "You're not worried about a revolt?"

He chuckled. "Come on, Steven, we haven't had a real revolution in this country since 1783! You think that's going to change just because of a song? Kids all listen to subversive music these days, but they have no idea what it means, and they can't remember anything the next day anyway. It's all designed to release energy—totally harmless."

I suggested helpfully, "Well, why don't we also do a biography about them while they're still living?"

He frowned sharply and replied, "Oh, we can't do *that!*"

"Why not?"

"Because those guys are heroin addicts, of course!"

I retorted, "Um, I've actually only seen that one guy who was probably using drugs."

The manager just shook his head knowingly and said, "Trust me; they all do it."

"Well, I've seen ... plenty of other people using drugs socially."

"Yes, but those are the ones we approve. Those guys out there are on street drugs, and don't forget, Steven, that heroin overdoses affect all of us."

"So?"

"So there is a huge risk that kids will idolize these guys, and you know what that will mean."

"Um, more overdoses?"

"Exactly, and that's a tremendous drain on the economy. Every time we lose a worker, it takes years to retrain another one. I tell you, in the dark times, we used to have a real opioid crisis. We knew that things were getting bad when librarians became first responders and we had umpires catching people before they jumped off bridges." Nodding assuredly at me, he said, "Now that's a far cry from what that Salinger fellow envisioned."

Struggling to follow his rant, I said, "What's a librarian?"

"Never mind. Check the archives. Fortunately, we keep plenty of spares around today."

"Spare librarians?"

"Heavens no! Spare people. Modern economies run best when we have approximately a 12 percent labor surplus."

Mildly shocked by his comment, I said, "Wait, that's 12 percent that can't find jobs?"

"Yep."

"So that's 12 percent who starve? What is that, twelve million humans?"

He waved a hand at me and said dismissively, "Approximately, but nobody really starves. Science proves that it's best to only eat at certain times of the day, so what you call starving we actually call maintaining good health."

Seeing that I was not overly convinced, the manager quickly added, "Besides, it used to be much worse. When we had robots running everything, unemployment was at 36 percent, but everything worked out just fine."

Exasperated, I said, "Fine for *who?*"

Unabashedly, he responded, "Well, at least for us. Oh, I admit that it's not an exact science, but we've gotten so many other things under control that we can still afford to fudge a little bit on the population."

It may have just been the gang's influence growing on me, but I reflexively challenged, "What have you gotten under control? From where I'm standing, it looks like everything is … a bit messy."

The manager finally sat down and wiped his brow. Assuredly, he replied, "It may appear that way to someone with your background, but it's all carefully controlled. Humans used to have to self-regulate in order to keep the climate in check. When temperatures rose, people would instinctively produce fewer offspring to help keep the earth in balance, and it worked quite well for a time. However, through aggressive emissions-reduction programs over the past hundred years, we have been able to keep global temperatures within acceptable limits despite rapidly increasing populations. That gives us the ability to produce as many humans as the economy needs and not worry about global warming. And let me tell you, people really love their naturally composting miniature virtual apartments!"

I raised a finger in further protest but then thought better of it and put my hand down. He clicked on without even noticing. "Yes, it's true that sometimes we do produce more lives than the economy needs, but those are just little externalities. The system itself works very well, and having a few extra lives that we can't fit into the scheme is actually a benefit for the overall economy. Besides, we take good care of them regardless."

I said, "You do? How?"

"Well, we feed everyone and give them space blankets, so without us, they'd definitely be in trouble."

I countered, "But those gang members seem to be doing fine without … us."

He waved a portentous finger at me and responded, "Oh, but that won't last. Steven, our economy binds us together and creates the very fabric of our society, and people who step outside of that never wind up doing well."

"Does that mean that we've set the boundaries too narrowly?"

"Not at all. The economy will take in almost anything as long as it has some value, and our incredible diversity these days is a testament to that. Look at it this way—two-thirds of our economy used to be based on domestic consumer spending, but now we're much more balanced. We are the world leader in the export of space blankets and space sushi. Thankfully, everything produced in space is reported in the export column, even if we buy it ourselves, but other countries love buying our products too."

I shook my head. "It still seems a bit ridiculous to make products in space."

He gave me a baffled look and shot back, "What are you talking about? It's ingenious! The lack of gravity on the moon and the planets makes workers more efficient. Plus we're making huge progress in terraforming!"

"Really?"

"Of course! We've been able to get a single raincloud to form in the atmosphere over Mars. Now, it did rain down sulphur that burned someone to death, but it was still a huge accomplishment."

"But you're still shipping materials and people all the way out there to make the same things you could make here."

He dismissed me with a hand and said assuredly, "Don't worry about it. It's still extremely efficient, and if you had an economics background, you'd get it. Anyway, in times of crisis, the government needs to step in and take money out of some policies and put it in others. That is from a brilliant economic principle discovered centuries ago."

I responded firmly, "Yes, and I understand that well enough. However, it seems like these days, instead of printing new money or raising interest rates, you just print more humans."

"Exactly. But don't worry; we take care of all of them, even your precious gang out there. Right now they're just the people the economy has to leave out for a while, and that's why we call them externalities. But the economy is a swinging door and always lets people come back in who went the wrong way." To emphasize his point, he added, "Didn't you read about all of the people in Hollywood that we kicked out and then let back in after a while?"

"No."

"Well, look it up. That certainly shows how kind we are to everyone!" Then, as if backtracking on everything he had just said, he waved a finger at me and scolded, "But Steven, you should be careful about romanticizing what they're doing out there. It's pure trouble; trust me on that."

Defensively, I said, "They don't seem to be doing any harm."

Astonished at the mere mention, he retorted, "You mean aside from attacking us with germ warfare?"

"Well ..."

He said firmly, "Look, that gang doesn't have anything to lose because they're not invested in anything. That's why all important aspects of society are linked to social standing. We can't just let anyone come in and disrupt what we have built. Steven, a great man once posted on the internet that poverty is just a state of mind. Now, unfortunately, the economy is too important of a thing to just risk on people knowing well enough to change their minds, so we simply have to put rational limitations in place."

Sensing that this conversation was going nowhere, all I could think to say was "So what do I do?"

"Keep trying to get them to come around and sign the licensing agreement, of course."

"And if they won't?"

He just shrugged. "Then they will come to an eventual end. That's just the way the economic machinery works."

Trying to mask my interest in their social statement, I said, "You mean that you're hoping they'll fail?"

He shot up with a wounded look. "Of course not! There's no economic benefit from failures! Well, that's not technically true. Seeing people fall from the top is a hoot and generates lots of money!" Then he quickly adopted a solemn expression and added, "But seeing someone fail who was already on the bottom is usually just sad and doesn't generate any readership."

Amazed at how easily he could shift from caring to uncaring about fellow humans, I just frowned at him, and he added quickly, "Look, don't worry about the intricacies of all of it. The takeaway is that we want everyone to do well."

"But not too well, right?"

"Right. Steven, the success of this country is really no big secret. All you ever have to do to stay ahead is handicap people a little bit— just enough so that they'll always be behind where you are."

"Kind of like dumping surplus crops on Latin America to keep them from gaining a competitive advantage?"

"Exactly. Well, no, of course not. We were trying to help them." Shaking his head in disbelief, he said defensively, "Geesh, Steven, since when is giving food to hungry people a bad thing?"

*　*　*

The longer I spent in that society, the more of a stranger I felt to it. I didn't even have the interest that night to call up a date. Instead I went home and was back to see the gang early again in the morning, where I asked them the very question the manager had posed to me and got an earful. They had either stumbled upon my college project or just felt the same way I used to. After that, I stopped trying to toe the party line but was still glad for the assignment. That ragtag gang was, in fact, the only group of genuine people I had met in the entire city.

One evening, I sneaked back into the newspaper and kept looking through the archives. Sure enough, there was a big hero story about the guy who was burned up by acid rain on Mars. The article concluded like this: "And looking down on us from the clouds, he'd say, 'Be safe—wear a helmet rated to prevent injury from acid rain.'"

After that, new sulfur-safe helmets hit the market on Earth, and there were fifty additional stories about the persistent dangers of acid rain caused by excess buildup of lemon rinds at the bottoms of landfills. That campaign helped sell millions of helmets for acid rain injury prevention, and through new legislation, all lemons had to be processed through the particle collider. The price of lemon juice went up overnight to $435 an ounce.

Eventually the manager grew tired of my continued failures to get the gang to come around, and I sensed that he might pull me from the story. I went back one last time, but they still weren't budging. Seeing that I didn't have any other purpose to be among them at the time, I bade them all a peaceful farewell, but I was secretly contemplating stopping back by later on to hang out with them some more.

Back at the paper, I tried to deliver the news as gently as possible. "Um, Boss, the gang won't agree to sell the rights to their story to us. They say no way, no how, and they've applied for a trademark for their name as well, claiming that they used it before the television characters came around."

He barely seemed affected by my presence. Unfazed, he said, "Oh, okay, Steven. Thanks, and good work for today."

I walked away in a cloud of confusion, but an hour later, there was a buzz in the office as one of the functionaries excitedly ran in. I looked up from my terminal and said, "What's going on?"

He responded wildly, "The leader of that gang has been assassinated and the others all disbanded!"

I shot up from my chair and said, "Who would do such a thing?"

The manager appeared from around the corner, as if on cue, already shaking his head in regret. "Oh Steven, the world is unfortunately full of mentally ill individuals who are subject to snapping at any moment. Yep, there are religious fanatics everywhere. We are, in fact, inundated by extremists in sleeper cells we just don't know about."

My bullshit meter pegged right at that moment, and I challenged, "Oh, really?"

The manager replied assuredly, "Yes, but it's not such a bad thing that they're gone. That gang was causing terror all over town."

Shocked at the mere suggestion, I said, "What? Where? I didn't see them do anything to anyone. They just wanted to be left alone."

The manager responded compassionately, "Well, it may have seemed that way to you, but you probably got too deep into the story and lost your own perspective. For the rest of the world, that gang was pure terror. Look, here's a survey taken of a thousand people. Terror. See? And here are the fifteen expert articles that followed."

What a fucking sham. I felt like decking him right there.

He added, "Anyway, it's better off now that they're gone. Look at the negative effects they were having on our people. These were Multiverse posts sent out right after the news came down: 'I hope that they rot in hell!' 'Death is too good for them!' Et cetera."

Still reeling from the shock, I said, "Well, there must have been some people out there who were saying positive things? I mean, the gang was just trying something different."

He conceded momentarily, "Oh sure, there were a few outliers who supported them, but look at this. This is a word cloud of the internet comments."

"What's a word cloud?"

"It shows an amalgamation of what people are saying on a subject. It groups some things that unimportant people are saying in smaller words, and the things that all the important people are saying in bigger words. Look here—the biggest message that everyone was saying about that gang was 'I hope that they rot in hell!' See, the words are bigger, so you know that's the most important message."

I was still fuming and challenged, "Are you sure that you didn't just make those words bigger to support your viewpoint of the situation?"

The manager put on an air of surprise and responded defensively, "Of course not, Steven! I don't get to make decisions like that. Someone upstairs does. Besides, it's all processed by AI."

"What does that mean?"

"It means that it's automatically valid." The manager turned to the guy next to me and suggested innocently, "By the way, Jackson, why don't you go back and round up the rest of the gang and see whether they're ready to sell the rights to their story. And Steven, we have an assignment about a three-legged service dog on Pluto for you to work on."

Not knowing what else to do, I quietly went back to my desk. Later that day, Jackson ran in with papers in hand and exclaimed, "Boss, Boss, it worked! They all signed contracts right away!"

After that, the story was out on the news board revealing one gang member's "confession" about how much they wanted to be just like the guys on the television drama, and predictably, the ratings for the show went through the roof. Over someone's radio playing in the office a few days later, I heard, "And new at number one is the hit song 'Lobotomize with a Side of Fries!'"

Fucking bastards. One of the girls next to me spontaneously pepped up and suggested, "Hey, let's do an article explaining what that song is really about! I think it's a period piece about the Mars colonists before we gave them jobs making space blankets!"

The manager patted her on the head and said, "Great idea, and spot-on interpretation of the lyrics! Let's run that immediately!"

It would be fair to describe my mood at that point as homicidally disenchanted. The manager eventually took notice and called me into his office. Closing the door, he said, "Steven, what's wrong? You seem a bit down today."

After being punished with fifteen pet-in-space stories, I didn't dare open my mouth. He guessed the source of my ire anyway and offered consolingly, "Look, I know that you miss talking to those guys, but it's much better now that they're gone."

Still wounded, I sat down numbly and said, "I just don't understand what happened."

He just shook his head regrettably and responded, "Oh, the gang eventually became radicalized, and when that happened, the formerly tight-knit group was bound to fall apart."

"What does 'radicalized' mean?"

"Look at the dictionary I gave you. In layman's terms, it means that they started doing things that we couldn't tolerate anymore. But Steven, as you know, the most stable economic systems in the world, including ours, are configured of a small number of people at the top who control most of the resources, with everyone else following rationally determined limitations to help the economy churn along. Our economic model also requires that those who can't adapt to fit into the system be weeded out, just like a bad part in a machine. Science has, in fact, proven that this is the only way to keep our economic miracle going."

I was too tired to get into a fiscal debate with him. Remembering the leader fondly, I lamented, "It just doesn't seem fair that the guy died just for being who he was."

The manager responded decisively, "Oh, that's not what killed him."

"It isn't?"

"No, the thing that killed him was trying to go it alone."

"He wasn't alone. He had seven brothers."

Assuredly, he said, "It may have seemed like that, but they were alone as well. See, Steven, some people suffer from mental infirmities which make them believe that they don't want to be part of our group, but humans are social creatures, and once you stop being part of our group, that's usually a sign that you're heading off a deep end. Now *that's* what really killed that guy."

"But I thought that he was killed by a religious fanatic."

"Well, there's that part too. But if he hadn't done ..." Then he pepped up and changed the subject. "Oh, don't worry, Steven; it doesn't affect you! Hey, why don't you check your phone and go out and get laid. That might cheer you up! And take the rest of the day off, why don't you. On me!"

Nearly numb at that point but operating on some kind of automatic instinct, I walked back to my desk and sat down. I stared at the blinking cursor for several minutes and then realized that my mind was completely disconnected from all of this madness.

I shut down my terminal and walked out for the day. I didn't dare go home–which would have only depressed me more. Instead I stepped out into the fresh air and walked around aimlessly, careful to stay away from any crowded locations. I watched and studied people from afar, trying to come up with some kind of greater understanding for the society I was supposedly a member of. The gang leader's words kept running through my head, and I wondered whether I would eventually share his fate.

How can these people just swallow everything that is put in front of them? Like that tow truck driver. He seemed like a normal human but couldn't question ... A cloud of opportunity suddenly opened over my head. *Holy shit! I can go around and find out how many of these people are really lobotomized! That might give me a huge clue as to what I'm up against! Why didn't I think of this sooner?*

Later that day, I found a science equipment resupplier and purchased a magnifying glass eyepiece and a high-power handheld magnifier. The next day, I went back to work to get to know my colleagues better.

I was the talk of the office that day. "Ooh, is that a new VR lens?"

"Not exactly. Hold still. I think you have something in your hair."

"Oh, thank you!"

My other experiments that day were eventually interrupted by an offsite assignment. A nerdy-looking fellow was addressing the manager. "Sir, we have the most amazing discovery!"

"What is it now?"

"Gingivitis is linked to Alzheimer's!"

Mildly annoyed, he said, "Yes, Poindexter, we already know that."

Excitedly, Poindexter responded, "No, no, look at *this!*"

The manager studied the report carefully; then suddenly his

brow rose and his face broke out in red splotches. Looking up at Poindexter, he exclaimed, "Holy pulverized cow! Excellent work!" In his excitement, he forgot who he was talking to, and a congratulatory pat on the back gave Poindexter his own field trip for the day—to the hospital.

The manager looked down at him on the floor and said apologetically, "Oops, sorry about that!"

Poindexter groaned obediently and replied, "*It's okay, sir.*"

The manager put his hands up to his face and exclaimed, "Shit, I completely forgot that you came over from the lab!" He whirled around and said excitedly, "I need someone to look into this! Hey, Steven, get over to the hospital ASAP, and while you're at it, help this guy down to an ambulance."

Confused, I said, "Why am I going to the hospital?"

The manager exclaimed, "Tell them to add 'My First Toothbrush' to the memoirs and count the number of people over there who have Alzheimer's!"

"How?"

He rolled his eyes and said definitively, "Look at their *gums*, of course. Christ!" Glancing one last time at our fallen comrade on the floor as he walked away, the manager observed, "I wish they'd send me more people with *hard* science backgrounds."

* * *

At the hospital, I was directed up to the third floor, where the man in charge whom I was supposed to speak with was in the middle of performing his rounds with the new medical students. His discourse continued: "This one looks like another case of hyperwrinkleism. As you all recall, skin naturally swells in old age, and if it doesn't, it is a clear case of hyperwrinkleism. Now what's the treatment for that? Judy?"

She replied unsurely, "Um, Botox?"

"Exactly. Now gather in close and look at how the condition manifests itself in a real-life subject."

One of the curious initiates said, "Doctor, how old is this particular patient?"

"Thirty-four. That is the mean age when this condition starts to set in."

The doctor finally noticed me standing uncomfortably behind the group and turned to address me while the students leaned in to pinch the patient's wrinkled flesh. "Yes? What do you want?"

I said, "I was told to check people's gums for Alzheimer's. Here's the letter from the manager at the newspaper."

He scanned it rapidly and then, looking up excitedly, said, "Sweet Jesus! We need to get toothbrushes into kindergarten classes, ASAP! And let's add my first toothbrush to the memoirs!"

One task down. While he ran around frantically, I started performing my examinations.

I spotted an elderly gentleman in one of the corner beds and gingerly approached him. He seemed to be resting comfortably and smiled as I grew nearer, and I said politely, "Good afternoon, sir."

"Hello there, young fellow."

"How are you today?"

"Oh, just fine."

"Um, have you been having any recent memory problems?"

"Nope. Not that I can recall."

"Oh, that's good. If you don't mind, though, I need to check you for Alzheimer's. Can you open your mouth, please?"

By the end of the day, I had covered nearly the entire floor. Walking out, I spotted a young boy on the other end of the ward. I was pretty sure that there was no use in even screening him, but I stopped by his bed anyway just to be thorough. With a warm smile, I said, "Hey, little trooper. How are you doing today?"

He was white-faced and huddled under the blankets and responded meekly, "I'm scared. I broke my leg."

I tried to be as consoling as possible and said, "Oh my, that's terrible!"

"There was a big fire in our apartment building, and I jumped out of the window to get away from the flames."

I sat down on the edge of the bed and responded reassuringly, "Well, that was certainly a very brave thing to do! Where are your parents?"

He shook his head despondently and said, "They didn't make it."

"What about your brothers and sisters?"

Pulling the blankets up tighter, he said, "I don't have any. I'm all alone!"

Smiling warmly, I patted the sheets and said, "Don't feel bad; I'm alone too. But your leg will heal up soon enough, and I'm sure they'll take good care of you while you're here. Have you talked to any of the nice doctors and nurses?"

He responded hollowly, "Yes. They come by to check on me every so often, and I heard one of them saying that I'd be released in a few weeks."

I smiled again and said, "Well, that's certainly good news! I have to go now, but I'll come back just as soon as I can and check on you. Hopefully I'll see you again before you get out!"

I had another date for that night. We finished up back at my apartment, but I could already tell that this wasn't going to be a long relationship. She came out of the bedroom and said, "Steven, Sophia tells me that your hangers aren't arranged properly. Wait; she just reminded me that there's a great article on this, and I'll give it to you tomorrow at work."

I sighed and headed to the couch. She sat down next to me and discreetly stretched her arm up, lighting tapping herself on the shoulder. Seeing this, I pleaded, "Come on, don't turn on your VR contacts!"

I presume that she rolled her eyes at me as they disappeared into the ether, and she said dismissively, "Steven, there's nothing going on right now, so why shouldn't I?" From whatever alternate reality she was entering, she added, "Hey, by the way, have you seen that new article about the right types of stories to read while you're in the bathroom? I had no idea that I was doing it wrong all these years!"

I took the opportunity of her distraction to get up and politely excuse myself, and then she blurted to me while still engrossed in her contacts, "If you're going to the bathroom, be sure to take that magazine on the counter. It's on the approved list."

I came back with my magnifying glass tucked quietly behind me, but she wouldn't have noticed anyway. She had apparently turned off her contacts and was fixated on a news break on the television: "Scientists announce that ninety-seven more planets have been discovered with two suns orbiting them, just like Luke's home planet of Tatooine!"

She leaned gently into my arm and closed her eyes. Dreamily, she said, "Oh, wouldn't it be great to live on a planet with two suns? Then I wouldn't have to turn over to get a tan!" I pulled the magnifying glass out of my back pocket just as the movie started back up.

Her eyes were still closed, but as the dialogue resumed on the television, she remarked praisingly, "Don't you just love this movie? Such emotion! It's sure to be an instant classic!" Then she yawned and curled further into me. I took the opportunity to maneuver the magnifying glass into my arm behind her and moved my other hand up. She moaned softly, "Oohh, that's nice! I love it when you play with my hair!"

I raised the magnifying glass and said in a low voice, "Just hold still."

*　*　*

The manager was waiting for me the next morning as usual and said eagerly, "What'd you find out?"

"Apparently everyone at the hospital over the age of sixty has Alzheimer's."

"Mother of God! This could be an epidemic! Quick, type up your results so I can get them out immediately!"

"What's the rush?"

He responded firmly, "Steven, running a scientific democracy is very difficult, and we have to latch onto developments as soon as they occur. Then we run a series of stories to support the new idea and generate public approval for an action plan. There may also be naysayers out there, and if so, we have to run separate articles condemning conspiracy theorists and then banning them from the Multiverse, but once the appropriations have been approved, we can move on to the next topic."

I took a step back and said accusingly, "So this *is* all about tricking people into letting you take money out of their insurance policies?"

The manager responded defensively, "Not at all! Steven, the process merely reflects the robust democracy we live in and the steps necessary to convince people that we know what's best for them. Oh, and anyway, these things all result in very minor withdrawals from the insurance system, so they're really nothing to worry about."

As I was walking away, he added, "By the way, they're still trying to fix your computer. Apparently you had pushed the override button too many times. Use Sally's terminal instead, and when you're done, I have a new assignment for you. An old man just died."

I turned around puzzled and said, "That doesn't sound very interesting."

"Don't worry about that. I need you to talk to everyone and gather information about the family members, their finances, whether he left a will, inheritance details, et cetera. Here's the address."

I took the paper from him and asked, "What does the apartment building look like?"

"It's not an apartment. It's a house—1117 Valley Drive. It's in the next town over. Well, technically it's on the edge of this town now, but it's still pretty far."

"Um, okay. Can I get there in a cab?"

"Sure. It's a long ride, but you'll make it if you leave first thing in the morning."

On the way out that day, I ran into the director, and he said cheerfully, "Hi, Steven, how's it going?"

"Fine."

"How's dating?"

"I'm done with it."

"Why?"

"I keep running into a lot of pretty, stupid people. They're gorgeous, but simply idiots."

He briefly put a hand on my shoulder as we walked and replied encouragingly, "Don't say that!"

"No, it's true. I think I like prostitutes better. At least with them you know up front what they really want out of the deal."

He nodded as we rounded the corner and said, "Well, I was young once and can certainly understand your difficulties with women. Most of them will wind up as prostitutes eventually."

I looked at him in astonishment and asked, "Really?"

"Sure, or doing porn. We made too many pretty people, and I'm afraid that there's an incredible surplus these days. And with nothing for them to do with all that beauty, we usually wind up putting them through the cycle."

"Cycle?"

"Modeling first, followed by seminude and stripping, followed by hooking or porn. It works very well. Most of them are having sex for money by age thirty-five. Of course, with the dismal performances at work, it's always good for them to have a side-hustle to help make ends meet anyway."

I looked at him skeptically and said, "That hardly sounds like gender equality."

"Oh, it applies to all sexes."

"Well, I don't remember seeing any males at the brothel."

He stammered for a minute. "Oh, well, that's just because most women won't pay for sex and gay men just go to the bathhouse. But equality of opportunity is really the important part."

Returning momentarily to the question of the companions, I said, "So why do you keep making more people? Or beautiful ones, that is?"

"Easy. It's good for business. Remember: one beautiful person suffering can attract a million lobotomy readers, but a million unattractive dead people doesn't make for a story." He patted me lightly on the back as we parted and said, "Anyway, good luck tomorrow!"

*

SIXTEEN

The ride took only two hours, and the first hour and a half of that was just getting out of town and past all of the delivery trucks. Once we hit the open road, however, it was smooth sailing, and I could smell country air for the first time since leaving the boys' home. I rolled down the window and stuck my head out, and the cabbie looked back at me as if I were nuts.

As we were driving down the highway, I glanced over to the right and saw a single telephone wire following us the entire way. We came over a ridge, and on the other side, about a quarter mile off the highway, sat a lone house up on a hill. The wire followed us all the way up the drive, and an ambulance crew was leaving as we pulled up.

I climbed out of the cab and signed for the bill with my thumb, thankful to avoid using retinal payment technology and leaving an involuntarily excessive tip. When I turned around, I saw a young girl standing out front. Despite her youth, it was obvious that she carried a heavy weight on her shoulders, but she appeared dutiful and purposeful in her actions nonetheless.

Her wizened eyes tracked me suspiciously as I walked the rest of the way up the drive. As I got closer, she put her hands on her hips and offered a curt greeting. "Can I help you?"

She was clad in plain-looking clothes—just jeans and a comfortable T-shirt. Nevertheless, I was instantly captivated by her beauty and nearly forgot why I was there in the first place. "I'm, er, I was supposed to … Hi, I'm Steven."

Her annoyance was evident. "Hi, Steven. Emily. The original question is still on the table."

"Oh ... he he! That. I was sent out here by my boss at the newspaper to cover the story of ..." *Jesus, I feel like an ass.*

She gave me a look of sheer annoyance and demanded, "My father's death?"

Sheepishly, I admitted, "Yes."

"Typical of those assholes to send one of their vultures out here." Motioning me toward the house irritatingly, she said, "Come on, then, and let's get your scavenger hunt over."

I scampered after her apologetically and responded, "No, I'm not. I mean, look, I'm sorry to be bothering you. I can certainly come back a later time. Or ... Are you doing okay?"

She stopped on the porch and sighed. Turning back toward me, she said, "Yes. I'm sorry. I don't mean to be short. You don't look very sinister, and I have no reason to be like that with you. It's just that I spent the last hour fighting with the ambulance crew."

"About what?"

Flashing her anger, she said, "About them not feeding my father into a furnace so that the center can save on energy costs!"

I nearly choked and responded quickly, "Excuse me, I must have swallowed a bug. So you're going to ... or ... Did they take him somewhere else?"

Defiantly, she said, "Nope. We're going to bury him in the backyard tomorrow, and my mother is paying her final respects right now. She'll sit with him tonight, and then tomorrow we'll dig a grave and bury him on our own property."

"That sounds ... nice." *Christ, Steven, you get stupider by the word.*

Emily finally said cordially, "Please, let me stop being rude. Would you like to come inside for a drink?"

"Oh, I don't, I mean, I don't usually, or I try not to ..."

She cocked her head in response to my continued awkwardness and said, "Water, Steven. We have cold water. And ice too, if that's your thing."

I finally loosened up and tried my best to discard the village idiot routine. "Oh, that sounds great!"

Emily turned to open the vast front door, and I politely followed. It was completely silent and peaceful inside, and I surveyed the interior of the house as we walked. The woodwork was more beautiful than I had ever seen, and old family portraits hung throughout the halls, some of them appearing to be generations old. Giant antique furniture also stood everywhere—a stark contrast to the preassembled, cookie-cutter furniture in most of the apartments in town.

I finally said, "This place is incredible!"

As we reached the living room, Emily replied, "Thank you. This house has been in our family forever. Till the day he died, my dad did everything in his power so we could keep it, but the damn taxes keep going up. Fortunately, we're pretty self-sufficient, and most of what we eat comes from here."

"You farm?"

"Yep. We have cows and chickens and grow our own corn and soybeans. And fruits and vegetables too."

"Do you have to ship the livestock away to go through the particle collider before you eat them?"

Shaking her head in disbelief, she said, "Are you nuts? We eat *real* food here. Most of the livestock we of course sell, and it becomes pureed whatever, but we save the best ones for us."

I was suddenly dreaming of steak, and I think my mouth was visibly overrunning with drool. I wiped my face on my sleeve and tried to recover, hoping she wouldn't notice, and then I asked, "But how do you eat that with a screen in your esophagus?"

Emily looked at me as though I were crazy and responded, "Who the hell would ever have something like that put into them?"

I laughed and just shook my head. "Frankly, I have no idea, but that's what they do in the city!"

Emily rolled her eyes. "Oh, that place."

"What? Do you get there much?"

She responded lightly, "I used to go in from time to time, but I hardly ever do anymore. Our house was previously part of a neighboring city, but brick by brick, that whole town was relocated into the center. We're the last house out here, so they eventually just annexed us into your town."

Feeling guilty, I said, "Oh, well it's not really mine. I just got there myself from ... Hey, but you were born there, right?"

"Oh, sure. In the lab, like everyone else, but Dad paid extra so I didn't have to be lobotomized. Our family has never done anything truly unique, and we were on the random lobotomy list, so when my number came up, he spent nearly everything to spare me. After that, my parents homeschooled me out here."

"How do you know you weren't lobotomized?"

I could not have possibly asked a more ridiculous question, but Emily didn't seem to notice. She just pointed and said, "That certificate of nonlobotomization hanging over the fireplace."

"Oh, wow! That's nice!" I was aware they issued those to people who actually paid to get out of the lobotomy lottery, but I had never seen one and walked over to study it. Turning around again and trying to keep the conversation rolling, I blurted out, "Um, did you get your tubes tied?" *Great question, Casanova—skipping right past third base.*

She didn't notice the inappropriate nature of that query and simply said, "Oh, sure, you can't get out of that, but my dad did talk them into making the technician come out here to harvest."

"Do they bring you your drugs?"

"Nope. Dad paid extra so I wouldn't have to take any."

"Wow, you're really a lucky girl ... um, woman! Say, how old are you?"

"Twenty-three." I had only met one girl younger, at the brothel. By that point, Emily was still on full duty and obviously not as interested in me as I was in her. Without further pleasantries, she just turned and started straightening things up a bit.

Finally, I asked, "So I guess you don't get out much?"

She looked up and said plainly, "Sure, I get out of here all the time. However, the city is not the only place to find adventure."

Continuing to scan the room, I noticed an old phone on the desk in the corner and said excitedly, "Hey, a landline! I haven't seen one of these since …"

She looked up and cocked an eyebrow. "Since what?"

"Oh, my, um, grandmother's house." I quickly added, "She's dead now."

"I'm sorry to hear that. And your parents?"

"Dead as well. It was … a car crash. Long time ago. I was raised by my grandmother … and she's dead too."

"Yes, I heard you say that part. Sorry to hear about your losses."

"Yes, I was too. I mean …" I suddenly realized my rudeness and dropped my voice to a whisper. "Hey, are we disturbing your mom by talking in here?"

"Oh, no. She's fine. She's just sitting vigil with him, as he would have wanted."

"Am I keeping you?"

"No. I said my goodbyes before all of the riffraff started." Bitterly, she added, "We wouldn't even have had to bother with any of it, except that my mother called one of our customers to tell them we'd be a little late delivering crops this fall, and the next thing I knew, the ambulance henchmen were here."

"Oh."

Appearing to remember her manners, she offered, "If you want to talk to her, I can go and get her."

"Heavens no! I wouldn't dream of doing that!" I was still taking in everything in the living room and said, "Hey, where's your television?"

"We don't have one." That floored me. I had never seen a house without a television and kept searching around with my eyes as if she might be mistaken.

She stood there politely, waiting for me to finish my inspection, but I could sense that she was restless. Finally, she said, "Look, I don't know you, but I need to get out of here for a while. You wanna go for a drive? You can keep asking questions while we're on the road."

"I, um, I didn't bring my car."

Emily said, "Don't worry; we have one here."

We headed out back to a stand-alone garage. It was stocked with more tools than I had ever seen, and most I couldn't even name. There was a giant tractor in one bay and an old truck in another. I couldn't even recognize the model of the vehicle and said incredulously, "Where on earth did you get that truck?"

She glided her hand proudly down its side and responded, "My dad built it! It's an old gasoline/electric hybrid, and it doesn't have any of the messy gadgetry or autonomous features of newer cars. He showed me how to operate it. Climb in."

We set out on the road, and amazingly there were no other vehicles that far out—just glowing sun and open space as far as we could see. And she was right; there were no electronic gadgets in the truck—nothing but a clock and some instruments, and we didn't even have a radio to listen to. Instead we just cranked the windows down and let the wind blow in.

I stole a glance at her while she drove. She wasn't smiling, but she looked more at ease than when I first met her. For my part, cruising down that road at highway speed with the wind whipping by was as close to normal as I had felt in a long time—maybe in forever.

Eventually we came upon an abandoned parade ground and parked. We got out and explored a little, and Emily had obviously been here before. She said, "This used to be the center of my town. As you can see, everything else is gone now except for these ramparts. This is where they used to hold democracy demonstrations, but I guess they haven't used it for a while."

"What are those buildings on either side of the grounds?"

"Bathrooms." We walked past them. One door read, "Men." The building on the other side read, "Women." Emily said, "They still maintain this place even though no one uses it. Some poor lobotomy has to drive out here every week to clean and replenish the supplies."

I just stood there in awe and observed, "Huh. So they had separate bathrooms back when they still had democracy?"

She laughed for the first time since I met her, and then she just smiled at me, and I ducked my head sheepishly, trying to hide my own grin. The sun started to dip behind the horizon while we meandered, and she continued. "Sure, I could have gone somewhere else, but when I got old enough, I realized what my parents were trying to do. I decided to stay home and help out in any way I could, since it seemed the least I could do for what they did for me."

I asked casually, "Pretty much a homebody, huh?"

Emily retorted, "Staying home doesn't mean I'm a homebody. It was just something I had to do, and I'm afraid that one day it will all come to an end. Now that he's gone, it will be very hard for mom and me to keep it up. She's pretty frail these days."

"You guys manage the place by yourselves?"

"No. We have a crew of workers who come out every day, but it's still up to us to keep orders going and keep everyone in line."

"Sounds like a tough life."

"It is, but it's our farm. Now it's just going to be a little harder without ..."

Emily grew silent for a good while, and I didn't dare intrude. She absently kicked a stone with her foot, lost in a thought somewhere. Finally she looked up and politely smiled, saying, "Hey, enough about me. What about you?"

I could scarcely remember who I was or where I had come from before we met, and I just stared at her blankly for a moment. I quickly snapped out of it and said, "Oh, I'm staff writer at the newspaper. Actually, I guess you could call me a mobile correspondent."

We started walking again, and she replied, "That sounds interesting."

"Yeah, some of it is. It's hard to maintain focus with all of the distractions around. You know, lobotomies are everywhere, and you never know if you're talking to a guy or a girl, what with the way people look these days."

She laughed again, and I redirected the conversation. After that, she took over and just talked for a while. Emily seemed to welcome the chance to muse a little bit, and I got the sense that she didn't get much time to just let her thoughts out when she was busy working at home. Frankly, I could have been listening to her read off the names of chemical components in a sludge factory and I would have been totally content.

She continued. "And I don't understand this whole equality battle. You and I are different, and that's okay with me. I like being a woman, and I like the differences between the sexes. If there is a strange noise at night, I don't want to be the only one who goes down to check on it, and I certainly don't want to go out on a date with someone wearing a matching onesie."

By then I hadn't even noticed that the sun was down. She finally did and said, "Hey, what time is it?"

I came out of my trance again and replied, startled, "Oh, I don't know."

She smiled and grabbed my arm. "Look at your watch, silly!"

"Shit, forgot I had the thing on." I looked down at the device, and it was glowing the color of an angry rooster.

She exclaimed, "Wow, great colors!"

I quickly said, "Oh, yeah, it just randomly does that." I shook it furiously to try to get it to go back to neutral, but my efforts had no effect. Finally I stopped and looked at the face. "Um, it says eight thirty."

"Well, it's too late to go back. They blocked the road just this side of our house because of the Heinz 57 incident. I guess they don't want traffic on the roads at night. Let's camp out."

I was shocked at how independent she was and that she wasn't concerned about being alone with me in the countryside. However, Emily went to the bed of the truck, and it was loaded with blankets and everything we needed to stay cozy and comfortable for the evening.

Eventually we settled in and lay there looking up at the sky. In the clearness of a country evening, I could finally see the flashing neon signs from the moon. At one point, she rolled a little my way, and I was completely intoxicated by her presence. Fighting against my natural inclinations, I decided to maintain the platonic pleasance of our company thus far, assuming she would let me.

I cleared my throat nervously and said, "Um, Emily, I'm having a really nice time, but I think that we should take things slow and ..."

She didn't even break her gaze from the stars, but she did let out a healthy laugh. When she settled down again, she answered, "Steven, I just met you. I'd like to get to know you first before I decide if I want to share the most intimate thing that two people can do."

I flashed back to a week ago and realized that she and I might have *slightly* different definitions of what "most intimate" really meant. Instead she moved a little closer and said, "Here, just lift your arm up." I did, and she nestled on my chest and kept looking at the stars. Our hearts and breathing eventually synchronized, and I believe that in that moment, I fell instantly in love.

For a long while, we just lay there listening to the night and the sound of our breathing. She finally broke the melodic silence and asked, "Have you slept with a lot of women?"

"Some."

"Prostitutes?"

I leaned my face toward her a little and said, "You know about those?"

"Of course. Who doesn't?"

I put my head back down and replied, "Oh, I did that once. Someone dragged me there."

She took a deep breath and sighed. "That must be a tough life. I'm lucky I didn't have to sell my body to survive." With that, she snuggled closer.

Lying there peacefully with her before we fell asleep, it seemed like the past however many days of waking nightmares I had experienced in that city were washed away and that I had been baptized as a human again.

* * *

The next morning, we woke up at dawn, gathered our supplies, and headed back. As she drove, Emily pulled out a scrap of paper and scribbled on it, holding the steering wheel with one knee while she wrote. Handing me the slip of paper, she said, "Here's my phone number."

I looked at it. *Jesus, even her handwriting is gorgeous!* My first thought was about getting her number tattooed somewhere on me. Instead I said, "Strange—your number has a different prefix than everyone else's."

"That's because we have a landline. I hear that it's the last one in town. If I'm out and I miss you, I'll call you back."

"What's your cell number?"

"I don't have one."

"Email?"

"Nope. Sorry."

"No cell phone, no email, no TV?"

She giggled. "Yeah, I'm kind of a dinosaur!"

And I love you.

On the way back, I sent an online request for a taxi to come and pick me up. Emily had offered to take me to town, but I didn't want to pull her away from her family any longer. Instead she gave me an embrace as I was leaving that almost buckled my knees. Reluctantly, I tried to play it cool and got into the cab, but I was admittedly delirious the whole way back.

However, as we rounded closer to the center, the panic set back in when I realized that I was going to be late for work. Worse than that, I hadn't collected any of the information I was supposed to. I walked right into the manager's office, ready to apologize, but to my surprise, no one was around anywhere. As I was walking back out, a note on his desk caught my eye.

Steven's Progress Report: Despite all efforts to the
contrary, Steven has developed an independent sense
of right and wrong. Appears compassionate. +7.

The plus seven was circled in red.

Huh. Maybe they give credit for things like that, and I'm back to G-7! Sweet! Looks like things are finally starting to turn around for me!

*

SEVENTEEN

Walking out of the manager's office, I heard some commotion going on in the back. Skipping over there, I found everyone huddled around the television monitors and said, "Hey, what's going on?"

One of them responded excitedly, "There's a high-speed car chase in progress! One of those guys who has been infected by that awful tree stole a police cruiser, and he's on the run!"

Someone else added, "Yes, and that's actually very clever. Police cars are the only ones with manual drive!"

I said, "Well, they're not the only ones," but no one heard me.

The manager was calmly surveying the scene and observed confidently, "Don't worry; we'll catch him. But watch this, because it's going to get very interesting. Steven is correct in that police cars aren't the only ones with manual drive, but they *are* the only ones without insta-flee."

I said, "What's that?"

The manager explained. "If an ordinary vehicle detects something coming for it, it will automatically get out of the way. That feature is responsible for most pedestrian deaths because pedestrians aren't on the same system. Unfortunately, as you know, lobotomies have problems walking across the street and will follow anyone in front of them, even if it's not clear to proceed." As an aside, he glanced over his shoulder and added thoughtfully, "We are working on a plan to install flashing orange lights on their heads." Then he turned back to the screens and said suspensefully, "But with a radicalized driver on the loose, he can force all of the other cars to move out of the way—even luxury cars."

One of the staff next to me exclaimed, "What a nightmare!" A few other people fainted dead on the spot.

As far as I could tell, the driver had not come across anyone else's path yet, and I asked, "What's the big deal?"

The manager responded definitively, "Steven, a single unauthorized person piloting a manual-drive car can wreak havoc, since he can force cars to move over even when he's not in the right socioeconomic group. That goes against all of our civic modeling!"

Someone else vomited. Still failing to appreciate the magnitude of the catastrophe, I said, "Um, is someone covering it?"

The manager replied, "We had a chopper following the car, but the chopper lost him and we're following him through remote devices."

One of the senior reporters had a microphone and was watching a combination feed from the car's dash-cam and various tracking devices in the car that were all triangulating the driver on the map. The reporter was giving the play-by-play to people listening and watching at home.

"Yes, people, this is terror like we have never witnessed anywhere in this country! A radicalized motorist is on the loose and traveling the streets without restraint or any regard for civilized behavior! Please stay inside and lock your doors and windows!"

I looked at the monitors on the screen, and he still appeared to me to just be driving steadily on the highway. He didn't even seem to be speeding. He did come across one other vehicle, and apparently that car's own monitoring system was on high alert. Before he even got within ten feet of it, the other car dived into a nearby hedge like a scared rabbit.

The reporter winced at the scene but continued bravely. "Don't worry, people! He's wearing his watch, so we know exactly where he's going!" At that moment, the driver rolled down the window and threw the watch out. Apparently he was monitoring the news feed in the car.

The reporter started sweating furiously and doubled down. "Don't panic, fair citizens, the car is still monitored by GPS! We can track him through the Wi-Fi signal beaming into the car!"

Someone tapped him on the shoulder and inferred otherwise. "Um, it appears that he has figured out how to disable the car's GPS." Sure enough, that blip suddenly went silent on the screen. The announcer started to turn white but didn't falter. "People, have no fear! There's a drive cam in the car that we're monitoring from the station!" At that moment, the driver hung a hat over the drive cam, and we lost view of him.

Now in complete shock, the reporter fell silent, convulsed, and threw up all over himself. The manager calmly walked right over to the mic and picked it up, saying, "Folks, folks, remain calm. We have him, and we'll pull him over shortly."

Sure enough, they had a barricade set up down the road. Strangely, it wasn't anywhere near the driver's original trajectory, but they got him nonetheless. A call came over the manager's phone confirming it, and everyone rejoiced and hugged after that. While several people muttered about feeling PTSD setting in and discussed establishing a new support group to recover and heal, I just went back to my desk.

Out of morbid curiosity, I did check the Multiverse activity shortly thereafter, and as expected, millions of people who didn't live anywhere near our town and had never met this person or could have conceivably been endangered by his actions were calling for his instantaneous cancellation from society and gruesome dismemberment. The level of mob rage concerned me once again, but I didn't think that it would do any good to raise the issue with the manager.

However, thirty minutes later, a blast went over the news service. "Kamikaze lunatic convicted of thirty-five charges!" That shocked me out of my chair, and I found the manager in his office, busy working on something, and asked, perplexed, "How'd that happen?"

He looked up absently. "How'd what happen?"

"How did he get convicted so quickly?"

Turning back to his work, he said reflexively, "Oh, we abolished courts years ago. People now just vote on the internet whenever we have a crime, but crime is rare anyway."

"Wait, who votes?"

"We have a panel of Multiverse judges."

"Are they real judges?"

"Oh, no—just people sitting at home on their computers."

"Who are they?"

"The fifteen wisest people on the internet."

Aghast, I said, "How the hell do you come up with that?"

The manager responded plainly, "We use the people who have the most followers."

I jumped back and countered, "Oh, come on! You just said that lobotomies will follow anything!"

He stopped writing for a second and looked up. "Steven, our system might not be perfect, but it's better than everyone else's. If you had studied democratic administrative science, you'd know that. In the old days, we did have a traditional jury system usually made up of twelve people who didn't know anything about the case. Now we find hordes of people who don't know anything about anything, and they make recommendations to the fifteen Multiverse judges, who then render a decision."

Still flabbergasted at the notion, I said, "And that's justice?"

The manager responded casually, "Well, yes. That's how we've been doing it for years. We do still have a Supreme Court, but cases are rarely decided up there. Besides, the only way to get the insurance companies to agree to the credit/insurance program was to get rid of messy due process. In a way, you could say that people ultimately waived their right to the courts in exchange for long-term security."

Taking a step forward, I said uneasily, "Are you sure that's a good idea?"

He finally put down his pen and leaned back in his chair. "Oh, it had to be done. In the dark times, people were just making up injuries and trying to get a free ride, so we frontloaded the system with the insurance program. People can still recover for their injuries, but it's a set amount and usually only pays enough for ancillary costs related to executing the larger insurance policy. It all works very well." Then he smiled and added, "Anyway, between universal insurance and the Multiverse, who needs to sue?"

I insisted, "Didn't the lawyers and judges—I mean the real judges—have anything to say about that?"

He laughed and replied, "Oh, a long time ago we ran out of people gutsy enough to be lawyers anymore! They wanted to participate in the justice system but preferred to stay at home, safely behind their computers and television screens. Once the lawyers went away, of course, we had no need for real judges. There was even a time when courts were closed entirely due to a virus outbreak, but the Multiverse still knew automatically how to judge right from wrong, so we went with them when the dust all settled."

The manager went back to work, and I looked out his window. The office was still very emotional, and people were breaking down and crying everywhere. Others were busy trying to revive people on the floor or catching those who were headed there. My watch was going off with posts flying around internet about PTSD related to watching the chase, and there were even posts about people suffering from PTSD from reading about other people suffering from PTSD.

I interrupted the manager again. Annoyed, he looked down at my watch to see what all the fuss was about, and I said, "How can these idiots be upset about that?"

Realizing what I was talking about, he looked up again and replied, "Well remember, PTSD is based on a frightening experience, and what constitutes frightening is determined by standards in the community. These people are suffering; that's for sure. Fortunately we have a whole slew of mental health professionals who help people deal with emotional issues related to these internet posts."

I took a step back and said, "What? You mean dealing with the hurtful things said to them?"

"No, dealing with reading hurtful things said to others."

"Seriously?"

Probably sensing that he wasn't going to be able to finish his work, he stopped again and looked up at me impatiently. "Yes. Say, what did you find out about that family's finances? Did they have a lot of expensive things around? Did you take a picture of the will?"

I fumbled nervously and backed away from where I was standing.

"Oh, um, everything was left to the mother, but no, I forgot to take a picture of the will."

He frowned at me and said, "Well, we'll deal with that later. But what kind of property did they have?"

"Not much that I could see. There was a house, a barn, and a tractor. The house was pretty much empty, and I think they sold a lot of the furniture and things at some point. The mother and daughter were both nearly catatonic, and I couldn't get very much out of them."

The manager leaned back, temporarily satisfied, and said, "Oh, very good. Write up the story and—" Just then his phone rang, cutting off the thought. "Excuse me for a second." He took the call. "Oh, I see. Thank you." He hung up and pushed the button on the loudspeaker. "Tomlinson, get in here."

An eager junior writer sprang into the office. "Yes sir?"

"Let's do another article about the most popular baby names."

"You got it, boss!" He disappeared as fast as he had arrived.

I asked sarcastically, "Economy in another slump?"

Absently, he said, "Yes. What? No, it's just, um, time to update everyone again." Shooting me a temporary look of disapproval, he dismissed me by demanding firmly, "Don't you have somewhere else to be right now?"

Walking out, I realized that he had forgotten to give me my deadline, but I took the excuse to try making this my best piece yet and pored over it endlessly for the whole night. I wrote and rewrote it ten times, making sure that I had captured everything I learned from talking to Emily. Then, after struggling for a while more, I finally hit on the correct title: "A Life Truly Worth Having Lived."

This was my crowning achievement. I proofread it a dozen times just to make sure it was perfect, and then I hit print and carried it to the manager's office like a jewel sitting atop a velvet pillow. He took it brusquely from me, quickly scanned it, and frowned at me. "It's not complete. Where's the stuff about the inheritance? And where's the will? We still need a copy of it."

I gently pleaded with him. "Shouldn't we wait a little while before doing all of that?"

He rubbed his chin and considered. "Well, we could wait for the probate proceedings, but it will take too long. It's a standard term in the agreement that they have to give us a copy of the will and all medical records. Get those and whatever else you can find, and then we'll publish everything ASAP."

The excitement at being able to see Emily again was indescribable, even though I knew that she and her mom would be going through tough times for a while. I fidgeted with nervous excitement during the whole ride and even left a tip so large with the driver that he shook my hand right before I bid him farewell, and then I sprinted up to the front door of Emily's house.

By the time I arrived, however, I had already missed the funeral procession. Emily's mom was still very tired, but she came out for a while and talked to us. She had fond stories to tell about all of the kind, good things her husband had done for the family and others. Later on she excused herself and took a nap. There were cards all around from the people he knew across the country. The ones who could make it to see him did; others just sent their wishes to the family.

Afterward, Emily and I quietly sat talking at the kitchen table for a long while. I was tempted to reach out and take her hand but didn't. Instead I just cupped the glass of water she had given me and said, "Will you and your mother be able to get along?"

She gave a dutiful half-smile and responded, "We'll manage. We don't have much saved up, but if we can keep this place going, we'll survive."

Warmly, I said, "I would have very much liked to have met your father."

She smiled quietly for a second, and then she fell into a thought, and it appeared that she might start crying. She finally looked up at me with glassy eyes and smiled, saying lightly, "Oh, he was just a regular guy."

I finally did take her hand and responded softly, "I know, but he got to be your father." She squeezed my hand a bit harder, and a single tear did escape her eye. After that, we just sat there listening to each other's gentle breathing.

I thought about staying the night but decided to get back to town. I didn't have any more financial details to add to the story, but I did have more to say about her dad. I reworked the story and made sure to include every wonderful nugget that Emily's mom had given to me, as well as what I had learned from the cards I read. I was anxious to get the story to print and wanted to take a copy of it to Emily as fast as possible, since I thought it might help her and her mother start to feel a little better.

Meanwhile, my phone was still up to its old tricks the whole time—more messages about shopping and babies. I ignored all of them and just kept working on my masterpiece. I was eventually interrupted by a conversation that made its way to my station, as one of the juniors was talking to the manager. "Sir, people keep getting infected when they go for coffee."

The manager said in disbelief, "What? How? The tree is boxed in."

Junior continued. "Well, apparently the roots have spread, and a smaller tree is budding on the other side of Joe's. People keep reaching down to touch it and can't seem to resist the colors."

The manager spat. "Goddamn lobotomies! That thing has to be stopped! Where is the infected guy now?"

"That's another thing. We can't find him."

"What do you mean, you can't find him?"

"He escaped from the hospital somehow and ditched all of his electronic goods. The last thing he said to the nurse was that he needed to go off on a pilgrimage."

I finally butted in and asked, "What's a pilgrimage?"

The manager looked at me and responded briefly, "Oh, just something that nutcase wannabe visionaries used to try. Don't worry about it; we have him on GPS."

Junior shook his head and corrected, "No, he ditched all of his devices."

The manager waved him off. "I said don't worry about it. But that damn tree appears to make people forget that they are tethered to a body and could wind up erasing centuries of social conditioning. We need a team of psychiatrists to help work with these newly infected people."

Junior countered. "But it will take years to train them!"

He responded, "No, it won't. We have millions working in low-wage service jobs because the market can't support them. Don't worry; I'll take care of it."

Junior saluted and scampered off, and then the manager turned to me and said abruptly, "By the way, Steven, why don't you call it a day. The director wants to see you." I shut down my unit and headed up to six.

I didn't even notice the current ads playing in the elevator, as Emily's face was running through my mind the whole ride. I stepped off on six and headed to the director's office, and he came around his desk and greeted me warmly. Studying my face as we shook hands, he said, "Well, I'd ask how you're doing, but I can already tell. You look like you're in love!"

I couldn't hide my smile. Nearly ecstatic, I said, "I met a girl!"

Hopefully, he asked, "At the brothel?"

"No, on an assignment."

"Oh. How old is she?"

"Twenty-three."

He frowned. "Steven, she's much too young for you."

Still smiling, I responded decisively, "I don't care."

He sat down on the other side of his desk, shaking his head. "Come on, Steven, don't take a risk at this point in your life. If you wait for her, you'll miss out on so many things. Hey, why don't we just go back to the brothel and you'll forget all about her."

I just stood there floating in the ether and said, "No thanks. I'm done with all of that."

"Then how about a nice trip to the bathhouse? Check your watch. It's probably glowing purple right now!"

"That's just because you're talking about the bathhouse and I can hear the Femboiz playing in the background."

Appearing moderately embarrassed, the director quickly

switched off the music and said, "Oh, he he! Very clever!" Changing the subject, he prodded unexpectedly, "By the way, what were you doing out at the old parade grounds?"

That brought me quickly out of my trance. Suddenly nervous for some reason, I stammered, "I ... How did you know that I was out there?"

"By the GPS on your watch."

"Oh. We just went for a drive. That is ... we took a cab." Trying to quickly deflect the conversation, I said, "Say, why are those vacant now?"

He shrugged and scratched his head. "I'm not sure. People just seemed to lose interest in public protests right around the time of the lobotomy program." Then he added enthusiastically, "But I think it's a sign of overall citizen confidence!"

"Don't people care about democracy anymore?"

He rocked thoughtfully in his chair and replied, "It's not that. In fact, we have an organization that gets people together to drink wine and monitor our democracy which works very well. As you know, 'wine-ing' is a staple of every robust free country!" He let out a little chuckle, but I was not amused. The director cleared his throat and added, for official purposes, "However, actual protests and political statements are limited to forty-five minutes these days, so they don't draw much notice."

"Why?"

"Well, they used to be longer, but no one would pay any attention to them. Heck, people were waiting outside for concert tickets longer than most sit-ins, so we just put a time limit on them to make things more democratically peaceful. Besides, you try getting lobotomies to pay attention for longer than an hour."

Then he leaned in and went back to lecturing. "Anyway, Steven, you'll want to be careful about getting mixed up with someone her age. It's just not a good thing for you. Are you sure you don't want to go to the bathhouse? I talked to them, and they don't have any HIV-infected needles over there today!"

"Thank you for the invitation to the bathhouse and for talking to me, but I'm fine. I'm just going to go home tonight."

I walked home in a love-struck daze. On the way, I ran across a scruffy-looking kid on the street. He noticed my watch, and his jealously was immediately apparent. From his ragged clothes and dirty face, he looked like he was from the B-class or below.

I held out my arm so he could study the watch. Turning it over in his hand, he said, "Wow, I've never seen anything like this in my whole life!" I took it off and held it out to him, and his jaw completely dropped. Nervously looking around, he accepted the gift from me, smiled, and darted out of sight. After that, I lay awake all night thinking about Emily and how best to finish the story.

* * *

I was still at my desk, clicking away, when I noticed the manager approaching. I stood up quickly to greet him, but he was halted a few feet away from me by another colleague who ambled up to him on a pair of newly mandated leg braces and said excitedly, "Sir, sir, the biggest story of the year just came in!"

"What is it now?"

"We just got a call from a female reported to have been molested by another Hollywood director!"

The manager beamed. "Terrific! Let's run with it and get as many witnesses as you can to call in with similar stories! By the way, we need someone to write a story about spontaneous cursing."

My colleague said, "What?"

The manager responded, "As in, 'That fucking tree is now causing spontaneous cursing'! Kids are spouting off words that they've never heard and appear to have developed Tourette's syndrome, so now they have to be sent to therapy for reprogramming."

"Right away, sir!"

As my colleague hobbled away clumsily, I said, "How many kids were infected?"

The manager responded, "Only one, I think, but the odd side

effect of lobotomies is that it causes people to parrot a lot of things. Now, that's usually good because they're reciting catchy slogans or pitching products. Say, did you get a copy of the will?"

I thought up a quick excuse. "Oh, there wasn't one. It ... burned in a fire a long time ago."

"Damn it. We can't do anything with that. Now the probate process will take years. Well, don't worry; I'll deal with it. I have another assignment for you."

"What is it?"

"I need you to cover a suicide story. A guy across town just blew his head off in his apartment."

Reluctantly, I got up from my unfinished work and headed out. By the time I got there, the emergency crew was just finishing scooping up the brains, and there wasn't anyone else around to talk to. However, on the bedside table I found a manifesto that the guy had written. It had every single detail in it about why he killed himself, how much he hated the government and all of the citizens and lobotomies, and how he couldn't stand to live one more day in a lie.

Walking back to the center, my thoughts of Emily were interrupted by the memory of my dead parents. I wondered briefly if suicidality might be hereditary and made a note to look it up. However, by the time I got back to my desk, the notion had faded, and I simply took the manifesto and pretty much weaved it into a nice, compact story. I completed it in less than two hours and handed it to the manager, but he threw it down after reaching the end and said angrily, "No, no, no! We can't publish that!"

Not having expected to be rebuffed on this one, I said, "Why not? That's exactly what he wrote down!"

Shaking his head, the manager replied, "Steven, we only have six or seven generally accepted reasons for suicides these days— molested as a kid, orphaned, drug overdose, brain disease, et cetera. It's obvious that this guy was suffering from one or more, or perhaps all of these. Don't worry; I'll take care of it."

Starting to get tired of all of my real stories being gutted, I protested one last time. "Are you sure you have to change it?"

The manager answered firmly, "Oh, yes. You should know by now that we don't recognize theories about mental health disorders that interfere with our economy. Now, run along."

The next day, my manifesto suicide story had been rewritten to warn about the dangers of untreated molestation among young people and was posted in the miscellaneous section of the news. The cover story was instead all about the diddling film director. My suicide story ended by saying, "And if he's looking down on us from the clouds right now, he'll tell you that early therapy is the best prevention your insurance money can buy." I recalled the earlier story about the Mars astronaut also looking down on us from the clouds and wondered how they both wound up in the same place.

Another excited writer limped up to the manager in leg irons and exclaimed, "Sir, another girl just called in on that molestation issue!"

"That's great; let's run it immediately! We're up to fifty now! This could be the biggest molestation in months!"

Having covered a dozen or so movie reviews while at the newspaper, 90 percent of which were reboots of things shown in the past few years anyway, I wasn't impressed. The film industry had even taken to making movies about a particular day or week in history—most of which involved something that had happened a few years prior—and were even doing rebooted reboots of those now, since the writers apparently couldn't come up with any novel ideas anymore.

I was even less interested in the molestation scandal, so when the other writer had clanked away, I asked, "Let me see if I have something straight."

The manager looked at me curiously. "Yes?"

"Thirty-eight of the people who have complained about being molested in the most recent scandal all posed nude in one publication or another last month?"

He shrugged. "Yeah, so?"

"So is it really a big deal if someone pinched them on the ass?"

"Oh, absolutely. Steven, it is one thing to go around in revealing clothing, or to even remove that clothing in public, or to sell photos, videos, or other media showing you nude. It is another thing completely to have someone engage in unauthorized touching of your body."

"Why?"

Firmly, he responded, "Because, Steven, our society is carefully constructed so that everyone's personal space is respected. Intimate personal touching is only allowed through express mutual consent, and that usually requires multiple shopping trips and at least a reasonable prospect of obtaining half of your insurance policy."

"Well, what about all of the people who get paid to have sex in movies?"

Exasperated with my continued lack of understanding, the manager said, "Duh, Steven, that's not the same thing at all."

"You mean that having to sleep with someone to get a part in a movie isn't the same as sleeping with someone after you get the part?"

"No, Steven, it's not. Besides, we use intimacy coaches for the on-screen action, so it's emotionally safer."

Unsarcastically, I responded, "Pretty confusing society you guys have out here. Thank goodness for prostitutes, huh?"

He frowned. "That's not funny, Steven."

"Sorry. But with directors who keep molesting people, and given that all they produce these days are reboots, don't you think that the movie people should take a little break?"

His patience with me was apparently done for the day, and he responded curtly, "No, Steven, that's not going to happen. Don't you have somewhere to be right now?"

As I was walking away and preparing to enjoy the privilege of living in a society where personal space is so deeply respected, a girl walked right into my path with a tear-stained, hurtful face, her left eye covered up with a bandage. I had no desire to talk to her, but apparently that didn't matter, as she was blocking the hallway with her huge ass. The notion of groping her to get her to go away crossed my mind. Instead I stood patiently and pretended to welcome her unwelcome advance.

She took a deep breath and steeled herself, her open eye already primed with excess moisture. As firmly as possible, she insisted, "Steven, I am very upset with you!"

I cocked my head and said, "Who are you again?"

She registered surprise through her good eye. "It's me, Julie!"

I shook my head confusedly and admitted, "I don't believe we've ever met. Say, why are you wearing an eye patch?"

Her good one finally let loose. *Sob.* "Because I tried to IM you, but it didn't work!" Snort. "The message just kept coming back as undeliverable, so I kept trying, and trying, and trying! Eventually I blinked so many times trying to reach you that I broke my contact and scratched my cornea!" *Bawl!*

Consolingly, I said, "Oh, I'm sorry; I turned off my messenger."

She wiped her nose on her sleeve and leveled accusingly, *"Thanks, Steven! You're a really insensitive human, you know?"*

I lightly patted her on the back as I walked past and replied, "Yeah, I'm working on that!"

*

EIGHTEEN

The following morning, the story broke about Emily's dad. I hadn't finished it myself, but I was certain that whatever the manager had added would only complement the heartfelt writing. Instead I discovered that story had been completely redone. The title read, "Rogue Radicalist Goes It Alone, Loses!" The whole story was about a stubborn, foolish old man who refused to follow modern scientific conveniences and who subjected himself and his family to unnecessary pain and suffering, when all he had to do was call on the blessed services of the government's health care workers. I was well beyond disgusted.

The manager, on the other hand, was thoroughly pleased with himself. When I confronted him, he just leaned back smiling and put his hands behind his head. Glowingly, he responded, "Yep, we have perfected the science of villainizing news characters!"

My face felt redder than his ever was, and I demanded, "How the hell could you do that?"

Innocently, he leaned forward and said, "Do what?"

"Change the story like that?"

He shrugged and responded plainly, "Makes it more readable. It also supports our health initiatives. Steven, we can't have people just taking their lives into their own hands like that."

I couldn't think of a credible rejoinder, but the notion of strangling him where he sat crossed my mind. Instead I shot back at him, "Well, what if it was your dad?"

The manager frowned at me and shook his head. "Oh, Steven, you can't use the Golden Rule like that."

"Like what?"

"You can't use the Golden Rule to censor the news. As responsible journalists, we can't let personal feelings get in the way of covering a story. And anyway, it wasn't my dad. My dad was sensible enough to go in peace at the hospital like everyone else."

I was terrified that Emily would see the story and somehow link it back to me. I called later that day, and she picked up, apparently unaware of goings-on outside of her home. From the other end, she said, "Yes, everything is okay. Mom is just puttering along, but she's holding together pretty well." Expectantly, she added, "Can you come out to see us?"

I said, "Um, not right now. Maybe in a few days."

Walking home, I prayed that she would never, ever see that story. The manager had changed the byline so it didn't have my name, but I was sure that Emily would think that it was all my fault anyway. I needed to be alone to think, and as far as I could tell, the best place to do that was at the soccer stadium. The anonymity of the crowd and unappealing action was good for me, and sitting there comfortably taking in the mindless activity, I finally relaxed a bit. The thought of purchasing season tickets actually occurred to me.

However, while I was trying to figure out how to make sense of everything and how best to help Emily, a commotion broke out on the jumbotron. Apparently one of the spectators was proposing to another while they were at the game, both of them wearing matching team onesies.

After the crowd applauded the ceremony, an announcement blasted over the screen: "And thanks to our lucky couple for helping us make this a very special day here at the stadium! They have won a chance to take the honeymoon trip of a lifetime, and everyone here in the stadium is automatically entered for a chance to win the second prize—a nonlobotomized baby!" The applause after that was deafening, and I got up and quietly left.

I didn't sleep at all that night. All I kept asking over and over again was, "How did everything get so fucked up?" I decided to go in early the next day and search through the archives again for more clues.

I was at the office by 4:00 a.m., where only a few of the wordsmithing sentries were busy monitoring in their leg braces for early-morning scandals. I nodded as I walked past and mumbled an excuse about a deadline, and then I sneaked into the archives room.

God is dead. God is not dead. Truth is dead. Truth is not dead. Aliens. No aliens. Coffee is good for you. Coffee isn't good for you. Chocolate is good for you. Chocolate isn't good for you. Government finishes war on terror; starts war on nightmares. Down's eliminated. Artificial placenta patented. Missing planet in solar system found, another missing planet detected. Pluto regains planetary status, loses it again.

No, that's not it. Try another search path. History of equal protection. Can own slaves. Now can't. Can beat spouse. Now can't. Sex with opposite, now sex with anyone. Marry opposite, now marry anyone.

No, that's not it either. Let's see. We're the best. We're still the best. Okay, we're not the best, but those guys are cheating. Okay, they're not cheating, but we have an excuse. Okay, we're changing the game so we can still say that we're the best. Oh no, here comes AIDS. Very bad because we're supposed to be the best. Never mind. Excuses are actually very good for us. Maintenance meds discovered; chronic diseases determined to be big boost to economy.

After that, there was a perceptible time when all of the stories were about churning every potentially offensive thing on the planet—mascots, fight songs, apparel, groping, language, racial differences, and so on. Parents were also publicly shamed—and then arrested—for choosing not to vaccinate their children, employing corporal punishment, letting children roam free without supervision, and sending the kids to school with the wrong kinds of snacks. Between that and a series of virus outbreaks, everyone had finally been beaten down to permanent milquetoast stasis by the Multiverse mobs, and then people willingly gave up control of all efforts at natural procreation, whereby the continued obedience of the citizenry had been permanently assured.

Not surprisingly, every exercise in further social control along the way had been initially supported by a study of a thousand people, and then cemented forever thereafter as truth in the name of science.

By then it was nearing 7:00 a.m., and people were starting to filter in, so I quietly slipped out and back to my desk. Shortly thereafter, I was diverted to covering another boring story. It was the foundation for the upcoming episode of This Week in History. A kid got lost on a field trip, and he didn't make it back to the group in time to eat lunch, and that wasn't even the worst of it. The lunch included his favorite dessert, but he didn't get any and everyone else did. When the story originally ran, adolescent watch sales quintupled.

A suspected lobotomy came up to me and asked me what I was doing. After explaining a bit to her, she said, sounding exasperated, "Well, why didn't they just save a piece for him?"

Dully, I responded. "One of the big kids ate the extra portion when no one was looking. Turns out it was an extreme case of dessert bullying."

She nearly fainted. "Oh, that's truly awful! I hope he's okay now."

"He is. He was in therapy for eighteen months over the incident, but he'll pull through now that they've put him on medications for the rest of his life to deal with the emotional trauma."

Her face lit up, and she said, "Oh good!" She looked over my shoulder and read some of the material herself. When she finished, she commented emotionally, "Wow, what a powerful story! I'm sure it's destined to become an instant classic!"

I turned to her plainly and replied, "Yes, I'm sure it is. Hey, could you hold still for a moment? I think you have something in your hair."

* * *

Still pleading unsuccessfully for a rewrite of the story about Emily's dad, I was caught in another debate with the manager, and he continued: "Steven, everyone is essential, and we treat all living beings as precious and part of our community. Excuse me for a moment. Zimmerman, can someone please hurry up and kill that fucking tree outside?"

I said, "Wait, I thought that all living beings were precious."

Backpedaling momentarily, he replied, "Oh, sure they are, but you have to understand that we can't sacrifice everything we have gained thus far in our society for one little rogue organism. After all, do you know what that tree just did?"

"No, what?"

"It completely knocked over the coffee bar!"

I feigned disgust. "That's terrible." Secretly, I was proud of the little guy.

The manager's ire continued as he shook his head in disgust. "Oh, you have no idea! Steven, that tree hates us. It hates our prosperity; it hates our technology. It hates the fun that we all get to have in society and the joy we get from working every day. That's why it is out to disrupt us!"

"But I thought that it was only a tree."

Sarcastically, he said, "So? Everyone knows that trees are dangerous! Speaking of, let's run a series of articles about all of the trees that have fallen over and killed people, disrupted power lines, or caused any other kind of damage. There are tons of them in the archives." Dutifully, I went back to the archives, and late in the afternoon, I did manage to pull together a dozen past references about tree disasters and turned in a decent piece.

Outside, however, everything they were doing to the tree just caused it to become even more robust and move in closer toward the center. They put a roof on top of it, and the roots expanded underground. They tried a controlled burn, but the tree just withered briefly and then then regrew in the same spot. It had also developed a defense mechanism that now made it impervious to fire. Then they tried to dig up all of the ground for one hundred square meters in front of the center, but part of the root system broke off underground in the process, and the tree regrew on the other side of the building.

The branches were now scratching some of the windows on

the upper floors, and as he watched them, the manager was beside himself. The law clearly stated that no trees located next to federal buildings could be higher than ten feet, but that creature didn't care. They had to amend the law to accommodate the unauthorized growth and still maintain an air of control, and the manager was out sick for three days as a result.

People were also still getting infected daily, despite the constant warnings, and what started as a pretty flower grew into a full-figured nuisance. Yes, it was weathered and scarred in spots and had lost some of its initial innocent beauty, but it had grown even more alluring in maturity, and people couldn't stay away. They sneaked out at night to see it, and the hospital emergency department was on constant alert for newly infected admissions. When the manager returned, he had a new plan to excavate all of the land immediately surrounding the center. People would be brought to and from work by helicopter each day.

When I heard the idea, I insisted, "Sir, don't you think that's a little extreme?"

With fierce determination in his eyes, the manager said, "Steven, that is a radicalized tree with a network of sleeper cell root systems just waiting to destroy us!"

I retorted, "Well, the recent readings actually show that the tree is soaking up huge amounts of pollutants from the air and that it's doing as much work as ten forests of trees."

The manager spat and said, "Oh, to hell with that! It ruined my favorite coffee bar! Look, just rerun that story about oxygen levels being dangerously high. Encourage people to talk more, text less. Also, be sure to remind them that oxygen has been found to be responsible for the hole in the ozone layer."

I dutifully obeyed. I was still trying to rebuild my credits to help Emily and had recently learned that I had, in fact, not gotten back to G-7. Apparently they didn't award any credits for morality.

However, to my absolute horror, the next day the Multiverse mob had been turned on her family. The cell phone shortage was not being blamed on the assholes who stole all of that money from the space program. Instead the blame was being leveled on that house outside of town that was supposedly draining our economy by requiring us to supply it with a landline. Other historical inefficiencies were thrown into the article as well to deflect from the fact that the landline service probably cost the government less than one of the director's shirts. The lobotomies were completely beside themselves.

Fucking hell! Thank God that she doesn't have a computer. Instead of going to my workstation, I headed straight for the manager's office and attempted to intervene.

He calmly dismissed my concerns. "Oh, Steven, don't worry about it. These stories have a way of taking on a life of their own, but no real harm will come out of it."

I was furious but tried not to reveal my inside interest in Emily's family. "But you're shifting blame to a completely irrelevant topic."

The manager responded plainly, "Well, I wouldn't say that it's *completely* irrelevant. Economic inefficiencies add up over time, you know."

I demanded, "You mean like shipping products to Mars to make goods to return to Earth?"

He shook his head and said assuredly, "That's not the same thing at all. Leaving out all of the subsidies, those are actually very profitable businesses, which you would understand if you had a stronger economic background."

Firmly, I said, "Look, I think it's time that we focus on something else."

"All in due time, my boy, all in due time. We have to let the process work itself out."

"Why?"

He smiled and replied, "Steven, the best way to promote togetherness and understanding is to have an army of people willing to step in and call people harsh names whenever they fail to conform. Besides, letting the Multiverse mob execute our initiatives is the last step in the Founders' grand dream."

That knocked me off base for a moment, and I said, "The which?"

"The dream to extend the power of the government directly to the people. With the Multiverse mob, we don't even have to pass through the Constitution to assert our will. We just set the mob loose!"

My temper started to show, and I stepped up angrily and replied, "Oh, that's just bullshit! Look, you don't take any responsibility for the stories you write! You just say whatever you want and don't care at all about the lives you ruin!"

He shot me a feigned look of concern and retorted innocently, "Of course we care. Steven, millions of people sleep very well in their beds at night because we are out here telling them what's happening. Consider this: we've made a promise to these people that we will be on top forever, and in the modern global economy, that requires that every one of our citizens agrees to participate in helping us achieve that goal. Doing anything less is a direct betrayal of the social contract."

I spat back, "Well, did you ever think that maybe it's not necessary to be on top anymore?"

He leaned in and shook a finger at me, scolding, "Steven, that's exactly what I'm talking about. Be careful who you say that to. That's a downright un-American sentiment."

Angrily, I said, "Did you ever think about just letting the world be whatever it's going to be?"

He scoffed at me and responded dismissively, "Now that's just your old pals from the gang talking. Put those ideas out of your head right now. People need to be able to dominate other people, and that's what's best for the world."

Backing off slightly, I asked confusedly, "But I thought that you said that we were working on getting rid of aggression."

"In our citizens, yes. Personal aggression is too dangerous of a thing, but public aggression is a very valuable tool in the modern world, and something Jesus would be proud of!" I didn't even know how to respond to that one.

Seeing that he had stunned me, he continued to wrap up his victory. "Look, Steven, I understand your concerns, and there are of course two sides to every story. However, we only tell the one that reinforces the fact that everything we're doing is right, which is naturally what our readers want to see."

Not knowing how to reengage the substantive topic, all I could think to plead was, "But don't they want the truth?"

The manager let out a small laugh and said, "Pssssshhh! What's that? Steven, our readers want to sleep well at night. And don't forget, we can't expect lobotomies to feel like they should actually do anything to help. Why do you think we leave the democracy gathering center way out on the outskirts? It just doesn't do them any good to even think about being civic-minded."

He stood up and added confidently, "Nope. Every day we ensure that all the people have to do is turn on the news and we will be there telling them what to think about whatever is going on. Now that, my boy, is just good ol' fashioned scientific journalism!"

Still angry, I fired back, "No, it's not! It's just biased news making!"

Opening the door to let me out, he just chuckled and shook his head. "Naturally, Steven! We haven't had unbiased news since Paul Revere made his famous announcement!"

*

NINETEEN

I made my way out to see Emily that weekend. Her mother was doing pretty well, so Emily and I took off for two nights and went camping again, and I was careful to leave my phone at her house. She didn't seem to be aware of the goings-on in town, and I didn't want to worry her at all. Still, I had a hard time hiding my true feelings about that place.

We sat in the bed of the truck next to each other, talking. Finally I said, "I'm sick of people."

She nodded gently. "I know what you mean."

I turned to her and asked, "Is that why you stay out here all the time? Are you afraid of the people in the city?"

"I'm not afraid. I just don't like them."

We were silent for a long time after that. Finally I realized that the only thing that really mattered to me was sitting at my side, and gently taking her hand, I said boldly, "Emily, I don't know how to say this, but I love you."

She covered my hand with her other, and all she offered in response was, "Thank you, Steven. Thank you for being out here with me."

As the sun started to go down, I said determinedly, "I'll do whatever I can to help you and your mom survive."

When I returned to the concrete jungle, there was a note on my desk to report immediately to the director's office. He stood in the doorway with his hands on his hips, and I approached cautiously. Firmly, he said, "Steven, did you go back out to the democracy center?"

"I, um … Yes, I did. How did you know?"

"Oh, well someone drove by there and saw a few people, and I just assumed that it was you." He walked around to his desk and sat down, and I stood there waiting for him to offer me a seat. Instead he just shook his head at me and lectured sternly. "I told you that girl is too young for you. She's nothing but bad news."

I remained planted and said, "I don't care. She's the one for me, and I don't know how I'll do it, but I am going to win her over no matter how long it takes."

He adopted a frustrated tone and pleaded, "Oh Steven, you're just holding on to outdated notions of what being a man is! There is no need to quest after females anymore, and there are no challenges left to conquer! It's all based on faulty programming!" He shook his fists dramatically toward the ceiling and added, "Oh, we should have made sure that those awful, misguided stories from the dark times were all destroyed so you wouldn't get ideas like this in your head!"

I just smiled at his theatric attempt and said, "Don't worry about me; I'll be fine." After that, I went back to my desk and doubled down.

Later that day, the manager was at my side and said, "Steven, be sure to do an 'Inside the Mind of' exposé on that story."

"What?"

"Go down to research and pull the file for 'Inside the Mind of a Saturn Goldfish.' It's sure to be there. They've been doing those for years."

"How the hell do they know what's inside the mind of a goldfish—wherever it is?"

He frowned at me and said curtly, "Never mind, Steven. Just give me the story and I'll finish that part."

One of the girls who had a firm sense of one-way personal space came up to me to tell me all about a new story she had just written. It was all about some star who had overcome years of shyness to be photographed in public. Deeply moved, she said, "It's so great that she can overcome her anxiety and zygote depression and let people take her picture!"

I just rolled my eyes and responded flatly, "Yeah, what's so great about it?"

"Steven, lobotomies get anxious seeing photos or watching videos of themselves, and that means that she has overcome a great disability!"

Becoming increasingly impatient, I spat back, "Sounds pretty ridiculous to me."

She insisted, "Oh, Steven, selfie photo–phobia is a tremendously debilitating disease. You may not know this, but these days all selfies are automatically photoshopped and filtered before viewing just to try to mitigate the harsh effects of that condition."

"Okay, but why is that news?"

"What?"

I raised my voice to help her understand. *"Why is it news if a self-absorbed human being goes outside to have their picture taken?"*

She finally retreated in tears. *"Waaaaaahhhhhh!!!!!"*

Late in the afternoon, I received an invitation to a team-building exercise, but I had better things to do and didn't feel much like being part of their team. One of the social coordinators came to find out why I wasn't participating and said, "Steven, this training is very important. Everyone puts on VR contacts for guided meditation, and then we have a sharing period where everyone IMs what they think."

I said, "Um, no thanks. What the hell is with these VR contacts anyway?"

"Oh, they came about because of autonomous vehicles."

"Why? Because people can use them in their cars?"

"Oh, no. When we made cars autonomous, most people just lost interest in driving, and as a result, they moved closer to the city. Eventually people developed agoraphobia because they never had to leave their apartments except to work, and the VR contacts help mitigate the harsh effects of being shut in all the time."

I said, "Well then, perhaps the people shouldn't have let someone take away their ability to drive. I still can't understand how that happened."

He responded plainly, "Oh, it wasn't too hard. See, the nature of change is actually very easy to master. If something is really unpopular, all you have to do is wait until the generation opposing it dies or until people get distracted enough by something else that they just give in. Most changes only take about six months, even with adamant opposition."

I didn't attend the group session that afternoon. Thinking about that conversation, however, I did come up with an idea for increasing my stock and value in town and potentially helping Emily.

Three days later, I presented the manager with a comprehensive door-to-door survey. I had interviewed two thousand people, just to cover my bets, and I asked all of them whether they would like to have cars with the ability for the driver to control the car's operations—and not just for passive-aggressive purposes. More than 80 percent of the respondents said they would like that.

The manager frowned and tossed the study aside. Decisively, he said, "There's no way we could ever do that." He reached down and pulled out a competing study and handed it to me. "Steven, look at this. People used to spend seventeen hours per year looking for parking spaces. That's a huge drain on the economy, never mind that people used to drive vehicles on sidewalks and kill innocent families. Nope, I'm afraid that autonomous vehicles are going to have to stay."

I pleaded, "But my results are overwhelming. We should at least consider giving people back *some* control!"

He responded automatically, "Oh, no, that's not going to happen. Besides, your survey is completely invalid."

"Why?"

"Because half of the people you surveyed have already been determined to be ineligible for surveys, and the other half don't own cars. I'm sorry, but we can't use the data."

"Wait, how do you know that half of them don't own cars?"

"Because, Steven, they're all in the C-3 class or lower."

Refusing to be defeated, I decided to regroup. "Well, can you give me the list of people who are eligible to respond to surveys so I don't make that mistake again?"

"Sure. Here you go."

I thumbed through it and finally looked up accusingly and said, "Wait a minute. This list is only a thousand people long?"

"Yep."

Floored, I said, "What, do you just use the same people?"

Unabashedly, he replied, "Of course." I shot him a scornful look, and he added lightly, "Oh, we used to randomize the studies and do all sorts of validity factors, but then we realized that ordinary people couldn't be trusted to answer correctly. We started doing that after banning all of the naysayers from social media."

But I had a backup plan and wasn't going to give up that easily. Tossing the survey list aside, I insisted, "How about this? Let's conduct another survey. Anyone who hasn't had a wreck is entitled to purchase a manually controlled vehicle."

The manager just shook his head and said automatically, "I'm afraid that won't work."

"Why not?"

"Steven, it's always the other car that causes the accident."

Floored, I exclaimed, *"What the hell does that mean?"*

Calmly, the manager responded, "Look, people can't be trusted to drive for themselves anymore and that's that. Anyway, I'd encourage you to stay out of the survey business, since you obviously don't have the background for it."

"How can you tell?"

"Because, Steven, surveys have to be capable of being proven correct. If you had any background in the survey game, you wouldn't have tried to study something that is incapable of opposition."

I shook my head and observed bitterly, "It sounds like we're all just living in prison."

The manager's face lightened, and he responded assuredly, "Oh, not at all! Sure, it may seem like there are walls and restrictions, but they're really for the people's own good. You have to understand that our citizens are tourists in their own lives and all they really want is to be able to take vacations and take things for granted. Heck, even when they come back from vacation, they just need another one.

That's called a vacation hangover, by the way!" He let out a little chuckle and said, "Isn't that clever?"

I was not even moderately amused, but he continued patiently having to deal with me. "Ahem. Anyway, we can't interfere with that just because a few people want to see change. Steven, over half of the economy is based on obedience. Can you imagine what would happen if that fell apart? Think of all of the little kids whose futures would be robbed from them."

Defeated, I started to head back to my desk, but my progress was halted by a group who stopped me in the hallway. One of the guys spoke up and said eagerly, "Hey Steven, come with us!"

Already skeptical, I asked, "Where?"

"We're going to a seminar on how to read your pet's expressions better!"

"Seriously?"

"Oh, yes, it's very serious! We've been doing it wrong all these years! Just think of those poor little pets freezing on the moon and the planets, and their owners are not even understanding them correctly! I sure hope that they do a live feed of this to the colonies!"

Backing away from them gingerly, I said, "I don't think I should go. After all, I don't even own a pet."

Their leader advanced unyieldingly. "Well, you can always help raise money for the cat overpopulation problem. Can we take a donation from you?"

I backed away further and stammered, "Oh, I'm … Things are a little tight this month. Look, here's an idea. Go to the conference and tell whoever is directing the pets in space program to only send one cat per family and spay and neuter them."

He shot back, "Steven, that's the most ridiculous idea I ever heard of!"

"Why?"

"Well, we can't interfere with nature!"

"Are you kidding me? You have a fucking human colony on the moon!"

With snooty confidence, he retorted, "Yes because nature wanted us to. If it didn't, we wouldn't have been given the ability to do so."

"Maybe you're reading nature wrong."

"Steven, the government says that we can do this, and if we were doing it wrong, the government would say so."

I finally suggested definitively, "Well, why don't you just wait until all of the cats die and then start over?" The six people standing in front of me all turned blanch-white, and one of them passed out on the spot as the rest just stared at me in horror. Not having the stomach to fight anymore, I finally sighed and said, "Okay, okay, what do I have to do to donate?"

"Yay!" He held out the scanner, and it panned my eye for a brief second. Checking the device to make sure that it registered, he looked up at me again and said, "By the way, could we also count on you to donate to help fight fake news?" At that, I just turned and walked away.

*　*　*

The continued inability to figure out a way out of my morass was starting to grind on me, and one of my colleagues found me at just the wrong moment. "Hi, Steven. Can you guess—?"

"You know, Greg, I've been meaning to mention something to you. I think that you might be coming down with nonselective non-mutism."

He was taken aback and muttered, in the apparent early stages of a panic attack, "What? I've never heard of that. Is it serious?"

I nodded grimly. "Very."

"OMG! How do I know if I have it?"

I adopted a solemn look and said, "That's the big problem; you won't. You'll need someone else to tell you that you have it."

He turned as white as a sheet and said frantically, "I need to go! I need to get to the hospital ASAP!"

As he scampered away in horror, the manager came around the corner frowning at me and chided sharply, "Steven, stop doing that!"

"Doing what?"

"You have to give a trigger warning if you're going to be that authentic."

I shot back, incensed, "Are you kidding me? The rest of these assholes just blurt out whatever is on their pea brains without even thinking!"

"Yes, but they can't help it. Look, maybe you should try to not talk to so many people. By the way, when you're done with the story you're working on, finish his up today as well, and then you can go home."

Fuck.

Just then a junior reporter ran up to the manager and said excitedly, "Sir, sir, another woman just called in and reported being groped in Hollywood!"

The manager fumbled momentarily and then said, "Er, we're onto something new now. Why don't you tell her to go out to eat so they can update her mental health profile, and we'll call her if we decide to reboot the scandal. Oh, and while we're at it, let's run a story about people leaving excessively large tips. That's always a boost to consumer confidence!"

After the other walked away, I turned to the manager snidely and said, "Still trying to recoup the money stolen from the space program?"

He shot me a look of disdain and retorted, "No, Steven, just doing my job." I left that afternoon without finishing mine.

* * *

The chopper dropped me off the following morning, and I tried to report to the second floor, but my card wouldn't give me access. I went up to the director's office to ask why, and he responded lightly, "Oh, we've moved you to the hospital since they're a bit short-handed over there. You don't mind, do you?"

That was actually the relief I had been waiting for. Eagerly, I smiled and said, "No problem!" I was, in reality, dying to get back to see that boy, and after the chopper came back to pick me up, I reported to the hospital with the new credential card the director had given me. I found one of the male nurses on three and immediately asked, "Where's the kid that was in this bed?"

"He was just moved up to the seventh floor for compassionate release."

I was shocked and exclaimed, "*What?*"

"Compassionate release. That's what we call it these days when they euthanize people."

Bastards! That's what they meant when they said he was going to be released! I tried to plead for him. "But he's only ten!"

The nurse clinically dismissed my concern by saying thoughtfully, "Yeah, but he was an old soul."

"What the hell are you talking about?"

"An old soul—he was born before the last upgrade came out to baby contacts. As a result, he's wiser than his contemporaries who were born after the new upgrade." While I was still trying to recover and process, he added, "Anyway, the kid chose God instead of pain."

"What?"

He produced a folded-up sheet of paper from his pocket and said, "Look: 'I, Timmy Smith, hereby choose God instead of pain. Duck stamp, smiley face.'" Nodding assuredly at me, he added, "We give them the stamps to cheer them up!"

"But all he had was a broken leg."

"Yep. Unfortunately, there was nothing we could have done for him."

"What are you talking about? Set the leg and let it heal!"

"No, Steven, I'm afraid his condition was much worse than that. He was an orphan."

I shook my head vigorously and insisted, "No, no, he had parents! They just died in the fire!"

"That's what I said. He was an orphan. He had no other family left."

Pleadingly, I said, "Well, why didn't you give him his parents' insurance policy to live on and set him up with a … conservator or something?"

"We couldn't. His parents used up their policies on their new apartment, and regrettably, as you may know, that burned down."

"What about his policy?"

"That was used up on gender reassignment surgery. I'm sorry, Steven, but there was just nothing left for him."

I started to feel sick. Still searching, I said, "I can't believe that you're going to ... terminate him!"

Putting a hand on my shoulder, he responded caringly, "Steven, look. It's really not as bad as you think. It is a completely gentle and humane process. Come with me."

We went up to seven and into a monitoring station that fed into the compassionate release room in the back of the hospital. On the screen, I could see that the little boy was all alone in the bed. He appeared to be sedated, and a nurse walked in to insert an IV in his arm. She struggled for quite a while, missing the vein several times. By the time she hit the mark, blood was running down his arm, and he seemed to twitch involuntarily, his glazed eyes fluttering rapidly.

My companion provided clinical narration: "Young people tend to have smaller veins, which makes them a little hard to find." The nurse attached a vial to the IV, and he added, "She's administering the first medication. This one produces a warm feeling of calm in the patient."

"I thought he was already sedated."

"Oh, yes, but being sedated is not the same as being calm. That's what she's doing now." When the medications hit his system, he took in one heavy breath and started choking violently and spitting up.

The guy next to me clinically explained, "In some people, that medication can make them a bit nauseated, but it's nothing to worry about." The nurse in the other room attached the second vial to the IV, and in seconds the boy's head fell over and his arm slumped off the side of bed. It appeared that he was gone.

A doctor walked in and certified the death. He nodded to the nurse and looked down and made a mark on a clipboard; then the two of them walked out, to be replaced by two orderlies who wheeled the bed out of the room.

Still in shock at what I had just witnessed, I said, "Where are they going?"

"Oh, they're carting him off to be taken to the crematorium. Look over here." There was another camera showing a large metal chute. "That goes directly down to the loading dock. From there they pick up the body and take it to the chute that feeds the furnace at the center."

The video was also hooked up to audio in the hallway, and the nurse with me cranked it up a few notches as we watched the body being loaded into the chute. It thumped on the metal like a sack of flour, followed by the sick sound of flesh rubbing down the slide; then I heard a small thud as the body hit the dumpster below.

Suddenly I started crying uncontrollably. The man standing with me patted my arm and said reassuringly, "Oh, it's okay, Steven. It's just part of life."

I tried to recover and in blind rage blurted out, "*Yeah, maybe, but the way he ended up, you might as well have shot him through a fucking particle collider!*"

His mouth dropped open, and he slapped me on the back. "Oh, crap! Steven, why didn't we think of that? A penniless, ten-year-old transgendered orphan with a broken leg! That could have netted a hundred times the prior results!" Then another thought halted him suddenly, and his enthusiasm waned. "Oh, but people might not think that was very cute."

The door to the monitoring room opened, and an orderly said, "Sir, excuse me, but they just wheeled another lunatic in who has been exposed to that tree."

"Shit. Sorry, Steven, gotta go." He walked out and gave me a nonchalant pat on the back. The other stayed for a moment, and I just lowered my head and bawled, hugging myself quietly to try to find some solace.

The other person put his hand on my shoulder and said consolingly, "Steven, you look a little upset. You'd better check your gender identity monitor. You might need some medications."

Sob. Snort. "I don't wear a watch."

"Huh? Well, anyway, whenever you're ready, please go over to the CPU and pick up some supplies for us."

I sucked up a load of snot and looked up at him. "CPU? What's that? The Central Processing Unit?"

"No. The Central Prescribing Unit."

"Where's that?"

"Third floor of the center."

*

Notes to Part II

---

3   *Federalist*, no. 59 (Hamilton), at 362.
4   *Federalist*, no. 16 (Hamilton), at 117.
5   *Federalist*, no. 6, (Hamilton) at 56.
6   *Federalist*, no. 11, (Hamilton) at 90–91.
7   de Tocqueville, *Democracy in America*, 131.

PART III
People Who Need Us Don't Know What Is Best for Them

TWENTY

The excavation plan had failed, and the tree was now located on the north side of the building, sticking up out of freshly compacted dirt and more robust than ever. It was also proudly blocking the back entrance. The branches had broken out a few windows, and those had been boarded up, but the people who had to cut the branches out were all at the hospital, under quarantine. A giant yellow tape ran the length of the building, keeping anyone from going near the menacing creature.

I stopped the security officer now guarding the tree to see what all the fuss was about, and he said bluntly, "That thing is under arrest for inciting reckless endangerment."

I gave a short nod and responded, "That makes sense." Then I went around to the front and made my way up to the third floor, explaining that I was there for a pickup. The pharmacist smiled politely and handed me a box marked "Poison."

I lifted it up, and it weighed a ton. Setting it down again, I said, "What's this?"

Without looking up from the form she was completing, she said, "The weekly stock of compassionate release drugs."

While I was waiting for her to finish, I looked around and noticed a sign on the far wall that read, "Compassion Strengthens Families." It was a picture of two kids dutifully smiling up at their parents. I interrupted as she was completing the paperwork and asked, "Say, are these the only drugs you send to the hospital?"

Finally looking up to hand me the completed form, she responded,

"Oh, no, but the vast majority. Most other drugs people just pick up from the dispensary around the corner, or they have them delivered to their homes."

I remembered that I went out on a date once with a girl who worked here, and I inquired about her. The pharmacist shook her head gravely and said, "I'm afraid that she's dead."

My eyes bulged out. "Dead?"

"Yep."

"How?"

She struggled lightly to remember the circumstances and then said, "I think it was cardiac related. Yes, broken heart syndrome. She realized she was never going to make it as far as she wanted and just couldn't handle the stress of disappointing her family."

With that I quietly turned to leave, carrying my burden with me. The box I left with was heavy, but my heart was even heavier, and walking back to the hospital, I felt as deadly as the contents I was carrying. Nothing I had done thus far had helped anyone, and I vowed then and there to try to be nicer to people and to continue working to boost my citizenship score to help Emily, no matter what.

I rode back up to seven to deliver the drugs, and the doctor in charge took them from me and handed them to an orderly who scampered away. The doctor finally shook my hand in greeting and said, "Thanks for picking those up, Steven, and welcome to the staff. You'll be mostly working up here with us on the seventh floor."

I was already familiar with the general order of business on this ward and instead asked skeptically, "What do they do on the other floors?"

"Well, we do gender reassignment down on one, and the second floor is for Botox."

"You need an entire floor for Botox?"

"Of course. Lobotomies have to constantly Botox past age twenty-five because the aging process freaks them out and they believe that youth is perpetual. The condition actually causes great difficulties, because they always expect their favorite stars to look the same until they're sixty. Anyway, the third floor is for the nonterminal diseases, although sometimes we have to use it for Botox overflow as well."

Remembering the boy, I said, "And how exactly do you figure out which diseases are nonterminal?"

"Oh, we have very sophisticated machines to help us with that. As you know, the human form is weak. Medical science has come a long way, but I'm afraid human existence is terribly perilous and has to be monitored constantly, since people could be diagnosed with a new condition any day. Thankfully we have AI supercomputers to assist us, and we apply algorithms to determine the level of care people need. Of course, if you don't meet the parameters, then you're incurable; and if you are determined to be incurable, we use another algorithm to determine release date."

"And the release date is based on what?"

"Well, it's a bit complex, but it is essentially a combination of your NarXex score multiplied by the probability of a pain-free recovery, and … other factors."

Recalling my study of the archives, I said skeptically, "Do you use the same algorithm that determines whether or not coffee is good for you?"

The doctor beamed and replied, "Oh, yes! It's such wonderful technology!"

Trying to mask my sarcasm, I said, "So it's about as good as the flip of a coin, huh?"

The doctor scratched his chin, and I could see him running the calculations in his head. He finally responded assuredly, "Well, in some cases, maybe. But don't forget it's a scientific coin and we've taken the thumb out of the equation."

Probably expecting me to be satisfied with that answer, we kept walking and he added, "Anyway, every person's information from their gender identity monitor is stored in the computer profiles right here. That helps form the person's overall health picture and lets us deliver personalized medicine."

"Okay. What else?"

"The fourth floor is for cosmetic surgery."

"Like what?"

"People born with the wrong feet or hands. Oh, and ears—we do that surgery now as well."

I halted and said, "You seriously give people feet transplants?"

Nodding assuredly, the doctor responded, "Oh, it's very serious. You wouldn't want to be trapped in a body with the wrong feet on it, would you? After all, that's an almost two-pound burden to lug around with you!"

I just shook my head and said, "I guess not. Where do you get them from anyway?"

"Organ donors. We give the patients surgery and then put them on antirejection drugs for rest of their lives, and it all works very well. The fifth floor is where we perform transgender pet surgery."

I jumped back. "Come on! You have to be joking!"

He peered at me over his glasses and responded, "Steven, you're obviously not a pet owner. Pets are people too. Plus, if someone wants to marry their pet, it might not be the right gender."

I just shrugged and replied lightly, "Yeah, that fits."

"And the sixth floor is the wellness center."

That was the first surprising thing I had heard. "Wellness? What do you do there?"

"We teach mindfulness and yoga."

Disappointed, I said, "Oh."

The doctor insisted, "No, no, it's very useful! In times of social catastrophe, we emphasize mindfulness stretching exercises. That, combined with medications, keeps people pretty well under control."

From all my time at the newspaper spent watching people fall to pieces with the slightest little social disturbance, I asked skeptically, "Yeah, and what if that doesn't help?"

The doctor just shrugged and responded, "Oh, we bring them up here for compassionate release."

"Seriously?"

"Absolutely. After all, people who witness emotionally charged events tend to suffer from survivor guilt."

"What the hell is that?"

"A condition where the survivors feel bad that some people died when they didn't."

I shook my head. "You mean that people actually feel bad about being left alive?"

The doctor replied knowingly, "Oh, Steven, you have no idea …" I didn't have any further response, so the doctor added, "Anyway, up here is where we do the most important work getting people ready for their trip to the afterlife. We like to call it Seventh Heaven!"

"Clever."

He shot back a smile. "Isn't it?"

As we walked along, I said, "Well, I was here a little while ago when they performed compassionate release on a ten-year-old boy, or girl. Or … I don't know what gender the kid was, but he, she, or whatever was killed."

The doctor nodded and said thoughtfully, "Oh, I remember that one. I'm so grateful that we could end his suffering."

Thud.

I said, "But all he had was a broken leg."

"Yes, but … Well, you probably know the rest of the story."

Trying not to let my exasperation show, I said, "Yes, I do, and excuse me for saying this, but it seems like he died because he couldn't afford to live?"

The doctor nodded. "Yes, that's true."

"But how could you do that?"

Absently, he said, "Oh, it happens all the time."

"Seriously?"

He stopped and responded, "Sure. Steven, there is nothing sadder than seeing a beautiful person out starving on the street, and as you know, lobotomies are incredibly attractive these days."

I retorted, "Wait, he wasn't a lobotomy?"

"Oh, of course not, but it happens to a lot of people in lower income brackets as well. See, for most of them, the insurance lets them live comfortably well into life, but then they start to realize that it's running out. They may make a final push to get up the ladder at work, but eventually they just give in."

"Then what?"

"Then we release them from the system. Of course the government takes a little cut, but the rest goes to the family, and it all works very well."

I tried to keep my tone curiously neutral and said, "But are you killing people just because they can't afford to pay for health care?"

Thud.

The doctor seemed not to register the sound and just rolled on, "Yes, but it's always been like that. In the old days, people would work and save and buy a house, and then some huge catastrophe would hit that landed them out on the streets where they would starve. All we're doing here is stopping it short of that final misery, and people are much happier as a result. Trust me, Steven; this is the pinnacle of humanity." Stopping again for a moment, the doctor shook his head and added mournfully, "I tell you, in the dark days, we had to use assisted suicide."

"What's that?"

"Oh, it was a horrible process. The decision to self-terminate was left up to each individual, and it was tearing families apart. The families didn't have any input and it just didn't work, so we gave them a stake in the game with the insurance policies. We also changed the program name to borrow from an old one they used to employ in prisons, since it's much more uplifting than that old, depressing term they used to have."

Thud.

"But how does the program work now?"

"These days, a community decision is made concerning when a person needs to be released. There are, of course, extreme circumstances, like what you saw with your young friend, but most of the time it's a joyous occasion that everyone celebrates."

Astonished, I said, "How could they ever celebrate death?"

The doctor waved a cheerfully impatient hand at me and responded, "Steven, you'll really need to spend some time here before you can comprehend it all, but the process basically works like this. The family comes together and votes, and everyone with an inheritance stake gets to decide what should happen. If a person has a terminal disease and the family consents, then we schedule them for release. That is again based on a very complicated formula, but in general, we usually give people six months to a year to live— depending on their credit score."

"Sounds pretty dreary to me."

The doctor responded enthusiastically, "Oh, not at all! In most instances, family members have presubmitted electronic orders to terminate the parents once they get within a certain percentage of being broke, so the actual processing at the hospital is sometimes fairly brief. And here—look at some of these scrapbook records."

The first photo showed a mom and kid setting up a social media app to track the compassionate release progress, and they were smiling brightly. The doctor handed me some more materials and said, "And look here. Here are some photos of the families as their date grows nearer. During that time, we provide caregivers to help them finish their bucket lists, and then they come over here with a few weeks to live. While they're here, we help them compile memoirs and prepare for the next phase in life."

Thud.

"Next phase?"

"Sure. You know, heaven!"

"Oh." More pictures showed families later gathered around the bed in the ward, and then the families were seen holding up their inheritance checks. They looked like sweepstakes winners, and I said incredulously, "You put leis around their necks?"

The doctor smiled broadly. "Oh, yes! That's a new positive encouragement tool we're trying out! But don't they look happy?"

Dully, I said, "Yes, they sure do."

Taking the promotional booklet from me, the doctor added reassuringly, "See, acting with the compassion that we do these days really does strengthen families." Then he handed me another promotional brochure. "And look at this list of all of the nice things a kindergarten class said about our program! How cute!"

Recalling the kindergarten class of lobotomies they taught the duck-and-cover method to, I took a step back and said suspiciously, "Are you trying to use a bunch of five-year-olds' opinions about a government program in order to justify it?"

Without faltering, the doctor responded, "Of course, Steven. Check the archives. That's been the standard for years now." He also added thoughtfully, "Anyway, compassionate release is what we doctors do for ourselves."

"Really?"

"Yes. See, I told you it was compassionate."

"How does that make it compassionate?"

"Well, if it's good enough for doctors, it should be good enough for everyone, right?"

Perhaps sensing that I was not entirely convinced, he hastily offered, "We also followed 'getting ready to die' events, and that helps us assist people in organizing their last year. Here, look at this."

He handed me another pamphlet. *Doctors Recommend How to Spend the Last Year of Your Life.* I noticed that getting enough sleep was high up on the list, and then he took it back from me and said confidently, "And who would know better than we doctors how properly to end life?"

Thud.

I couldn't ignore it any longer and finally asked, unnerved, "The families don't hear that, do they?"

"What?"

"Can't you hear that thud every time they drop a body down the disposal chute?"

Dismissively, the doctor said, "Oh, that. We time it carefully so the survivors are in the elevator on the way to collecting their checks before we dump the body."

"And what if their parent spent everything and there is no check?"

He paused for a second and looked at me, calculating the possibilities. Finally, he said, "Well, those people might hear a thud, but don't worry. You'll tune it out after enough time."

* * *

Later on, we were still touring the ward, and he said, "Steven, you'll see that compassionate release is the most relaxing experience there is. People suddenly realize that all they have to do is let go and let God, and it is most moving to witness!"

"Are the families standing around when you ... pull the plug?"

"Oh no. The bodies—I mean people—are wheeled down the hall. Here, let me show you."

We opened the door on someone about to undergo compassionate release. It was the same room that the little boy had been in, and the patient was heavily sedated and lying on a bed covered with rubber sheets.

The doctor said pleasantly, "See? The family never has to actually encounter the corpse." With that, he nodded, and the technician injected the body, and then whomever it was expired in seconds. After that, two orderlies pushed past me and grabbed the gurney, and we followed them down the hall to a metal chute mounted on the wall. The door swung down on hinges, and the body was loaded onto it; then the two orderlies slammed the plate door shut, and we heard the body screech down the shaft. They listened for the thud and then briefly high-fived.

Cringing, I said to the doctor, "And his family was here?"

"Oh yes, but they're downstairs now, finding out about their insurance payout." The doctor smiled broadly and added, "Yep, thanks to us, most people think that death only happens in the news, but studies prove anyway that the best thing people can do when they die is get over it ASAP."

While the doctor turned and addressed the orderlies, I thought about Emily's dad and was eternally grateful that they kept him out of this place. Then I heard the doctor say to the orderlies in the room, "Thank you, I'll take it from here." They walked away, and he turned to me expectantly and asked, "Steven, wanna try one?"

My face probably registered somewhere between horrified and blank, and I asked hesitantly, "Try one what?"

"You wanna chuck a body down the incinerator chute?"

"Oh, I'm not ..."

He grabbed my arm and said, "Sissy! Come here!"

We went back into the compassionate release room, and another person was in there and had already been injected. The body was completely lifeless but still warm to the touch, and the doctor went around the bed and said, "Steven, we also have a chute in here. See?"

I looked up on the wall behind the bed, and he added, "We use this one in case release has to be performed at night or the orderlies are on their lunch break. Watch." The doctor pressed a button on the side of the bed and a panel slid open on the wall; then the bed tilted backward to forty-five degrees. The rubber sheets had apparently been lightly lubricated, and the body slid right into the chute. The familiar sound of flesh on metal was followed by a thud, and I shuddered noticeably and closed my eyes.

The doctor slammed the chute closed and wiped his hands together. "See, nothing to it! We designed it so that the two chutes go to the same place."

I opened my eyes to look at him. Trying to control my nausea, I said, "Why don't you put some padding down there?"

The doctor responded with a smile of oblivion. "What for?"

"So you're not just dumping bodies straight into a garbage container."

He waved a dismissive hand at me and responded, "Oh, don't worry about that. The fall can't damage the body too much since we're only seven stories up, and they still burn the same even if the bones are broken up a bit."

Holding back the urge to vomit, I managed to ask, "But what about the body parts you remove for transplants?"

"Oh, those. We preselect people who will be donating body parts, and they undergo release in a special wet room down on four."

"I presume there's a chute down there as well?"

"Of course!"

I just shook my head, dreading the notion of ever having to participate in a dismemberment while working at the hospital. Then the doctor added, "Now sometimes when we're really busy, the bodies can get jammed up if we're using both chutes at the same time. In the hallway storage closet, there's a twelve-foot spear you can use to unblock the jam, and they have one on four as well in case bodies wind up twisting and contorting on each other and messing up our neat system."

The doctor ushered me out of the room and continued unfazed as I fought the oncoming vertigo. "Anyway, having people go through compassionate release is the most pleasurable experience they have ever had. Out here, we give them a special bed all to themselves and put them on a cocktail of drugs so they'll feel like they are in a nice, warm cocoon the entire time."

Trying to shake off the nausea, I asked, "If it's so pleasurable, why do you have to drug them?"

Thud.

The doctor smiled and replied, "Well, some people are naturally nervous when they come to the hospital. That's all."

"Is that part of what I picked up from the pharmacy?"

"Oh, no. The cocktail we give them out there is a bit of fentanyl mixed with morphine and meth, and we pick up that stock on a different day. Of course, we do give them one last jolt of morphine with the stuff that sends them over the rainbow."

As we walked back out into the main area, he continued. "After a few days of getting them to relax up here, we slowly titrate the cocktail, and any available family members get to come in for the whole day and say their good-byes. FFLA provides workers a day off for that purpose."

From the look on his face, it appeared that the tour had ended, which he confirmed by saying, "Now, is everything clear to you?"

Thankful that I didn't feel like vomiting anymore and still resolute in my promise to Emily, I simply said, "Yep. So what do I do?"

"Help restock supplies, change bedpans, sweep, and anything else that comes up. And when you're walking around, feel free to talk to people if they don't have any family around. That helps calm them."

With unconcealed irony, I said, "Jeez, thank goodness for twenty-five years of schooling, huh?"

In all earnestness, he responded, "Oh, yes. The application process for this position is actually very competitive, since we usually only take people with hard science backgrounds who have a thorough understanding of the compassion that comes through the work we do here."

Thud.

* * *

As I was making my rounds with supplies, I noticed an elderly lady siting all alone in her bed. Mindful of the doctor's instructions, I went over to pay her a visit.

She said, "Oh, I'm doing just fine, and thank you for stopping by to say hello!" She reached out and grabbed my hand, patting it warmly and counseled, "You know, if you're lucky, young man, you'll make it to my age. Then you can go out in the hospital, the natural way!"

I muttered reflexively, "I'm not interested in just making it to the end."

She leaned forward and said, "Huh? Speak up, sonny."

I quickly changed tones and asked lightly, "Are you're happy to be here?"

She nodded thoughtfully and replied, "Oh, yes!" Then she motioned me closer and said, "I'll tell you a secret. A long time ago, I was very, very depressed. I even contemplated suicide at one point." I nodded solemnly, and she sat back and added, "I'm so glad that I got over that and waited so that I could die the way God wanted me to!"

The next day, I had to make a run to the center for more drugs. On my way out, I ran into two young guys down in the lobby whom I had seen with their father up on the ward. They smiled and waved as I passed, so I stopped to chat briefly. Trying not to be intrusive, I asked respectfully, "Are you here for your dad's release?"

The short one gave an oddly satisfactory response. "Oh yeah!"

Slightly surprised by this, I said, "Must be very sad."

The taller one laughed. "Are you kidding? The joke's on him when he dies! We inherit everything and get to live free, and we have been biding our time all these years just waiting for the bastard to croak!" With that they gave each other a high five.

Coming back upstairs later on, I saw that same gentleman sitting alone, and I walked over and greeted him. "Hello, sir. How's it going today?"

He was beaming. "I'm having a great day now that my two ingrate sons left!"

That was again surprising to hear, and I said, "You guys don't get along?"

"Are you kidding? I couldn't get here fast enough to finally get away from them! Little freeloading weasels! But I'll tell you a secret." He motioned me to come closer, and when I bent down, he whispered gleefully, "The joke's on them when I die! Not only have I been able to exercise complete control over them for their entire lives, but I spent almost everything in the last six months! Ha!"

Shocked, I said, "You did?"

"You bet! I ran up a huge tab at the brothel, went to the racetrack, and incurred a ton of other debt that won't be called in until after I die!"

I stood up straight again and asked, "Um, don't you know that they were relying on you to be able to get ahead?"

He smirked and replied vengefully, "Ha! Serves those little leeches right! If they'd actually gotten off their asses to work for a living like I did, they wouldn't need me. Now we'll see what happens to them when I'm gone!"

"So what are you dying of, anyway?"

Crossing his arms in front of him, he boasted, "Nothing. I'm just sick of them, and now that I've spent all of my money, I have to go anyway."

"Why?"

"Because that's the law. When your money runs out, you get released. Fortunately, I'm old already and got to do everything I wanted to. I went out with a bang, not like the rest of these sucks!"

I walked away from him in a state of partial shock and wound up running right into one of the doctors, whose head was buried in a clipboard. Embarrassed, he said, "Oh Steven, sorry about that. I didn't see you."

"No, that was my fault."

"Are you okay?"

"Well, I was just over talking to that old man in bed 432."

"Yes?"

"He said that he spent all of his insurance money and his kids don't know about it, but earlier I saw them downstairs, and they were counting on getting money from him after he died."

The doctor just shrugged and said, "Well, it can't be helped. Sometimes things just go that way. But don't worry; we'll have beds available for the kids as well when their time is up. Excuse me, I have to go."

That evening as I walked home, I saw another ad on the street for the insurance program: "Strengthening Families, Protecting Lives." *What a joke.*

When I got to my door, there was also a giant box waiting for me. I hadn't ordered anything lately and had no idea what it could be. When I brought it inside and opened it, I found dozens of different condiments and foodstuffs, all of which had apparently been auto-reordered by my pantry as a remnant of my days spent cooking for sex. Fortunately, out in the hallway was an axe stored next to the fire extinguisher, and that put an end to my home economics reordering assistant. The pantry and shelves also wound up being shoved down the incinerator hatch in my building, which was one chute that actually had some use in this screwed-up society.

* * *

The next day, I was interviewing another middle-aged lady who was going on about the most recent director / coach / yoga trainer who had been caught molesting people. Quietly, she beckoned me to come closer and whispered with small excitement, "I tell you, that almost happened to me once! I was alone in my doctor's office, and he tried to feel me up!"

"What were you there for?"

"A breast exam. Thankfully I saw what he was up to and got out of there." Reflecting momentarily, she added, "I tell you, that frightful moment was really the defining one of my whole life."

"And what did you do about it?"

She shrugged lightly and said, "After I got him fired, not much at all. Naturally I've suffered from extreme PTSD since then, and having PTSD, I was far too afraid to do anything at all."

"Why didn't you just do what you wanted with life?"

She responded thoughtfully, "Oh, I was waiting on a cure for Alzheimer's."

I stood up again and looked at her confusedly. "But you don't have Alzheimer's. Your gums look fine."

"Yeah, but I didn't want to take a risk. Fortunately, this place is full of kind, trusting people!"

I said, "Well, you don't look very old to me."

She smiled gently and responded, "That's kind of you to say, but I'm already fifty-seven, and it's my time."

"How do you know?"

She just shrugged and responded, "Someone IM'd me to my VR contacts. Anyway, it's better this way. I sure don't want to run out of energy before I get to heaven!"

One morning I walked onto the ward and there was a fellow I recognized from television—a returning hero from the Pluto colony. Stopping over to pay my gratitude to him, I said, "Hey, wow! You're a real American hero and it's a pleasure to meet you! Was the space adventure wonderful? I've seen pictures, and the digs they give you on Pluto look really amazing!"

He raised his head from the pillow and responded bitterly, "Are you kidding me? It's all a sham, and the space colonies are just another way to skim money. They put us in tin shacks that barely keep oxygen in, and those phony artist's renditions you saw are just a way to generate public support."

Suddenly the doctor appeared. "Hi, Captain Jackson, how are we feeling today? Still having paranoid delusions?"

The astronaut spit at him. "I'm not deluded, you asshole! I know what I saw! It's a trick; it's all a trick!"

The doctor ushered me away and closed the curtain around the space traveler, quickly signaling to two orderlies who rushed behind the curtain to put restraints on the once weightless man. The doctor just shook his head and said regretfully, "Ah, his is a very sad case. He suffers from extreme schizophrenia caused by the outer space experience."

I said, "Does that happen a lot?"

"Oh, yes."

"To how many of them?"

"All of them, of course. I'm afraid the colonists from the moon and the other planets who return are just an unfortunate externality of the economy. They come back expecting a reality that isn't here for them."

"What do you mean?"

"We never expected them to survive, of course, so the only thing we can do is send them to the hospital to die immediately. He's going to be released later today."

"Is he really in that bad of shape?"

"Oh, no. His condition would likely go away at some point, but the space colonists have to give up their insurance policies to participate in the adventure of a lifetime, so there's nothing left over to take care of him."

"How long was he up there?"

"Six years, but most don't make it that long. Heck, some don't even make the trip."

"What?"

"Oh yes. We send shrinks with them on the spaceships, and it's a sort of chicken exit, but some of them crack up right after leaving Earth's atmosphere, so we have a shuttle pick them up on one of the outposts and bring them right to the hospital."

Looking back at the curtain covering the soon-to-be extinct hero, I said with growing concern, "Isn't there something you can do for them?"

When I turned around to the doctor again, he was looking at me like my question had originated from another planet, and then he queried with an odd expression on his face, "You mean *without* an insurance policy?" He stood there waiting for me to clarify, and finally understanding that I was actually serious, he just shook his head and said, "No. I'm afraid that the space experience completely ruins them." He quickly added, "But don't worry; we're just doing things the same as nature does."

"Huh?"

"Even cats and dogs know when their time is up. We put pets to sleep all the time in space."

"Really?"

"Sure. They usually last about three years and then just fall apart. When that happens, we have to show compassion and put them to sleep."

I took a step back and said, "So you drag pets up there and let them live three years, and then you kill them?"

"Yep. Why?"

"It just seems like a waste of life."

Putting a consoling hand on my shoulder, he responded, "Steven, when a horse can no longer do what it is meant to do, you put it down. That's compassion, and we do the same thing with all living creatures who are dying."

*

TWENTY-ONE

After that, sleeping at night became more difficult. I kept having visions of them shoving needles into that poor kid's arm and killing him, and every morning it was getting harder and harder to get out of bed and participate in that process. Still, I kept my head down and tried to endure, for Emily.

However, after a few weeks, I started to notice that the conversations the families were having were all the same, which the doctor explained: "Oh, we give them scripts of suggested things to talk about during their last few days. Most people can't remember anything that has happened, but they all experienced pretty much the same things. As you can imagine, it is very embarrassing to have nothing to talk about with your loved ones when the end finally arrives."

"How do you know what to tell them to say?"

"Science provides the answers. Look, here's a famous article detailing what people talk about when they're dying."

When the doctor left, I chucked the list of canned heartfelt discussions in the trash and rubbed my face. None of it seemed to justify any part of the experience—either living or dying. On one of my breaks, I thumbed through some of the old memoirs that had been left behind, whether by people who died alone or by families who didn't need the keepsakes. They were designed like Mad Libs with blanks to fill in.

> When I was twelve, I saw _____ movie, and
> it was great. When I was fourteen, my favorite doctor

who harvested my eggs was _____. When
I was fifteen, my favorite onesie was _____.
When I was forty, my favorite pair of yoga pants were
_____. The best thing the government ever
did for me was _____.

Users could also get their memoirs in alternate electronic tablet
form. On those, the blanks were actually drop-down menus with
about eight selections per topic. Most people opted for the electronic
memoirs these days.

The next day, a girl who also worked on the ward walked up to
me, sighing heavily. I hadn't slept the previous night and had my own
problems to deal with, and I was hoping that if I didn't acknowledge
her, she would vanish like a body down the corpse chute.

Unfortunately she just kept shuffling her feet loudly, walking
slowly around me like a shark closing in on its prey. She let out one
heavy sigh, followed by another, and another, and another. Finally,
pretending that it was an accident, her orbit reached terminal velocity
and she ran right into the back of me. Barely looking up, I said
unwelcomingly, "Oh, hi, Constance. I didn't see you there."

Hollowly, she spoke toward the ground. "Hi, Steven."

Crap. Be nice, be nice. "Are you doing okay?"

She sighed heavily. "Oh, no. I'm a little down today. I woke up
with a persistent inability to get out of bed."

"Sorry to hear that."

"Yeah, I'm going to try to press on. We'll see what happens." She
shuffled off.

Exactly three minutes later, she was back and hovering right
over my shoulder, and I could actually feel her breath on my neck.
"Steven?"

I clenched my teeth and slowly turned around to give her time to
back away. "What?"

She sighed again and said hollowly, "I don't think I'm going to
make it through the day. Can you finish my work for me?"

I turned back to what I was doing and said curtly, "Fine. I hope you recover."

She responded weightily, "Thanks, Steven. That's really nice of you to say, but my medical condition is a tough burden to bear."

* * *

The doctor grabbed me later that day and said, "Steven, I need you to make a pharmacy run."

"More release drugs?"

"No. The third floor ran out of their supplies. Pick up the delivery and take it down there, and be sure that when they sign for it, you take the invoice back over to the Administration Office on the sixth floor at the center."

In addition to medications, the pharmacy also had a new stock of brochures, and they gave me those as well to take back to the hospital. The top one in the stack was chock-full of advice. "Putting our dad through compassionate release was the best thing our family did! Save plenty of energy for the afterlife! Don't go to heaven suffering!"

While I was there, I struck up a conversation with the girl behind the counter, hoping to delay the need to return to the hospital. She said, "Oh, yes, we sell tons of other drugs besides the one for the seventh floor. We have a pickup location just around the corner from the center."

"Yes, I've seen that."

"And other people get theirs delivered directly to their doors. We have delivery people ready to go twenty-four hours a day."

"What kinds of things get sent to their homes?"

She replied lightly, "Oh, emergency medications mostly—benzos, fentanyl, meth—those kinds of things."

"Huh. I'd think that with the drugs you can buy in the bars, there wouldn't be much of a need."

She beamed. "Don't you know? The stuff we have is ten times better than that! And besides, most people are terrified to go outdoors, except for work and to eat."

"Aren't you worried about all of these people taking drugs?"

She shook her head and replied assuredly, "Nope. The government says it's okay, and if there was a problem, I'm sure they'd tell us!" Hearing that did not make me feel very reassured anymore, but she thoughtfully added, "Plus it's much better than it used to be. A long time ago, we started legalizing marijuana and found out that the increase in weed consumption equaled a decrease in opioid consumption. We realized that people just need something to numb the pain and that the gradual approach works best. That pioneered our whole revitalization of the maintenance drug program."

"Huh."

She also said, "Besides, not everyone uses our drugs."

"How many do?"

"Only about 60 percent of the population. For the rest, a little estrogen or Pitocin usually does the trick. If they're really agitated, we can throw in a small shot of meth or weed with their monthly refill medications."

"It sounds like you have a pretty easy job."

She shook her head decisively. "Oh, not at all! We have to run a very tight ship, and we're constantly under pressure. Otherwise we can cause people to develop a persistent fear of not getting their meds on time."

Dismissively, I said, "Well, it sounds like we have a nation of addicts, huh?"

She shrugged. "Yep, but with the paltry substance we had to work with, it's to be expected. Fortunately, things are getting better."

"They are?"

"Sure. Not too long ago, we discovered that moon dust cures fibromyalgia—well, moon dust mixed with shark fin and koala embryo."

"What causes fibromyalgia?"

"Overactive nerves."

"What causes that?"

"Sitting around too much."

I just shook my head and walked out with the giant box of supplies.

When I got back, the charge nurse on the third floor thanked me profusely for the medications. They were swamped, and she asked me to stick around to help out, and I looked around and asked, "What's wrong with these people?"

Shaking her head and starting to dispense frantically from the box, she responded, "Are you kidding? What *isn't* wrong with them?" I followed her as she started down the line of beds, and she said, "This gentleman suffers from the newest phobia we've discovered—fear of walking through a door alone. That's the result of that damn tree over at the center!"

"Did he work there?"

"Oh, no. He used to work here on six."

I said, confused, "But there aren't even any manual doors around here?"

"It doesn't matter. Psychosis spreads like wildfire among our tender population. Lobotomies, as you know, will somatically inherit diseases from other lobotomies."

"Shouldn't we teach them how to go through doors on their own?"

As the beleaguered man swallowed his meds dutifully, she said over her shoulder, "What for? The condition is actually great for promoting togetherness!"

I stayed around and learned about other maladies people suffered on that ward and talked to several people and handed out pills of one kind or another. Most of the patients were nice enough, and all of them were diagnosed with at least one form of depression, usually mixed with early-onset adolescent anxiety. Studying their charts, I saw that it looked as though the markers had been tracked from about the fourth month of gestation. Many of them had also developed mild schizophrenia and reported hearing voices in their heads and kept mumbling about someone named Sophia.

As I walked home, I realized that the more I learned about that place, the more I started to doubt the ground I was actually walking on. It seemed to me that the firm stones beneath me might suddenly open up into a chasm at any minute. Still, I kept my feet under me, for Emily's sake, and the next day, they moved me back up to seven.

When I got there, I noticed a lovely young lady whom I had seen down on three the day before. Shocked, I said, "What's she doing here?"

Absently, the doctor looked up from his clipboard and said, "Oh, she's just been scheduled for release."

"Why?"

"Uncontrollable anxiety. She's afraid that she could be diagnosed with autism at any moment."

"Why don't you give her treatment?"

He just shrugged. "Can't. There's no treatment for that."

Later that week, I was back on three, and the nurse shook her head again and said, "I'm afraid it can't be helped. A large portion of these people will eventually wind up on seven. As you know, all sprains are permanent, and some people just can't handle that. Most of our patients are, of course, also people in lower income brackets, so they tend to have more trouble coping than others. And because they can't afford all prescription drugs, they will often turn to street products."

Attempting to be helpful, I suggested, "Have you tried taking them off their meds?"

She gave a jelly-roll laugh as if that was the funniest thing she had heard in weeks. Still shaking her head in amusement, she said, "Ha! Steven, I'm afraid that our budget is only so large! We can't justify experimental treatments for everyone!"

I retorted, "But taking someone off their antidepressants is not an experimental treatment."

She replied knowingly, "Well, it is these days, and especially with people like him."

"What's his problem?"

"He was waitlisted to go to the moon."

"So?"

"So you have to bet your insurance policy to get on the waitlist for the moon or any of the other space colonies, and if people aren't selected after a time, they can develop the newest form of depression. It's called 'I didn't get picked for the list' depression."

Feeling the desperation build, I said, "Can't we do something about having to kill all of these people just because they run out of money?"

She responded nonchalantly, "'Fraid not. Lobotomies fret terribly about personal finances, but most of them eventually succumb."

"Then why don't they do something about it?"

The nurse shook her head with practiced regret. "Unfortunately, the human form is weak. Have you seen the experiment they did over at the lab? Anyway, can you imagine all of those beautiful lobotomies out on the street just because they spent all of their money? Now, that would be too much to bear."

"Well, this morning I was talking to a lady who had carpal tunnel syndrome. Surely she's going to recover, right?"

The nurse paused between tasks to shrug lightly. "Maybe, but the types of workplace injuries people suffer these days are usually unbearable."

"Why?"

She responded thoughtfully, "Sitting at a desk all day depressing push-button emojis, you get carpal tunnel, but all you really get in exchange is the experience of sitting at a desk." Wistfully, she sighed and added, "It's just not the same as the good ol' days when you could lose an arm but also had the benefit of going to war or defending your own property. You know, like you see in the movies."

Still confused, I said, "But why can't people do things like that now?"

She laughed lightly and said, "Because the mysteries of life have all been solved! The closest thing we have now is the space experience, and you see how those people turn out ..."

*　*　*

I eventually stumbled upon a truly interesting case down on three of an elderly man suffering from Parkinson's disease. He shook horribly when sitting down, but his condition completely resolved when I gave him a sawed-off broom handle he had asked for. He was able to stand up, and his tremors completely subsided as he went through an elaborate swashbuckling routine.

The doctor came on the ward later in the afternoon and saw the performance. Frowning at me, he immediately snatched the broom handle away, and they strapped the man to his bed. After a few seconds, I could hear the entire bed shaking along with him, like one of the vibro-pleasure ones they had over at the brothel.

I followed the doctor to the back of the ward, and when we were alone, I demanded angrily, "Why don't you leave him be?"

Tucking the broom handle neatly in the back of the closet, he responded definitively, "Because it's ridiculous! No one gets to do that all of the time. Besides, it scares the hell out of people. Why don't you just tend to the gentleman in bed 46?"

"What's wrong with him?"

"He has AIDS."

I jumped back and said, "Holy cow! When's he scheduled to be up on seven?"

"Oh, he's not. We're just upgrading his nanobot to deliver postdiagnosis medications to him. Fortunately, AIDS is not a terminal disease unless you can't pay for the medication. Otherwise, as you know, chronic diseases are a great boon to the economy." As we turned to walk back onto the ward, he added cheerfully, "Say, did you know that Napoleon died of AIDS?"

I responded flatly, "No, I wasn't aware of that."

I spent the next few days tending to one patient. He was an eight-year-old boy who had been diagnosed with severe zygote depression. They feared that he might turn into the next serial killer, but he seemed harmless enough to me.

He confessed to me one day when no one was around that he didn't like how he felt on his medications, so I went out on my lunch break and bought a large stock of sugar pills. In the afternoon, I told him that the doctors had said that he needed a new medication, promising that this one would taste better.

He sucked one of the candies down and beamed at me. "Mmm! This is great! Will it help me feel better?"

Enthusiastically, I said, "You bet! I'll come back and check on you later." After that, I offered to take the kid's medication monitoring off of the nurse's plate, and she gladly agreed.

Three days later, he was bouncing around and behaving just like an eight-year-old should. He stood up in bed and hugged me when I walked over. "Thanks for curing me! I feel great!"

The doctor finally realized what was happening and pulled me aside. Accusingly, he demanded, "Steven, have you been giving this child *sugar pills?*"

"I, um ..."

He leaned into me angrily. "We tested his urine, Steven, and this boy has a dangerously low level of benzodiazepines in his system! Now explain yourself!"

I tried to provide some clinical justification for my efforts. "Sure. I read a lengthy article in the archives about how the placebo effect works, so I decided to try it on him. Doesn't he look great?"

The doctor looked over at the toddler in his improved condition. Turning back to me and calculating his next response, he said, "Well, maybe today he does, but his blood pressure is also dangerously elevated."

"How high is it?"

"One hundred over sixty."

"I thought that was normal for a kid his age?"

"Oh, it may well be, but we're probably going to lower the range again sometime soon, and then he'll be at risk for an early heart attack."

I pleaded, "Come on! He's a little kid, so let him be a little kid!"

The doctor finally sighed. Putting a patient hand on my shoulder, probably because of my lack of medical background, he said authoritatively, "Steven, look. This one particular child may have responded to your tricks on a short-term basis, but you are messing with a dangerous method, and science proves that this child won't be able to maintain his condition forever on just sugar pills."

"Why not?"

The doctor responded with stressed absolution, "Because, Steven, this is the real world, and in the real world, little, happy children grow into neurotic, anxious adults. Plus, with his zygote depression, he is in an increased risk category."

I tried to plead one last time. "Can't you just let him be?"

The doctor shook his head firmly. "I'm afraid not, since it could be catastrophically dangerous to our population." He could see the look of malaise in my expression, and trying to show that there were no hard feelings, he added, "Look, Steven, if it was your child you'd certainly want the best for him, wouldn't you?"

Bitterly, I replied, "I don't have children."

He smiled. "See what I mean?"

"Well, what about some of these others? Why can't we try it on all of them?"

He responded conclusively, "That can never work."

"Why not?"

"Because placebos are only effective if *some* people are actually getting drugs."

After he left, I completely ignored his admonishments and kept up my routine anyway. The air on the ward was light and happy, but the doctor was furious when he returned. In the middle of my rounds, he came over and snatched the tray away from me and demanded, "What the hell are you doing?"

Innocently, I responded, "Oh, nothing! Just a little side-hustle giving placebo drugs to these patients!"

Mockingly, he replied, "Well, are you charging them for it?"

"Of course not."

He leaned in accusingly and said, "*Then it's not really a side-hustle, now is it?*"

I shrugged and shot him an innocent look. Several patients on the ward were studying us in their unmuddled conditions, and the doctor noticed and gave them all a nervous, reassuring smile. Turning back to me and lowering his voice, he said, "Goddamn it, Steven, you're not their physician! Any more stunts like that and you'll be out on your ear. Now go and see the director!"

*

TWENTY-TWO

Sitting calmly at his desk, hands clasped behind his head, the director responded lightly, "Steven, I can completely understand your compassion, but you mustn't interrupt the scientific process."

Standing my ground, I said, "Look, half of the people on that ward came in initially for the flu, and they were eventually sent upstairs for compassionate release."

"And?"

I stomped my foot and insisted, *"It's the flu, goddamn it!"*

"Yes, but if you look closely at their charts, you will see that all of those people have birthdays that are close together."

"So?"

"So flu exposure is linked to people's birthdays."

Angrily, I said, "No, it's linked to living in cramped, crappy dwellings!"

The director just shook his head knowingly and responded, "Sorry, Steven, but science has already come up with the answer. Those people run the risk of repeated flu exposure just because of the date on which they were born. And as you know, it gets harder and harder to survive the flu after repeat exposure—never mind the potential for exposure to other airborne viruses."

I had absolutely no response to that, so the director leaned forward and lectured firmly, "And you have to understand something. All science is based on the notion of general acceptance. If you go around questioning the doctors, that hurts the ability to get people to accept what we are telling them. That's why surveys are so important these days."

"Why?"

"Steven, if a thousand people accept something, that's general acceptance."

"But that's only a thousand out of what … one billion?"

He sat back again and responded knowingly, "Yes, but then that survey turns into fifty papers on the subject, and … Well, you know the rest."

Still frustrated, I said, "So, what, we're just keeping people complacent long enough to be able to kill them?"

The director shook his head defensively. "Oh, no, not at all. There are a lot of overlapping principles at play in our society that might be a little difficult to understand, but they all work perfectly once you see them as we do. One thing is for sure, however, and the doctor was right to call you out on it."

Finally sitting down, I said, "What's that?"

"Unconventional treatments double the risk of death, and they also greatly upset our system."

"Well, I'm starting to seriously doubt the usefulness of your system." Right after I said that, I realized how risky the comment actually was.

The director just gave an innocent smile and responded, "Why? It all works very well for those who cooperate! After all, the credit system gets you from a dingy apartment with thin walls where you can hear everyone to a very robust apartment where you can't hear your neighbors and added security is present in the building. And if those people had worked to get to that nicer building, they wouldn't get the flu as often. Unfortunately, science proves that poor credit management is linked to people who have certain birthdays and who also live in the same neighborhood."

I finally insisted, "Why can't you just give everyone nicer accommodations?"

He shook his head and gave a dismissive chuckle. "I'm afraid that is due to the age-old problem of scarcity of resources! I'm sure you know that the darn law of supply and demand never goes away. It is, in fact, the most challenging problem that the social planners have ever had to face. But don't forget things are much better than they used to be."

Acridly, I said, "That is becoming harder and harder to believe. My first experience at that place was watching them kill a little boy, or girl, because ... they didn't have enough insurance left over to survive."

The director responded assuredly, "Yes, but in the dark times, that little person wouldn't have even made it that far. Steven, I can't tell you what it was like to be around when people were shooting each other during gender renaming parties."

Shifting sideways in the chair, I said, "Well, I still can't see how anyone actually 'makes it.' Most of these people aren't fit to manage a linen closet."

Unfazed, he acknowledged unabashedly, "Probably not, but that doesn't mean that we can't still eke a little economic benefit out of them before they die."

I gave up on the director and went back to work. Despite my best efforts, the old Steven was emerging again among my colleagues. "Hi, Steven. Do you want to know what I'm thinking today?"

I pretended not to hear him, and when he inched closer to ask me again, I whipped around and shouted, "*No!*"

The frightened orderly scampered away. "*Waaaaaaah!*"

One of the doctors came up to me concerned and said, "Steven, what's wrong?"

I sighed and tried to remember my promise. "Oh, nothing. I just think this place is starting to get to me."

He rested a hand momentarily on my shoulder and counseled, "Steven, compassionate release is just the natural progression of things. Years ago, we had people who would suffer auto accidents and have minor soft tissue injuries, but for some reason, they would never seem to get better. Soft tissue injuries led to fibromyalgia, and fibromyalgia led to addiction to pain medications. Then surgical intervention left the people paralyzed and even more depressed, and depression led to suicide. Now we've simplified things and made them much better!"

I took a step away and turned toward him. "How? By killing people before they realize what's happening to them?"

"Of course. Look at it this way: if you come down with a disease but were ready to die anyway, it wouldn't matter that much to you now, would it?"

I pondered that for a minute and finally conceded sullenly, "Probably not."

"Exactly. And that's what we do here. Besides, we don't want to force them to choose between having the drugs they so desperately need and being able to put food on the table, so we don't. When they get within about 20 percent of not being able to afford one or the other, we just end it."

In a slightly accusing tone, I said, "I would think that all of this medical technology would help people live longer, not cut their lives short."

The doctor held up his hands innocently and responded, "Oh, make no mistake—people can live nearly forever these days. However, most don't want to because of bowel problems. A lifetime buildup of dark matter causes loose stools—which isn't very glamorous, as you can probably imagine. Lots of other people also ask to be released because of pressures from social media."

"Huh?"

The doctor shook his head. "Yes, for some reason lobotomies have a desperate need to find acceptance. Oddly, they only know where to look for it in electronic mediums, and I'm afraid that getting PTSD from reading a news story is now one of the most frequently utilized methods to trigger insurance coverage—right up there with hearing persistent voices in your head. But it's all part of the marvelous democracy experiment we live in!"

I responded incredulously, "Democracy experiment?"

"Oh sure! You watch the news, don't you?"

I thought for a second about diving into that conversation but instead chose my words carefully. "Yes, I do. However, from what I can see, the two factions of the government appear to be largely fighting over whether people should get 20 or 22 percent of the leftover insurance proceeds."

The doctor shook his head and laughed. "Yeah, those hippie liberals are always trying to give too much back to the people! But Steven, the more time you spend here, the more you'll see that people truly live a rich tapestry of experiences. The workday has been reduced to four hours during most weeks; all of their needs are taken care of, and they have nothing to fear. In reality, it's a modern paradise!"

I finally just demanded, "Well, when the hell did human beings lose so much of their substance that nearly anything could kill them?"

He responded compassionately, "Oh, I'm afraid that that's the result of there not being much out there for people to do anymore. In reality, all we are left with around here is to count up the bodies, tally the insurance numbers, write a brief eulogy, and go on. But what we do is absolutely essential to overall well-being, since these people want to be able to look back when they get to heaven and know that they spent their lives well."

Accusingly, I said, "Yeah, well the other day, I saw that you wrote memoirs for an eight-year-old."

"Sure." He rattled off the list: "Baby's first medication implant, baby's first inhaler, et cetera. Now, of course, we have baby's first toothbrush!"

"But how could you kill an eight-year-old?"

"Oh, it happens all the time. Don't worry; he was an old soul."

I snapped. *"What the hell does that mean?"*

Unfazed, he responded, "He was born before the last technology upgrade."

"No, no! Why the hell does that have anything to do with being able to kill him?"

"It means that he knew what he was giving up. Actual awareness is essential for choice, and if people can't make a choice to die, then it's the same as murder—which we *certainly* do not do. Thankfully, everyone up here knowingly chooses their fate!"

Exasperated, I said, "How? How can they possibly know what they're agreeing to, no matter how old they are?"

The doctor smiled assuredly and answered, "Because we advertise it to them every day of their lives! Life is, after all, really just a timeshare arrangement. We let them live for a while in exchange for their obedience to us, and we have the system down to a true science. We don't let people live too long, or not long enough. After all, time famine leads to Einsteinian depression."

Still bitter, I said, "What the hell is time famine?"

He responded solemnly, "Well, sometimes lobotomies want to do so much but realize that to do it they'll have to spend energy. I'm afraid that it can be terribly upsetting." Then he smiled and added, "But thank goodness for the lobotomies! Did you know that parents used to lock their kids in sheds in the backyard for months on end?"

I finally sighed, deflated, and said, "Yeah, things are much better now."

* * *

I left early that day, thankful that it was Friday. My seams were starting to come apart, and the only thing that kept me sane was my weekly call to Emily. She never broke character, even though I know she was struggling very hard, and from the other side, she said, "Things are going as well as they can. You?"

I didn't want to add to her burdens, but I couldn't hide my mood. "Bad."

Sounding preoccupied, she tried to be helpful nonetheless and suggested, "Well then, why don't you do something about it?"

"Like what?"

"I don't know. You're the one with the fancy education. Put your mind to it and come see me the next chance you get. I miss you!"

I promised to be there in a week. Calling her on Friday was better than any shot in the arm, and after a meditative weekend and a long, hot shower on Monday morning, I redoubled my efforts. I was convinced that I could prove them wrong this time.

My new survey was flawless. It asked one single substantive question: "What would you do if you could live one more day?" I was convinced that if I showed them all of the things these people would actually want to do, they would have to recalibrate the algorithms—whatever those were. The survey, of course, had an initial validity factor. The first question was "Have you ever been surveyed?" If they answered no, I was sure I would have a legitimate sample.

The doctor on seven studied it and laughed. "Oh, Steven, these are completely invalid! People who need health care can't possibly know what's best for them. Here's the famous study to prove it." And with that, my next great idea was in the tank.

I was tempted to break our schedule and call Emily midweek, but my phone was at home. Later that evening, I called anyway. She answered concerned and asked, "Steven, is everything all right?"

"Oh yes, and sorry for bothering you during the week. Are you okay?"

"Yes. Mom is still in a bit of a slump. She's been shuffling around the house all day today, but she'll come back around. I'm looking forward to seeing you on Friday!"

That was music to my ears. When Friday came around, I sneaked out at 10:00 a.m., blaming it on a massive migraine. I ran out to the street and excitedly summoned a cab, but my online request was denied. I tried again but still couldn't get a cab to respond. Unsure of what do to, I quickly made my way over to the center and found the director in his office. Confused and starting to panic, I said, "Why can't I get a cab?"

He shot me a quick look of surprise and responded innocently, "Gee, I'm not sure." Pulling up my profile, he said, "Let's see. Oh, here's why. Look at your citizenship score summary. You've dropped so low that you can't afford cabs anymore."

I sat up and said, "What? How the hell did that happen? And wait, I thought you told me that people couldn't get an accounting?"

He smiled and responded quickly, "Oh, well, we're trying it with you! This says that your original G-7 score was reduced by .5 for poor performance. You also lost a point for throwing away your watch."

I shot back quickly, "But I didn't throw it away! I gave it to a poor kid!"

Unapologetically, the director responded, "That's pretty much the same thing. I told you about gray market goods, remember?"

"But wasn't it mine to give away?"

"Oh, no. Those products are owned in trust. That's part of the contract you signed."

Starting to fume, I said, "That's just a fucking trap!"

The director shook his head lightly and responded, "Not at all. Those devices help us know where everyone is. That way we can do our best to make sure that no one has to sleep in the cold or gets lost, and they're vitally useful for keeping the populace safe."

Slumping down in the chair, I said, "Crap. How did you get everyone to wear watches in the first place?"

He smiled and responded, "Easy! We actually gave them away by having people send in elevator selfies, and it was like shooting fish in a barrel and killing two birds with one stone! They wear the watches, and we get the selfies for the news!"

"But then people have no choice except to wear them?"

"Yes, but as you know, we have the power to regulate interstate commerce, and that now includes people. After all, it was the Framers' great dream to extend the reach of the government directly to the people themselves."

Still struggling to follow the reference, I was stuck without a response, so he read on. "Then you lost a point for destroying your auto-reordering pantry."

Starting to sense a trap, I said defensively, "Wait a minute. What am I, a slave to all technology devices?"

"Of course not, but a long time ago we had to build in loss of points to consumer purchases to protect the market. So many people in the past couldn't honor their contractual obligations that incorporating material possessions into the points system was essential." Shaking his head knowingly, he added, "And if you would have read the contract you signed when you activated them, you agreed to hold all of those pieces of property in trust for the people. They were, after all, given to you by the government."

Under my breath, I muttered, "Fucking fine print."

The director laughed and said, "Oh, Steven, don't feel bad! No one has bothered to read the fine print since we inked the Constitution!"

Seeing that I was not amused, he continued plainly. "Anyway, you violated the terms when you destroyed or gave those goods away." Then, waving a lecturing finger at me, he added, "Don't forget that you can tell the level of people's contribution to society by looking at things they own. Watch, shoes, car, you name it—they all help to instantly identify class; it's just like stripes on military professionals, but without the uniform. Isn't that great?"

I slumped down even farther and responded bitterly, "Yeah, terrific."

"You also lost another point for not purchasing a car."

I shot up again and said, "But I didn't even want that car!"

"Well, when you took the test drive, the button you pressed to open the passenger door triggered an agreement that you would faithfully support world automakers. You didn't buy the car, so you didn't fulfill your end of the bargain."

I slammed my fist down on the desk and shouted, "Look, that's just unfair!"

Trapping me again, he responded plainly, "Well, since you didn't have a car, you also took a lot of cabs, and those cost money. Here's the bill summary." As I looked it over, he added sarcastically, "Getting out to see that little floozy of yours sure racked up some hefty bills!"

"Shit."

"And here's the bill for all of the consumer things you spent on those other girls."

Taking it and looking at the string of useless dating events that never meant anything to me, I said, "Fuck. What a waste."

He laughed and added, "And by the size of the tips you left at all of those restaurants, I guess you never got the 12 percent look down correctly, did you?" I shot him a "zero" percent look, which only made him chuckle, and then he added, "Oh, and here's the bill for your biweekly contribution to the cat rescue fund on the moon."

Under my breath, I said, "Fucking cats. Fucking autotip technology."

"You also lost a half point for hitting that drug addict."

"What? I thought physical contact was no harm, no foul."

"Yeah, but you intentionally hit him."

"So? What's the difference?"

The director shook his head and said, "Intent, Steven. Intentions are everything. Heck, even your dog can tell the difference between being kicked and being stepped on."[8]

Bitterly, I said, "I don't have a dog."

He just looked at me and replied definitively, "Well, there you go. Anyway, you are now at G-2, and G-2s can only afford to ride the bus."

I pleaded, "But what about all of my credit for working?"

"Well, at the lab you were up to eight hundred hours, and at the newspaper you worked twelve hundred. So far at the hospital, you've worked four hundred."

"Then I should be up some more, right?"

"Yes. One half of a point. But you already lost five and a half points from all of your stunts and reckless consumer spending."

Eternally frustrated, I said, "Shit. How the hell do people ever make it in this system?"

He shook his head knowingly and replied, "Frankly, most don't."

At that point, I was utterly trapped. I asked a question that I knew had no real meaning, but it came to me anyway. "If I had purchased that car originally, would I still be able to use it now?"

The director laughed. "Of course not! We have to automatically repossess all expensive consumer items once your score gets down as low as yours did!"

I muttered, "What a sham system." The director didn't respond and just sat there waiting for me to try something else, but all I could do was continue griping. "So I'm stuck taking the bus?"

He nodded coldly. "'Fraid so." With a final hint of mockery, he added, "And if you want to take the bus to see your little girlfriend, the next one going out there leaves on Tuesday."

Hearing that, hopelessness settled in, and then I whined, "Are there no other ones?"

Unapologetically, he responded, "'Fraid not."

I was completely defeated. Finally the director leaned forward and folded his hands together on the desk. Firmly, he said, "Look, Steven, if you would only play by our rules, you'd be okay. The rules about technology purchases are there for a very good reason, and they're only a small part of the overall insurance program, but for someone like you, they can cost a lot when you don't want to follow along." Leaning back again, he added definitively, "And I told you, you need to forget about that girl."

I shot him a challenging look but could see that I wasn't going anywhere—literally. Disgusted and without any other recourse, I finally said emptily, "I just think it's all a big trick."

Standing up to show me out, he said cheerfully, "Oh, not at all! Lobotomies love their technology, and the Latin American countries that make them are doing very well—much better than they ever did trying to sell corn!"

Bitterly, I retorted, "Yeah, as long as they always cooperate with us to feed them."

Closing his door behind me, he flashed a conquering smile and said, "Exactly!"

*

TWENTY-THREE

I was almost too ashamed to tell her that I couldn't make it, but I had to say something, so I finally called to break the news. "Look, I'm sorry, but I won't be able to come and see you this weekend. Is there any chance you could get away and come to town?"

On the other end, Emily took a long breath, obviously to hide her disappointment. Finally she regrouped and said, "Well, I'd like to, but I should stay with my mom. She's still struggling a bit and needs me around."

"I understand. I'll get there as soon as I can, and I'm sorry."

The next morning, I asked for a double shift, and I smiled at everyone and listened to anyone who wanted to tell me anything about anything. I just nodded my head and agreed with everything. "Yes, yes, yes. Oh, that's brilliant! You don't say? Wow, that's really interesting!" Ad infinitum. *Thud, thud, thud.* Nothing got to me.

I kept calling to check in on Emily, and they were managing, but just barely. She said that her mom was sleeping a lot lately, and I told her to hang on. I said I was working on a plan to be able to give them some permanent relief, but it would take time. She, of course, understood, and never let on if she was upset with me. She just said thanks for taking time to call and hoped to see me soon.

I was a man on fire. I barely slept. I just worked and worked and worked, and at night I lay awake thinking about her. After two months, I thought it would be safe to take a few days off of work. I had the bus schedule memorized and could leave on Tuesday and be back on Friday. I found someone to cover my shifts and was all set to leave.

The Monday before my trip, I was so excited to see Emily that I couldn't concentrate on what I was doing. I was handing out memoir tablets, and for all I remember, I may have given the children's memoirs to some of the older people. They didn't seem to notice and just started filling them in.

Late in the afternoon while I was doing my rounds, however, Emily slowly walked onto the ward, and I nearly fell over. I saw her from across the room and it is a cliché to say so, but my heart leapt. I didn't want to look too eager, so I kept doing what I was doing.

She didn't notice me off in the corner and seemed to be in distress for some reason. Moments later, her mother was wheeled in on a gurney, and they parked her in the far back corner of the ward. She was secured to the bed and was apparently heavily sedated. Her face was also sheet-white, and she seemed frozen in place.

Emily finally turned and saw me, and I was about to smile at her when I registered the utter fear in her eyes. I nonchalantly made my way across the room and grabbed one of the passing doctors, asking casually, "What's going on with her?"

"Who? Oh, that lady they just wheeled in. She's in catatonic shock. It's truly horrible. She had an extreme reaction to the death of a loved one."

Pretending to be merely curious, I said, "What are they going to do?"

"They have a crash team coming in to perform an emergency release. Unfortunately, there's just nothing that can be done."

With academic surprise, I replied, "Huh. Thanks."

I made an excuse for something I needed to grab down the hall and started walking. Emily saw me, and I discreetly motioned for her to follow. When we were safely around the corner, she threw her arms around me desperately, shaking for the first time that I had ever experienced. I pulled her away after a moment and said in a low, panicked voice, "What is she doing here?"

Still trembling, Emily said, "I don't know. She was doing fine at home ... well, she was still a bit down, but she was able to carry through the day—and then came a knock on our door. A mobile medical crew announced a report of an emergency situation. Grand mal depression and rapid-onset schizophrenia, they said. I told them that I didn't know anything of the sort, but they pushed past me and went into her room. They checked her vitals and gave her a shot, and she's been mostly out of it since. The next thing I knew, they threw both of us in the back of a white ambulance and brought us here."

I grabbed her by the shoulders and looked at her with dire urgency. "You need to get her out of here. I can't tell you why, but get her out of here *right now!*"

Helplessly, she said, "I can't! They said that her condition warranted emergency intervention and that if I couldn't prove I was her authorized legal representative, there was nothing I could do about it." Pleadingly, she looked into my eyes and asked, "Can you do something?"

"I ... I ... I ..."

Just then, the doctor came around the corner and said, "Ah, Steven. There you are. I need you to come over here and assist me with restocking the fentanyl drips."

I responded quickly, "Sure, Boss. Be there in a second. Um, ma'am, the cafeteria is located down in the basement. Just head for the elevators and you'll see it."

When the doctor was safely gone, I said, "Look, there's nothing I can do. Maybe they just want to run some tests on her?" I knew that was a lie. Holding her by the shoulders one last time, I said, "Let's just see what happens."

Emily walked back to her mother's bed, and I went over and started helping to unload the boxes with the fentanyl bags, but I could see what they were doing out of the corner of my eye. They hooked Emily's mom up to the bedside computer, and I heard one of them confirm, "Yep, she's in a dire state. Her algorithms are completely off the chart. She's suffering tremendously, and we need to act quickly." The doctor turned around and saw me watching. He frowned at me and sharply closed the curtain around the bed, and Emily was lost to me on the other side.

A few minutes later, Emily slowly emerged with her head down.

She wouldn't even look in my direction. Then one of the insurance representatives, dressed in a sequin jacket, put his arm around her and led her out, probably to go over the estate details.

One of the doctors came out and shucked off his rubber gloves, and I tapped him on the shoulder as he passed by. I already knew the answer, but I had to ask. "Hey, what happened to that lady?"

He just shook his head mournfully. "Oh, it was a very, very sad case. That lady completely lost the will to live. Her husband died recently, and it broke her heart, so the best thing we could do was put her out of her misery."

Still trying to conceal my true interest, I said, "Did she ask to be terminated?"

"Oh, no, but it's okay. Steven, people in her condition don't know what's best for them."

"What about the daughter?"

The doctor responded astoundingly, "Are you kidding? She was too grief-stricken to say anything!"

"You did it right there? Behind that curtain?"

"Yes."

Shaking my head in deplorable shame, I said, "Why didn't you wheel her back to the termination room?"

Earnestly, he responded, "There wasn't any time. She was in a horrible state."

"How could you tell? It looked like she was all but knocked out to me."

The doctor responded clinically, "Oh, she was placed on a slew of antidepressants before she got here. Those medications, as you know, can cause violent behavior, and we've learned that in order to effectively maintain people on antidepressants, we have to sedate them as well. Plus, as you know, being in the hospital makes people nervous, and the sedation also helps with that, but her condition couldn't have been starker. She was showing all of the classical signs of schizophrenia."

I tried not to sound aggressive but insisted, "Such as?"

He laughed ironically and said, "Well, for starters, they were trying to keep that farm going, which is about as delusional as you can get, especially when science has proven that people prefer living in our cities! She had also lost the desire to do much of anything, and to boot, she was showing extreme signs of negativism."

"Negativism?"

"Yep. When we got to her place today, she said that she didn't need any of our help. I tell you; we should have seen it coming. A while ago, she refused to let us bring her husband to the center to be cremated."

My blood started to boil at hearing that, and through clenched teeth I said, "How did you find her in the first place?"

The doctor didn't notice and replied plainly, "Oh, it was an anonymous tip. The poor woman was so distraught over her husband's tragic self-guided termination that she couldn't even cook—an obvious sign of schizodepressive syndrome. She phoned in a delivery order yesterday, and a mental health food technician on the line immediately recognized the signs of distress and called us."

At that point, I lost it. I grabbed the front of his shirt and shouted, *"You mean you murder people based on anonymous tips from takeout operators?"*

Startled at my nerve, he shucked my hands away and took a step back, saying defensively, "Hey, whoa. Slow down there, bub. I'm her medical doctor, not you. That patient was in great suffering, and there was nothing we could do, and compassionate release was the only option left to save her. Now please excuse me."

He brushed past me in a hurry, and I just froze and stood there in a daze. A short while later, someone came up and tapped me on the shoulder. I turned sharply and realized that it was a functionary from the lab, and he said, "Steven, the director wants to see you back at the center right away." *Fuck.*

I looked for Emily on my way out of the hospital, but she was nowhere to be seen. All I could do put my head down and proceed briskly over to the center, where the director was waiting for me when I got off the elevator on six. He demanded sharply, "What the hell happened at the hospital? Do you know who that doctor was that you mouthed off to?"

I was still livid. "No."

Firmly, the director responded, "Well, he's a very well-respected man. He's not just the chief physician, but he's also a vice clergy at the church. You can be assured that whatever happened to that woman was absolutely correct under the circumstances." He motioned me into his office and closed the door.

He took a seat behind his desk and started quietly tapping with his fingers while waiting for me to explain myself, but I was starting to go numb and just sat down. Finally, I said defenselessly, "I don't know. It just didn't seem right."

His fingers stopped tapping and he leveled accusingly, "Well, you don't really have the background to make that kind of call, do you?"

"I ... I guess not."

"Steven, many people who need home health care don't know it. That's why they need us."

Finally my emotion burst through and I shouted in a rage, "*But they killed her!*"

The director nodded plainly and said, "Yes, and it was the best thing for it, really, since she was only going to go downhill. Look here. Here's the mental status exam they did of her mother."

In my mixture of grief and anger, I blinked at the form, trying to decipher the neuropsychological data. The test entailed recognizing current events, people who won Oscars last year, the six most recent government initiatives, and trends in social media. These were basically the same questions the idiots I worked with quizzed me on every week, and Emily's mom failed all of them.

I looked up pleadingly and said, "But it's obvious that you gave her the wrong test! They don't even have television out there! I know! I've been there!"

Glaring sharply, he replied, "Yes, Steven, I am abundantly aware of that. But you have to understand that these tests are standardized and clearly show that she was delusional. After all, if you don't know and you don't care, you're obviously losing it."

In a rage, I ripped the test into shreds and started to cry. "*It's not fucking fair! She didn't have to die!*"

Instead of his usual concern, he just leaned back and frowned at me, and then he asked accusingly, "This isn't about that girl again, is it? Steven, Emily is just a baby. She's only twenty-three."

I sniffled and tried to defend myself. "So? I've had younger!"

He responded sarcastically, "Sure—at the *brothel!* Look, Steven, I'm only going to tell you this one last time. You need to put her out of your mind."

I took a deep breath and closed my eyes, but all I could see was Emily's betrayed face staring at me over and over and over again. The full weight of the losses she had endured finally hit me, and I felt truly helpless. I suddenly started crying harder than I think I ever had before.

The director just sat there and let me weep. When I finally began taking in deep breaths to try to get myself under control, he got up and came around the desk. He put his hand on my shoulder and said, "Listen, son, you've had a hard day. Why don't you just go home and rest and you can start again tomorrow."

*

TWENTY-FOUR

I left the center a broken man. I hadn't done anything right since getting to that city, and now someone I dearly loved had just been rendered parentless by the system. I was walking aimlessly and not paying any attention to where I was or what I was doing, and the next thing I knew, I was on the other side of the building, where my tree was standing tall in the encroaching dusk. The creature was beaten and scarred, but it still stood proudly, and its branches were gently rapping at the fiberboard covering the windows.

I didn't know what else to do, so I crossed under the police tape and sat down at the base of the tree. It may have just been the wind, but I felt the branches overhead sway in my direction, as if forming a protective layer over the top of me. I fell asleep and woke long after it was dark. There was no one around, and I was thankful for that. If someone had seen me, they probably would have branded me a complete lunatic.

As soon as I stood up, Emily sprang into my mind and I ran home as fast as I could. I tried to reach her, but the phone just rang and rang. After a few tries, I gave up. I wouldn't blame her at all if she never wanted to talk to me again.

After that, I did the only thing I could and went back to work. I didn't take on extra shifts, but I didn't put up a fight when others had better things to do with their days and needed me to finish their work. I kept mindlessly refilling medications to deliver compassionate release and stopped whenever patients called my attention, reassuring them that they were headed to a better place.

During the middle of the next week, the doctor stopped me to express his concern. "Steven, what's wrong? It looks like you're suffering from a little ennui not otherwise specified."

I just sighed and responded emptily, "You could call it that."

He patted my back reassuringly and said, "Don't worry; it happens to the best of us." Then, putting an arm around me, he said, "Let's take a ride down to the cafeteria and get some coffee. After all, science proves that walking reduces anxiety."

As we strolled past the patients, I said, "Then why are all of the people on three strapped down to their beds?"

He responded officially, "Oh, well, we can't try experimental treatments on everyone." We reached the elevator, and as he pushed the button to call it up to our floor, he continued. "As we have discovered over all of these years, people have been infected with this horrible energy that wants them to go places and do things, but unfortunately it's not at all suited for our society."

I had no will to fight with anyone, but on some internal instinct I had to respond. Hollowly, I said, "Why don't you do something about it?"

"Oh, we do. We prescribe them with medications."

"No, I mean, why don't you open society back up so people can use that energy?"

He laughed. "Are you serious? Do you have any idea how long we've been working to get to this point? We're not going to risk the chaos and uncertainty of the past just because a *few people* don't want to play by the rules!" I looked over at him weakly, and he added, "In reality, drug medications are part of our compromise with the citizens. We keep them sedated, and they agree not to try to deal with things that are bothering them."

"You really think that's all it takes?"

"Oh, yes. As you'll learn, the best way to ensure the personal freedoms we all enjoy is to lobotomize people sufficiently so that they will follow whatever you tell them. Fortunately for us, science proves that people are really just the sum of their parts, so it's pretty easy to do once you get the hang of it."

The elevator finally opened, and we stepped in. As the doors closed, the doctor said, "Steven, this is what I wanted you to see." The ads started scrolling, and he said, "Look at this. Wait … Not that one, not that one, not that one." We watched an ad for a raffle, the next awards show, and the latest advancement in pet transgender surgery. Finally another one popped up, and he said, "There it is. That study shows that 85 percent of people are satisfied at work. Now, what's wrong with you?"

Hollowly, I replied in complete sincerity, "I don't know."

We proceeded to get coffee, and he continued lecturing. Then, as we made our way back to the elevator bank, I stopped and told him that I needed to grab a delivery from the pharmacy. He smiled and said, "Atta boy! Keep your chin up and things will work out just fine!"

* * *

After the elevator doors had closed behind him, I turned and just walked out. I was effectively leaving two hours early that day, on the verge of complete collapse. However, I couldn't go home. My phone was there and would just remind me of the failure I had left on the other end. Instead I went to Ophelia's Pond and sat by water.

There weren't many people there during the day. A couple had shown up early to get a good seat for that evening's new birth announcements, and one of them said to the other, "Did you see that article about the excessive tip that someone left the other day? The economy must be booming!"

"Yeah! Hey, let's order a new baby!"

"Great idea! Oh, I can't wait until we get to unpack our own little bundle of joy!" *Sure, then wait until it's ready to pull the plug on you.*

After a little while, I gave up and headed home. Along the way, I saw a slick-backed luxury vehicle rip through an unsuspecting pedestrian as he was crossing the street. The car didn't stop, and there was no one else around to witness the event.

I approached the motionless body in the street and had seen enough people compassionately released from this world to know that this guy just had his number called up; there wasn't any algorithm necessary to figure that out. All of his pieces appeared to be accounted for in various spots on the roadway, but there was definitely no one home. I picked up a nearby stick and poked him gently, but he didn't respond. It appeared that he may, in fact, have been more than just the sum of his parts.

As I was looking down at him, I spotted a faint blinking light underneath a large brown organ. I lifted the organ up with the stick and saw a little electronic device seemingly embedded in something below, and it was flashing a steady blue.

Seconds later, sirens came around the corner and another blue flashing light appeared. It was the emergency crew, and one of them sprang from the ambulance and came up to me, saying urgently, "What happened?"

"Hit-and-run."

"What kind of car was it?"

"I don't know. Looked like a luxury model."

He just shrugged and pulled a set of rubber gloves out of his pocket. "Figures."

"Why?"

"Those kinds are not programmed to stop for pedestrian collisions. Anyway, let's see what we have here." The technician checked the victim's pulse, and then he looked over his shoulder at me. Apparently presuming that I wasn't any kind of threat, he proceeded to turn back to the body, pulled out a small set of shears, and clipped out the man's organ with the flashing device inside. After neatly separating the two, he shoved the device discreetly in his front pocket and pitched the organ into a nearby sewer drain.

Then he stood up and shucked off his rubber gloves, saying lightly, "Well, nothing more to do here." Two other technicians came around with a stretcher and loaded up the body. The first one gave me a cursory salute and climbed back into the driver's seat, and they slowly made a three-point turn and headed away.

I was still taking in the whole scene, but something told me to try to follow them. I started running after the ambulance, being careful to stay out of their line of sight and taking several shortcuts to keep up. However, after a few blocks, instead of turning right to the hospital, the ambulance turned left to go to the crematorium at the center. When I realized they were just doing a direct delivery to the furnace, I stopped my pursuit. Instead I went into the center and proceeded upstairs, finding the director still working in his office.

He seemed to have forgotten the whole episode with Emily's mom, and rocking his chair gently from side to side, he said, astonished, "Wow. I must say, that's quite a sight you observed! That containment crew you saw is there to keep people from witnessing the harshness of death. As you can imagine, seeing a sight like that could be extremely tragic for our fragile lobotomies."

"How often does that happen?"

"Oh, two to three times per day. The technology in cars is pretty good at spotting larger objects and stopping in time, but pedestrians are still a big problem."

"He said that luxury cards aren't programmed to stop after pedestrian collisions."

Unabashedly, he responded, "Yep."

"That's a little barbaric, don't you think?"

The director stopped and shrugged gently. "Steven, in a no-fault system, what's the difference?"

Wishing I still had that stick to poke him with, I challenged, "Isn't that just an excuse so the super-rich can get away with murder?"

Leaning forward, he retorted firmly, "Steven, don't play so high-and-mighty. You've benefitted plenty from our no-fault system. Tell me this—how many people did you send to the hospital?"

I gulped. "Um, a lot, I think."

He nodded and said definitively, "That's right, and you didn't have to pay for anything you did to those people, now did you?"

Sheepishly, I responded, "No, but those were all accidents." He just sat there looking at me. "Okay, okay." I changed the subject. "But the containment crew sure got there fast."

"Well, the products are very expensive and have to be recovered before someone steals them."

"The what?"

"The tracking device and nanobot. The CPU and GPS units in the people. That flashing blue thing you saw. They're virtually indestructible and usually last for eighty years or so, and we can reuse that guy's unit on someone else. Of course, we'll have to find someone who will probably only live to be thirty or forty, but there are plenty of those around, as you know from seeing all of the poor souls who start out with zygote depression."

Floored that my suspicions were confirmed, I said, "You put *tracking devices* in people?"

He responded plainly, "Sure. They're very useful for preventing disease."

"What?"

"Oh, yes. There was a monumental study years ago that tracking people's online search habits helped prevent disease. We do that as well, of course, but physical tracking also helps so we know where everyone is. That way, if they're stuck out in the cold, we can find them and get them a space blanket." He looked at me as if he were explaining the simplest civics lesson and asked innocently, "Didn't you learn about the tracking modules when you were over at the lab?"

"No."

"Well, you can't do everything on one job. Anyway, don't worry about those too much. They're standard protocol these days. Heck, we even put tracking devices on livestock to measure speed and location." Slapping his knee, he added, "And you should see some of the record times we've clocked running them down the particle collider!"

I was neither amused nor willing to be distracted by him at that moment, and I simply demanded, "Well, do you have one?"

"Oh, heavens no! But hey, you don't either!"

I was not overly trusting of what he was saying anymore and continued prodding. "But you track people from the day they're born?"

He went back to swaying in his chair and said reassuringly, "Of course not. We can't turn them on until you do something to indicate that you are a potential danger to society—pesky Fourteenth

Amendment, I'm afraid. Most people don't have them turned on until they're about eight years old."

He pulled one out of his desk and slid it across to me. I picked it up to study, and it looked like the same thing I had seen him fiddling with a while ago. He continued the lesson as I examined the device. "The tracking module was ultimately a compromise between the old world, where your phone could track you but everyone else could also see where you were going, and having no technology at all. They do also help prevent school shootings, which as you know were a big problem in the past."

"How much do you charge for it?"

"Seventeen ninety-nine, but that's just to defray a portion of the cost for the cardboard box the device comes in."

Finally starting to see the lunacy in this society come around full circle, I said incredulously, "Then why the hell don't you connect the tracking module to crash avoidance systems in cars to keep people from getting run over?"

His chair stopped moving for a moment, and then he responded earnestly, "Look, Steven, people generally don't know about the tracking modules and wouldn't want to know. After all, they might not trust us if they knew we were following their every move." He smiled and added thoughtfully, "We are working on a system to wire blinking orange cones to people who don't own cars, and that should be a big help in the future!"

Putting the device down on the desk, I looked up and scowled at him, demanding, "But why the hell are you tracking people?"

Innocently, he responded, "I told you, for health concerns, but that doesn't mean it's any of their business. Now, I admit that the monitoring is a *slightly* controversial practice. In the past, everyone was leery of it because they thought we would want to monitor them for some puritanical, quasi-fascist notion. However, as you know, we don't care what people do these days. There are no social taboos anymore, and we let people do whatever they want, as long as they are civic-minded enough to not to disturb us from doing our jobs."

"Who pays for tracking modules? I mean, for the development of the product, not just for the box it comes in?"

"The people do, of course." He quickly added, "But it's only a small fraction of their overall insurance policy."

"Yeah, but you're wasting money on things like this, and when the government runs out, someone is either born or dies."

"So?"

"So you're trafficking in human beings!"

He let out a healthy laugh and said, "Oh, Steven, we've been doing that since the time of Adam Smith![9] After all, money is not the real value of wealth. In the modern economic age, the real measure is the number of people you command and the goods they consume."[10]

I felt like throwing up. Seeing this, he said, "I'm sorry you had to learn all of this, my boy, but it's a necessary part of our economy."

Still floored, I asked, "So they're paying you to track them and eventually tell them how to kill themselves?"

He pursed his lips and shook his head, chidingly gently, "Steven, that's an awful way to look at it."

"But is it true?"

Flatly, he responded, "Yes. And I'll tell you, these sudden accidents cause a huge problem."

I sat forward and demanded sarcastically, "Why? Because you have to go through the burden of growing and fitting a new cog into your machinery?"

He responded, unaffected, "Well, there's that, but if you die in a sudden accident as opposed to in the hospital, the government only gets to keep 60 percent of your remaining insurance proceeds—assuming, that is, that you die with heirs. And if you die of natural causes, then the government only gets 50 percent."

"And what if they die in the hospital?"

"Then the government gets its standard 80 percent—well, somewhere between 78 and 80." Laughing gently, he added, "The damn hippie liberals are always trying to increase the payout to the citizens!"

That's why these bastards villainized Emily's dad! Someone has got to stop this!

Satisfied that he had thoroughly shot down all of my argument, and apparently sensing that I was no real threat to him winding down his day, he said, "Say, it's still early. You want to go out for a drink?"

I measured my response carefully. I was finally convinced that I was, in fact, convening with the devil, but I didn't want him to know it. Still, I thought that if I accepted one more thing from him, I might very well wind up in hell for eternity. Instead I politely stood up and said, "You know, I'm a little shaken up from the whole event. I think I need to go home and lie down."

*   *   *

My anger gave me clarity at that point, and I felt a little vigor return. When I got home, I tried Emily again. No answer. From what I could recall of her, I sat down and drew a picture of her face and hung it over my mirror. I wish that I had thought to take one with my phone, but it didn't matter. I could hold her in my mind forever, and that was enough to keep me going.

I went back to the hospital, and they needed me down on three. I decided to forget all about the medications and just tried to talk people out of their beds. Two days in, an angry doctor stopped me and scolded, "Steven, quit that! You're just impeding these people's treatment! And anyway, what you're doing won't work."

"Why not?"

"Because mental conditioning only works in one direction. Science proves that you can't make people more robust than they already are."

She gave me a stern look to make sure that I understood this time, and I stepped away and held up my hands in surrender. "Okay, okay. Fine." But I didn't really mean it.

Satisfied, the doctor nodded at me and paused to stretch her back. Surveying the placid ward, she said, "I tell you, it's amazing that all of these people survived before we told them that it was impossible to do so without our instruction."

Maintaining an innocent tone, I said, "So you think that there's nothing we can do?"

"Unfortunately, no. Steven, you can't cure anyone who winds up here. You may be able to buy them time, but the disease will always be there. Take the gentleman you were just talking to."

"Yeah?"

"Well, he's addicted to opiates, and the vast majority of addicts never recover."

"But I thought they used to."

With undisguised irony, she let out a short laugh and said, "Yeah, like a hundred fifty years ago! However, the same treatments don't seem to work anymore."

"Then maybe you're doing something wrong."

"No, Steven, that's not it. We've been tracking this for years, and the data unequivocally show that we were doing it right the whole time. However, the power of addiction is a strange beast and is just too strong to cure, no matter how technically advanced we become in our treatment methods." Shaking her head with honest regret, she added, "It truly is a baffling disease."

"Well, what about the drugs we give to them?"

She waved a lighthearted hand and responded, "Oh, those aren't addictive at all."

"But people can't function without them."

"Yes, Steven, but there's a huge difference between dependence and addiction. If you had studied hard sciences, you would know this."

"Okay then, how many people ever stop being dependent on their drugs?"

She scratched her head for a moment and said, "Well, none that I can recall."

"So it's the same thing."

She laughed. "Not even remotely! Look at it this way, Steven. You can't stop eating. That's just the way it is. You have to eat to survive, and some people are born with genetic flaws that will require them to be supplemented their whole lives in order to function normally." She could see that I was not overly convinced, and trying to hammer the point home, she added, "Plus, you have to consider this: the economy is very good for all of us. Fortunately, the human form is weak, and we have an endless supply of people who will wind up fitting neatly into the new chronic conditions we make up for them. And without that and the need to purchase new medications, well … Trying to change things could be terribly damaging to the economy and might wind up hurting the children."

Bitterly, I said, "All you're doing is selling out your own kind so you can sleep very comfortably in a big bed."

She took a step back, frowning deeply. Finally, deciding that further efforts at explanation would be lost on me, she simply concluded, "Like I said, if you had a hard science degree, you'd get it. Now go away. I have work to do."

In the doctor's absence, I decided to take up my frustrations on the next girl who stopped by to give me the weekly civics quiz. She was also a big fan of the Kool-Aid they were peddling and wasn't backed down at all by my skepticism.

She had originally come over to ask me whether I had seen the latest rebooted reboot, but I cut her off and gave her an earful instead.

She nodded confidently in response. "Yes, she's exactly right. I should know; I'm premed."

I leveled angrily, "Well, it sounds like a bunch of made-up bullshit!"

That apparently pushed one of her buttons, as her face grew bright red and she screamed, "Steven, it's *science!* Now if you're not going to believe in generally accepted theories, I'm just going to have to stop talking to you!"

I clasped my hands together and fell to my knees. "Hallelujah!"

She started crying and said accusingly, "Look, Steven, now you've upset me! I'm afraid that I'm going to have to go home. Can you do my work for me?"

I got to my feet, dusted myself off, and then said, "Sure, but just answer this one question: if you have enough energy to throw a tantrum, why don't you have enough energy to work?"

Her face turned beet red, and she screamed at me, "Steven, that's actualization shaming! It's not my fault that I don't want to work! I have a mental health condition!"

Glaring at her, I said, "No, you're actually just a shapeless pile of goo."

With that, she fainted dead away. The doctor came back around as the crew was taking her up to seven. Looking at me sideways, she finally said, "You know, Steven, maybe we should put you on the graveyard shift so you won't interact with so many people."

* * *

I couldn't tell whether I cared about potentially getting fired at that point—or anything, for that matter. I hadn't talked to Emily for so long that I was just surviving on raw instinct, and I eventually learned that the graveyard shift had its own store of gameshow hosts. A scrawny, unshaven manlike being tapped me on the shoulder in the early morning and said, "Name something that nearly all people have in their homes but most don't use."

"What?"

"Name something ..."

Aggressively, I grabbed the front of his shirt and pulled him to within inches of my face. I gritted my teeth and growled, "*I'm sorry; you lost me when you opened your mouth to start talking!*"

Terrified, he stammered, "You ... you wouldn't hit someone with VR contacts, would you?"

I gave no sign of backing down. Finally he just quivered for a second and then devolved into a blubbery mass. "*Waaaahhhhh!*"

Letting go of his shirt and gently straightening it out, I said in my most consoling voice, "Oh, I'm sorry. I was supposed to give you a trigger warning, wasn't I?"

Sucking up snot, he said, "Yes ... *snort* ... you were!"

"Here it is: *stay the fuck home if you can't handle what people say to you!*"

"*Waaaahhhhh!*" He ran out. Fortunately, my outburst didn't wake any of the soon-to-be departed, and I had a quiet evening all to myself.

After that, I simply comported myself like the Incredible Hulk, appearing menacing to anyone who tried to come my way. At one point, I was restocking the new pamphlets that had just arrived, and they showed an elderly woman who was smiling, despite obvious signs of hyper-wrinkleism. It was entitled *Why Ending Your Life Is a Good Thing.* When I opened it up, I saw that the inside began as follows: "Do you suffer from Newtonian ennui? Are you worried that you may be losing your place in the world? Come see us!" Two grinning doctors held their hands out to the reader.

At the end of my shift, I foolishly asked whether it was necessary to use these new pamphlets, to which the doctor coming on shift replied, "Oh, yes. Education is the only way to stop the problem. As you know, we sent people to the moon to test Newtonian ennui, and so far we've determined that it is a useful thing to have, because people seem to die up there for some reason."

"Maybe they die because humans are not supposed to live in space."

He looked at me as if I were from another species. "Steven, where did you ever get such a crazy notion? That's not published anywhere! In any event, if it's not one thing that gets them, it will be another. Everyone is infected with the same illnesses, all the time, and it's just a question of when they manifest."

Two days later, the stock market dropped several points as a result of some international mineral shortage, and the medical staff immediately sprang to action. I was even kept after my graveyard shift had ended to help with the crisis, and the doctor screamed as he ran from bed to bed, quickly calling out people's numbers. "There's no time to waste! These people are locked in a death spiral! They're all exhibiting signs of tremendous anxiety, and some of them are even wrinkling at an excessively high rate!" Pointing frantically to the corner bed, he added, "And look, that one could develop anti-NMDA receptor encephalitis at any moment!"

I was back up on seven by then to help with all of the rush jobs, and the doctor up there could obviously sense my distaste for the process. Putting a hand on my shoulder as we walked away from the last body that was still screeching to the corpse bin, he counseled, "Steven, you just have to learn how to smile as you lead patients to their promised land. It's very helpful and reassuring to them."

Half-exasperated, half-weary, I said, "How on earth could you ever smile doing this? Like those ridiculous people on the brochure?"

As we reentered the main area, he answered, "Oh, well, it's against the law to make people feel bad about the decision to undergo compassionate release."

"What about suicide?"

He looked at me sideways and responded assuredly, "Well, there's certainly no law against that. Steven, we are just a part of the circle of life up here. We have to release people because eventually the human body loses control of itself, which leads to suffering."

I finally stopped in the middle of the room and said, dumbfounded, "Why don't you just admit that suffering is part of life?"

Since the panic for the day had worn off, several others who were standing around celebrating overheard my question and joined the discussion, and six blank faces now stared at me. One of them robotically responded, "Steven, there's basically a straight line from prescription drugs to needles, so once people need prescription drugs, we give them the opportunity to undergo release." Nodding proudly at the others, she added, "It really does a nice job of reducing illicit drug use."

Another concurred and said, "Oh yes, and it also helps to eliminate the huge problem of long-term care."

I jumped in and retorted, "Yeah, by offing them prematurely!"

A third responded clinically, "Well, I'm sorry to be the one to break this to you, Steven, but there's no such thing as a cure for these people. They have a disease at the genetic level. It can't be fixed, and it never goes away, so the best we can do is keep them medicated until youth wears off."

Feeling as though I were being encircled, I backed up a step and challenged, "People, these patients come in with sprained ligaments, broken bones, and acute depressive episodes."

One stepped toward me and responded thoughtfully, "Well, those are all gateway illnesses."

"Gateway to what?"

Another followed. "A lifetime of suffering."

I took another step back and pleaded, "But some of them are just kids! Why don't you give them a chance to have a life before you condemn them?"

A third stepped forward, and I realized that the group was instinctively forming up to attack, just like a flock of birds. "Well, if they have zygote depression—"

I waved her off and took another step back. "Leave that aside."

"Or back-to-school PTSD—"

The mob kept advancing. Another one added, "Oh, and don't forget that new form of disorder that was just added into the *DSM*. It's called UPD."

"What the hell is that?"

"Unpatriotic disagreement."

The doctor finally raised his hand, and the flock halted. Firmly, he said, "Look, Steven, letting them live longer than we need them to would just be hopeless. Trust me; we've been tracking these things for years. We established that the type of Instagram filter you used showed that you were depressed, the color of clothes you wore showed that you were depressed, the length of time you spent in the bathtub showed that you were depressed, and on and on. And because we have been tracking these milestones for all of these years, we are now able to save people from their own personal hells."

Taking one more step back, just for good measure, I said accusingly, "How? By drugging them and then killing them?"

He responded with studied compassion, "It's the only way to stop the pain." Everyone else nodded firmly in agreement.

One of the underlings added, "People who have reached their time to go usually don't know it."

And another said, "Steven, it's Novocain for the soul."

Bitterly, I shot back, "Yeah, more like opiates for the masses."

The doctor's face lit up and he said, "Hey, that's a great one! We should change the marketing materials to …"

The guy to his left pulled at his sleeve and interrupted him in midthought. "Um, sir, someone already used that."

Stunned, the doctor turned to him and said, "Who?"

"Karl Marx."

With that, the doctor frowned at me, and the attack formation dispersed, leaving me alone again in my non-science-background, uneducated shame.

*

TWENTY-FIVE

I still hadn't been able to reach Emily. Thankfully, the Multiverse fervor about her family had died down, but the campaign apparently did its work. Appropriations had been granted to start a new road paving project, and sixty-seven new studies conclusively established that the precise stretch of road where Emily's house was located constituted an excessively dangerous risk for highway marauders. The route was being redone to eliminate any side roads that could provide access for potential bandits.

No one even questioned the budgetary line item when it was proposed. The result was that the only access to Emily's house was by going to the next town over and then taking an old river road. Online GPS services no longer showed a residence there of any sort.

They also passed the Cell Phone Bailout Act to provide assistance to all those so devastatingly affected by the earlier crisis. Conveniently, a new, immediately lethal nanodisease was also discovered, and about ten thousand people received letters, texts, or IMs asking them to report immediately to the hospital for treatment.

Not knowing what else to do, I was back in the director's office. He may in fact have been the devil, but he was the only audience I had left. I pleaded, "Look, you're killing people way before their time!"

Calmly from behind his desk, he said, "Steven, compassionate release is a huge part of the national economy. If we can't have some hand in the timing and manner of people's exit from society, it could tremendously affect the debt ceiling."

I shook my head and asked, "What's that?"

"That is the limit of debt that the country can take on to keep supporting its citizens and their wonderful lives. It has historically always been right at national gross domestic product, and currently we have as much debt out there as the number of insurance policies we produce here. So naturally we have to keep expiring people and releasing their insurance policies back into the economy so we don't run out of money to cover the debt."

I said accusingly, "Then you're treating these people as nothing more than pawns for the good of the economy?"

With studied arrogance, he responded, "Well, if more people would keep their end of the bargain in supporting our GDP, we wouldn't have to do this."

"What are you talking about?"

"Consumer debt. Take, for example, the nanobot and tracking device module. There are lifetime lease contracts that go with those."

"Wait. I thought you said that they only cost seventeen ninety-nine?"

"That's the charge to implant the device. The lease contract is for the continued upgrades, and most people don't live long enough to finish the payments."

At a loss and feeling as if I had entered a time warp, I responded, exasperated, "Yeah, because you kill them!"

Calmly, he shook his head and replied, "Of course. It's the only way to keep them from spending everything we're entitled to. After all, science proves that people who buy things with credit don't expect to have to pay it back."

I threw up my hands and exclaimed, *"Then why the hell do you give them huge sums of money at birth?"*

"Because that's the law."

My confusion only deepened, and I sat there without any way to respond. Finally he sighed and revealed, "Look, Steven, the truth is that there is simply nothing for these people to do. Oh, we give them plenty of distractions and let them live what appear to be nice, quaint lives, but the reality of it is that we keep them around only as long as is necessary to justify the total withdrawal that is culminated when they die. Still, it's all based on scientific principles that were around long before you got here."

I shifted defensively in my chair and said disgustedly, "I'll bet."

Still trying to justify everything, he added, "Look at it this way: states had always made it illegal for doctors to advertise the ability to cure a clearly incurable disease, so we just decided to open the floodgates by recognizing that all human conditions are inherently incurable. We have determined that anything we can't cure with a pill is a terminal disease, and that's science."

I sat forward and demanded, "Then tell me this: if everything is based on science, why do you let people spend almost thirty years of life earning non-science degrees?"

He leaned back in his chair and responded assuredly, "Personal choice, my boy, personal choice!"

I was nearly defeated by that point, and rather than continue to fight, I simply decided to throw in the towel. "Look, I can't go back there."

Unapologetically, he said, "You have to. There are no other jobs open at this point. Sorry, but you'll just have to tough it out."

* * *

My phone kept going off. I started keeping it with me on the off chance that Emily would call and give me another shot in the arm. However, I was no longer responding to text or email messages.

My auto response read as follows:

> Thank you for your friend request. I am so busy ignoring requests from other people that it may take me quite some time to get around to ignoring yours. On the bright side, I haven't met anyone online that I would actually consider as a true friend, and I doubt that you are any different. Please stand by and I will attempt to deny your request in the order in which it was received. Have a nice day.

I was still checking my citizenship score daily, but I didn't know whether I could keep things up, and the prospect of being able to afford cab rides again seemed like a distant dream. With still no contact from Emily, my hope was starting to fade anyway.

Admittedly, by then I had contemplated a few times just giving in and going to the brothel. I needed some real companionship, and none of the idiots I worked with even came close. By the end of the week, all I had left in me was a continuous volley of insults for everyone, and I made my rounds doling them out as though I were delivering medications.

"You know, having to listen to you is its own kind of cancer!"

"No one is judging you because of the anatomy you were born with! They're judging you because you're a moron!"

"What's your name?"

"Um, Davis."

"No, your full name," I demanded in a sinister voice.

He backed away slowly and said, panicked, "I don't see how that really matters."

I advanced. "What's your address? I'm going to pay you a visit later on!"

"Steven, you're scaring me!" He took off running in the other direction, and I was finally alone again, thank God.

Around 7:00 p.m. that evening, the doctor asked me to come in on Saturday afternoon to meet the delivery truck. He said that there was a new load of catheters coming in and I needed to sign for them and have them ready to go for Monday morning.

As he turned to leave, he instructed, "Get them hung on beds 435 through 610 for some new arrivals, and don't forget that the original invoice needs to be dropped off back at the center on the sixth floor. You'll see the administrative clerk's office when you go up there."

"No, I know where it is. I've been to her office before."

"Good. Leave the invoice, and then you can take Sunday off."

When I left, it was raining and my feet made two steady lines on the pavement all the way to my apartment. I tried Emily again when I got home, and to my surprise, she picked up.

I was so ecstatic that I barely knew what to say. However, she was back to being as short with me as she was on the day we met. From the other end, she said, "Look, I can't talk right now."

Wounded, I asked, "Are you mad at me?"

She sighed momentarily and responded, "Steven, I'm not mad at you. I'm just fed up with whole system and I'm trying to figure out how to keep this place afloat by myself."

Knowing that it was an empty gesture, I said, "Want some help?"

"No, I need to be alone. Thank you for calling, and maybe we'll get together in a while. Goodbye."

My medications had just run out. I slumped down in a chair and couldn't move. I felt as if the last thing I had to believe in just died.

The only unexpired item in my disassembled pantry was an old bottle of liquor I had purchased long before I met Emily. I pulled it out again and had a small drink to see whether it could dull my senses. The first drink did nothing; neither did the second. When I had finished that bottle, I headed out to get another one.

Later that evening, I wandered back by the brothel. Some of the girls outside recognized me and beckoned me in, but I was in shambles and couldn't stand the company. Even in my inebriated state, I knew that none of them was Emily.

Somehow I found myself on the far end of town. I was nearly exhausted, and my bottle had run out miles ago, so I decided to just lie down in a ditch and take a rest.

Eventually a bus passed by, and the driver saw me on the side of the road and probably took me for someone who lived in that shabby neighborhood. He stopped and opened the door, so I climbed aboard and collapsed into a seat.

There were maybe ten people on the bus, and all of them looked completely whipped. There was a shower in the back, and I thought about getting in it to try to revive myself, but I couldn't muster the effort. On the wall facing me was a giant SWAGSA poster advertising for the next round of space adventurers: "Sign up for a trip to the Mars colony! Share the adventure of a lifetime!" I have no idea how, but the bus eventually made its way to my neighborhood and I stumbled off and went upstairs.

That night I kept hallucinating. I was shaking uncontrollably, and visions and voices of everyone that I had ever wronged were filling my head. I doubt that I slept more than two hours.

The next morning, I woke up with a pounding headache but remembered that I had to work restocking the catheters. I pulled myself out of bed and went to work without even bothering to shower. I met the delivery truck out back on the loading dock, and the driver and I rolled four pallets of catheters into the hospital. I was groggy, but everyone else there was sedated and sleeping and didn't notice. I hung all of the catheters in a daze and then shoved the delivery invoice into my back pocket and walked out.

The glaring sunlight was there to greet me and almost made me retreat into the hospital to join the others in one of the beds. Instead I pressed on to the center and instinctively pushed open the back door without even stopping to notice the tree.

I slowly ascended the stairs. My head was down, and I wasn't even paying attention, and when I got to the fourth floor, a door was propped open. Without even realizing where I was, I walked through onto the floor. Where I emerged was not the administrative wing. Instead there was a giant sign in the hallway that read, "SWAGSA: Planetary Watch Command Division."

I was about to turn around and head back when I heard commotion up ahead. I kept walking forward and emerged into a giant room filled with wall-sized computer screens. In the room were two men sitting in front of the screens, and on the displays were images from some distant galaxy that I couldn't recognize. I suddenly realized that both of the men had their pants down.

One of them exclaimed, "See, I told you that fucker wasn't out there anywhere! We can do anything we want! Tighten my nipple clamps a little more! Yeah, that's it!"

The other said, "Yeah, and when it's my turn, use the whole fist! Really jam it up there!"

"Oh yeah, that'll be hot!"

One of them sensed my presence and turned around suddenly. He cleared his throat and pretended that nothing had happened. Glancing at my name badge and probably realizing that I was authorized to be in the building, he said, "Ahem. Hello, Steven!" He looked down and flicked off the nipple clamps as though they were flies that had randomly landed on his chest. Then he paused for a second, stood up, and buttoned his pants.

Immediately shocked out of my stupor, I said, "Uh, what are you guys doing?"

The first one tried to distract me while the second similarly put himself back together. "Oh, nothing. We're using the super telescope on Pluto to peer into the deepest reaches of space."

As I watched the second pull up his trousers, I realized that he was also sporting an odd undergarment and asked awkwardly, "Are you wearing … a diaper?"

The second looked down and laughed nervously. He said, "Oh, he he, that! Well, we used to use them as part of missions, and they were necessary because astronauts had to go long periods of time without being able to use the bathroom. We've solved that problem, of course, and now we just keep them around for … nostalgia."

"Are you two astronauts?"

"Oh, no. We're planetary protection officers." He turned to the other guy and whispered, "Psst. Hey, you have a little lube on your chin. There, you got it." Turning back to me casually, he continued. "Anyway, what we've got here is a telescope that peers into the universe a thousand times farther than anyone ever thought possible."

The first licked a bit of lube off his finger and said, "Yeah, and we're searching for the next Earth. We've found about five hundred so far, but we don't want to pick just any old substitute planet."

The other added, "We want to find exactly the right one. Not the smallest."

"But not the biggest, either."

"Somewhere in between."

I felt as if I were back watching the Punch and Judy routine at the director's place and said, "I thought that you were up to about ten thousand by now."

The first one responded, "Oh, most of the other ones look enough like potential earths, but they'd never do. As you know, however, lobotomies love hearing about all of the new Earth-like planets that we discover."

The second added, "Yeah, especially ones that have two suns, just like Luke's home planet of Tatooine!"

My hangover was in full swing, and the nausea was creeping in slowly. The first officer sat back down and focused on the screen. Gazing at it eagerly, he said, "Can you imagine all of the great things we'll be able to do with a new earth? On the next one, we're going to do it better! We'll start the civilization with no memory of all of these ridiculous superstitions and create an entire society where everyone can be free to do what they want." Running some calculations in his head, he added, "And we'll lobotomize 60 ... no, 70 percent of the population, just to make sure that everyone is content."

I said, "If you get rid of superstitions, do you really think the lobotomies will still be necessary?"

He laughed nervously and responded, "Oh, very clever, Steven! Well, we may still need to have a few—you know, for economic reasons."

I stepped forward and said curiously, "Why are you guys working on the weekend?"

The second answered, "We run twenty-four-hour shifts. We have to keep searching constantly because there are still things out there that break our fundamental understanding of how the universe works."

I retorted, "Why don't you just admit that you don't know how the universe works?"

I was met with blank faces. The first finally shook his head decisively and then corrected by saying, "Duh, Steven, we know everything about how the universe works. We just have to verify it."

His colleague added boastfully, "Yeah, and don't forget that we put a missile site on the moon. Now, of course, we're having to install artificial illuminators on the moon because it no longer shines at night."

I said, "How'd that happen?"

Second replied, "Oh, we kicked up so much dust on the moon that it doesn't reflect anything anymore. Plus, the moon dust is now being used in fibromyalgia treatments and to 3-D print materials for the colonies."

Scanning the screen momentarily, I said, "Yeah, and you guys got a single raincloud to form on Mars, right?"

Number One responded proudly, "Oh, yes! That was a huge accomplishment for the colonists!"

I replied, "I thought that one of them burned to death."

Number One paused for a moment and then said, "Well, not for that guy, of course, but the rest appreciate everything else we've done up there."

I said, "And then they come back here to die?"

Number Two piped up. "Sure, but the space explorers don't mind. Steven, a lot of the Mars colonists are actually outcasts who got kicked off their own planet. As you may know, most people have to give up their insurance policies to participate in the Mars colony."

"Why?"

"Because it's useless in space. You can't have kids up there anyway, and when you get back, you're just immediately sent to the hospital."

"Then why send them?"

Innocently, he said, "How can we take people's dreams away from them?"

"But don't they get paid for working up there?"

Number One responded, "Sure, they do. However, the short time they survive is only enough to buy them a return ticket."

"Then why don't you pay them more?"

Number Two answered boldly, "What for? It takes two Mars years to equal one Earth year, so they're really only doing half the work that we can do down here. As a result, we pay them at one-half the customary rate, and that helps us keep the space venture profitable."

I had been there for only two minutes, but I felt as if I were in lunar orbit listening to these guys and I was thoroughly disgusted. Desperately needing to find a sane foothold, I insisted, "Wait, wait. I read the archives, and you convinced people to go to Mars. Hell, you even advertise for it today."

"Steven, it's still their choice, isn't it?"

Appearing to want to get off that subject, Number One quickly added, "And let's not focus on Mars. That's just a stopping-off point anyway."

His buddy took the cue and followed. "Yeah, we figured that when we opened up a non-GMO sushi joint on the moon, the aliens would see how civilized we were. When that didn't work, we kept opening up sushi restaurants on all of the rocky planets going toward Pluto, but that didn't work either for some reason."

Leaning forward and squinting at the screen, Number One said, "Yes, the current scientific thinking is that we have to open one on the missing planet in our solar system."

I shook my head and responded, "Hold on. You already found the missing planet?"

Number Two replied confidently, "Oh, well, we did find *that* missing planet. Unfortunately, it's not very suitable for colonists, so we'll have to find the other missing planet before we can open the sushi restaurant which will finally establish first contact!"

Number Two nodded assuredly at his colleague, obviously proud that their searching efforts would eventually lead us to discover alien races, and I asked, bewildered, "How do you know that there's another missing planet out there?"

Number Two answered sarcastically, "Steven, there's always going to be a missing planet until we find it."

Number One added, "Yeah, and since we got rid of Mercury and Venus, we still have room in our nine-planet model for one more."

I stepped back, astonished, and said, "Why the hell did you do that?"

Number One replied, "Oh, we finally realized that we wouldn't ever make any money off of them, so we just don't count them anymore, and that frees up plenty of expenditures to keep searching.

Fortunately, our budget is inexhaustible these days, thanks to all of the marketing campaigns we run through the movies!"

I watched him enhance the screen endlessly in a completely dark area of space. He panned in and out, in and out, and the puzzled look on his face only deepened. Frustrated, he added, "But we still can't find the damn thing!"

You two probably couldn't find your own assholes if you had to. I said, "Um, I don't think there's anything there."

Number One finally gave up and moved the field of vision. "Well, maybe not ... yet. However, we still have to be on the lookout for aliens."

I said flatly, "I don't think there are any of those out there, either."

Number Two responded, sounding astonished, "Are you kidding? Steven, read the archives; you're an alien in your own life, made up entirely of stardust."

"I am?"

Snidely, he said, "Of course, and you're lucky we were here to tell you that." Swiveling back proudly toward his colleague, he added, "Yep, we've developed some amazing discoveries right in these two chairs!"

I said accusingly, "Like how long you can go wearing nipple clamps before your flesh goes numb?"

Number One was focusing on something else on the screen and responded absently, "Well, there's that, but we've also spent trillions researching the cold spot in the universe. Understanding that could overturn mankind's vision of our place in reality."

Number Two nodded and added helpfully, "Plus, it could explain why the universe is so cold!"

"We're also working on an expedition to see if they can shave off pieces of the sun. We're going to put them in giant heating lamps and turn Pluto into the next vacation destination!"

I said, "Don't you think we'll need the sun to keep the earth warm?"

The second looked at me and laughed. "Steven, there are so many greedy planets out there with extra suns they don't need that we'll have a replacement sun in no time! We're working on the technology, and pretty soon we'll be swimming in suns. Heck, we'll have extra suns coming out of our asses!"

Incredulous, I challenged, "How do you plan to make that happen?"

Number One pulled up the screen. "Look; it's right here. That's the artist's rendition of the three-million-mile-long scooper that will be used to capture part of the sun." Looking over his shoulder at me, he added for my educational benefit, "That's as close to the sun as we can get without mucking up our instruments. Then look here. Here's the giant net we'll use to lasso other suns and pull them into our galaxy."

"Aren't you guys being a little overconfident? After all, all you've managed to do so far is put a sushi joint on Pluto."

Number One said, "Steven, you're missing the big picture. Through our telescopic and microscopic efforts, we have all of creation mapped down to the molecule—*with artists' renditions*. We tell people where they fit into the universe, and not the other way around."

"Yes, Steven. If you had a scientific background, you'd know this."

I wondered if Number Two's diaper was as full as he was, and I said, "Look, the last time I checked, all you people were doing was running bogus studies filled out by the same one thousand people and then convincing everyone to follow along. I hardly call that controlling where people fit in the universe."

Number One, who obviously had the duty to address similar inquiries from naysayers, responded, "Yes, but you have to understand, Steven, that when deciding what studies to run, we use whatever information we have available under the circumstances, and the people never doubt us for a second. Years ago, when we wanted to handicap people by making them pay exorbitant taxes to subsidize nascent and highly uncompetitive eco-friendly businesses, we would publish studies linking everything in the world to climate change: lung disease, obesity, increases in skin cancer, and, of course, the corollary famous links between sunscreen, ibuprofen, and infertility in males. You name it, we've done it."

"So?"

"So, the infertility studies, combined with the invention of the artificial placenta, were instrumental in helping us start lab births. We convinced men that if they didn't let us test their sunscreen-damaged semen, they would never wind up having a healthy baby, and it was brilliant!"

Number Two jumped in to demonstrate his prowess and asserted, "So you see, we *do* control where people fit in the universe! And thanks to their subsidization efforts over the years, we got them to pay for terraforming technology for us!"

Number One added, "However, now that people are auto-paying 15 percent of their take-home pay for carbon-reducing technologies, we're on to new topics."

I said, "So, you're just duping people to line your own pockets and make the universe your unsupervised playground?"

Number Two blurted out in overeager fashion, "Oh, it's much more than that! If we hadn't done what we did, the people would be completely lost once the surface of the earth finally crumbles away!"

I asked, astonished, "It is actually crumbling?"

Number One quickly shot him a nervous glance, as his colleague had obviously let me in on something that he wasn't supposed to. Finally, Number One sighed and confirmed. "Yes, it is—a little at a time—but that's just the natural result of all of the materials we've shipped to the colonies."

Seeing that he was free to divulge further, Number Two added, "But don't worry; we have emergency shuttles ready to go."

I said, "So can you get everyone off the earth when it starts to fail?"

Number One laughed definitively. "What are you talking about, 'everyone'? We have enough emergency shuttles for two hundred thousand people."

I said, "That's it? How are you going save the rest?"

Number Two answered, "Are you kidding? We're not. After all, a ticket to get on the emergency shuttle costs fifteen trillion dollars, and most people could never afford that."

Number One nodded at his companion and added, "We do sell raffle tickets for six hundred million."

I said, astonished, "But that's more than any one person's insurance policy!"

Number One switched back to his PR voice and responded, "Yep. As you can guess, most people don't buy the raffle tickets. Instead they contribute indirectly through taxes, preferring to invest slowly in the prospect that we'll get everyone off the planet over time."

I exclaimed, *"But you just said that you won't get everyone off the planet!"*

Number One just shrugged and replied lightly, "Probably not."

"Then how can you keep doing what you're doing?"

Unapologetically, he said, "Because we're the government."

Stepping forward angrily, I insisted, "If … *When* someone finds out about this, you're going to be in big trouble!"

Number One laughed and said mockingly, "With who? The lobotomies? They'll never stop us!"

I said, "Wait, but the lobotomies are only 17—no, 35—percent of the population?"

Paying more attention to the screen than my protests, Number One said, "Come on, Steven, you're smarter than that."

"There are more?"

"No, but there's more than one way to lobotomize everyone." The horror hit me like a freight train. He added boldly, "Anyway, by the time the earth is ready to fall, do you really think that we will care one whit what the majority thinks of us? All we're going to do is take the ones that we can and then start over somewhere else."

Number Two said, "Yes, and every week we do a feature about another new earth. We show different models of houses that will be available to everyone, what the dog parks will look like, et cetera. It's a very popular program!"

Number One switched screens to one of their other creations and added, "It's even more popular than our longest-running show, which depicts what it will look like when we offer adventure cruises through black holes! Neat, huh?"

Looking up at the 3-D depiction, I said, "Do you actually know what's inside of a black hole?"

Number One admitted, "Well, technically, no, but we've combined twenty-seven of the most generally accepted theories on the subject, and we're pretty close to figuring it all out. And look at this. Here's a roller coaster we're going to build through one of them. Won't that be fun?"

I said accusingly, "I'm pretty sure that you're just making all of these things up."

Number One responded haughtily, "Not at all, but it is pretty complex, and I'm not sure you'd understand it."

Finally losing all of my patience, I blurted out angrily, "I won't understand it because it's just crap piled on top of crap! All you guys are doing is drawing concentric circles around things and calling it truth!"

Number One turned briefly away from the screen and addressed his sex partner. "Ahem. I'm afraid, Harold, that we need to explain some basic fundamentals to him. Steven, to truly understand science, you must understand the first two principles: one, whatever we're doing is right; and two, any answer that is not generally accepted must be rejected."

The one who I finally figured out was the junior among the two, because he didn't have any nipple clamps, chimed in to show how much he knew, and he added snootily, "Actually, anything that is unexplainable is simply disregarded as a statistical fluke."

I said, "So then, what's with the clamps and the fisting?"

Junior blushed and responded, "Oh, nothing! We're just trying to let loose on the weekend! You know, when you have so much knowledge at your fingertips, it's important to keep a little levity around."

"I heard you say that 'he' isn't out there anywhere. Who are you searching for? God?"

Senior let out a nervous laugh and said, "Oh, heavens no! We debunked that myth years ago!"

Scowling at him, I replied, "Yeah, somehow I don't believe you."

They both exchanged cautious glances, and then Junior shrugged and Senior finally nodded and turned back to me. "Look, Steven. Okay, yes, that is also part of our mission, and we'll tell you why and let you in on a little secret. But this is *top secret*, in fact, and you have to swear not to repeat it to another living being—even lobotomies."

"Okay."

Senior looked at me sternly and said, "Swear to it."

"I said okay."

He insisted, "No, you have to hold your right hand up and make the Vulcan salute with your fingers." I complied. "Now say, 'I swear.'"

"I swear."

"Good." He took a deep breath to steel himself, and then, with stark dramatism, he declared, "Steven, we have been *abandoned!*"

I took a step back and shook my head. "Huh? Is that what this is all about? Being able to make a new home where you don't have to be shackled by your disapproving father who hasn't returned from work yet?"

Senior said, "Oh, it's so much more than that! Come closer." He clicked several buttons on the screen, and the view changed, and he narrated as he panned across the galaxy. "See, Steven, over time we discovered dark matter in the universe. You can see several patches of that in these views."

Wondering if my eyesight was failing, I said, "I don't see anything."

Without a hint of irony, he responded, "That's why it's called *dark* matter. Anyway, through new imaging techniques, we also discovered dark whiskers, and continuously scanning the entire universe, we have also found clumps of dark substances scattered everywhere. However, the real horror didn't surface until we got nearer to the great attractor."

"The what?"

"The mysterious force that is pulling all matter in the universe toward it. Fortunately, we used infrared X-ray spectrography that bends around matter to finally get to the bottom of things. All along, we thought that the great attractor was merely a hologram, and we eventually confirmed that it was, because it never moved no matter how much we cursed it and told it to go away."

I swear that I heard anticipation music cuing up somewhere, but it may have just been my imagination. Senior continued narrating as he panned through the screens: "Now, using the same math equation we used for the big bang, we have been able to recombine all of these dark objects into their original form, and here's the artist's rendition of that."

On the screen was a cosmic picture of God in a bowling shirt.

I laughed and said mockingly, "That's it? You've put out an APB for God?"

Senior, however, was not amused, and in a completely animated state by now, he exclaimed, "Absolutely! That bastard has caused misery for our entire galaxy, and now he's left us all alone! Steven, you can't possibly know what it feels like to be abandoned like we do!"

I shook my head and said mockingly, "Oh, I might know a thing or two about it."

Senior's face was nearly white with terror, and he added ominously, "No, no, you can't! You can't know *this!*"

By now my hangover was gone and I was just annoyed. "Know what?"

His voice grew quiet and he confided direly, "Listen; this is also top secret."

"Fine." He sat there for a moment and then nodded his head toward my right hand. I sighed, formed my fingers into a V, and said, "I swear not to tell."

Satisfied, Senior turned back to the screen and continued, "A long time ago, we sent out thousands of postage-stamp-sized spacecraft, and their original mission was to explore the universe and take pictures. Now look here. Here's a picture of an infrared scan of a planet we call Jealousy 42. It's in one of the farthest corners of space, in the Globula Nebula. Do you see that?"

Squinting, I said, "I see a big red smudge on the screen."

Obviously annoyed with me by now, he said, "Well, if you had sophisticated training like we do, you'd be able to see deeper into that smudge, and what you would see is this." He pulled up the artist's rendition, and I leaned in to look at it. It was a picture of a lawn chair with an empty beer can lying beside it.

Leaning back again, I realized that there *was* actually music playing. I looked over, and Junior was amping it up and down from the controls on the arm of his chair. I shot him a sideways glance and said, "Um, you don't need to play the music for dramatic effect."

He looked over at Senior, who just nodded for him to stop the music. Deeply disappointed, Junior crossed his arms, sulking. "Fine, I guess we won't get to have any fun today."

Senior continued. "Steven, even without a background score, you can realize how absolutely, intensely devastating this is!"

With unmasked sarcasm, I responded, "I'll say. How did you spot the objects in the first place?"

"We observed the lawn chair when a shift in the magnetic field of the planet's core, combined with solar winds, caused the otherwise opaque atmosphere to clear up and offer us a glimpse of the betrayal."

"Wait, how do you know that's what caused the shift?"

Senior responded assuredly, "Steven, in the absence of anyone who actually knows what happened, science always prevails."

Not having any more music to make, Poopy-Pants added, "Yes, and the backbone of science is to discover observable, repeatable phenomena and then take credit for it."

I just rolled my eyes and challenged, "So?"

Finally losing it at my continued nonbelief, Senior jumped up from his chair dramatically to confront me. However, when he did, a butt plug thumped to the ground behind him. He glanced at it briefly and then continued undaunted by glaring at me and pointing an angry finger back at the screen. "So? *So?* Obviously that asshole has been out having fun with someone else while we're all here, stuck in the misery he left us! He made other intelligent beings and probably favors them over us and has left us here to rot in a barren universe!"

Holding back the urge to laugh, I said, "How do you know that they're intelligent beings?"

He was almost screeching by now. "Steven, didn't you see the *beer can?* And the *lawn chair?* It is abundantly clear that we are dealing with an advanced species!" He finally collapsed back into his seat, covered his eyes with his hands, and cried out, "It is horrifying, truly horrifying!"

I tried to sound consoling and responded, "Yes, apparently it is."

Junior quickly sprang to the rescue of his beleaguered colleague, but when he stood up, a raunchy smell rose with him. I tried not to show that I noticed. However, still defiant, even with an apparently full diaper, he screamed, "Yeah, and when we find that SOB, we're going to tell him that we've taken over things and that he needs to make a few changes!"

I looked down at the clamps and plug on the floor and finally put it all together. I was tempted to pinch my nose but just battled through the smell to deliver my point. "That's what this is all about? You're perverting the whole galaxy to prove that God can't punish you?"

Senior had partially recovered and was obviously not interested in trying to educate me any further. He simply said, "Steven, our mission is to find out the mysteries of the universe, and in doing so, we obtain a greater understanding of our own humanity."

I laughed sarcastically and retorted, "You mean greater than *zero?*"

He paused to measure a response. However, the pungent air had apparently aggravated his already lightheaded condition, and he may have realized that he was going to need to change Junior's diaper fairly soon. Finally he looked up and curtly asked, "Did you want something?"

Shaking my head in disbelief, I simply responded, "No. I accidentally walked through the wrong door. Excuse me." And with that, I plugged my nostrils and exited the way I came.

*

TWENTY-SIX

Having now confirmed that the whole universe was fucking nuts, and knowing that Emily didn't want me to call, I was completely in the dumps. Sunday, I went on another bender. Monday, I called in sick, which was true by that point. I had the shakes, and the visions were worse. Tuesday, I managed to drag myself out of bed. I made it a half day, but the visions were still there all night long.

Wednesday, I made it through the whole day, and everything just passed in a blur. I mumbled responses to people, but I can't tell you for sure what I said. By Thursday, I had found some of my old pep again, but I didn't seem to be making any progress, even with the new tactics I tried.

"Steven, can you do my work for me today?"

"You know, I just learned a new word in the dictionary. No!"

And later: "I'm sorry, you have me confused with someone else."

"Huh? You're Steven, right?"

"Yes, but you still have me confused with someone else."

"I don't get it."

I spat back aggressively, "I'm the guy who doesn't care what you think! You're looking for the other guy!"

"Waaahhhh!"

By the evening, the staff was wise to my techniques, and one of the defiant girls came up to me, intent on getting me to do her work for her. Before she would grant me the opportunity to do so, however, she had to set the record straight. She stood there blocking me in between two beds with her fat hands on her frumpy hips and proclaimed, "Listen, Steven; I'm not afraid of you or your bad attitude!"

Moderately homicidal, I glared at her and said, "That's nice."

"Now listen up. I will let you be equal with me as long as you concede that my sufferings outweigh anything you could ever experience in your life."

"What the fuck are you talking about?"

On cue, her demeanor softened, and she said fawnishly, "Steven, I was molested as a kid."

At that point, I lost it. I took two steps forward and screamed right into her face. "Are you *kidding* me? Who *wasn't?* Look, every person on the planet is going to wake up one day and realize that they've been betrayed! You probably should have figured that out just about the time that you were having your tubes tied! And here's another thing for you—it doesn't fucking make you special! It's not new news! Just be glad that they didn't feed you into a fucking particle collider!"

She collapsed in a blubbery mess. That freed up my path of travel, so I deftly stepped over her and out into the main aisle. Looking back, I realized that I had perhaps been a bit too authentic with her and sighed as I returned to where she was. Leaning down, I gently offered, "Come on, get up. Look, I'm sorry. That was probably a little harsh."

Accepting my help, she stood up on shaky legs, wiped her tears away, and gave me a faint smile. Releasing her hand, I gently guided her shoulders off in the other direction, and as she walked away unsteadily, I said coldly, "And when you get over your past experience, let me know and we can talk again."

She immediately began to bawl.

Insufferable bitch.

Later on, someone approached with a peace offering. "Hi, Steven, we're going to the soccer game! Come with us! The halftime show will be all about togetherness and unity!"

I didn't even look up. "Yeah, I'd rather be alone."

One of the girls who stayed behind felt an undeterrable need to keep trying to be my friend. Seventy-two text messages and six accidental bumps from her later, I finally whipped around to address her. "Look, I don't like you and I don't want to be your friend. We're not going to order a baby, and we're not going to go shopping. Now leave me alone!"

Tears forming in her eyes, she immediately went on the defensive. "You're just picking on me because of my gender!"

I scowled at her and fired back automatically, "Your gender is *questionable!*"

Later in the evening one Saturday, I cornered the doctor, having discovered something shocking in the medical literature. He was the only foe worth fighting with, as the rest of the so-called hardy ones were either at home or down on three recovering. I might have been losing it, but I was going to take him with me if I could and gave it to him with both barrels.

Leaning in aggressively, I said, "Look, pal, I've figured you out!"

He just studied me curiously as if I might have been developing a bit of schizophrenia. "You have, have you?"

"Yes! Right here it says that benzodiazepines cause dementia!"

"So?"

"So? So it's not gingivitis or rayon socks or anything else! You're drugging these people, and that's the reason why they lose their memories!"

He just shook his head at my novice misunderstanding and corrected, "Steven, the drugs cause an entirely different kind of condition. We monitor that with a simple test to measure blood flow in the neck."

"Yeah, and when it shows positive, you send them an IM to come in for compassionate release!"

"Naturally."

In a spouting ramble, I said, "Then all you're really doing is creating a nation of zombies who can't remember anything and don't appear to do much of anything anyway, and then you're just offing them to free up their insurance policies!"

Unmoved, he responded, "So?"

"So it's a huge fucking human tragedy!"

With his usual clinical compassion, he said, "Steven, of course everything looks tragic from close up, but when you stand back as far as we do and just consider everything based on generally accepted theories, you see it all happens for a reason. That's the great benefit of administering a scientific democracy."

I shouted back in response, "You're not administering a democracy! You're just making up shit as you go and slapping Band-Aids over the eyes of citizens so they can't see what's in front of them! And if you had any kind of a soul, you'd question some of these *generally accepted* notions!"

He just shook his head and wrapped up the conversation by saying, "Oh, it's sad that you don't have the understanding that we do. Why would we ever question anything that benefits us? Look, maybe you should go home."

"Way ahead of you, pal!" I kicked over a mop bucket as I headed for the elevator.

*　*　*

On the way home, I passed by the brothel again, and maybe I did it intentionally. Still, I ignored the catcalls and that feeling in my gut telling me to just give up and get stoned.

On one of the billboards I passed, another ad was playing. "Do you suffer from Newtonian ennui? Is gravity too tough to deal with? We here at SWAGSA are committed to working toward a solution!"

The next thought that popped into my mind was heading straight to the bathhouse and just getting it over with. Instead I forced myself to go home and tried to find sleep. The visions from the previous bender were gone, but a new one woke me in the middle of the night. I suddenly realized that I could just buy a gun and end it. That would be so simple and would take a lot less effort than all of this other shit.

Trying desperately to shake off the thought, I got up and turned on the scalding hot shower, standing there under the water until the top of my head seemed as if it would turn to mush. After a while, I switched the temperature to cold and let the frigid stream pass over me.

Then I opened my eyes wearily and saw the water circling down the drain, the same as my life was doing. I also realized that I was starting to give up, just as my parents had.

Sunday morning, I went to the dispensary around the corner from the center and picked up a bottle of sleeping pills. I took three at noon that day and had a small nap, but the pills couldn't keep me under. I took five at seven o'clock that night and slept until 3:00 a.m. Sitting there feeling my brain outpace my body after waking again, I realized that I needed help. I wasn't going to make it like this and decided to talk to the director again and tell him that I would have to quit. I didn't know what that might mean, but I had reached the end of my own sanity by that point.

I arrived at the center before it even opened. Since I wasn't working there anymore, my card would give me access only during the daytime hours, or on the weekends for deliveries. I had stopped along the way and picked up a fresh cup of coffee for the director, perhaps as a peace offering, and I was waiting outside for him when he arrived.

He was partially surprised to see me and said warmly, "Well, good morning, my boy! How are you?"

"I'm … I guess you could say that I'm not well."

He put on a momentarily concerned air and responded, "Oh, that's too bad. Say, thanks for the coffee! Now come up to my office and we'll talk about it!"

We rode in silence. I couldn't even bear to raise my head and see what was playing on the screen, but the director whistled quietly as he studied the ads, pausing to take small sips of his morning treat.

The director nodded pleasantries to everyone as we headed to his office, but I just stared straight ahead in desperate trepidation. Behind the closed door, I sat down and measured where to begin. Finally I said, "Listen, sir, I don't know how to say this, but I don't think that I fit in very well over at the hospital."

He gave me an inquisitive look over his coffee cup and asked, "Is that right? What's the problem?"

"I, well, I don't feel comfortable pretending that I know how to advise people on their health care decisions."

Setting down his cup, he said, "Oh, that's certainly understandable. After all, we struggled with that at the very beginning."

"You did?"

"Sure. It's perfectly natural. People like you and I expect that other people would want to feel the same way we do. That is, we expect that they would want to be able to make decisions for themselves. Unfortunately, as we have found over time, people like giving us the ability to make decisions for them."

"I ... I guess that could be true. And excuse me for saying this, but it does seem like there is a bit of gentle persuasion that goes into it."

He smiled. "Oh sure, but that's also part of what they want. Steven, I know how you really feel deep down. You feel like we're using these people, and perhaps we are, in a sense, but it's really not our fault. Every year, fewer and fewer people stepped up to take responsibility, and they kept insisting that we give them more freedoms."

"You mean distractions?"

"Yes."

"But you didn't do anything to stop them."

He gave me a politically regretful look and said, "That's democracy in action, I'm afraid. But we don't force people to do anything. They've mostly all been lobotomized and will respond automatically to the slightest suggestion. Usually they'll just do whatever the person next to them does, and it all works out very well."

"But you're treating humans like cattle."

He responded thoughtfully, "In a way, yes, but controlling the market of human capital is the most important thing for a healthy economy. Once you control the number of human inputs and where they want to direct their energy, you can accomplish nearly anything."

Slumping down in exhaustion, I said, "I don't know how you do it."

He cocked his head in confusion and retorted, "How we do what? All we do is what they ask us to. Steven, these people asked us to control every single aspect of humanity, from birth to death. Sure, these girls may suffer small breakdowns, and we do cut life short these days through compassionate release. However, the overall quality of life is as high as it's ever been, and that's because we've eliminated eternal suffering. As a result, any amount of suffering as a daily dose can be tolerated. It was really the eternal nature of uncertainty, chaos, and existence that people needed to get rid of, and that's precisely what we did."

Weakly, I protested, "Well, something still seems wrong about it."

The director responded confidently, "Steven, don't forget that these problems have been around since the birth of our nation. Remember George Washington's famous internet quote: 'Lobotomies left to themselves are unfit for their own government.'"[11]

I started to raise a finger in protest but then just let it drop. He continued: "Besides, the Framers were wise enough to put plenty of checks in place to make sure that people are always protected. Just read *Federalist* 46 and 60."

Not having seen an inkling of public protection anywhere in that society, and not having been able to find a single copy of that book, either online or in print, all I could do was ask, "Why? What do they say?"

"Basically that there are multiple tiers of protection for the people, and for anything to ever really get out of control, they would all have to fail at once. But you see how happy these people are, don't you? After all, studies show that 90 percent of all workers are happy in their jobs!"

"I thought it was 85 percent?"

"It's going up every day, my boy! And don't forget: the government employs nearly a third of the population, so we have plenty of people to keep the happiness growing!"

I was too tired to fight anymore, and I shivered involuntarily and said, "Something still makes me uneasy about this place."

Consolingly, he responded, "Steven, that's because you can only see a small part of it. When you've been doing this as long as I have, well, things become much clearer." Then he put his hand to his chest and said, "And I tell you this as an oath as solemn as any James Madison ever gave. Were there something actually wrong with this society, my voice would say, 'Down with it, down with it, I tell you!'"[12]

I tried not to roll my eyes. Then, proudly picking up his coffee again following that gallant speech, he added, "Look, don't try to analyze things too much. They're not your problems; they're mine. And believe me; you wouldn't want my job."

I sighed and conceded, "Yeah, that's probably true."

"Of course it is. In the end, we are exactly what is necessary. The world—nay, the entire universe—is filled with too much uncertainty, which has led to periods of extreme fear, depression, and chaos. I tell you, there was a point in history when people were secretly longing for Armageddon, a zombie apocalypse, or an alien invasion. They wanted anything to relieve them of the pressure of trying to listen to what the world was telling them. They couldn't handle the weight, and the best they could come up with was to fantasize about ending it all, so eventually they asked us to take the misery away, which we did."

Knowing the truth of his words was nearly crushing me in the chair. The director saw this and leaned forward, counseling firmly, "Listen, my boy; here's a piece of advice that might help you. You have to realize that you won't be able to change everything. You just have to focus on being happy if you can."

At that point, his kind words nearly brought me to tears. Choking them back, I said, "Thank you. That certainly sounds like sage advice. But I came here this morning because there is something I really need to tell you."

He leaned in even farther and said expectantly, "Yes?"

I bowed my head in shame. "I don't think I can go back there. I've had enough experiences with death to last me a lifetime."

He was silent for a moment, and then I looked up and saw him frowning at me, knowing that I was doomed. He finally nodded his head firmly and responded, "Yes, then that is a problem ..." My hope sunk, but suddenly he broke out in a smile and finished by saying enthusiastically, "... that I think we can solve!"

I sat up surprised and exclaimed, "Really?"

"Sure! If the position doesn't suit you, we have something else you can do to still be useful!"

Feeling like I had just received a pardon, I said incredulously, "But I thought that there were no other jobs."

He smiled and responded casually, "Oh, one just happened to open up last week."

Nervously, I said, "You're not going to fire me?"

"Of course not."

"You're not mad?"

"Not at all. Steven, you're not the first orphan we've had through here, and we all understand what you go through and how hard it is for you to fit in. So if death doesn't suit you, we're going to send you to the place where they actually work on combatting all of the awful maladies that get people sent to the hospital in the first place. I'm talking real frontline prevention stuff. Interested?"

I sat up even further and said, "You bet! Gosh, I'd love to be able to really heal people!"

He nodded reassuringly and replied, "Then it sounds like this will be a good fit for you!"

"Really?"

"Yep! It's real palliative care on a daily basis and plenty of opportunities for compassion."

I sighed heavily and admitted, "That would be a *big* help!"

He looked at his watch briefly and said, "Tell you what. Today is Monday, so why don't you take the next two days off and come back on Thursday and we'll start you down on the fifth floor."

Panicked at the notion, I said, "But I don't want to lose more hours."

Cheerfully, the director offered, "Let's try this. I'll give you a whole year's worth of credit, and that'll wipe away that little brawl you got into from your score. How's that sound?"

My eyes shot open. "That would be great! But you can do that?"

He just smiled warmly and said, "Oh, sure. We all understand what you go through and how hard it is to adjust to our environment coming from yours. Now go and rest up, my boy!"

*

Notes to Part III

---

[8]   Oliver Wendell Holmes, *The Common Law* (San Bernardino, California: Empire Books, 2017), 2.

[9]   Adam Smith, *The Wealth of Nations*, ed. Edwin Cannan (New York: Bantam Classics, 2003), 112–13.

[10] Ibid., 43–44.

[11] George Washington's actual quotation is "[M]ankind left to themselves are unfit for their own government." See Joseph J. Ellis, *The Quartet – Orchestrating the Second American Revolution, 1783-1789* (New York: Vintage Books, 2016), 102.

[12] *Federalist*, no. 45 (Madison), at 289.

PART IV

Your Obedience Has Been Predetermined

TWENTY-SEVEN

I went home with reignited hope. I thought about calling Emily to give her the good news, but that felt selfish. Instead I told myself that the best thing I could do was help her in the long run, and I promised myself not to get caught up in my petty ego—no matter what they did to me.

The rest of the day, I lay in bed calculating the glimmer of light in front of me and trying to steel myself to endure whatever was going to happen. In the middle of it, I thought about all of the fucking people who had been tortured because of the quest for science. Other thoughts also came to mind, and before I knew it, I was talking to myself.

"Why haven't they fired me yet? Maybe they're not allowed to fire orphans from the government. That would make sense with all of the other fucked-up labor laws they have. You need fresh air, Steven. If you sit in here alone, you'll crack up. Now get up and go outdoors."

Walking out of my building, I sucked in a deep breath, feeling completely detached from everything and everyone around me. I wanted desperately to find my purpose in life again, and that didn't have anything to do with any of these other fools. I started walking with a determined step, and for some reason, I found myself back at the pond. A mother and daughter were sitting close by, and I heard the mom say sternly, "Now dear, next week is your thirtieth birthday, so don't forget everything we've been practicing all this time."

The daughter rolled her eyes. "Yes, Mother. I got it."

Her mom chided, "You may think you do, but if you don't land the right mate when you turn thirty … Well, the next thing you know, you'll be an old maid with no one to take care of you."

"Yeah, yeah."

"And don't forget that you could be diagnosed with autism at any minute."

The girl just rolled her eyes again, and then her gaze shifted longingly to the far end of the pond. Her mother saw this and said firmly, "Oh no, don't even think about going for a swim!" Grabbing her arm tightly, the mother said, "Now let's go home and get you prepped for your date tonight."

There might have been something wrong with that conversation, but I didn't care. I just remembered what the director said and tried to filter everyone else out.

There were also a few couples around, and on the other side a lone girl was kicking pebbles into the water. She seemed to be eyeing the pond intently, as if contemplating her next move, then I overheard the couple behind me, and one of them said, "Hey, I saw that fuel prices are down again! Let's order a baby!"

"Great idea! Oh, I can't wait until it arrives and we can unwrap our little bundle of joy!"

I said, "You'd better hope it's lobotomized."

They looked back at me, seemingly startled, and I quickly got up and scurried away with my head down. *Jesus, Steven, you've really become jaded.*

Eventually I found myself wandering toward the church, and this time not just because I wanted to use one of their segregated bathrooms. It was the third-largest building in town by volume, behind the center and the hospital, and it was packed for a Monday evening. When I got closer, I saw that the doors were wide open, and I could hear the sounds of celebration inside.

The explanation for the crowd was a wedding that was taking place. That seemed like as good a distraction as anything, so I went in and sat quietly in the back, and no one seemed to notice me.

Everyone was dressed very nicely, and after a few minutes, the crowd quieted down. The bride and groom—or at least two people who nearly passed as members of opposite sexes—were already on the stage, and the priest walked in and waved to the crowd. I thought that it might have been the same guy I saw at the hospital, but it wasn't.

He began the service. "Beloved are we who have come together to witness this sacred union. Before we proceed, however, is there any person who has cause to know why these two should not be wedded by the bonds of holy matrimony? If so, please speak now or hold your peace for approximately four to six years until the statistical probability for divorce arises."

Everyone smiled politely and looked at each other, but no one spoke up. The priest continued by introducing the couple and going into a speech about the tough trials that a marriage can bring and how people need to learn to respect their spouse's space, especially as pertaining to the eventual carnal desires that creep up.

Then he said, "And now I shall read from John's letter to the Corinthians. 'Love is patient. Love is kind. Love doesn't argue about going down to the bank immediately following the ceremony to assign insurance proceeds. Love understands if your spouse feels the need to sleep with other people, as long as it's more than three days after the wedding is over. Love doesn't judge the buildup of excess dark matter that comes after a new baby is ordered ...'"

Somewhere in the middle of it, I lost track of what he was saying. I looked down in front of me and noticed that there was a device embedded in the back of every pew for thumbprint tithing. Below that, there were two giant books.

Christ, I haven't seen a real book since the orphanage.

They had *Scripture's Greatest Hits* and *The King James Revised DSM XLV.*

I muttered to myself, "Huh. I wasn't aware that science and religion went hand in hand."

After the ceremony, everyone was filing out. Many were openly weeping at the joyous nature of the occasion, but I was still sitting quietly, just taking in the scene. A few people were handing out church pamphlets to the wedding guests containing information about recognizing the right time to get a divorce. Then suddenly, the director's wife emerged out of the crowd. I was hoping to avoid her, but she eventually noticed me and came over with a broad smile and open arms, so I stood up to politely greet her.

"Oh, my boy, my lovely boy! It's so good to see you!" She leaned in to give me a kiss. I turned my cheek, and she grabbed my face and plunged her tongue into my mouth while her other hand went straight for my crotch. After a second, I managed to discreetly pull her away and wiped my lips with my sleeve.

Just then I spotted the officiant coming down the aisle. The director's wife saw as well and beckoned him over to us. "Oh, Bishop! This is Steven! He's an orphan, you know, but he's the sweetest, most honorable boy you'd ever meet!"

The bishop extended a scrawny hand, and I wasn't sure whether I was supposed to bow, kneel, kiss it, or what. Instead I extended my hand, and he shook it like a fish.

Everyone had nearly filed out by that time, and the director's wife excused herself, stealing a grope of my ass on the way out and winking suggestively at me. As the bishop made his way back to the front, I finally sat back down and just stared up at the stained-glass images of all of the religious figures.

He looked back and apparently thought that I was in some distress, as he gradually returned to where I was sitting and said, "Is something troubling you today, my son?"

Not sure whether I welcomed the company, I shifted uncomfortably in the pew and stammered, "Oh, er, not too much."

Adopting a concerned expression, he pressed. "Steven, I see a lot of troubled people in my work, and you certainly look like you're suffering."

I didn't know where to start, or what to even say, having never even remotely participated in a confessional. However, seeing that he wasn't going away, I finally said, "Well, for starters, I met a lobotomy a while ago."

"Yes?"

"He couldn't remember anything about yesterday, and he couldn't even think about tomorrow."

"Yes?"

"Well, it's a little troubling to me!"

Smiling broadly, he said, "Oh, Steven, that's perfectly natural!"

"How can you say that?"

"There is absolutely no conflict between science and religion. A wise man once posted on the internet that all power comes from God, but so do all diseases, and nothing prevents you from summoning a physician, now does it?"[13]

"No, I guess not, but I'm still a little worried about how far they have taken things."

Reassuringly, he said, "Let me tell you; you're not the first to come in here with that concern."

"I'm not?"

"Oh, no. Every so often, a young man like you—and sometimes an orphan—will come in and question their faith in the system, but it's a perfectly natural part of the process and nothing to worry about. As for people who can't remember things, that's nothing to be concerned about either. After all, you're not upset about having strong teeth, are you?"

"What the hell does that have to do with anything?"

"Well, fluoride has long been known to cause a decrease in IQ, but people still want to have attractive smiles." He finished by flashing his shiny choppers at me.

I thought about wrestling with him on that score and decided to just let it be. Instead I said, "So you think that it's consistent with God's plan for us to be lobotomizing citizens?"

"Naturally. Steven, the church's greatest aim is to help end human suffering. That was, after all, Jesus's mission, and that's why we keep the King James Version of the *DSM* in here, right next to *The Big Book*."

I observed, "Actually, the *DSM* is *bigger* than *The Big Book*."

"Oh, well, we had to cut some materials out of the other. I'm afraid that many of those old stories used to give people nightmares, and that wasn't good for anyone. Now we just use the best parts, which are, of course, the most popular passages."

He sat down in the pew next to me and continued. "In any event, lobotomies are not new. Pacifying man and his inherent longing for meaning has been the work of society since before Christ, and Steven, we make those people into lobotomies because they were put here to be so. God created the entire universe and gave man a special place in it so that we could discover all of the wonderful treasures of creation."

"But don't you think that it's taking something away from them? I mean something that God gave them?"

"Not at all." Clasping his hands together momentarily, he said, "Steven, we have really created heaven on earth, especially for them. All we do is follow a very simple model these days. We permit society to flow by the path of least resistance, and if they want it, we give it to them. We got rid of that messy, fussy morality that they used to use in the old church. You could say that this is now the church 2.0, and the people have never been happier, as scientific polls show."

I pressed uneasily, "But they can't remember anything."

He pointed to the manuscripts confidently and responded, "That's why we record everything for them, right here!"

I picked up the Bible and thumbed through it. It was pretty bare— mostly just pictures—and he slid closer to me and pointed as we turned the pages.

"Look; it's all been written. In the beginning, God created man, and then he created woman. Then he created gene splicing. After that, Daniel went to a zoo and communed with lions, and they played around, and it was pretty cute. Then David slung a rock and knocked out Goliath's VR contact so that he couldn't send any more hurtful messages." He looked up at me and added instructively, "We call people who say mean things on the internet 'Philistines.'" Then he went back to the book. "After that, Joseph and his FTM lover ordered a new baby from the center, and that was the joyous discovery that ended all suffering for humankind."

Shooting him a sideways glance, I said dubiously, "Um, I remember being taught Bible stories when I was younger, and I think that you may have mixed up a few things."

He replied lightly, "Oh, they're not mixed up. Maybe rearranged a bit, but it's all for the good of the people." He waved a hand and added, "Those old lessons they used were horrible anyway. You may not know this, but in the dark times, priests were being sued for giving people PTSD with their sermons."

"Doesn't that upset you?"

He shook his head solemnly and replied, "Oh, there's nothing sadder to a parishioner than someone with PTSD."

"No, not that. The fact that you had to change doctrine that was more than two thousand years old."

He replied jovially, "Not at all! Steven, eternal damnation does not make for good consumerism, and as you know, the prosperity of commerce is acknowledged by all to be the most useful end of our society."[14]

I chewed on that for a second and then finally said, "Well, what about procreation?"

He leaned back with a curious look and asked, "What about it? Look at page one. 'And the Lord said go forth and multiply and enter into as many raffles as you can.'"

"Yes, but I heard that a man and woman used to be able to do that naturally."

He gave a frail laugh and slapped me on the back with his dead fish hand. "Well, there's not much difference between them these days! And anyway, we've done our best to mitigate the effects of that meddlesome impulse of procreation." Nodding sideways at me, he winked and added, "It was the original sin, you know, so it's certainly a good thing that we got rid of it. Ha!"

I didn't laugh with him, instead saying, "But women are going crazy and trying to drown themselves."

He responded plainly, "Oh, that. Well, some women hold on to the incorrect notion that they can reach God directly by giving birth, which is, I'm afraid, an unfortunate remnant of bygone programming. Most people gave up that delusion long ago, and the few that still struggle with it wind up in that pond." For emphasis, he rested his clammy hand on my shoulder and pronounced, "Of course, communing with God is left up to us in the church."

Doubting the pious nature of my company, I leveled: "Well, do you know they killed an entire gang just because they wouldn't play along?"

He smiled warmly and replied, "Oh, that little thing! It couldn't be helped. Steven, homeless people don't qualify for insurance, so it would be no good for them to undergo compassionate release, although a bunch did it at the very beginning."

"Really?"

"Yep. We promised them that even though they couldn't participate in the insurance program, they could still inherit the earth, and they signed up in droves!"

I was beginning to get sick. Seeking confirmation, I said, "Then the church is in it for the profit as well?"

He responded benevolently, "Oh, no, we're here to minister to those in need." Then he laughed and added, "But profit is certainly a necessary part of the equation! After all, we can't give to those in need if they don't need in the first place!"

Putting the book down and looking up again at the glass images, I said, "I don't know. It doesn't seem very ... righteous?"

He responded assuredly, "Oh, Steven, God wants us to make a profit, and it's detailed in all of the most famous sayings on the subject. Don't forget: the economy pays for our freedoms, and freedom is the only tent big enough for everyone!"

I looked at him again and insisted, "But everyone is going crazy."

Crossing himself, he said, "Don't worry, my son. Jesus died for our sins."

I shot back, astonished, "What the hell does that mean?"

"It means that everything is taken care of. It doesn't matter what we do on earth, because heaven will set everything right. Don't forget, the Bible says, 'Give me your tired, your poor, your huddled masses yearning to breathe free, the wretched refuse of your teeming shore. Send these, the homeless, tempest-tossed to me, I lift my lamp beside the golden door!'"[15]

I shook my head and asked, "It really says that?"

"Of course! Look right here in the *Revised Abridged Pope Caesar New Edition to the New, New Testament.*"

True enough, it was in there. Then he added affirmingly, "And sure, some people lose it and a few people suffer, but look at all of the economic benefits we'd be missing out on if we did things any differently."

I decided to change tactics and demanded further, "Then what about the puritan ethic and hard work?"

He gave me a half-frown, half-smile and responded chidingly, "Steven, you should really stop reading outdated books. The people who wrote those original principles were so guided by religious dogma that our laws had to be rewritten once we obtained a more enlightened perspective."

"How so?"

"Well, for example, we used to have people fixated on retirement, but that's obviously not very useful anymore!" With that, he let out a short laugh.

I said despondently, "But all you've created is a society where people fake illness to get out of work so they can go home and play, shop, and avoid ever really doing anything."

"Naturally, Steven. In case you didn't know it, the human form is weak, but don't worry. There'll be plenty of time to work in heaven."

Finally pressing him hard, I said, "So you agree that it's in keeping with Jesus's teachings to just keep people sedated long enough for them to accept their fates?"

He put his hand on his heart and replied, "My boy, I dare say that everyone should have the opportunity to live with such humanity. If you can keep people relatively sedated until they die, there aren't any problems." With a small chuckle, he nudged me and added, "After all, what are they going to do after that—ask for a refund? Ha!"

Looking up at the image above us, I said defiantly, "Well, I'm pretty sure that he'd be disappointed."

"Oh, not at all. If reincarnated today, Jesus would be one of us. He'd love Botox, lobotomies, and compassionate release. After all, they are all tools to help ensure eternal life—for the state, that is."

"What about … God?"

He clasped his hands together and pronounced, "Steven, we are God's prized children. After all, at no time since science replaced superstition has God tried to smite us."

I finally glared at him and leveled, "Maybe it's that at no time since you started making up your own rules have you *recognized* that God was trying to smite you."

He leaned back with disdain and replied, "Well, I'm not going to get into that with you, as you obviously don't have the theological background to understand all of it. But I will say this: our scientific democracy makes no distinction between the truth and theories tending to establish the truth, and with all the benefits we provide to these people that they never had before, the least they can do is have faith in the system." He nodded disapprovingly at me and added, "That goes for you as well, my son."

Hearing him call me "son" made me as disgusted as when the director did it. Firmly, I said, "Well, I just don't like it. There's something not right about the world being controlled by generally accepted truths."

Leaning back, the priest said innocently, "Okay then, what should we be doing differently?"

Completely at a loss to answer that, I responded emptily, "I don't know."

He smiled briefly, as if knowing that he had won this battle, and said, "Steven, compared to what other people have done, what we're doing is really not that bad. When you know your history, you know that this is true."

I still tried to argue with him and pointed out emphatically, "But you just gave a speech at a wedding about the statistical probability that the couple would eventually get a divorce."

"Sure, I did. That's science. But look at it this way: the number of divorces performed by the church are way down from past numbers, all thanks to the compassionate release program. And remember Madison's famous internet post—'It doesn't matter if things are a little messy now, as long as they're better than they were.'"[16]

I retorted bitterly, "I seriously doubt he ever said anything like that, and I already knew that things were more than just messy. This state is downright rotten!"

The bishop stood up and frowned at me, insisting firmly, "My young man, you would do well to put these wicked notions behind you. After all, we can't leave society up to the people. Can you imagine if people had to decide whether to fix the road or not, or how much to spend on this building? There'd be nothing but continuous fights, and in the end, there would be no house of worship. If the Bible teaches us one thing, my son, it is that we must have a common good."

I stood up as well and glared at him. "And what if you don't fit into that scheme?"

Compassionately, he said, "Oh, Steven, you're a young man, so why worry yourself with things that are never going to matter to you? Don't forget that First Corinthians says, 'When I was a child, I talked like a child, I thought like a child, I reasoned like a child. When I became a man, I realized that all of that worked pretty well, so now I have faith like a child.'"

Defiantly, I said, "Well, I'm not a child anymore."

He laughed gently and shook his head, adding as a final comment, "My boy, people your age can't change! Once you're thirty, you're stuck!" Finally turning his own gaze toward the stained-glass image of Jesus above, he concluded knowingly, "Just ask him."

*

TWENTY-EIGHT

My auto-reply had been recently updated:

> I'm sorry that I missed your text / email / friend
> request / offer to have sex / invitation to purchase
> a baby. I'm absolutely swamped ignoring similar
> requests from other people, and it could take me quite
> some time to get back to you. In the meantime, stay
> heavily medicated and trust that someone is minding
> the light at the end of the tunnel.

I did know one thing, however: I might have been the only sane person in the whole fucking town, and I didn't care. I was going to save Emily and her house, even if it was the last thing I did. I didn't even care what they wanted me to do, and I knew I could survive anything if it was for her. I could clearly see my plan to build up my credits and use my government job to help her survive. I would buy her nice things and give her the kind of life that these people just took for granted, and as long as she was alive, I promised to stay alive for her.

On Wednesday night, I started penning a letter to her. I knew her address at least, and I thought that a letter might help bring her back to me. "Dear Emily: I don't even know you, but I promise that nothing bad will ever happen to you while I'm by your side." After that, the words fell short and everything else I tried to write came out clumsily. I longed for auto-fill to explain my heart to her the way that I wanted to, but I knew that was not possible.

Just then, my phone rang. My chest started pounding immediately, hoping that it was her on the other end. Instead it was a telemarketer indicating that I had won second prize in the drawing at the soccer stadium for having been there when that couple got engaged. I was now in the running for a nonlobotomized baby. I hung up before he had even finished his spiel, put the phone in a drawer, and went for a walk. When I got back, I finished the letter to Emily as best as I could and sent it out, but I had only a faint hope that I would hear from her again.

On Thursday morning, I rose ready to confront my new task. Walking toward the center, I wondered whether it was too late to request a lobotomy for myself. Dismissing the idea, I tried to give myself a mental one so I could handle whatever confronted me at this new place, remembering that my only goal was to be with Emily.

A sleek, stylish woman in an open-bust suit greeted me when I emerged from the elevator. She had obviously benefitted greatly from the tube-tying process, and her proportions proved it. Sticking her chest out at me, she said, "Hello, Steven, and welcome to the fifth floor of the center. I must say, you're really going places in our grand society!"

I tried to sound as enthusiastic as possible and responded, "Gosh, I'm glad to be here! You can't imagine what I've been going through, and I'm dying to do something that really helps people!"

She replied knowingly, "I'll bet, what with you being an orphan and all." She ended by giving me a pitying smile.

That almost set me off right out of the gate. *Restraint, Steven, restraint.* I just smiled and politely answered, "Yes, that's right!"

"Well, you've come to the right place. Let me show you around. Over here is where we create jingles."

"Jingles? Is that a cure for shingles?"

Briefly annoyed, she said, "Huh? Steven, this is where we assign little jingles to stories that people read. You may have noticed, but all of the news stories that we show to people these days have background music to them. Of course, some are shorter than others, and the length of the jingle is tied to the length of the story."

I was instantly confused but tried my best to follow along. "And that's important why?"

"Well, the shorter attention spans that humans have developed over time has shaped music—and stories, for that matter—but lobotomies will follow anything if you put music to it."

"No, but—"

She was moving swiftly but somehow still managed to swing her ass as she chugged along, and I tried to keep up as she continued. "Over here, we also do all of the music that kids listen to, and over here is where we write scripts for movies."

"Movies?"

"Yes. You've seen the wonderful movies that we make?"

Starting to feel like I had gotten off on the wrong floor again, I answered unsteadily, "I've … seen some movies; that's for sure."

She looked over her shoulder at me with a patterned smile. "Aren't they great? Of course, we don't actually make the movies here. We just write the stories and review the proofs of the screenplays before they go out."

"Well, I covered a number of movie busts at the newspaper, so I don't know if I'd call a lot of them 'great.'"

In complete lockstep, she said dismissively, "Oh, you still have to get over a certain bar, and sometimes we miss it just a bit, since we have to compete with technology upgrades. But we're getting better every day, and we've almost gotten the formula down to a science." As an aside, she remarked, "And thank God for lobotomies. There was a dark time when people wouldn't even go to see the movies we had worked so hard to make for them."

Dully, I said, "You've got to be kidding me."

"I know. Horrible, right? They just didn't understand that it really benefits everyone when they pay their small share to make sure a movie is successful, but it was really awful—or at least that's what I've been told." Continuing to move down the hall at an efficient pace, she added, "Of course, most of the time you don't really have to sell anything to these people. You can usually just dangle an item in front of their faces, and they'll grab it like a cat with a string."

Skeptically, I said, "So you're telling me that what you do here is trick people into buying products?"

She responded lightly, "In part, yes, but we also do lots of other things that I'll show you in a minute. Steven, what we do today is not much different from the past, and we've always used the news media to sell goods for us. You read the archives, right? Half of the articles used to be about a new product. The stories were, of course, cleverly designed to look like news, but they were really intended to draw people's attention to a new car, razor, or whatever. In the end, it all benefits the economy, and the economy is good for stability."

I was starting to realize that I had been tricked, but I didn't know whether there was another job out there. I decided to play the part of the curious new initiate and said, "Yes, and stability is good for me, but how did you do it?"

"Well, it originally started with the experiment of raising and lowering gas prices for decades. We learned through that process that people will buy some things no matter what the cost is, so we just figured out how to get rid of that little factor that made them consider some things more important than others. Now they'll buy anything we put in front of them at whatever the expense, all thanks to the quiet pressures of social media."

"So you're scaring people into buying things?"

Shocked at the mere suggestion, she said, "Heavens no! Fear is what the news is for."

"Huh?"

"Steven, the way our system works, we keep people terrified with the news, then we show commercials where everyone is perfectly happy. That way the people's brains are wired to only associate happiness with spending."

Starting to feel ill, I said, "Do you think that's how we should be doing things?"

"Oh, absolutely. Look at it this way: the human as a free-standing participant is largely obsolete these days. Humans became obsolete when we mapped the entire universe and came up with generally accepted answers for everything. The rub, however, is that we still need humans to give value to the economy, but other than moving pieces back and forth on the chessboard for us, they're no more valuable than their allegiance to what we're doing. Now thanks to the Multiverse, we've fulfilled the Framers' intention to make whatever we do the law of the land."

I started to open my mouth, but she stopped abruptly and whirled around, so I quickly stood at attention. My heart was pounding from her steely gaze and the pace we had been keeping up. By contrast, she was completely at ease and took a moment to undress me from head to toe with her eyes. With mild interest, she said, "My, my, you're good looking! We can definitely use you here!"

"Huh?"

She just turned and continued chugging along. "Anyway, there was a very dark time when people had to sweat and toil and do backbreaking labor just to survive."

"You don't say."

"No, and it was horrible because they were all so beautiful and photogenic and couldn't sell their looks."

"That sounds pretty tough."

"I'll say. Thank goodness for lobotomies, although most of those don't end up very well."

"No, really?"

"Oh, we give them plenty of opportunity to make it—internet commercials, television, then maybe movies or reporting. Then we leak a sex tape they've made, and we sometimes combine that with filler pieces about them having been groped, molested, or whatever in the past. And they also get to publicize if they get a disease—the cute ones that everyone likes, you know, not the really awful ones that no one wants to hear about—and then, of course, there's always the chance to do some good porn. If they don't take advantage of those opportunities, it's certainly not our fault."

Still trying to sound obediently curious, I said, "What if they start out in porn?"

She responded in lockstep, "Well then, it's harder to go in the other direction. That career path is mostly frowned upon in primary school education, but it's never too late to start if you do it right. We've had plenty of famous flesh-peddlers who were glad for the late start they had in life, and lots of stars have posed nude into their forties and fifties. Anyway, as you'll see, movies are easy to make. Do you remember seeing a movie as a kid?"

"Sure."

"Could you tell what was real and what was fake?"

"No."

"It's pretty much the same thing these days with the lobotomized population."

I decided to test her level of infiltration into the conspiracy and asked unassumingly, "But that's only 35 percent? How do you get over 80 percent of the population to watch movies?"

"Come on, Steven, there's more than one way to lobotomize people. You should know that by now." *She was one of them.* The fear crept in.

With mechanical efficiency, she continued on. "And over here is where we do commercials, which of course rely heavily on the jingle department. The most important thing to remember about commercials is to always work a child somewhere into the pitch."

I had taken to staying three feet away from her at all times, watching for bats to fly out of the back of her head. When she turned around to see why I was lagging behind, I pretended to be looking at something else on the other side of the room and then snapped to attention quickly. "Oh, and why is that again?"

"Well, as you know, all commercials are product placement ads, and since we're responsible for all products sold in society, that also includes children. Putting a cute little kid in a commercial is as effective in keeping new birth orders up as is showing someone relaxing at a beach with an umbrellaed drink!"

"So part of what you do here involves all of those ads I see in the elevator?"

She responded proudly, "Yep—all as part of the American Dream we're selling!"

"What dream?"

"Oh, ages ago, everyone wanted to be a princess or a prince. It always involved marrying someone in royalty, but that fantasy fell apart when the monarchies disbanded. Now we sell vacations and nonlobotomized kids, and whenever possible we like to show kids and vacations together in the same ad, which basically kills two birds with one stone."

"And what's with all of the vacations again?"

"Steven, science proves that taking regular holidays lengthens life."

She moved on and kept explaining more of the process, but after a while my mask of sanity started slipping. Finally I halted and said, "Excuse me for interrupting, but I thought the director said you were curing diseases?"

She stopped and turned around, responding with the utmost sincerity, "Oh, but we *are!* Every day, we help to cure brain tumors, quadriplegia, and thousands of other maladies."

"With what?"

"Distraction, Steven. That's the best thing that we could ever provide to these people, and it works for nearly everything."

I finally showed some opposition and insisted, "Look, I don't just want to distract people. I want to cure them."

"Well, some of the things we can't help."

"Like what?"

"Take cancer for example. Sure, you can keep it away for a while, but in the meantime, you'll lose your hair, your digestive system will go to pot, and the rest is very ugly stuff. Now we just, you know …" She made a slashing gesture across her throat. "Swish, swish, and it all works out much better in the end."

I finally said challengingly, "Listen, I've just spent months working in the hospital, and I know damn well that people are still dying of all of the maladies you just mentioned—including cancer."

With calculated regret, she responded, "Well, you have to understand that we can't fix absolutely *everything*. Human knowledge has grown only so far, I'm afraid."

"No, no, no. They're cutting people down like trees out there, and I want to stop it!"

She shook her head compassionately and replied, "But there's no way to do that, Steven. The best we can do here is to keep people from noticing it."

My disguise completely slipped at that point, and I leveled accusingly, "Yeah, and rake in the profits along the way!"

She didn't break character for a second. She just started walking again, and all I could do was trot after her. "It's not just about money, Steven. Well, the money is nice too, but it's about etching events into the fabric of society. Every time we allow the public to see us doing something, it creates permission for them to do the same, so we are literally creating freedom as we speak."

Well, you're all fucked in the head as far as I can tell.

She continued unapologetically. "I'll tell you, thank goodness for lobotomies. Do you know that there was a time when people actually claimed we staged certain tragic events?"

Exasperated, I said, "But you did! The archives show trillions spent to increase patriotism!"

"Oh, sure, we did stage those. But the rest ... Well, people just don't realize that disasters actually make the citizenry stronger."

"Really?"

Pausing momentarily, she remarked, "Of course. Science proves that disasters help to bring people together—especially lobotomies who are terrified of even a thunderclap." I had absolutely no response to that, so she just turned and continued. "Anyway, these days people are ready to accept the things we do before they even happen, and as people want to roll over more and more, we simply have to find new ways to exploit their earning potential—for the economy's sake."

Struggling to follow her again, I said, "Is what you do here really that big a part of the economy?"

She looked over her shoulder knowingly for a moment and answered, "Steven, if you buy something that is regulated by us, you're buying from us." Then she turned back and continued trucking along, adding, "In the end, the frozen resources that make up these citizens all come back to us, which is why we lead the world in the export of lobotomization techniques. Everyone wants the same ones we use on our people."

Finally I halted, which she noticed, and turned around, surprised. I made an X with my arms in surrender, saying firmly, "Look, I don't think I belong here. I wanted to be somewhere helping people."

Suddenly her lips formed into a deadly, vengeful grin that she was obviously very accustomed to flashing, and she took two steps toward me. Hissing sharply, she proclaimed, "But Steven, this is the *last* place left for you!"

I stepped back and involuntarily gulped. "What?"

Her advance continued. "There are no other jobs out there. Look, we know all about your employment history. You've been through every position the government can offer someone like you, and if you can't do this job, you'll get fired."

My voice cracked as I backed into one of the walls. "And … then what?"

"Then what nothing. That's it. You'll be kicked out of society and wind up as just another penniless orphan on the streets. As you know, there used to be a gang of people just like you, but they're all gone now."

Shocked at the reference, I said, "Those were all orphans?"

She was now less than twelve inches from me, her lips still parted in a crimson grin, and her menacing tone continued. "All except the gang leader. He had extreme mental health issues and refused treatment, and you know what happened to him."

By then my testicles had fully ascended back to first position, and I choked in response, "I do."

"Well, we're all you've got left. If you can't fit in here, we'll have to boot you, and then you'll be out on the street with nothing."

She stood there glaring at me and waiting for a response. *I won't let Emily down; I won't let Emily down.* Instead I lubed up and got ready to start my new job. Obediently, I said, "Okay, okay. Just tell me what you want me to do."

With that, her wicked smile cemented. Turning away and raising a manicured hand over her shoulder, she curled a finger at me and ordered, "That's better. Come with me, please."

* * *

"Want to add some laughter to your life? Science proves that the youngest child is always the funniest! Call or click to order a new jokester for your family today! Hurry, supplies are limited!"

The madam was back and very pleased with my turnaround. Smiling approvingly at my new ad campaign, she said, "Steven, that was brilliant! How did you ever come up with that?"

"It wasn't too hard. I just read through the archives and found the study and put two and two together."

"Jesus Christ, you'll be getting a bonus in no time! The director just called and said that they now have a twelve-month backorder at the lab!"

Well, I hope to God that they're lobotomized. In full propagandistic swing, I added, "Of course, the oldest child also gets into the best schools. Hey, let's run a separate promo for that and target first-time families!"

"Great idea!" she said. "I tell you, Steven, for a long time we've been worried about how to keep our population up, what with everyone going gay all the time. But thanks to you, we won't have that problem for decades to come!"

I was fairly well numbed to the idea of caring about the implications of my actions by then, and the madam added, "And don't forget: next week we're hosting the Academy Awards."

Someone chimed in. "No, next week we're hosting the pre–potential nominees' celebration."

She raised a theatrical backhand to her forehead and said lightly, "Oh, my, I completely forgot! We have so many awards shows these days that it's hard to keep track!"

That's the stupidest thing I've ever heard. Feigning ignorance, I asked, "Um, why would they do an award show for pre–potential nominees?"

The madam said, "Because we need it now. With the number of orders for new babies, we had to make a whole new list of criteria for winning a nonlobotomized kid. We have to do that one so that we can later have the potential nominees' show, then the nominees' show, and then the actual Academy Awards."

As innocently as possible, I offered, "That sounds like a lot of work just for people to congratulate themselves."

She nodded assuredly and responded, "It sure is, and we're going to have to repeat that whole process every four months, but we're sure lucky to have lobotomies around! One year they almost found out that we keep multiple envelopes for most major awards."

"Why?"

"To see how the betting is going before the awards are announced, of course."

I was no longer fighting with people, but my basic nature hadn't changed. Wearily, I asked, "Doesn't that seem a little disingenuous?"

The madam replied, "Oh, no. After all, it benefits the economy." She lightly patted me on the head and added condescendingly, "And you know how good that is for you, right, Steven?"

I said nothing, and she addressed the larger group proudly. "We once even had an actress wear a pin to the Oscars to support Planned Parenthood, which helped fuel the battle over reproductive rights and eventually led our citizens to throw up their hands and ask for guidance. Yes, we are truly powerful people!"

The minions all nodded along with her and then one of the eager propaganda technicians added proudly, "A long time ago, people weren't even watching the awards ceremonies because they had better things to do outdoors for some reason. Fortunately, these days, people get to experience all of the life they need through the movies!"

The madam gave her a curt nod and then turned to leave. Stopping back by my station, she said praisingly, "Steven, we're sure glad that you're here, because we need the extra help. Everyone will probably be working overtime all week."

Standing right behind me, she ran her hand down the front of my shirt and squeezed my pec. I thought about calling the newspaper, but then I realized that they were probably still on to churning the next bit of social drama to fill their pages. Besides, I needed the points for Emily.

I responded compliantly, "No problem. Just tell me what you want me to do."

* * *

As the days went on, I realized that there were no lobotomies working anywhere on this floor. Instead I was surrounded by robots. I would call them fembots, but some of them could have been males for all I know.

Bot Number One said, "Television, news, and movies are our most important means of communication, and everyone accepts that. As a result, we're able to cite to our own programs as authority for how society should live."

Bot Number Two nodded. "Besides, the only real history is what you see on television, and it's much more important than what actually happened. The history shows we make also turn into great true-to-life movies."

Bot Number Three chimed in excitedly, "Like *The 57!* That one was absolutely groundbreaking! Of course, it was only partially true. The real story is that the driver got a flat and couldn't make it into town. However, with that movie we were able to change the route of traffic to make it safer for people."

Bastards. I said, "How, um, did you make that happen?"

Bot Number One explained: "Steven, people naturally can't sleep at night unless we implement changes that the movies call for. We show them terror, then we show them a solution—or at least we suggest a solution. The actual solution may not be shown until the sequel. However, with the movie plus all of the studies we did afterward about the dangers of the very road where that particular movie was based, we obtained appropriations for a new route." The bot nodded around the room and added, "And a good thing too. There was a house out there that was sucking up resources with a landline. Can you believe that?"

* * *

The next day, the madam was back. Her nearly translucent blouse displayed her ample cleavage prominently, and her heels clicked along as we walked. "Steven, we're big fans of anything nonthreatening that slows people down and keeps them distracted. You should have figured that out by now. Apropos, as you may know, this is also where we create social messages for the Multiverse voters, and we need you to work on one for us."

"Like what?"

"Look at this. Here's a kid who destroyed a whole shipment of newborn pamphlets and obviously deserves to be sent to jail. Now, no one knows about it because it's not very public yet, since we didn't want to scare prospective parents by having them think that they'll have to wing it during the first few days after unwrapping their shipment. However, once we print the replacements, we can run the social media campaign."

The bile was already creeping up in my throat, but I said nothing, and she continued. "Meanwhile, why don't you do a mock-up for the social media announcement? We'll have someone get you relevant data from the newspaper about the dangers of doing things like this, and you can put together a nice, scathing piece to take care of this little miscreant. After that we'll notify the newspaper so they can run a complementary article which agrees with our position; then we'll publish the mock-up you create on our internet feed, and the Multiverse judges will convict the guy instantly."

I started to open my mouth in protest. Immediately silencing me, she turned to address the larger group, obviously meaning to shame me into collective obedience. "Don't forget what Hamilton said, people: 'Laws are a dead letter without the Multiverse to expound their true meaning!'"[17]

Everyone nodded in mechanical agreement, and she turned back to me to see whether I would dare try to defy her. Instead I smiled and took the assignment sheet from her and read the background information. It turned out that he was an orphan, but without hesitating, all I said was "No problem."

She nodded firmly and gave my backside a loving pat as she walked past. "That's my good boy!"

Later that afternoon, as I was crafting the rope to hang one of my own, the crew next to me was working on the next sci-fi addition to the SWAGSA budget. The screenwriter-turned-cosmonaut explained: "People in space are working on a plan to temporarily stop the earth from rotating. That way, if we're ever hit by an asteroid, it will only affect countries that we don't care about."

The guyish creature next to her said snidely, "Yeah, like all of those countries that still don't care about greenhouse gas emissions!"

The other nodded assuredly. "Yeah, that'll teach 'em!"

I said, "I'm not sure that's possible."

"Oh, yes, it is. Take a look at this. This is the visualization of how it will work. See how cool that is?"

"Yes. I see the visual creation you've made, but I still don't think it's going to be possible."

"Oh, Steven, of course it will. After all, space may be the final frontier, but we create the truth about it here first! Anyway, this shows that we can just turn the earth like a giant shield and make the rocks hit all of our enemies." She made a shooting gesture. "*Pew, pew, pew!* Won't that be fun?"

Wearily, I said, "It sure will."

"And at just under six hundred eighty-five trillion, it's a remarkable steal for space projects!"

She looked at her finished project lovingly and added, "This one is sure to make it to ten on the charts!"

I said, "Huh?"

"Every time we have a hit movie, we do five sequels and five prequels. That's ten total. And nearly all movies are hits, since most people can't remember anything and just watch whatever we put in front of them." As an aside, she added, "Thank goodness for lobotomies! By the time they came around, Hollywood had already used up all of the good ideas in the world!"

The following week, my pit deepened as the madam gave me a new proposition, worse than the other ones she had made before. "Steven, we may want to use your face for some of our projects."

Oh God, no! I stammered in protest. "I, um, I'd prefer to stay behind the scenes if I can."

"Come on! You're not shy. We've all seen that sex tape you made!"

"I … um, yeah, but that was just a one-time deal."

She cooed demandingly, "Oh, Steven, we need you! Attractive people like you are our best asset to convince people to accept what we're telling them! Besides, if you don't do it, then it will be an affront to every other beautiful person who never got the opportunities that you and I have!"

Confused, I said, "What, to be on television?"

"Yes! That is, of course, the loftiest goal in our society!"

Reluctantly, I caved, just as I had been doing all along. "Okay, but let me finish what I was doing here, and then we can talk about it." *Thank God Emily doesn't have a television.*

Patting my backside and pausing momentarily for a healthy squeeze, she said, "Oh, I almost forgot. Before we get to that, I need you to write up something to send to the newspaper."

Hesitating again, I said, "Oh, I really shouldn't. The manager over there didn't like my stuff very well."

She responded dismissively, "Steven, we tell the second floor what to publish, not the other way around, so don't worry about it. We need you to write a 'What the Movie Gets Wrong about Planetary Rotation' article."

"Wait a minute. You write those here too?"

"Of course!"

"But you wrote the script for the movie."

"Oh sure, but it doesn't matter. You can't fit everything into a movie, and we can make money on the front and the back end by including an article like this. You think you can handle it?"

I just sighed and said, "Sure, no problem."

"Good boy! And be sure to include a pitch for the SWAGSA show about the new roller coaster they're designing for black holes. The newspaper needs that to go along with a story they're running about people who leave excessively large tips. I say, things like that always help to boost consumer confidence!"

I dutifully saluted in acknowledgment, and she smiled authoritatively. As she walked past, she unmistakably rubbed her massive knockers up against me, but all I could do was sit down and get to work.

* * *

By then, thank God, Emily and I were back on speaking terms. My letter appeared to do the trick, and I spoke into the phone cautiously. "You doing okay?"

Her weariness was apparent for the first time since I had known her, and she responded in exasperation, "*Barely.* It's getting harder and harder to keep this all up. Can you believe that they just built a road that completely bypasses the bypass to my house?"

"What?"

"Yep, and now the crops have to be shipped to the next, *next* town over just to be picked up to get to get to your town."

"Can you just sell them to the next, next town over?"

"Well, sure, but the population of that town is only four hundred people. The shipping costs are nearly killing me, and I'm barely breaking even these days."

"Is the crew still coming out to help you?"

"Yes, but I'm also now paying double for labor because of how far they have to drive to get to me."

Finally I hazarded a dangerous suggestion and said, "Look, have you thought about giving up that place and moving to the city with me?"

She responded with instant conviction, "Steven, there's no way I can do that. I can't give up on my dad's dream that easily."

"Oh, I understand. Listen, I'd love to come out and help, but I've got some things I need to take care of here. I promise I'll be there as soon as I can."

* * *

I went to the director's office to check my citizenship score, and he confirmed my progress. "You're doing very well, and in another week you'll be able to afford taxis again. You've almost completely wiped off all of the missed days you had at the hospital, although those will also likely keep you from getting a promotion anytime soon."

I said, "That's fine. I just need the points."

He looked at me suspiciously and asked, "You're not still interested in that girl, are you?"

"I, um … no. Not at all."

"Good. There's no future there for you." *That's what you think. I can wait you out, bub, and she can too.* Nonchalantly, he continued. "You may have noticed that the town is slowly walling her house off."

Trying to play it cool, I said, "Yeah, what's up with that?"

"Oh, that route was notorious for bandits, and we've determined that bypassing that area is best way to ensure safe commerce across the country."

"But I thought that it was illegal to enclose real property?"

He looked at me suspiciously again and said, "Steven, where did you ever come up with that notion?"

"I, er, I saw something about it in the archives."

"Oh, okay. Well, actually it's only illegal to *completely* enclose someone's property, and we've still left her a route of ingress and egress." He let out a small chuckle and added, "It is sure a damn long way for her to enter and exit, but it's still legal!"

I tried pleading undetectably, "Couldn't you have done so without cutting her—I mean, the location—off from regular traffic?"

He shook his head and responded plainly, "I'm afraid not. The geological formations in the area just wouldn't have allowed us to do it that way. Besides, the address was on Valley Drive, and everyone knows how dangerous valleys are."

"Yeah, but her house was actually up on a hill …"

"Well—"

He was interrupted in the middle of another excuse by the buzzer on his desk. "Director, you must get down to the lab! We have the most amazing discovery!"

He responded and clicked off, and then, standing up, he said, "Well, the scientific process calls, so I've got to cut this short. You know how to find your way out, don't you?"

I nodded dutifully. "Yep. I'll see you soon."

I stood up and was getting ready to walk out when suddenly I noticed Emily's mom's name on a scrap of paper under a pile on his desk. It was the original order to send her for compassionate release, dated a week before she phoned in the food delivery order. Under my breath I said, "What the fuck?"

The order read, "Emily's mom determined to be chief barrier to new transportation route. Can still remarry and leverage influence. Once she's gone, will have no problem getting route approved. Daughter too young to do anything."

Motherfuckers! Steven, calm down. You know you can't do anything about it right now. Just go back to work and keep earning credits. There's still time to save Emily before it's too late.

*

TWENTY-NINE

The next day, I was fidgeting at my station, half anxious for Emily and half annoyed by my colleagues. Next to me, Sleepy, Dopey, and Doc were working in collaboration, as they were part of a team I had been assigned to for my new role.

Sleepy corrected me. "No, Steven, that's just the artist's rendition of what the new colony will look like on the missing planet—that is, whenever we find it. Don't forget that with modern technology, we can put up fake buildings as fast as we can make a fake movie!"

Shaking my head and turning back to this uncomfortable new assignment, I asked, "So what do you want me to do about this ad?"

"Well, you'll have to memorize this short script, and we want to use your face on the promo for a new television drama we're showing starting next week."

I said, "Am I going to be in the actual show?"

"Oh, no, but it's useful to have an outsider do the promo. That will help increase the legitimacy of the project."

"Okay. What's it about?"

Dopey chimed in eagerly: "What we're developing is a riveting tale! There aren't a lot of special effects, but it's very powerful stuff and based on a true story which is a follow-up to *The 57!* Say, did you see that one?"

I stammered, "Um, parts of it."

"Anyway, it's about this family who live way out in the sticks. They have this ominous house located at 1117 Valley Drive."

I choked so hard I almost threw up. Everyone looked at me in surprise, and I quickly recovered and said, "Uh huh?"

- THE MADMAN -

Dopey continued the suspenseful explanation: "Anyway, the dad is a crime syndicate boss, and he hijacked a truck full of medical supplies years ago so he wouldn't have to go to the hospital." As an aside, he said eagerly, "As you can imagine, we splice in lots of really moving clips of all of the people who were deprived of treatments because of his hoarding the supplies all for himself! Now with all of the supplies and super-tech know-how, he turned himself into part man, part machine, and he also has eleven henchmen working with him to attempt to overthrow the government!"

Trying to remain as detached as possible, I asked innocently, "Are you sure that's based on a true story?"

Dopey nodded assuredly and said, "Oh, yes! Well, we embellished some of it, but these days all you need in order to say that it's based on a true story is one factually correct detail."

I asked sarcastically, "Let me guess. The address?"

"Exactly. And thank God someone went out there and got the story in the first place so we could use it!"

I finally did start choking. Doc looked at me with concern and said, "Steven, are you okay?"

"I, um, yes, I'm fine. Sorry. I could use a little water. Ahem. So, did someone get them to sign a contract?"

Doc finished the story. "No, but everyone was dead anyway."

Feigning ignorance, I said, "What do you mean? I thought they had a daughter?"

Doc looked around momentarily to make sure that no one outside of the loop was listening; then he turned back and said excitedly, "Well, this part is technically not public yet, but I heard that she was on the verge of a mental breakdown! Oh, it's going to be such a riveting story! First Dad dies, then Mom goes nuts, and then daughter does too! I'm very excited to have you work on it with us!"

Trying to mask the panic that was quickly overtaking me, I said abruptly, "I, um … I actually think I'm not feeling too well. Would you mind if we picked this up tomorrow?"

Doc said, "Oh, sure, no problem. I hope that you feel better." Then he winked at me and added, "And have fun shopping while you're on sick leave!"

I sprinted out of there as fast as possible. Fortunately I had my phone with me, and I tried Emily's number, but there was no answer. I wondered if she had made any phone-in orders lately and prayed to God that she had not. I decided to run over to the pharmacy pick-up station to see whether I could intercept what I feared was happening.

I tried to remain calm as I walked up to the counter, where a scrawny gentleman politely addressed my arrival, and I said, "Excuse me, have you sent anyone recently over to 1117 Valley Drive for … anything?"

"Oh, let me check. Why, yes, in fact, we just sent a delivery driver over there."

The calm ended there, as I reached over the counter and grabbed his shirt, demanding, "Listen, give me your keys, right now!"

He stammered, petrified, "But I don't drive!"

"Does anyone in here drive?"

I caught the faint odor of urine as he started shaking and blurted out, "I don't know for sure? I only live two blocks away, so I don't get out much with other people—except for work, that is!"

Releasing my grip on him, sheer terror took over and I searched frantically for a solution. *Fuck! Let's see … I can't take a taxi, and the bus is no good. I could steal a police car. No, I already saw what happened to that guy.*

Unfortunately, the pharmacy was buzzing with activity that day. It was the monthly refill period for people with the last names beginning in L through R, and people were busily filling out orders and separating drug vials into little home-delivery packages.

I tried her on my phone one last time. No answer. *Shit, shit, shit!* I lost it. I threw my phone on the ground and smashed it into a million pieces. Everyone stopped for a second at the commotion and then all started commenting to each other.

"I wonder if he's having a seizure."

"Maybe it's a brain tumor."

"I can't believe he smashed his phone like that!"

"Well, that was a pretty old model anyway, so he's probably better to be rid of it." And on and on.

Finally I stopped and threw up my hands, shouting at the top of my lungs, "Listen everyone, shut the fuck up!"

Someone from the back said, "What language! This must be a robbery. No one else would dare talk like that!"

Someone else recognized me and replied, "Wait, it can't be a robbery. It's Steven. He's an orphan."

I vaulted onto the counter and screamed, "*Which part of shut the fuck up didn't you understand?*"

The general incomprehension continued, "Oh, he must be low on estrogen?"

"No, Pitocin?"

"He could be one of those that needs lithium?"

"Ooohhh! Let me get a good look at him!"

A girl approached the counter and looked up at me compassionately. Cocking her head to the side, she said, "Steven, you look a little tense. Have you checked your gender identity monitor lately?"

"ARRRRRRRRGGGGGHHHHHH!"

* * *

I have no idea how long I was in there; nor do I know how long I sat out on the street afterward. I finally looked down at myself as my breathing started to slow. My clothes were half-torn, and I had blood all over me. All around me were broken bodies in white coats, moaning in and out of unconsciousness, and pills, pill dispensers, pill boxes, computer terminals, and other equipment lying in waste all over the street. I was sure I would be executed in a matter of seconds. Oddly enough, however, the police were not on the way, and I suddenly remembered why.

There was a giant soccer match going on that day, and the president and vice president were going to be in attendance. I knew this because I had written the ads for the event. Suddenly I sprang to my feet and took off running. I might have been doomed, but at least I could warn someone. I considered that maybe the president had no idea what was going on. I had to try something to see whether I could help Emily.

Like a rabid beast on the hunt, I made my way through dark alleyways, being sure to duck behind barriers every time a car passed by. When I got to the stadium, the gates were wide open, as a parade float had just pulled out at the end of the halftime show.

I bowled right over the lone security guard, who noticed my rapid charge a second too late; then I sprinted over to the announcer's booth and grabbed the portable microphone. Running onto the field, I started screaming as loudly as I could. "People, listen to me! Stop requesting new lives! It's a fix! You're all being lobotomized! You are as shackled as these players on the field, but your shackles are on the inside, and you let them do it to you!"

One of the other announcers still had a microphone, and I heard him conferring with his colleague. "What's he talking about?"

My shouting continued: "The economy is not based on anything real! It's just fake numbers! The ground is falling out from under you, and it's a trap—a trap, I tell you!"

Annoyed, the other announcer said, "I don't know, but that SOB is disrupting the game!"

His colleague nodded knowingly and responded, "Well, Stu, he probably has a mental health disorder."

"No, the booth informs me that the guy on the field is named Steven, and that he's an orphan."

"Awwww! We should probably show him a little compassion for all that he's gone through."

Raising my voice even louder to drown them out, I said, "Madam President, you can hear me up there! Listen, they tricked you too! There is no fucking dormant commerce clause! Even if there was, a piece of paper doesn't make you gods! Humans should not be born into slavery in the name of the state! They should be born into freedom!"

Announcer Number One shook his head and said, "Yep, he's definitely lost it."

"Right you are, Skip, and I still can't understand what he's talking about."

Stu said, "I don't know, either, but the players are ready to come out onto the field, and the report from the locker room is that they're too scared to do so. Hey, he's interrupting our game! Boooooo!"

Someone ran up to the announcers' table with an urgent message. Taking it, Skip stood up, incensed, and shouted into his mic, "Hey everyone, Steven trashed the dispensary! They say that it will take weeks before we can get our regular medications again!"

The crowd was on their feet immediately.

"Let's get him!"

"No, let's stone him!"

"Yeah!"

It turned out that it was tethered bobblehead day at the stadium. Section by section, the fans started hurling bobblehead dolls in my direction, and they swooped down on me like boomerangs. I tried to shield myself from the onslaught as best as I could, but they were coming at me from all directions. Finally one of the polyurethane dolls caught me right between the eyes, and I fell to the ground nearly unconscious.

Then, as the souvenirs continued to rain down on me mercilessly and I struggled to my knees, I looked up toward the heavens and saw those two assholes from the sushi joint on Pluto staring down at me and laughing. Apparently the powers that be had expanded the broadcast of the game on the jumbotron to let the whole solar system watch my demise, and thanks to artificial intelligence monitoring of the crowd reactions, no human being missed the highlights of my downfall.

Frantically coming to my feet, I ran for the exit. The security guard I knocked over had recovered by then, however, and he pulled out his gun and shot me right in the leg. I was fortunate—it was a ketamine bullet and not a regular one—and I passed out shortly after that.

I woke up handcuffed to the rail in an ambulance, and the doors were open and I could hear people talking all around me.

"Where are they taking him?"

"To prison."

"What are the charges?"

"Disturbing the peace and excessive zealotry!"

"Ooh! I'll bet he became radicalized!"

"I hear that no one ever makes it out of that place!"

"I hear that it's worse than death on the inside!"

"Good! He deserves that!"

"Wow! It feels good to be part of a mob—other than on the internet, I mean!"

"Oh, me too, but I think I'm developing a little PTSD over it as well."

A calming, familiar male voice chimed in and said, "That's certainly to be expected, since science proves that unusual bursts of emotion can cause PTSD. We'll get you all scheduled for group support sessions and provide notes excusing you from work for the next few weeks."

They exclaimed in unison, "Oh, great idea! Thank you!"

Slowly, they all dispersed to collect their doctors' notes; then, through the open doors, the man I knew it was stuck his head in. With a playful grin, the director held out a standard-form contract to me and said, "By the way, Steven, can you sign this so we can use your story?"

I glared at him and spat back vengefully, "*Go to hell!*"

His wife appeared at his side, ready for instant condemnation, and retorted sharply, "No, Steven, that's where you're going!" With her best Christian pity, she shook her head regretfully and added, "And we thought that you were a good, upstanding young man, but you betrayed us!" They exchanged agreed looks of disappointment and passed out of sight; then I just closed my eyes and laid my head back.

After a short while, the engines started up and they shut the doors, and I sat up momentarily to look out the window. To my shock, Emily was standing quietly in the back of the crowd, a slow trail of tears falling down her face. My mouth fell open with some voiceless message I wanted to scream to her, but as the ambulance started moving, I saw the director come up beside her and grab her by the arm, quietly ushering her away from me forever.

*

THIRTY

I slowly roused from a temporary sedation, but my head was trapped in a persistent fog of some kind and there was a throbbing pain deep under the covers. I couldn't reach down to inspect it because my hands were secured down with straps. Looking up, I saw two orderlies standing over me, and they appeared frustrated for some reason I could not quite understand through the medication-induced haze.

"Damn, he takes good pictures! And we can't find any selfies out there? We can't find a single horrific picture of Steven to use for his mug shot?"

"I know. And no social media memberships, either. It's like this guy doesn't exist."

"He's been here since last night. I wonder why he hasn't grown any stubble yet. At least we could use that."

"Duh, look at him. It's obvious that he's naturally hairless below the scalp. You've seen his sex video, right?"

"Yeah, like fifteen times!"

"Well, that settles it. I guess we'll just have to shave off a portion of his head."

"Great idea, and that'll go perfectly with the article! Hand me the clippers."

I mumbled, "What the hell are you guys talking about?"

The one now holding my head firmly on both sides said, "Steven, we can't precondemn you if you still look like someone who belongs to our group. Now hold still." I passed out again to the sound of a buzzing razor.

I woke up sometime after that but still wasn't quite sure where I was. Looking up at the wall in front of me, I saw a sign that read, "Prison Hospital. The End is Nigh." There was a newspaper on the table next to me, and the front-page headline read, "Madman Taken Down!" My hands had been untied, so I reached over and studied it a bit closer. "Sources confirm that the lunatic who was pelted and then shot by the heroes at the soccer stadium suffered from seventy, maybe even eighty, different mental illnesses, all at the same time!"

I tossed it on the ground and closed my eyes. Just then, however, the door opened and the director walked in. Terror stricken, I bolted upright and said, "Oh my God! Are you here to kill me?"

Approaching calmly and pulling up a chair near the foot of the bed, he chided, "Well, technically we should. Breaking your phone and then that stunt at the stadium knocked all your points away, but the law also says that we can't grant compassionate release to criminals anymore."

Unsure whether that was a welcome reprieve or not, I leaned back and said bitterly, "I take it that the hooded Multiverse judges have already done their work?"

"Oh, yes." Looking down at his watch, he rattled off the results. "You have been convicted by an anonymous jury of your peers of excessive zealotry, disturbing the peace, twenty-four counts of assault, and twelve thousand seven hundred thirty-four counts of causing unpatriotic traumatic stress."

I didn't even bother to respond. I just started at the ceiling; then he added jubilantly, "Yes, my boy, you proceeded straight to your destruction, largely as expected!"

Shocked, I sat up and said, "What the hell are you talking about?"

"We predicted that you would eventually land in here before you even arrived for your first day on the job!"

"*You what?*"

He let out another satisfied laugh and said mockingly, "Oh, you didn't know that? I figured that a smart guy like you would have at least guessed it by now. What, did you think that we plucked you out of the orphanage and gave you all those things because we were hoping that you would actually succeed? Come on!"

My blood began to rise, and I thought about getting up to pummel him, but my leg was swollen from where the bullet struck me. Digging into me a little deeper, he said, "By the way, you should know that the little citizenship score we gave you … Well, for orphans it's really a countdown to their eventual self-destruction. We also never gave you insurance because we knew that it would wind up just being voided."

I didn't fully grasp what he was saying at that point, but my impression of him was now confirmed. All I could do was wish him back to where he came from and mutter sharply, "Go to hell!" Then I rolled back toward the wall.

He simply retorted, "Oh, Steven, my silly boy! You should know by now that science has disproven the idea of hell—well, everywhere but in this place, that is. Nope, I'm afraid that I'm going to be just fine on the outside. You, on the other hand, are right where you were meant to be."

I didn't say anything, and he continued. "For a while there I was actually a little worried that you wouldn't wind up in here. You were nearly on your way to fitting in before you snapped."

I finally said, "What the hell are you talking about?"

"You had demonstrated the ability to betray everything you believed in while you were working in the production studio. You supported new births, condemned fellow orphans, and prostituted yourself in nearly every other way." Laughing gently, he added, "Funny that it was that girl who finally made you lose it!"

The mention of Emily stung, but I tried not to show it and grumbled back at him, "I wasn't trying to fit in. I was just trying to survive, and it's a damn shitty system you have if that's what it takes."

He responded lightly, "Oh, it's really not. Everyone was doing exactly what they were supposed to, with the exception of you. I tell you, after all we've done, it was actually a tremendous disappointment to your mother and me."

I whipped around in my bed and said, astonished, "*Who?*"

He adopted a playfully apologetic smile and responded, "Well, we weren't *actually* your parents, and you know well enough what happened to them. But we always thought of you like a son, and even though you're in here and we knew that it would happen all along, it still hurts a little. Your mother couldn't even bring herself to come over here to see you."

Exasperated, I said, "My what? Are you kidding me? That lady tried to sleep with me!"

Innocently, he smiled and responded, "Well, there's nothing wrong with a little motherly love these days!"

"And you almost gave me AIDS!"

With a gently loving tone, he shook his head and insisted, "Steven, it was all for your own good."

"How the hell can you say that? Oh, who cares about you? I didn't even meet you two until I was thirty."

Fondly, he said, "Well, we always watched you at the orphanage from afar. I did read stories to you when you were three—along with my first wife, that is. Don't you remember that?"

"No."

"Well, I did, and we also chipped in so you'd have special things that some of the kids never had, and we were very proud of you when you were younger!"

I said bitterly, "Yeah, then why didn't you bother to adopt me?"

Grinning mockingly, he responded, "Oh, we were pretty busy, you know!" He shook his head and added, "Now, of course, you've just become a total disappointment."

"Humph."

"And to think of all of the money we spent to subsidize your education."

I shook my head confusedly and said, "Wait, I paid for that."

"Well, it would have cost more if we hadn't helped. And you don't know this, but we also gave a little here and there to the orphanage so you could have decent food, clothing, and special things on Christmas."

I was fuming by this point. My mind searched frantically for some truth in the middle of everything he was saying, and I shot back in anger, "So, for the price of covering part of my education and some basic sustenance, you think that you own me? You're no father! All you ever did was quote rules to me and make me want to turn gay!"

Still speaking in his mentor voice, he said, "Steven, I was trying to make things easier on you. You never had a chance and certainly would have never made it as far as I did. I was just trying to take the burden off you, but now you're a branded criminal."

I sat up and shouted at him, "You know damn well that it is absurd to call me criminal with all that goes on out there!"

He just laughed and responded innocently, "You mean our little human experiment? Why Steven, you're one of the few people on the planet that it didn't work for."

Wearily, I just shook my head in absolution and replied, "You're telling me? I had a rotten start and a rotten finish. But answer me this: why did everyone keep saying I was an orphan?"

He leaned in and answered coldly, "Because, Steven, they knew that no one wanted you."

That hurt more than where the bobbleheads or bullet hit me. Settling in comfortably, he added, "But I forgot to tell you that you were part of another experiment."

I didn't much care to listen to any more of his lies, but I asked flatly, "What experiment?"

"Raising a kid in the wild without access to technology or modern societal developments. We knew that you would never be able to cope with our advanced civilization, but we also knew that you would try, and we knew that it was impossible for someone in your position to survive with everyone around you trying to dodge responsibility."

Recalling all of my coworker experiences, I sat up again and asked incredulously, "So you made all of them do that just to set me up?"

He laughed gently. "Of course not, but why would we ever encourage people to try any harder, especially when we get paid no matter what? Their own frailties keep us in power and keep us prosperous, and the truth is that our economy is too intertwined to ever let anything change—unless, of course, it generates more money. That's why people have no problem condemning a miscreant like you." Then he laughed and added, "Oh, and a funny haircut never hurts!"

I rolled back toward the wall and muttered sourly, "They just faked that for the news photo."

Plainly, he retorted, "It really doesn't matter, does it? Steven, in every generation there is a wild-eyed kid born who refuses to be broken. That was you, and now you're broken. But don't feel bad. You actually lasted far longer than most."

Hollowly, I said, "So, I was just … a science project?"

"Oh, yes, although the outcome was virtually guaranteed from the start. See, ever since the third great American Revolution, we have known that humans like you cannot survive in our modern environment."

I turned back toward him again and said, "What the hell are you talking about? There's only ever been one American Revolution?"

He shook his head definitively and responded, "Nope. The second was way back in 1933, when people started allowing government intrusion into private life, and the third—and coincidentally the final—was when they gave up all control to us through lab births. Yep, we've been testing them all these years: depressions, recessions, horrible conditions, never-ending government shutdowns, and, of course, unpopular wars—yet not one single sign of real rebellion. The masses just take whatever we feed to them and ask for seconds."

Trying not to let him get to me, I observed vacantly, "It's all just a cruel joke."

He shook his head playfully and responded, "Oh, not on them! They're perfectly content, since they can't even remember yesterday. In fact, it only took one generation after we started lobotomizing everyone for them to forget the past. The only real joke we played was on you. You were handpicked to fail from the very beginning, and it was all for our own amusement!"

I thought about spitting on his freshly pressed suit but didn't bother. Then he added, "Ironically, the orphan program you were a part of was modeled after our last lost generation."

"The what?"

"A generation of people born before virtual reality took over. They were continually unable to adapt or be at ease with the instant-gratification nature of the electronic world, and like you, they distrusted phones, computers, monitoring devices, and every other sort of contraption. We raised you at the orphanage as they were brought up, and we even used the same kinds of devices they had back then."

Realizing the true nature of the devil I was now talking to, I asked, astonished, "What is all of this, some kind of sick torture?"

He replied plainly, "Of course not. It's a staple of the new economy. What'd you think this was all about? It's about controlling resources, and it doesn't matter if it's credits, allowance, or people exchanging little scraps of paper with each other. As long as we control the medium and have more people in the galaxy than we have room for, someone is always going to wind up on the bottom."

Bitterly, I said, "Well, it's sad to know that I was part of the 12 percent you don't care about."

He laughed again and responded, "Steven, you weren't part of *that* group! The 12 percent are the ones who keep our wages stable. The orphans are part of the 1 percent. I told you; you're just like us!"

Scowling at him, I said, *"I'm sorry you think so."*

"Well, technically you're correct. Unlike us, you were part of the most popular betting program that we have out there."

Shocked I said, *"Betting?"*

The director calmly crossed his legs and set into a lecture, just as if we were back in his office. Unfortunately, by then I was trapped with nowhere to go, and he answered, "Sure. The economy is largely stagnant these days, owing to all of the things we automatically provide to these people; and as a result, we simply have to find ways to make money elsewhere. Conventional investments still work, but the profit margins are very low, so the real money is made betting on orphans. That is also, by the way, how the insurance carriers make most of their profits for the year. All around the country, millions of participants bet on orphans just like you, and it's the most elite program of all. The 1 percent elites bet on the 1 percent orphans, and you are all handpicked by us. Each elite gets to sponsor an orphan, and that elite is in charge of the betting rules."

I felt a sickness coming on but tried not to show it. "Then what about the 98 percent others?"

Dismissively, he laughed and said, "What about them? They don't matter and never have! Steven, they're little more than economic data points on our giant balance sheet!"

Mustering up a small bit of defiance again, I leveled accusingly, "Then they're nothing but your slaves, and that makes you a slave master!"

He shook his head with patent regret and responded, "That's an awful way to look at it, but you're probably correct."

"Well, I'm not one of them and I never will be."

"Oh, you're right about that. You were never going to be one of them in the first place, but you're a slave nonetheless." He sat forward and glared at me again and added, "*Mine!*"

I shot back. "Bullshit!"

"Steven, the truth is this: I am your father because you are my creation. After all, I gave the order not to terminate you when your parents killed themselves."

I was completely shocked when he said that, and he simply grinned and added lightly, "And when you're gone, I will win enough money not only to erase what my last two money-grubbing wives have spent but also to retire completely!"

Sickened by what he had just told me, I tried to piece it all together. Still confused, I said, "Wait, you bet that I couldn't handle technology?"

"No. We bet that you'd have a meltdown out there, and it worked just like everything else we predict these days. I told you, we are inevitable!"

Angry and unable to make sense of anything anymore, I said, "Then why the hell did you bother giving me relationship advice?"

He let out a tremendous bellow in response. "Are you kidding? If you had gotten married, you would have wound up in here twice as fast! Now *that* would have really helped my odds!" Settling down again, he said, "But you pretty much stayed on pace anyway, so I still stand to make a mint after you're gone."

As he sat there grinning, the reality of it all started to sink in. I was alone. I had always been alone, and my life was nothing but a practical joke. I finally just laid my head back and started crying.

He coldly ignored my state and kept talking, digging into me deeper. "Fortunately for us, even more than the revenue you'll generate, your tree stunt was also a great boon for the economy."

Shocked once more, I looked at him through glassy eyes and said, "You knew that was me?"

"Of course. Well, it took a little while to put two and two together, but we figured it out soon enough. And sure, it made a mess, and we did lose some people before their timed releases, but we also had fewer Ph.D.'s working in fast-food joints than ever, and people had to phone in orders to even be able to reach a shrink."

Christ, Emily ...

"And not only did we figure out that it was you, but we also figured out what you had done. Then we realized why the tree was so difficult to control. Steven, you let a child's soul back out into the world completely unmitigated. We haven't permitted that for centuries, so naturally it was bound to cause some havoc. Plus, because that tree hadn't been conditioned to accept our methods of modern horticulture, it didn't respond to any of our attempted interventions." He grinned confidently and added, "But don't worry about your little wooden friend! We'll find a way to kill that thing eventually. We always do!"

I sucked back my tears and sat up, shouting angrily, "Fuck you!"

He just shook his head and chided, "Tsk, tsk, tsk. Typical response. Steven, don't take it so hard. You are simply the result of modern predictability, and what you did, while not entirely foreseeable, was certainly inevitable within the confines of our scientific democracy."

I wiped my eyes on my sleeve and tried to fire back at him. "Bullshit! Following people around and making up new laws or diagnoses any time they defy you is not a democracy!"

He was unmoved and conceded, "You may be right, but you're

not of any concern to us anymore. I do have to admit that you were the most exciting orphan we've had in a long time. You broke the record for the quickest physical injury to another; quickest to bring someone to tears—that's a separate category, of course—quickest to cause PTSD, anxiety attack, fainting spell, and about a dozen other categories." He nodded proudly and added, "I tell you; you generated the highest betting odds of all time just based on your volatility! By comparison, most orphans check out early and are relatively boring!"

I shouted angrily in response, "Well, you're all fucked in the head as far as I can tell!"

In all sincerity, he replied, "Oh, Steven, that's not true at all. We administer a perfect society where we have created a virtual reality a thousand times better than anything from a computerized device. Every day of a human's life is filled with preprogrammed instructions, rules, and boundaries. People are compelled to check their messages every single second, to respond to all the latest social trends, to watch the right shows, to eat the right things, and to stay obedient and get married at the right time. All told, there is not a single inch of free disk space left for independent thought."

Feeling the rage get the best of me, I spat back, "All you've created is a living nightmare, you butcher!"

He responded unfazed, "No, Steven, we haven't, because the truth is that this is the only way to ensure safety and prosperity. People need us, and they actually prefer these limitations being placed on them if it enables them to sleep at night."

The sickness of it all was overpowering me, and my anger was met only with growing helplessness. All I could do was roll back toward the wall and wish that he would disappear. Instead he just continued mocking me. "What do you think we've been doing this whole time? Every study we perform tells us about people's weaknesses, and every time we publish a study giving them permission to be weaker, more and more people accept it. They're just like that ooze in the basement, and even those people who do exercise are little more than hamsters on a treadmill, spinning along for our benefit while going nowhere."

He added arrogantly, "Steven, people think that physics is the oldest science. It's actually fiefdom, and we've been studying how to control the world's population since the very birth of groups."

I turned and snapped back at him. "All you're doing is passing laws that benefit you!"

Quizzically, he replied, "Of course. Why would we ever pass a law that didn't?" Then shaking his head gently from side to side, he said, "But Steven, it's not me. It's the law of economics."

Still trying to fight on some basic level, I challenged, "Well, if everything you've done is so great, then why do people still need to be medicated and eventually murdered at the hospital?"

He laughed again and responded, "Oh, my boy, nothing we do is a contradiction! We've pulled the curtain down over the top of the universe, so there's no one else to judge what we do. The only reality left is that what we say is the truth and what we do is the truth."

"If you're so all-powerful, then why do you dumb down society to suit the lobotomies, but you can't bother to make enough room for someone like me to survive?"

He almost doubled over at that, and it took him a few seconds to collect himself. "Room? Are you kidding me? We haven't left enough room for the next generation since the projects were first conceived! Why do you think apartments keep getting smaller and the buildings keep getting taller? And as for the orphans, well, we do what we do to you precisely because we are so all-powerful. Besides, there are no real adventures left to pursue, so everyone might as well be lobotomized. It's much better for them in the end." He shook his head and added dismissively, "I'm afraid that those lobotomies, much like their music, are simply disposable these days."

I responded accusingly, "Well, it's a pretty fucking sick society where five-year-olds can have gender reassignment surgery before they even know what the hell that all means, but I'm not allowed to say what I really think!"

He shook his head softly and said, "Oh, Steven, that's where you failed. You never understood that all we permit these days are things that are cute and nonthreatening, which are the perfect tools to keep everyone distracted." Waving an accusing finger at me, he said, "You, on the other hand, became a menace."

Finally lying back in exhaustion and staring at the ceiling, I admitted defeatedly, "And now I'm just another one of your casualties to be swept under the rug."

He calmly sat back and replied, "I am afraid so, but don't worry. We have so many new units being born every day that the world will never even notice your absence. Steven, in the end you were just one person, and you were the child of suicides. You couldn't have done anything to stop us anyway."

Fleetingly, I sat up and challenged, "Well, maybe not, but someone will!"

Overcome with amusement, he said, "Who? Steven, we have an entire society frozen in its own narcissism! We have people struggling just to maintain a basic economic existence while the threat of euthanasia nips at their heels, and we have perpetual children obsessed with fashion and playing sex games. No one can stop us, and pretty soon, we'll own a majority share of the whole galaxy. Do you really think that anyone cares what we do to a few unwanted orphans if it keeps our economy going?" He shook his head gently again and said, "The answer is no. I'm afraid that you were one of the last freestanding humans out there, and look at what happened to you."

Attempting one final act of defiance, I proclaimed, "Well, I'm going to find a way to fight these charges!"

Continuing to mock me, he said, "How? With what help? Steven, you're all alone. You don't belong to any groups, you're not part of any clubs, and you have no friends in the world."

Realizing that he was right, all I could say in empty response was, "Yeah, but I know that I lived better than any of you, even if it was only for a short time."

Flatly, he countered, "Your experiences are invalid. We didn't let you live and give you all of these advantages just so you could try to ruin our society. Christ, Steven, you act just like the people out there who think we give them things for free! As you know, of course, we always take back more than what they got in the first place, which is really just good, sound economic policy. After all, we can't avoid the chance to turn a profit!"

I scowled at him, but I was out of clever retorts by then and just leaned back and stared at the wall. However, twisting the knife even deeper, he laughed and added, "Oh, and it's a shame about all of the new lives you encouraged to be born!"

The mere notion of that truth made me cringe, and he saw this and took full advantage. Nodding mockingly, he continued. "Oh yes! Your ads have continued to generate record-setting orders for new births, and now they'll all have to endure the society you so gravely despise! Fortunately you won't be able to interfere with how we raise them." Cracking a small smile and clicking his tongue, he finally plunged the knife all the way in and declared, "Nor will you be able to stop what happens to your precious little Emily!"

I tried to jump up at hearing him say that, but the pain in my leg set me back down again. Angrily, I demanded, "What the hell are you going to do to her?"

He just smiled playfully and answered, "Oh, nothing that you need to worry about!"

"You son of a bitch! If you try to murder her like you did her mother—"

He waved a gentle hand at me and replied, "Steven, calm down, calm down. We would never do that to someone like her."

"But I heard them say that they were sending someone over to her house."

He finally admitted, "Oh, that was just a ruse to see how you'd react! I told you that she was bad news for you. And as for her mother, well, that was really just an economic necessity. After the old man kicked it, we saw our chance to finally take that property back. It had been in private hands for so long that it was really becoming a menace. Imagine it, Steven—having to supply a landline for one household? What a waste of government expenditure!"

I stared at him in utter disbelief and said, "Your hypocrisy is boundless."

He responded easily, "Oh, it's not. Plus, they were growing crops but refused to use the same AI technology that everyone uses these days and were actually doing *better* than some of their competitors. It was really disheartening to our other clients, so we simply took her by eminent domain."

I shook my head violently and said, "You *what?*"

"Steven, because the state is the one responsible for creating life, we own life and can take it back for whatever reason we want. Nope, I'm afraid that the algorithm was correct when it finally called her number."

"Fuck you and fuck your ridiculous algorithms! They're all worthless, and they all come up with the same answer!"

He conceded with pleasure, "Oh, you're right about that! They do all come up with the same answer!"

Confused, I said, "What?"

"While it is true that AI technology can run on its own, AI programs are completely useless without a predefined goal, so we gave them one: figure out how to maximize our profits, for everything! And with that goal applied to every aspect of social programming these days, all we really need to do is wait for new developments, pass laws to box them in, and then rake in the benefits!"

Finally glimpsing the heinous ghoul behind the curtain, I said incredulously, "You're one sick bastard!"

He shook a finger at me and scolded, "Tsk, tsk, that's not a name you should be calling anyone now, is it? But thanks to that ridiculous *The 57!* movie, the new road project, and now not having to supply a landline, we've done quite well off that family! Yep, with our sophisticated modeling, we can add or subtract an organ, a planet, an orphan, or even an entire family whenever it suits us best!"

With one final effort, I threatened emptily, "You'd better leave Emily alone or I'll—"

"You'll what?" Smiling warmly, he said, "I told you, don't worry about her! We'd never terminate a pretty young thing like that; we'll just put her to work in the city. She was, after all, on the way to move in with you when you blew up!"

My jaw dropped and I said, "What?"

"Yep. She came into town with that beat-up old truck and a suitcase. Looks like she finally realized that country life is obsolete these days, and she's bound to eventually ask us to just take the property off her hands, especially with the ever-increasing taxes. In the meantime, however, we've cancelled the phone service, and I'm sure that we can find some way for her to make money." He shot me a playful grin and added, "After all, she's still a virgin, in case you didn't know, and people will pay extra for something like that!"

Nearly insane with rage at that point, I clutched the bedsheets and screamed at him, *"You're … you're nothing but a heartless monster!"*

Apparently deciding that I was finished, he stood up, smoothed out the crease in his pants, and said, "No, Steven, I am the director of this scientific democracy. Goodbye."

*

Notes to Part IV

---

13   Jean-Jacques Rousseau, *The Social Contract*, trans. Maurice Cranston (London, England: Penguin Classics, 1968), 53.

14   *Federalist*, no. 12, at 91 (Hamilton).

15   Inscription on Statue of Liberty.

16   *Federalist*, no. 38, at 237 (Madison).

17   *Federalist*, no. 22, at 150 (Hamilton).

Printed in the United States
by Baker & Taylor Publisher Services